BLOODROCK

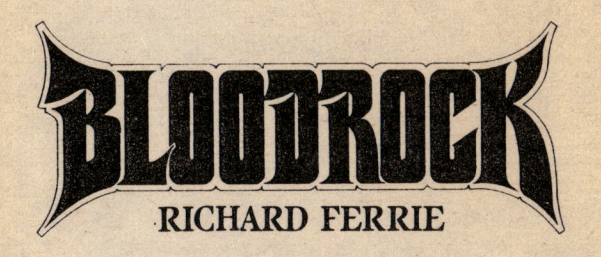

RICHARD FERRIE

LEISURE BOOKS ∞ NEW YORK CITY

For Josephine

This novel is a work of fiction. Names, characters, places, and incidents are either the product of the author's imagination or are used fictitiously. Any resemblance to actual events or locales or persons, living or dead, is entirely coincidental.

A LEISURE BOOK

Published by

Dorchester Publishing Co., Inc.
6 East 39 Street
New York, NY 10016

Copyright © 1987 by Richard Ferrie

All rights reserved. No part of this book may be reproduced or transmitted in any form or by any electronic or mechanical means, including photocopying, recording, or by any information storage and retrieval system, without the written permission of the Publisher, except where permitted by law.

Printed in the United States of America

BLOODROCK

Prologue

July 13, 1923
The provincial countryside, eight kilometers outside of the city limits of Paris, shortly before midnight.

"See me! See me!"

Edna chose a large elevated gravestone for her stage.

There, on the slightly raised stone, she danced the jig she had learned that evening on the Rue d'Orsay. Ray, who claimed credit for the child she was carrying, joined her after a moment's hesitation.

"See me! See us!" Edna cried.

The balding Parisian cab driver watched them prance on the tombstone, while he huffed a plume of disapproval into the unseasonally cold August night.

"Prohibé," he muttered under his mustache. "This is all wrong."

Laughter bubbled out from the back seat of the cab where a middle-aged French couple snuggled together beneath a blue and red coverlet.

"*You* are the repulsive one," said Marelle, who often spoke better English to those who could not understand than she did to those who could. "Ils sont trés belles, les jeunes Americains. Very wonderful, very beautiful."

"Do not scold him, darling," whispered her husband. "They have less of beauty, I think, than of the energy."

"Of course," Marelle said, "but you are more of a fool than the driver. Come out now a little with me. I have a grand idea for what we will do next!"

Marelle and her husband had been enjoying the company of the hedonistic young American couple for only three days, but those three days seemed like a glorious eternity. Was it really so short a time since they had met at the Cafe Etranger? So short a time that they had shared what they discovered to be certain mutual exotic interests? In particular, Marelle found the young American woman's self-absorbtion amusing and delightful.

Struggling out of the idling cab, they saw Ray cup his hands together to make an imaginary trumpet into which he tooted an imitation of the new jazz they had heard in the club. Catching on, Edna clapped and shouted, an audience of one for his musical efforts.

"Bravo, darling!"

How comical they were, how innocently decadent!

Ray, momentarily fatigued, stopped his fantasy performance to stoop and snatch a bottle of inexpensive red wine from their picnic basket. Slurping down a big mouthful, he passed the bottle to his swaying fiancée.

"For the child," he suggested.

Edna patted her slightly protuberant belly. "For posterity," she agreed, taking the bottle. "For the good life—the kid's gotta learn some day, right? A bon vivant!"

She thrust back her head at the dark sky, the brilliant crystaline stars, and let the wine flow into her mouth and down her chin. Some drops drizzled like dark rain onto the stone beneath her moving feet.

In the darkness of the cab the driver crossed himself

once, and then again. "Monsieur Méchant," he whispered, "pardonnez-moi! They are young; they do not know what they do!" Then he began to cough, quietly, desperately.

Shrugging, the Parisians left him to climb across the graves and join their young friends.

"That's enough, honey bunch," Ray said, wrestling the sloshing wine bottle from Edna's hands. "We want to baptize the kid, not drown him."

Edna grabbed hold of the bottle with both hands again and tried to win it back.

"Careful, darling," called Marelle as she stepped over a large puddle left by the rains. "No accidents, please."

Lifting her head like a defiant stallion, Edna clung to the spurting bottle. The carbide glow of the taxi's headlamps flickered and dimmed, touching the tombstones at odd angles to cast unsettling abstract shadows.

"Don't tell me *no* tonight, Marelle," Edna said, the volume and emphasis of her voice close to song. "Tonight I am free of life. And free of life means free to live. Look at me! See the wonders I feel? I am everything, therefore I must *do* everything. Aren't I profound? Aren't I . . .?" Groping for a word, she faltered, suddenly unsure.

Reaching the raised stone, the two Parisians applauded the foolish girl and cheered her on, a habit they had fallen into these last few days. "Bravo! Encore!"

Edna, suddenly confused, glanced around at the dark sprawling graveyard. "But what do I *want* to do? I've done everything. Everything! There must be something more . . . oh!"

The bottle she had been slowly waving slipped from her grasp to shatter with a soft explosion on the dark impersonal stone, the sweet blood brew of the grape spreading out in a cunningly suggestive pattern over the middle of the death monument.

"Tsk, tsk," Marelle preached, wagging a finger at her pregnant young friend. "When you are our age, darling, you will know better than to waste the wine of your life. But come, why are you crying?"

Ray, drunkenly kicking at jagged shards of glass, saw Edna's convulsive sobs at last and belatedly enveloped her shoulders with a strong arm. "There, darling. There, there."

But Edna, face in hands, frozen on the grave stone, the puddle of wine fleshing out the boundary around her, could not stop crying. "I want . . . I need . . . I need something *new* to do! Now! Oh please, there must be something I haven't done?" She turned her beautiful oval face imploringly to her French friends. A little ground mist nestled lovingly about her ankles, carrying an uncanny green patina as of aged brass.

Shaking his head, fed up at last, the aging Frenchman turned away. But Marelle strode over to offer Edna a helping hand down. "Darling, I have just the thing for you—for all of us. Something new, something special."

Pawing at her wet eyes like a spoiled child, Edna took the extended hand but pretended to resist being consoled. "Don't be nice to me . . . I don't want to be treated like you treat your stupid husband. I want to be . . ."

"No, no!" Marelle promised. "It's you who've made me think of this, dear one. Your choice of marble dance floors is peculiarly appropriate on this particular night. Here, see? Note the name. There, raise your lovely heel a little to see it."

Edna reluctantly lifted her dripping foot, and Ray struck a match as they bent to scan the inscription. Marelle translated aloud.

"ANDRE MECHANT — 1841-1904 — THE MASTER.

'He knew the spell that killed him.

'Rest fitfully, wayward soul.'

"Is that famous? I am not sure," she mused. "Oh, there is a little more here . . . 'The universe return unto itself again.' Something like that. His daughter is the most famous witch in all this region. She is responsible for this stone."

Edna grabbed her friend's shoulder and began a jumping dance. "A witch, really?" she cried. "Around here? How can I meet her? I must!"

Marelle touched her cheek. "Yes, exactly what I had in mind. Shall we?"

"No!" Edna cried. "Now, everybody must hurry. Hurry! Before I absolutely *die* of curiosity."

The two men laughed and clapped each other on the shoulder, taking great pleasure in catering to the whims of their irrepressible women.

"Oh, what an adventure!" Edna proclaimed once they were back in the dark cab.

Suspicious, the driver inquired as to their new destination.

"Fermez la bouche," Marelle instructed. "Shut up and drive."

Grumbling, thrusting his neck forward as if to stick his head through the wheel, the driver steered the wobbling vehicle along the rutted unlit road leading out of the graveyard and deeper into the provincial countryside.

Haggard trees fingered the highway with low-hanging branches; signposts loomed like disjointed pencil sketched figures; an unexpected set of muddy train tracks protruded from the ground like the backbone of some subterranean beast. Mist coagulated around the cab, and all the while Edna bounced ecstatically in the back seat.

"A witch! A real witch! Oh, I love life so. There'll always be something new to do, won't there!"

The driver coughed fitfully as the cab bounced on the treacherous road.

"Down this lane, imbécile," Marelle directed. "You know the way now?"

"Chez Méchant? But, madame, I beg you . . ."

Marelle snapped the driver's ear with her thumb and forefinger. "Fermez!"

Listening for once, Edna was delighted by the exchange. "He's scared!" she sang. "Oh, yes, it's dangerous! It's dangerous, isn't it? It's sooo dangerous! I just lo-o-ove it!"

Marelle laughed and Ray followed suit. He laughed when others laughed, drank when others drank. Only Marelle's husband did not laugh, his fingers twining and retwining themselves under the rainbow coverlet.

The road dwindled down to a rut between two twisted trees, a bit of slanted dirt bank, a turn and a radical drop-off down between stacked logs. The cab bumped impossibly through, Edna screaming in mock horror as she arched her hands up over her head as if cresting a thrill ride.

The cab slowed. Someone exhaled nervously inside. Something appeared in the light of the dim headlamps—a fence, a luxurious but unkempt garden bounded by wire, steps, a railing, the uneven clapboards of a farmhouse or cabin. The lurching cab slammed to a stop, its poor headlamps full on the small dwelling. The driver turned to face his eager passengers. "Madame, je vous implore . . ." No response. "Mademoiselle, I beg you . . ."

"Quiet, coward," Edna instructed. "My sophisticated friends are giving me the grand tour! Keep the motor running."

Jumping boldly from the cab, Edna strutted a few steps toward the cabin before stopping to wait for the others. "So dark. Are you sure someone's home?"

Marelle took Edna's arm to urge her on. "She is always home. Where else would she go?"

An ember of fire in the blackness beckoned them up the steps to the porch. A scantily clad young girl, barely more than a child, sat smoking a hand-carved pipe in a straight-backed chair near the door.

"Bon soir," Marelle said.

Shrugging her tiny sensuous shoulders, the girl puffed rapidly on the pipe and slumped lower in the chair.

"Her hair . . . uggh!" Edna whispered as they bunched together before the door. Tangled and twined around her thin body and bulbous abdomen, the girl's hair overgrew her body like some uncontrollable weed.

"She's . . . preggy, like me . . . so young but . . . uggh!"

The cabin door swung open for no discernible reason. A blazing fireplace illuminated the rustic interior. Beside the fire in an antique rocking chair carved with the likenesses of ancient beings, a shrunken old woman inclined her body back and forth with the slow certainty of a pendulum.

"Bon soir, Madame Méchant."

Because the old body did not stir, the dry and guttural yet powerful voice that came from it was shocking. "Faites attention. Ma petite fils n'aimes pas le . . ."

Marelle fronted the old woman like a movie narrator comandeering the foreground. "She warns us that her granddaughter is fascinated by strangers but that we must not . . ." She winked at Ray who burst out laughing. "She knew we would come because everyone wants to see a pregnant girl who is . . ." Marelle tilted her head to listen, nodded. "Who is unknown to man. That is, she herself, Madame Méchant, rendered the girl pregnant by means of . . . Repetez, s'il vous plais?"

Ray swung the older Frenchman around to whisper loudly, "Unknown to man, huh? I've got something here that'd like to know her real good!"

Edna, overhearing, laughed with raucous abandon. "You sexy rascal! Just can't wait 'til after the harvest, can you?"

Marelle shouldered her way casually between them. "Madame Méchant is trying to tell you that she collaborated on the pregnancy with her grandfather, the man whose grave you danced . . . that is, whose grave you visited tonight. No *living* man was present at the conception."

Ray hitched his pants up repeatedly. "Well, *I'm* alive—and I can prove it! Let me at her!" He crouched as if to spring out onto the porch to assault the long-haired girl; Edna, playing along, grabbed him around the throat. They slumped together, laughing uncontrollably.

Smiling a little, Marelle waited until her young American friend caught her breath. "Do you have any questions to ask Madame Méchant?"

Giggling, Edna started to shake her head then seemed to reconsider. She winked at Ray. "Okay," she said to Marelle. "Ask her when the last time was . . . the last time she *did it*."

Momentarily puzzled, Marelle cocked her head quizically. "Did it? Ah, bon! Le paff-paff! Mais oui . . ." And she turned to the elderly woman who, for all the life she had shown, might just as well be dead. "Madame Méchant, tell me . . ."

Children overwhelmed by the wonder of their impertinence, Edna and Ray held each other tightly, shaking, muffling their laughter with mouths buried in each other's shoulder.

Marelle's husband tried to catch Ray's attention with little warning gestures, at last tapping him on the shoulder. "Non, mon ami, my friend!" he whispered urgently. "No . . ."

Apparently oblivious to all this, Marelle, having listened attentively to the old crone's reply, turned to Edna to translate. "Madame Méchant did not hesitate a moment before telling me that she *did it* less than an hour ago."

Ray blew out a *whoosh* of wonderment and flopped his hands up at shoulder level as if they were burning from the supercharged eroticism emanating from the old woman.

Marelle gave him a glance. "She also foretells that within a fortnight she will do it with young Ray here. Also, she promises that Monsieur Méchant will surely find an appropriate time and place to do it with you, Edna. Unfortunately, these pleasures will be followed by a . . ."

"Cockadoodle-doo!" Ray drunkenly retorted. "Buch of frog hogwash! Let's get out of here."

He made a grab for Edna, who flung her arms into the air to do her dance.

"Witch! Witch! Witch!" she sang triumphantly. "I'm the real witch! Bitch, bitch, bitch. She's the only . . . Marelle, how do you say *bitch* in . . .?"

"Come on," Ray said. "You're drunk." He pushed her out the door to the porch where they carried on a mock fistfight, Edna landing one accidental glancing blow to Ray's chin.

At last, Marelle emerged from the dark interior of the musty cabin, closing the door behind her in a painfully decorous manner.

"You two were rather rude," she said quietly as they

descended the dilapidated wooden steps. "I suspect that you have a few rather serious and shocking surprises ahead in your future as a result . . ."

She stopped when she saw the girl, her filthy hair twitching spasmodically as she strove to twist free from Ray's strong grip. "Come on, baby," he said. "Come on. We had a great time, didn't we? Here, take this. Yes, take it. Take it!"

When the girl saw what he offered, she stopped struggling and took it from his hand.

"That's right," Ray approved. "You earned it. You were the best. And we'll get together again real soon."

Screeching with appreciative laughter, Edna pounded his back with her fists. "Oh, you're a filthy thing!" she cried. "Just for that I'm going to make you make love to me in this stupid taxi. And you have to tell me, 'Witch, witch, you're a juicy little . . .' "

"Come on, you two," Marelle instructed, perhaps the slightest little tremor entering her voice. "Before you get into some real trouble."

The swollen child rose dreamily from the wooden steps where she had been studying her prize under the protective covering of her unwholesome hair. She stepped toward him, holding out the squares of paper. "Encore un peu?" she said. "Encore."

Marelle directed them all into the cab.

Languorously, the pregnant child began to follow them.

Coming to life, the cab driver lifted his head from the wheel to cross himself and start the motor even before the two couples had entirely situated themselves.

"Tomorrow I will take you to see that young writer I told you of," Marelle announced. "Edna, remember? The one who keeps company with the strange woman who is anciently middle-aged, the one with the cats? And the . . . friend? Yes. And, oh, you will admire his strength. That is, of course, if the weather . . ."

"Encore un peu!"

Running toward the cab, the girl raised her pale thin arms to signal them.

Ray hung far out of the open window of the moving vehicle and waved a new bottle of wine at the running girl.

"Here you are, my dirty little French pig of a knocked-up lover!" he called to her. "Here, you little frog whore, come and get some wine, a whole bottle to go between your legs!"

"Ray," Marelle's husband cautioned. "My friend . . ."

The cabbie, frantic to get away, wheeled the taxi around wildly in the darkness of the dangerously confining farmyard. The pregnant girl trotted to intercept the cirling vehicle, running awkwardly, as if in slow motion, with annoyingly desperate patience.

"Oh, this is the real fun!" Edna cried out. "What all the civilized fools hide from, cringing in their safe little houses, the sweet bloody center of life! This is it! More! Oh, more life! Faster, coward, faster!"

Cursing, the cabbie maneuvered the vehicle around a fruit-bearing tree and, brushing an untrimmed hedge, regained the rutted road that led back to the highway. He crammed his foot down on the accelerator just as Edna playfully punched the back of his hairy neck.

"Coward! Wonderful cow . . ."

"Oh, no!"

They lurched forward and to the right as the wild dark-haired girl emerged, all big eyes and belly, in the carbide headlamp glow of the uncontrollable taxi.

A little ground fog eddied like water over the silent scene.

BOOK I:
INITIATION

Chapter One:

Blood Show

June Lockwood watched her former idol raise the glinting machete over the feathered throat of the struggling creature.

An unexpected smack of the gong made her cringe back against Duane's formidable shoulder. Was it cowardice, sensitivity, or just the fact that she loved animals? June would have hid her face in the safe cascade of her manager's shoulder length blond hair if it weren't for the fact that the concept of public decorum had been drummed into her since childhood. What would her famous mother think to see her cowering at a mere show, an entertainment?

The Club Crater showcased the best '80's rock acts to tour the South Bay. Many name bands were lured into bypassing San Francisco on their concert route, instead heading straight for Herm D'Angello's San Jose club chicly housed on the wrong side of the tracks. Its California rustic decor featured rough hewn wooden fixtures, gouged chairs, paneling and supposedly authentic early California relics such as old wash tubs, gold panning paraphernalia, plows, and sections of an original buckboard wagon.

June and her manager Duane Lombard sat along the wall to the left of the stage in a clawfooted bathtub that, with one side cut away, served now as a sofa.

"Oh, bird of death," Bosley Broderick chanted from the strobe-lit platform.

The peacock squirmed in its chains, indifferent to Bosley's masterful showmanship and to the machete he held high over its gorgeous head.

"Oh, feathered midwife of eternity, you whom I rescued from the place of tombs, recieve now my swift and just caress of steel. Carry my flaming soul with you into the night!"

The droning guitar reached an otherworldly climax. Bosley's roadies, dressed as unisex demons in leotards and chains, held the brightly plumed bird rigid, its head pinned to the stage floor. The thousand eyes of its translucent tail flashed in response to the theatrical lighting.

"What a bunch of bull," Duane said. "Are you ready to go?"

June flinched as she watched Bosley hitch his arm in readiness. Then he leered an enormous make-up enhanced smile in her direction. He closed his eyes and tottered, seeming to lapse into a trance.

"Go with my dark hopes to the True Shadowed Father of Us All," he whispered as if the words truly were intended only for the sacrificial bird.

The gong rang fiercely. June plunged her face into the crook of Duane's taut neck. "It's too . . ." She shut her eyes, also trying to shut her mind.

Everybody knew about Bosley Broderick's band, Children of the Night. They knew that a different animal was allegedly sacrificed each night and that the sacrifice took place on the third stroke of the bronze gong he was rumored to have stolen from a Tibetan monastery. Not every fan believed that the sacrifices were genuine. Until tonight, June had been one of the skeptics, until. . . .

Duane shifted and pulled her closer. "Should I tell you when?"

"No, No, please don't say anything."

That's all right, darling. Hide your face. Mother will look for you. After all, it's mother's show. You be the baby and I'll be the eyes. But one day. . . .

"Whhyeeee!" A crazy laugh rang out with the spooky resonance of a countertenor singing voice.

"I thought you said this guy used to be mellow?" Duane said, angrily firming his grip on her shoulder. "Do you want me to take you out of here?"

She shook her head, pulling away. "It's just that Bosley's . . . evolved," she tried to explain, aware that the words sounded lame (as her mother often enjoyed reminding her). "I mean, he started out mellow, very accoustic, but he seemed to be one of those artists who can't—or won't—stand still and he just progressed through blues, fusion, acid rock, heavy . . ."

"You call that progress?" Duane nodded up toward Bosley towering above the defenseless bird.

June shook her long auburn hair and tried not to use her peripheral vision to see that area of the stage. "He's a genius, Duane. Since I first heard him when I was a little girl, I've spent hundreds of hours alone in the dark with Bosley Broderick's voice. I feel that he's part . . ."

"Sorry, June, but I think that bald character's going to beat the gong again. Did you . . . ?"

No, she did not want to see it happen. She bit her lip and tried not to cry. She couldn't begin to explain how she felt toward Bosley Broderick and his music. She loved his records—even the ones with the Children of Night—loved them so much that she felt that she needed to communicate something of her love directly to Bosley.

Hush, now. Don't look, Darling. Don't. . . .

She shook herself through the abruptness of a shiver. Oh yes, that music of his had got tangled up with her own creative development, her music. So she had to look; she would resist portraying the wounded female because . . . because she felt like one.

It was the blood. The bleeding. Oh, she didn't regard her menstrual period as a wound or affliction, but she hated the way that men tended to use the knowledge of its advent against her. (The way they phrased it—"It must be *that* time of month, huh? Don't worry, *I* understand.") No, she hadn't told Duane; she had no reason to, since they didn't know each other that well—not yet. Still, she found herself thinking of creativity and blood, all that blood she'd lost all these years, that blood that under other circumstances might have become. . . .

The gong made its shattering clamor for the third time.

"Oh, Dark Father," Bosley's voice boomed from the stage, "I launch my living vehicle of love to You, only You."

A hush.

The music stopped.

A hiss of air being sliced by sudden slick thin motion. Then a horrible silence in which, if one cringed, one heard nothing but. . . .

Hush, little girl. Everything is going to be all right. Everything is. . . .

A sickening thunk, the sound of something soft striking the hard wooden surface of the stage.

Cheers of triumphant revulsion from the audience. Yes—yes! Just like Greek tragedy, there had to be catharsis! There had to be that final moment.

Yes, she had to see what happened now. She hadn't waited all these years, hadn't yearned in private to see this special public show, this brilliant performer, only to turn coward now and regret it the rest of her life.

June heard the audience growl at something they were witnessing, a sound of such forlorn pleasure. She thought of an animal with a bone caught in its throat still warding off the others that want the prize. What did they see up there? Why?

Hush! No, don't. . . .

June wished immediately that she had not looked. She saw Bosley cup his hands to catch the pulsing blood as he used a finger like a brush to paint his own face. She saw him go to each member of the band in turn, dancing, pirouetting across the stage to finger paint the face of each with the drying blood of the sacrificed bird, to mark everything he could reach.

June struck a fist to her cheek. Had she meant to hit her eye? "Oh, Duane, it's awful! How can he do . . .?"

Young men with bare chests rushed the stage to be anointed, but Bosley seemed to prefer the willow thin girls with streaming hair who offered their foreheads and wrists to the touch of his sanguine art and to the sacramental kiss of his grinning lips.

"Is this what we came to see?" Duane wanted to know. "I don't know which I find more disgusting, the performance itself or the audience's response. And now . . . all this. June, are you okay?"

She did not dab at the tears sliding so foolishly down her face, tracing itchy trails across her cheeks. Why did she still love Bosley after what she'd seen? She only knew that somehow he had offered her the world the way it had been when she was still very little. And that offering remained, remained to be grasped, to be taken hold of. And somehow what she had seen tonight was still part of it, her life, inexplicably innocent, yearning.

Oh, sure, she wanted to be a rock 'n' roll star, didn't everybody? But she also wanted a grand house, a baby (did she dare pray for a daughter?) and love, of course. And somehow behind every dream she saw the face of the man who had just performed an absolute atrocity on the stage in front of her.

"June, have you had enough? Let's get the hell out of here!"

She heard Duane's annoyance, his anger and his impatience, but she could not take her eyes from the stage, from Bosley Broderick. Through that facade of bloated warpainted skin she saw all too easily the sensitive elegant young singer and composer he had once been. She remembered the first shock of recognition on hearing the voice of a kindred soul as if from inside her own head. *I understand. I understand everything. My art is only for you.*

"I said *let's go!*" Duane repeated, trying to pull her up out of the modified bathtub. "That guy isn't one tenth the musician you are, June—and you know it! He covers up his lack of talent with a sordid show and gimmicks. June—look at me!"

She knew that to Duane she must appear foolishly dreamy, ogling an aging rock singer who'd smeared himself with the blood of a slaughtered animal.

Don't look again, dear. Mommy will do the looking for both of us. And the performing.

"Duane, I *have* to see him."

"What? You're kidding!"

Applause. Stomping. Bosley and his band bowed separately, joined hands, then bowed again and fled the stage.

Despite the screams from the Club Crater audience, there would be no encore, June knew. The other loyalists knew it too and vacated with surprising rapidity. The club became itself again, a big ugly room that affected a rustic atmosphere. The lights went up. Hanging at odd angles on the wall the miner's lanterns, pitchforks and horseshoes appeared no more decorative than debris deposited by a high tide.

"I have to see him," June repeated. Without looking at Duane for confirmation, she started walking toward the partition on the far side of the elevated stage.

"Hey, wait," he called. "I don't think they're even going to let you . . ."

Members of the road crew efficiently mopped the splattered stage, from which she averted her gaze. Would Bosley see her? Would he speak to her?

June bumped into the chest of a man with a shaved head whose arms were locked behind him. She recognized him as the one who had bashed the gong three times with the enormous mallet.

"Hi!" she said. She twisted a hand slowly through her hair in a way that she had been told was irresistible. "I just want to . . ."

"No admittance."

"But . . ."

Coming up behind, Duane gripped her elbow with his hand. "Come on, June. It's not worth the hassle to see that fat has-been."

But June did not disengage her eyes from the eyes of the man with the shaved head. "Look—I promise that I'll only take a minute."

"No admittance." His frown gave the definite impression that it didn't take him long to reach his boiling point.

"June, let's . . ."

Jumping down off the stage, one of the roadies brushed by them, almost swinging the mop into the bald man's face. "It's okay, Reformer," he said as he slid by. "That's June Lockwood. She played with Blithedale Romance when they toured through last month. Bos'll see her."

Reformer looked over his shoulder at the retreating roadie as if considering taking a bite out of him. Then he glanced back at June, eyeing her up and down. "You go—but *he* stays here," he said at last.

"Wait just a minute," Duane said. "I don't think . . ."

"It'll be okay," June said, smiling assurance.

Reformer shifted his great mass slightly as she tried to get by. "I ask nothing of you but that you respect his age and poor health. Do nothing to antagonize him. And if he asks you to do a thing for him, you must pledge to do it. You agree?"

June nodded without hesitating. Shoving past, she whipped the green curtain out of her way and slipped backstage.

Chapter Two:

Prophecy of Blood

June angled down the narrow dimly-lit passageway. Loud music and pungent smoke seeped from under a heavy door which she tried and found securely locked. Somehow, she just couldn't believe that Bosley relaxed like that after his show. Perhaps it was no more than the romantic image of him she still clung to, but she felt sure that. . . .

She stopped dead at the sight of the hideous old man slumped back in a folding chair in the room at the end of the passage. Of course it couldn't be Bosley, who was still young.

Unmoving, he held a discolored rag in his lap; make-up had been wiped from half his face. Had his energy failed him before he could finish? Naked old man's breasts sagged on his chest like deflated balloons.

June pulled back into the shadows. It was obscene—this candid tableaux of a man in his prime given over to premature senility, more obscene than the beheading of that beautiful bird. Then she thought how foolish and narrow she was to find the onslaught of age obscene. Just because this backstage glimpse at the real flesh and blood didn't meet her expectations, that didn't mean she had a right to judge.

"I sense a presence."

June felt the words as one does a breeze.

"I sense beauty, great beauty! Approach me."

Why comply? Perhaps, hallucinating, he spoke this way following each performance—then what embarrassment for her! And if somehow he was addressing her, why leave the safety of the shadows?

June moved forward without knowing she moved. She knew only that the voice must have come from some source other than this empty shell of an old man because it had resonated with strength, vitality, conviction.

She stopped walking, realizing that she *had* been walking, and found herself knee to knee with the rouged corpse slumped in the chair, the rag dangling from its lifeless hand. "I know you," it told her.

"No. No, you don't."

It raised its head with a magnificent expenditure of effort, like a great whale breaking the surface of the sea. "Oh, yes." The eyes exulted as the rest of the face remained dead. "I know everything but who you are."

You can look now, darling. Here's someone I'd like you to meet.

June's eyes darted around the bare dressing room. A once-lustrous sequined robe was draped over a small sofa flanked by a wastebasket and two lamps with dusty tinted shades. She stared through the single streaked window to the darkness outside.

"I . . ." What had he asked? "I . . ."

Something magical happened then. The face came to life in a smile that seemed to have been there all the time, a rich radiant smile that made June want to hold her hands up to receive the warmth. No fatigue, no age, no despair.

"Come, now. Don't be awe-struck. I'm not Mick Jagger or Michael Jackson—or even Gordon Sumner, hah! Everyone says I can't sing—and I agree. Can't play an instrument. In short, I'm just an old fake, a charlatan."

"No! June cried, her hands almost touching his face. "No, don't say that."

"I write some songs," Bosley said, staring with the directness of a challenge. "And sing them—or pretend to. That's about it. Now, the hell with this psychic stuff, do you want an old phony's autograph or don't you?"

Leaning back, June almost stumbled. "But you knew that I was standing there . . ."

He chuckled. "I saw you; that's all."

"But you couldn't have. It's impossible."

Bosley's smile locked into place, as if to keep from dwindling. "Autograph or not? Going, going . . ."

Less than half the light bulbs around the make-up mirror had life, giving the effect of a dust-muted glow, yet his whispy hair and broad head were brilliantly backlit as if his body attracted light.

"Well?" he demanded. "Want it now, or are you going to wait to try to get it posthumously?"

The way he scrunched up his parched earth face, sending surface cracks spreading out from his eyes and nose and mouth, June knew that she was supposed to laugh. "I don't think I want your autograph," she said. "I think that . . ."

"Yes?" He arched a single formidably bushy eyebrow.

"I'd like to know . . ." Her voice dropped to a whisper as if she could barely manage to get the words out. She had to know. ". . . the blood, the peacock. Is it . . . is it dead? Please tell me."

"Ah. I see," Bosley did not move; only his voice showed comprehension. "Yes. And what instrument do *you* play?"

Even his aging pectoral muscles seemed to have pulled up into place. June twined a knot of hair with three fingers. She wouldn't let him divert her from finding out what she needed to know. Still. . . . "I play keyboards a little but mainly I sing . . . like you. And write my own songs. But what does that have to do with the peacock?"

"Of course you sing and write, as you say, like me." Bosley looked toward the dirty window as if gathering the darkness with his eyes. "Of course you do," he said. "And so you know that what you saw tonight is all an act, an entertainment, a diversion, a bit of theatrical business to enhance the music. Yes? Slight of hand, electronically augmented sound, blood bags, illusion —isn't that how *you* do it?"

She could not keep her lips from parting in surprise. "But you *did* kill that bird. I saw it."

"And when you entered this room, what did you see then? A dead old man? And what do you see now?" He gestured to his body with an unmistakably erotic flourish.

June took a full step back from that gravitational field of flesh and blood she found it hard to resist. "But I don't . . ."

"Of course you don't, darling. You are very new. You are a baby. You have just begun to find yourself. Does that help?" He waited for a response. "No, then try this. I have *given birth* to you tonight. Nothing died, no animal, no human—but you were born from the blood. And now you must cry. You must scream for breath in the limitless darkness if you are to live in this world."

June smiled mildly, as if she did not understand. What would happen if she acknowledged that she did?

Bosley jerked into animal alertness. "I said. . . ."

He came up out of the folding chair so quickly, so violently, that it collapsed behind him with the clatter of metal cushioned by cheap carpeting. ". . . *scream!*" He raised his large meaty hand like a holy book and brought it down toward her face with a stylized swing that, when it seemed to strike, made a muffled smacking sound like that of a stunt punch in a movie.

"Scream," he urged. "Cry, fellow musician! Force back the horror of the darkness with the power of your wonderful lungs. Bring your blood to life."

June told herself to get a logical fix on the moment. But it was all too fast, too fast. Her mind felt mixed and scattered and scrambled, a slot machine with its handle pulled and all the slots in dizzy motion—thoughts, feelings, associations, nothing would stop, nothing would line up and come together and pay off with some sort of good sense.

June shook her head, forcing her eyes fearfully wide. She could not clear her brain. She felt that she had lost herself, perhaps forever.

Bosley shook her with passionate intensity.

"No, dismissing it will not work! Live it, suffer it, feel!"

Her lips pulled back and her throat opened wide. June screamed. She screamed to let out the frustration and dread of seven years of struggling to succeed as a rock singer, seven years of mortifying failure with teasingly brief moments of qualified success. June screamed for all the renewed dreams that she thought had died forever.

"Yes," Bosley crooned in her ear, "that's right, yes. That's good, my luminous darkling, my own June Lockwood whom I now baptize in the name of . . ."

"How did you know my name?" June said. Yes, the scream *had* helped. Enough, at least, for her to recognize this logical impossibility. "You couldn't possibly know my name."

"It's nothing." He did not even offer a token smile. "A trick, a tiny little trick which I may teach you. Now I've given birth to you, baptized you, and you must do something for me."

June felt a bewildered sort of trust for this strange large man. Had she passed some sort of test? How? Why? The thought lingered for her that perhaps failure might have been preferable. And now he wanted something. "Yes?"

"Tell me, June. You've begun your lunar cycle tonight, have you not? The cycle of the blood? Good, good. Now, if you will . . ."

"You couldn't possibly know something like that. Or do you have cameras hidden everywhere in this club?"

Bosley threw the make-up rag at the mirror, a gesture of satisfied finality. "I saw *you*," he said. "Only you. I know blood; I have the gift of blood." He leaned forward to emphasize the directness of looking into her eyes. "And so do you. I knew it the moment you entered this room and began to watch me. We share this dark sanguine secret."

June could not stop shaking her head. She tried to avoid his gaze. "I don't know any of your secrets."

"Ha! So you say. We will share gifts, eternal gifts, infinite gifts." He cocked his head to the side like a quizzical bird. "Or am I just an old sham, an old sham of a shaman? Huh?"

Shutting her eyes, June tried to separate the effect of Bosley's playful manipulations from her previous expectations, impressions, misconceptions, fantasies. She heard maniacally inspired music. She saw his face come closer, looming, smiling its benevolently corrupt smile. She knew nothing, nothing except what he told her. How could this happen to her?

"I'm sorry. I have nothing to give you."

"You do not need to lie to me, June. I understand. You are your mother's child. You will do anything to please her. You will become a monster being her good little girl."

"How do you know my mother?"

He took her two lovely white hands in his husky one and pulled her closer. His smile staked a claim in her soul. "You're very young. You misunderstand."

Close your eyes, darling. Don't look at the man. There's no need. You'll never understand. Mommy will look for you. Mommy will. . . .

Sudden anger flared her nostrils; resisting him, June pulled free. "Not so young," she said. "I know how old you are to the *day*—and there's only seven years difference between us. I'm old enough to know exactly what so-called *gift* you want from me. And if you hadn't been so patronizing about it, I might have considered." She didn't mean it and knew she lied, yet. . . .

"Hoooo-yes!" Why did he laugh with such ferocious pleasure? Why did he now pull on her hands and make her sway like a dancing child, laughing, giddy with some secret joke he could not keep to himself?

Lights blinked once, flickered, then settled down to reveal the dead seriousness of his deep blue eyes.

"Don't think I'm patronizing you when I laugh or say you misunderstand, June. Sex with you would be delicious bloody bliss but I . . ."

"Wait," June said. She hated thinking of herself as a comic figure, fleeing this sort of intensity. But nothing in her experience permitted her to see herself staying in this weird scene. "I'm sorry, Mr. Broderick, but I'm going to have to leave. I have to admit that your energy is overwhelming and I'm flattered that you think there could be a bond between us, but I'm not the kind of person who can . . ."

"Oh, but you are," he said with incredible gentleness.

He smoothed back what remained of his whispy hair. "Just one little insignificant secret—my potency is gone, taken from me. Taken by a vengeful woman whom you know all too well . . . but more of that later. I don't expect to regain it, at least, not in this lifetime. So you see . . ."

Should she apologize? Nothing seemed appropriate. She touched his red-streaked body near the armpit. "I didn't mean to hurt you."

"Not at all," Bosley said, his crafty virile grin making her wonder if he'd told the truth. "Sex is one little secret, just one. Love is more and larger. And the deepest push of love is blood. Remember, June. Without feeling the blood, human life is mockery and misunderstanding. People like us, like you and me, cackle at the bloodless robots that flood the streets of these cities with their empty bodies."

Now he sounded like an old beatnick or hippie, yet June's hands on his naked torso began to burn as if she were touching a furnace.

"Let me show you," he said, sinking to his knees. June had to drop her hands, which fell naturally to his sloping shoulders. Raising his hands up to her hips, he worked them into her form-fitting jeans. Clutching the blue denim, he began to pull them down. She was not prudish but. . . .

"No, I'm on my . . ."

"Ssssssh," he soothed. "Sssssh, easy, little girl, my new born woman of blood. Easy."

Why did she let him do this? What if someone came in and found them? What if Duane came in? How would she explain? ("Oh, sure, he's a little eccentric. I was just humoring one of his little pet theories about blood and all and . . .") June held his shoulders and looked down at his balding head, then up to the cracked plaster ceiling where deep shadows accumulated like fears in the far corners. She did not want to think what he would do. She did not want to think what it meant. Yet she did not want him to stop.

The lights in the dressing room blinked once again.

Bosley stood before her, one clean hand rising up as a fist beside his face as if moving upward on its own, a single finger held aloft, wet and red to the second knuckle. It glinted dully in the dim light.

"Oh, I . . . I'm sorry, Mr. Broderick . . ." She was sure the finger accused her.

Bosley Broderick did not laugh at her. "It's all right, June, dearest June, my dark sister of blood. This is your gift to me. It is the only gift we can give, since every other is sham. And now . . ."

Coming regally to his full height, he lifted the finger high as if it were a wand, a weapon, a bloody beacon of truth. Then, turning to sit in the folding chair, facing the mirror, he touched his forehead. When he turned back toward June, all the make-up was gone from his face. A single mark adorned his forehead. A cross, an inverted cross. In her blood.

June's hand fluttered instinctively to the bare space between her breasts where nothing had hung for all the years of her professional struggles. Suddenly Bosley Broderick shivered, as if stricken by stroke, some convulsive nausea, an icepick of bitterly personal pain. June knew her blood had hurt him, the blood he'd been trusting enough to touch to his own dear balding head. She had hurt him—a horrible accident, almost worse than an intentional blow to his vulnerable skull.

June groped to take it from him, to wipe it away, to take the curse back upon herself. Her hand trembled as she reached for him.

Bosley stopped her with a gesture of his left hand.

"You must . . ." His voice was that of a dying man. "You must . . ."

June touched cold fingers to her warm lips. He was going to die right there in front of her.

"What, Broderick? What?"

His eyes—was it a trick of the light, or did they actually roll back in his head? "You must . . . you *will* perform, on stage, a more outrageous act than any I have ever conceived. You will erase my memory from the annals of grotesquery. *You!* You will grow to become one of the greatest artists in the history of this music. You will marry, you will conceive, and then, using your own child alive on stage, you will . . ."

June laughed at the image of herself as the distaff version of Spinal Tap! What a perfectly absurd misunderstanding!

Bosley's head lolled dangerously on his shoulders, as if his neck must certainly be broken, the cord itself snapped in two. "But . . . but first . . ." Somehow the lips moved. "First you will deny your mother, once, and then once again. For she is the prison in which you do not know what you do. She forms your bars. Deny her. You must!"

"I'm perfectly able to cope with my mom's eccentricities. I've always been taught that an adult should learn to tolerate and compro . . ."

"It is the key!" His torso writhed, his arms to his sides. "You must deny her to save your child, save your life . . . save me."

"That's absurd," June muttered. She turned away to finger one of the squashed tubes of greasepaint on his dressing table. The cap had been screwed back on cockeyed and paint slurped from one side of it; a gash in the tube, a false mouth, had become the orifice used by the artist to draw out another of the the theatrical colors with which he disguised his fundamental shabbiness. What a careless, tired trickster he really was! What a poor excuse for an artist, no longer even a credible performer.

"June?"

When she turned, she saw the blood mark gone from his forehead. He had smeared it off with his thumb, surely. But how had he reinvigorated himself like this? His very presence in the minutes she had been with him had gone from disintegration to rebirth to dissipation. Well, he seemed lively enough now, almost youthful.

Bosley came toward her, confident now, one hand a happy claw out to catch her, the other hand hidden behind his back.

"I could wait to give you this, June. I could insist upon another meeting, a third—and more! I could make you come back again and again and again, an acolyte, a supplicant, but I will not play such pretty little fantasy games. What I offer you is *real*. We recognize each other. Isn't it true, June?"

What did he have for her? She'd gone this far. She had to know what came next. "No. This is all ridiculous. Nothing has happened here tonight, and I *don't* recognize you as an artist! I would never resort to your sort of cheap . . ."

"Theatrics!"

June shrugged at the enthusiasm with which he mocked her, that hideous huge smile. "I don't want anything from you," she said. "In fact, I'd rather forget everything that's . . ."

"Well, let us see." Bosley reached down into the deep pockets of the robe. His hand came out closed around something.

"Those of us who are of the Blood never lie," he said, still smiling defiantly. "We leave that to the organized metaphysical systems—to manipulate and damage the truth. So, in giving you this, I will not swear that what I have heard is true. I will only report the words I have been given."

Did he hold a diamond in his hand, in his palm? A precious stone? June leaned closer, looked at the small precious object framed by his thick parchment palm. The glow was illusory, the stone dark and impenetrable. The voices inside said her name, made beautiful promises, showed her how to enter. June blinked, shook her head; dizzy and disoriented, she felt as if she'd looked down from a great height and now could not judge her distance from the edge or secure her footing. June steadied herself against the dressing table.

"The man who occupied my rather infamous abode before me—the one they called Sorcerer, the Great Dark One—gave me this little trinket two years ago in the very moment of his transition."

The absurd formality did nothing for June's vertigo. Magnificent in his gold and crimson robe, Bosley held the black stone up high near his squinting eye. "He told me with his dying words the history I shall now relate to you. This rock was formed from the pure distilate of Aztec sacrifice, the blood of myriad virgins . . ."

"Is this supposed to be funny?"

". . . caught by the fount and preserved, compressed by the forgotten alchemical skills of Quetzalcoatl's minions. And so you see before you, safe in the bower of my naked human hand, this impossibly hard, impossibly dark jewel of power. They say that once it is put on around the neck, it may be removed only after death. Silly, isn't it?"

June backed away, feeling that it was the wrong thing to do. Smiling, Bosley came toward her with the dark stone that she saw now to be attached to an almost invisible chain. He held the links loosely open like a noose.

"Won't you wear my silly gift?"

June reached out tentatively to stop him, unsure that she dared to touch the stone. She remembered having felt like this when she'd extended fingers toward a coral snake—in the moment before she'd been assured that its venom was delightfully lethal. The smile grew, the stone touched her hand, and June forced herself not to recoil. But Bosley did not relinquish his prize.

"Marvelous things have transpired for me since I owned this priceless object d'art—some of which you have observed tonight. You have heard my records. I don't have to tell you what power means. Here, June. Yours."

She would not take it.

"Do you imagine that I have worn it and that in removing it I have vouchsafed my own death? Do not concern yourself. Do you imagine that I could prize the success of a total stranger so highly? Here—take it."

He placed the stone in her hand, the chain lapping down across her knuckles. Gently, he tried to close her fingers into a fist, but she resisted. He moved quickly then, behind her, over her, putting a hand to her throat.

June felt a burning sensation on her neck, like a bee sting. She wanted to swat the thing away.

"No, no, don't fight it. Let me . . ." It settled into place like membrane, like emotion, like the acceptance of a title. June felt for her throat."

"There. Thank you for your blood gift, my dear. You'll hear it returned on my next album. For now, wear the rock, go out in the world and prevail."

June looked down to her sweater, tucking her chin in to see the stone that seemed to pulse in place. "What you said about my career . . . about how I'll become famous for doing something outrageous with a baby . . . it'll never happen. I'm not married; and besides . . ."

Bosley kissed her full on the lips and made what

seemed a terminal flourish, a gesture of dismissal. June could hardly wait to get out, get the damned thing off her throat. The tingling sensation had eased but what she felt now was no less irritating. It seemed as though a fine line of coarse material constricted her throat. To her fingers the stone felt cool and delicate and tiny, but the second she took them away. . . . June hesitated to leave.

Smiling hugely, Bosley spread his robe like wings and pointed toward the door. "Go!" he said. "Go with blood!"

Chapter Three:

The Writ

June was trapped by other browsers in a pie wedge of bookshelves.

Poetry/Literary Criticism said the wooden flag that marked the aisle. She let her hand wander up to the strange medallion on her throat. Last night, after Duane had taken her home from the club, she had tried to remove the bloodrock and found that. . . .

"Never overtip," came an authorative voice from the café area. "Besides—look at this!—they sprinkled chocolate on top of the cappuccino. I knew we should've gone to Lucchessi's instead."

It sounded like Duane, whom she was supposed to meet here at Faust's Choice, perhaps the most fashionable café-bookstore in one of Silicon Valley's most fashionable shopping centers. Yet when she had searched the serving area minutes before she'd seen neither Duane nor either of the two men he'd arranged for her to meet—Pete Robinson of RMA records and Crater Club owner Herm D'Angello. Still, it sounded like Duane. She would have checked immediately except that her way out was blocked by a bearded young man, quite tall, with a pleasant curious smile, who seemed totally engrossed in flipping pages of *The Oxford Book of American Literary Anecdotes*.

"So I heard this scream," boomed the voice beyond the shelves. "I mean, she sounded like . . ." The volume dropped to signal confidentiality. ". . . like she was getting *raped* or something."

"Well, why didn't you go in there and see?"

June peeked between shelves to see the second speaker, a small slick-haired man chewing on an enormous yellow cigar. He had to be the record executive. Sitting across from him, as she'd guessed, was Duane Lombard, wearing what used to be called an ice cream suit, an elaborately knotted Florentine tie adding a dash of a crazy color to the overall effect of white. She saw him casually scratch his carefully coiffed blond head.

"Well, to be honest, I didn't really have much of a chance of getting past that Reformer character without getting my ass kicked. So I waited until she came out."

June made sure that the bearded fellow remained thoroughly entranced with his big paperback, therefore effectively preventing an exit, before again peeking out through the shelves. One must earn one's guilty pleasures. Again, her hand went instinctively to the bloodrock which she had been unable to remove from her throat. She had spent from 11:30 until after midnight trying to decipher the secret of the stubborn clasp that held it to her body with such irritating intimacy. Finally, deciding that the next day would be soon enough to ask her sister Betty to pry the clasp with pliers, June had given up the project as hopeless.

Memories of that frustration came back now and she could swear she felt heat coming from the rock and a corresponding tingling in her fingers. She could hardly wait to get the thing off her neck. It was a talisman, surely, a charm of some sort; but did it offer protection—or threaten harm?

"You sound pretty worked up about this, Lombard," said the second man. "I thought you were the perfect business manager, practical and objective. Your response seems pretty emotional to me. If I were you, I'd be looking at the publicity angle, you know—the occult stuff. Instead, you seem to be worrying about your client's uncertain mental stability. Am I right?"

A plume of cigar smoke wafted expansively toward the book shelves, and June jerked her head away. Suddenly afraid of coughing, drawing attention to herself and being caught spying, she grabbed a book, any book.

"You'd have been spooked, too," Duane said. "She didn't say a word to me after she came out of there. And you should have seen the look on her face—like one of those portraits of Nefertiti—pure stone. It frightened me, as if she'd got into some kind of danger that she couldn't . . ."

"You're behind the times, Lombard." Another aggressive plume of smoke homed in on June as if programed to seek out hidden women. "What you don't understand is that this client of yours needs to get involved in more of this mock-danger stuff. She plays it too safe; that's her problem."

Flinching, June looked away, almost dropping the book. Was that true? Did she play it safe?

"You call a great voice with more high and low octaves than any other girl rock singer *safe*?" Looking through the crack in the shelves, she saw that Duane had risen angrily up out of his seat and was hovering over the record executive. "You call writing lyrics about nuclear disarmament and women's rights and gay liberation *playing it safe*? How about hiring two black guys when the lily white FMers were shivering at the sight of . . . ?"

"Enough! Enough, Lombard!" The executive hid his face and waved his cigar like a flag of surrender, "No one's saying this girl isn't a great talent, a nice person—the Second Coming, for Christ's sake! That's the problem; she does everything right. Show me the pop singer since Pat Boone that's sold nice. When I say she's too safe, what I'm trying to get across to you is that . . ."

"She'd make it big if she did dope or got involved in S & M? Or maybe you'd like her to perform unnatural sex acts on stage with snakes and other . . . ?"

"No, no, no! Let me breathe, huh?" He expelled prolific volumes of smoke. "Ever hear of show biz? Or doing an act? Look at this guy Bosley Broderick. Do you think he really bites the heads off rats and chickens on stage? Do you think he really believes in all that devil-worship crap? Look, I know his ex-manager and, straight from the horse's mouth, Broderick's a pussycat, a family man, and a great artist to boot, huh?"

June saw Duane rock back on his chair to make the front legs smack down on the hardwood floor of the cafe, startling students and chess players throughout the serving area. "Sure, just like Jack the Ripper was a good family man and Adolph Hitler loved his maiden aunt Matilda!"

"See why I hate boyfriends?" Pete looked up to the ceiling and held his cigar high as if soliciting divine aid.

"I'm not her boyfriend," Duane said softly. "I happen to like her. We happen to be friends as well as business associates. She's a brilliant, attractive, remarkably committed young lady—and you say she's got to pretend she's the opposite? I don't understand your logic—to me, it seems twisted. And, in turn, you tell me *I'm* thinking emotionally because I'm in love with her or something."

June snatched her head out of the opening between the shelves. She asked herself what she felt—a kind of pleased embarrassment?

"Of course you are," the record executive said gently enough. "She's a great little property—clean, wholesome, perfect, a rock 'n' roll Shirley Temple, right? But look, Mr. Lombard, when a woman's been around for ten years trying to break in, you've got to start wondering."

"Seven years, buddy. Seven years of . . ."

"Hello, gentlemen!"

June's heart fired off one ferocious cannon shot of a beat at the proximity of the voice. Certainly she had been discovered! Loud, right in her ear, the voice carried the mocking sense of triumph of a cop catching a crook with the goods.

"I was only . . ." She began to apologize before she realized that someone else was talking and she was not being heard.

"Looks like you two are getting a little heated up over the belle dame sans merci who is the subject of our little get-together. Am I right?"

The booming voice belonged to a tall square-shouldered man in a Hawaiian shirt and designer jeans that rode low on his hips.

Duane had risen to extend his large hand and the two locked into a handshake that looked like preparation for mortal combat. "Good to see you. June and I enjoyed the show at your club last night—Bosley's really something, huh? Want you to meet Pete Robinson of RMA records. I was just telling Mr. Robinson that June would be the perfect act for a club like yours that caters to the real rock connoisseur."

"Exactly," Pete Robinson said as they shook. "Whereas my company feels that Miss Lockwood is too sedate and traditional to stir up much enthusiasm with the target audience. I'm sure, however, that your mature and discerning clientele will immediately embrace such an artist."

June felt the shelf sway as she slumped against it. Three men wrangling over her career, her life, her fate. She felt that her body had been locked into a very subtle sort of huge invisible vise and that what she heard out there was the sound of the handle turning to tighten it. With one hand she gripped the book she had plucked from the shelf for a prop, while the other homed in inevitably on the blood medallion hanging from her throat.

"Let's get to the point, Mr. Robinson," the big club owner drawled. "Is your company signing Duane's girl or not? I called in a sign painter this morning who's ready to give me a nice little two-color broadside for the lobby with your company and June's name in equally large script if you give me the okay."

Turning back to the opening, she saw Pete Robinson feeling all around his jaw as if the answer to this question was somehow coded there. "Well . . . that's hard to say, Herm, hard to say. At this point in time we find it difficult to commit . . ."

Herm D'Angello raised his eyebrows in exaggerated contempt. "Come on, Pete," he said. "Are you signing June or not?"

Pete glanced around the room at those reading and writing and sipping coffee or chewing pastry. Then his eye lit on the crevice through which June peered. "Like you, Herm, I'm a businessman. And like all businessmen, I'm willing to take a risk now and then. Now if June were to add . . . a little spice to her act, that

X-factor that distinguishes just another talent from a recognizable performer . . ."

"A gimmick, you mean," Duane blurted. "Well, my client won't . . ."

Pete held the cigar up to request silence. "Who says it has to be a gimmick? Is it a gimmick to add a little brandy extract to get the right taste in a fruit cake?"

Duane seemed to mutter something personal and nasty.

Pete took another thoughtful puff on his stogy. "No, if June could add that certain spice, that little dash of controversy or . . ."

"Controversy!" Duane pounded the table with his fist, making the demitasse cups spout like tiny geysers. "What do you call lines like: 'Outspoken survivors without tongues/Fingers miming the holocaust song/Fallout's just another name for censorship.'?"

"Come on, Duane," Pete chided. "You've been in this business long enough to know that message, no matter how strong, isn't controversy. It ain't what you sell, it's the way that you sell it."

Invisible fingers dialed out the Stravinsky piece that had been brewing toward a climax on the in-shop speaker system and homed in on some fast bluesy rock.

"Like that," Pete proclaimed, snapping his fingers and pistol-pointing toward the sound. "That's Beelzebub—the latest thing in acid rock. A bunch of nice guys knocking around for years as Albatross—a band that was going nowhere until they got a new name and an identity and—bango! overnight gangbusters! Selling like wildfire! Just by reviving an old '60s sound, concert dates up the . . ."

"Okay." Herm contemplated the raucous music. "I'll admit my audience ain't so sophisticated—that's exactly what *they're* asking for. But I figure you got to take a chance on quality once in a while. And that's why I'm booking June Lockwood for a two-week stint whether you sign her or not. Hell, if she doesn't get support here in her hometeown, where . . ."

The bearded browser having long since cleared out, June had no excuse not to show herself. She glanced at the book she'd been clutching—*Les Fleurs de Mal*—and, shaking her head, strolled around the shelves into the coffee shop area. Did heads turn? The idea of being a femme fatale frightened her.

"Hi, June!"

Seeing Duane stand, the other two stood as well. June stopped several feet from their table as if arrested by the collective force of their intent gaze. Did they know she'd been hiding, listening? She refused to be timid or guilty.

"If every audience was as attentive as you three gentlemen," she said, "performing would be a snap!"

Laughing nervously, Pete blew smoke and jerked his head away. Herm pulled out a chair for June, and they resumed their seats. Duane prolonged the unnecessary introductions.

June, smiling warily, scanned the male eyes ranged so closely around the table. "So how's my future? Which is closer—skid row or the Nobel Prize?"

Herm laughed. Duane pulled her close for a quick peck on the cheek and signaled the young waiter to bring another cappuccino, while Pete emitted a ruminative puff of smoke. Each darted secret looks at June. With her full-skirted summer dress gathered around her, big brown and blue flowers keying subtly into imperceptible make-up, she did not feel like the center of attention. Having previously arranged to see her mother for her monthly visit, June felt her sense of self-importance to be already preshrunk for the scene tonight at the mansion. Mother always occupied center stage, leaving room there for no one else. June became aware that Duane was snapping his fingers in her face.

"Are you on drugs or something? That'd be just perfect according to Pete here. Right, Pete?"

June bit her lip, angry at having embarrassed Duane, whom she trusted more than any other man since her step-father died. "Sorry, Duane, I . . . What were you saying?"

"I said—should we dispense with the preliminaries and get down to it? Look, here's Herm's contract for two weeks at the club. I know we're not used to being so formal, but I figure since we're here and all . . . I recommend signing that, by the way."

June took the proffered contract, no more than a form available in any stationery store, and scanned it as the young man brought her cappuccino. He almost spilled the contents in his efforts to sneak a frontal look at June.

She smiled openly. "Just fine," she said. "Here's my John Hancock."

Duane nodded with disconcerting seriousness. "Okay, now for the nasty part. Robinson, let's see what you got."

"You got a real charmer here for a manager, Miss Lockwood," Pete said. "You're lucky I'm a good-natured guy and can take the kidding. Because, I mean, these guys were really ganging up on me before you got here."

Duane snapped his fingers impatiently. "The contract, Robinson. Let's see it. You're wasting everybody's time."

Pete Robinson reached a hand into his breast pocket and withdrew a thickly folded packet with maddening slowness. Grabbing the papers away, Duane angrily backhanded them to make them stay flat and open on the small round table. He leaned threateningly over the document.

"Now let's see . . . very interesting. *Very* interesting. Take a look at this, June." Duane slid the contract in front of her while squinting straight into Pete's eyes. "See that part that starts, 'In the event of fiscal difficulties regarding the project in question'? That's what you call a no-risk clause, isn't it, Pete? And where it says, 'copyright considerations in conformation with previously established company policy regarding incipient artists'—ah, lovely, Pete, just lovely. June?"

Winking, June pursed her lips, feigning puzzlement. "It couldn't mean that, ah, RMA assumes copyright control of all my songs for the next three years if I sign this—could it?"

Someone out of sight behind the serving counter fiddled with the cafe radio again, dialing rapidly between stations, yielding a not unpleasant but utterly atonal John Cage effect.

Duane threw his hands up, apparently nonplussed. "Sorry, Pete. My star and I just can't make heads or tails of this thing. Come back and see us when RMA's big wigs learn to write the English language."

Pete snatched the contract and stood in one motion. "Okay, yokels! I tried to be nice. I'll take this contract and my report of your attitude back to Mr. Chives, the company president, along with my evaluation of Miss Lockwood's . . . opportunities. We gave you your chance. Don't ever look to RMA to give you a break again."

With that, he squirmed his way between tables and out the bookstore door.

Herm covered the hand June rested on the small table with his own massive paw. "I'll bet Robinson's threats have you just terrified, right?"

June peered off into the night for such a long moment that neither man was sure whether she'd caught the sarcastic question. She wanted to touch what hung from her throat but did not. "Yes," she said at last. "I am terrified."

Duane laughed—hadn't she made a joke? "Hey," he said, "what's that around your neck, that weird looking stone? I've never noticed it before."

"Nothing. I mean . . . it's really nothing."

Herm shook his head and laughed uninhibitedly, his big guffaws filling the polite academic cafe with unaccustomed energy.

"You know, June. You're hilarious! You *do* look terrified. What an actress! Wait till I get you on stage at my club—you're going to make Bosley Broderick look like Cinderella!"

Chapter Four:

Larry's Fantasy

The dragon vomited plumes of spiky fire. Heels boldly planted in crimson clouds of nostril smoke, the Nordic warrior, clad only in animal skins knotted at the loins, flourished a sparkling sword long as a sapling. The beast's curling talons striping her naked body, the wild young temptress snarled in anguished defiance. Her black flowing hair twined around dragon and hero alike. And through the tableau streamed a banner of psychedelic flames, "Heavy Metal Rules."

June had seen the mural often enough, though she'd never before been inside Larry's van. The airbrush painting stretched from front door to rear left bumper—art, 1980's style. Hardly Keats' Grecian urn, yet to June, reminiscent of it—the dragon always threatening, the hero untested, the voluptuous female terrified but unravished. Forever—or, at least, until the van's next paint job. Better that way, she thought. Better if you could stop the story before its climax. Real life had a tendency to get ugly when you let it play out to the end.

An interior junkyard of discarded and cannibalized guitars littered the van's rear compartment. Once in a while, however, Larry became dissatisfied with his present axe and delved into the harmonic graveyard to resurrect one of these old wrecks on which he'd proceed to lavish hundreds of dollars and many hours of his own time. More than once in a while, too, he cleared a space amongst the wood and fiberglass debris to entertain a young lady here with his high-energy approach to love.

"I really appreciate this, Larry," June said, settling herself tentatively in the black leather bucketseat.

"Don't worry. You'll have a chance to pay me back later." He jerked a thumb toward the back of the van and eyed her appraisingly. "Just kidding. Don't you think Neil'd do the same for Pat? What's a lead guitarist for if not to give his gal singer rides to her mother's stately mansion in his humble and highly vulgar van? And to make the de rigueur lewd suggestion, right? Right, June?"

Giving a little giggle, she eyed Larry right back. Maybe it hadn't been so smart after all to ask him for a ride.

Gangly, still plagued by complexion problems, a faint sneer always dancing across his big lips like some fleshly St. Elmo's fire, Larry Ludwig drove with the same distracted abandon with which he played guitar for June's band. The van ate up the dark streets that connected the south valley to the Willow Glen area of San Jose as if, for Larry, negotiating a dark corner on an unknown street at top speed was the ultimate form of improvisation.

Despite (or because of) her nervousness, June could hardly keep from laughing. "Larry, could you . . . uh, slow down just a little?"

"Honey," Larry drawled, "people been tellin' me that all my life. Mom, that's what she always said. 'If'n you don't slow yer ass down, sonny boy, you gonna buy yerself a mighty skinny lookin' early grave.' Colorful talker, my mom. Then there was Gertrude, my first eternal flame, who'd always roll over in bed and say, 'Whooshew—eight cylinders is right! But could you please shift back to . . .' "

June laughed openly and punched him hard in the arm, harder than she'd meant to. "Larry, aren't you ever serious?"

"You know I am," he said. "Whenever I'm near you I'm serious, dead serious. Hit me again like that and my unrequited passion may get requited real quick with our bodies fused together along with one of our fair city's venerable telephone poles."

Ready to extend an elbow into his ribs, June considered his words and thought better of it. He was, as he'd said himself, unpredictable, dangerous, and had been addicted at one time or another to "just about every drug known to man." He liked to brag that he was a master fisherman, a superior angler; his catch, of course, consisted of those groupies foolish enough to swim his way backstage. Ironically, her step-father had used a similar metaphor to warn her against such men years before. "Don't bite the first flashy lure you see, honey. Find the one where you have to scratch the surface to see the shine."

How Larry did shine! A ferocious, relentless guitarist, he sometimes came close to stopping the show with his blistering solos. June didn't mind; in fact, she relished every deflection of attention away from herself, that shift of focus. She thought that taking the backseat occasionally might benefit the longevity of her career.

"I'm sure grateful to you for driving me—even if I can't come through later on as you're hoping. It's just that Duane couldn't break away from Herm D'Angello; they still had some . . ."

"Ah, Duane couldn't break away. A pity, that. But just remember, sweetums, if the young manager ever gets hung up permanently—know what I mean?—old Larry here's not proud and he's jus' a waitin' an' a pinin' to get somethin' permanent goin'."

"Oh, Larry!" June didn't know what to say. No matter how much he kidded, it seemed pretty obvious that he was unfortunately serious about his affection for her. "Don't lead me on, okay?"

But he spoke as if he hadn't caught her attempt at casual humor. "I know musicians aren't supposed to get . . . hung up on each other. It's supposed to be bad for the artistic distance and all, but you're the woman I've always dreamed . . ."

"Sssssh," June said. "What good is that talk going to do either of us. I have to visit my mother and you . . ."

"Me? I'll head back to the club to dip my dorsel fin in the waters and see what luscious bodies are lolling on the surface. Dah, dah, dah . . ." Larry did a mock-menacing version of the *Jaws* theme, crouched over the wheel as if the van itself had suddenly become a cruising Great White.

Laughing appreciatively, June failed to notice the houses increasing in size. "Oh, Larry! Turn, turn!"

Larry twisted the wheel and screeched the van around the corner down a narrow tree-lined street. Homes became estates as Larry sang, " 'Turn, turn, turn, there is a season; turn, turn turn . . .' "

"I'll bet you don't know where that's originally from—no, not the Byrds. Would you shut up or you're going to miss . . ."

"You say 'shut up' to a pious and reverend preacher of the Word? Shame, shame, shame! For every treason there is a . . ."

"Larry!"

"Don't be irreverent, June." His head swiveling from

side to side, Larry slowed the van. "What house number are we looking for? Want a toke?"

"Right here, Larry. The three-story house with the Hollywood sheers."

He dredged the half-smoked joint from the ashtray and raised it up for her inspection. Almost as an afterthought, he parked the van.

"Larry, you know I don't use chemicals and . . ."

"First off, you need to relax before you go in to face that ordeal you've described to me. Second, pot's no chemical. Hundred percent natural homegrown. Better than booze. Have I ever told you my fantasy of the ultimate experience that . . ."

"Larry, I have to go in now. Really."

He grabbed June's arm, not roughly, but with a firmness she was afraid to resist. "My ultimate fantasy, June—some very good grass, for both of us, and then to find out what you're all about. Because sex and pot go together like honey and . . ."

"I've *got* to go," June insisted, pulling away. She unlatched the door.

"June, listen . . . don't . . ."

"Never mind, Larry." Throwing the van door open wide, June jumped down into the mouth of the massive circular driveway that curled up to her mother's rambling estate.

"Just . . . thanks for the ride." She slammed the door and began to run toward the house before slowing to a trot. She had to have time to brace herself for what was coming. Yet she'd felt the need to put physical space between herself and Larry, whom she found intimidating. He'd probably meant to relax her by joking around, but. . . .

June found herself at the base of the stone slab steps looking up, caught herself counting them. Looking back over her shoulder, she saw Larry burn rubber as he rocketed the van down the narrow regal road. Anger? Exuberance? Just good old plain irresponsibility?

In a moment, she knew she would have to order herself to quit stalling and begin to climb.

Chapter Five:

The Door in the Silver Screen

Twenty-three stone slabs. Steps. A short climb, really. Then why did they always seem to June an insurmountable obstacle? Why did this mosaic of her childhood descend on her like a rock falling irrevocably into place?

Always the spinning spool of frayed celluloid. The pretension of on-going life just a series of still shots linked together by a machine that took advantage of the eye's willingness to be tricked. Any life will do. Always. *I want you to meet Henry, dear. Hug your teddy bear, mommy won't be long. Mommy's private time is very, very important, darling, so please don't dare to come looking for her.* So the lines of fantasy and reality in her life became fouled. How come you don't know the way to your mother's house, little girl? How come you don't climb up there? June climbed up to the top.

She lifted the hefty discolored brass knocker and, as if it were something repugnant, let it drop to clang hollowly against the impenetrable door. Why, in this moment, did June always feel so cold?

Always, great segments of time seemed to pass before the door rolled open, as if of its own volition.

"June, how nice of you to visit us!"

She recognized the lilting voice as the one that all airline stewardesses were taught to strive for but which few achieved.

"Mother will be so pleased to see you."

June extended her hand, embarrassed at not remembering the girl's name. "Hi!" She compensated with a big smile. "How are you?"

Always amazing how Amelia found the exact look she sought in each of her "young ladies" for whom she declined to use the term "servant." Amazing, too, how many of them there had been, a never-ending succession, seemingly. Tall, beautiful, full-figured, and always, always cheerful, each approximately the image in Amelia's memory of the leading ladies under whom she had played for so many years. Because June's mother had never landed a starring role, she recollected herself as having been habitually cast as a "lady-in-waiting." Once, June remembered, mother had slipped and referred to her latest acquisition with that very term.

"Mother is in the drawing room this evening," the girl confided brightly. "Earlier tonight she told me, 'Alice, if anyone should call on me . . .' "

Of course the girl would notice June's discomfort! Of course she would find a way to insinuate her name into the conversation with supreme subtlety! Of course, Amelia always managed to select surrogate daughters with more presence of mind than her real ones.

The drawing room opened up like a set for the narrator of Masterpiece Theatre. In fact, June realized, she did not so much visit her mother as she did participate in a tour, a tour conducted by the world's foremost authority on Amelia Lockwood. Utterly excluded from the tour, of course, was the present moment—Amelia Lockwood today. Visitors were allowed access only to the Amelia Lockwood captured on celluloid and displayed on the screen magically unfurled from the drawing room ceiling.

"Well, June." Amelia rose precisely, both civilized hands gripping her teacup and saucer with the gentlest of all possible pressures. "How nice of you to drop in on your mother on such a pleasant night. I would have thought you'd be out playing that loud noise you call music—or dancing with that gorgeous blond Viking of yours at one of those hoedown places." Smiling, Amelia bowed almost imperceptibly as if to restrained but enthuisastic applause and settled back down onto her Queen Anne highback. "Well, dear, what *have* you been up to? Sit down, please. You know how I detest it when you stand by as if you were one of my young ladies. Now . . ."

Like a captured soldier in the study of an enemy general, June sat as instructed, tense, dutiful and wary. She did not want her mother to scold her. True, her name was more common now in the media than that of the famous actress. But no matter what perspective she put it in, no matter how philosophical she tried to be about it, June had not yet learned how to avoid reacting—even overreacting—to being scolded by Amelia.

"Well, Mom, exciting news—I'm going to be on a two-week engagement . . ."

Amelia waved her to stop. " 'Mom'? Please, darling, you know how I feel about sentimental familiarity. We have a mature relationship as one adult woman to another. Isn't that the way it's supposed to be in the 1980's?"

June knew better than to attempt any logical fencing with her mother. What was the percentage in dueling a woman constitutionally incapable of acknowledging defeat or even yielding up a begrudging *touché*. "Anyway . . . Mr. D'Angello over at the Club Crater has agreed . . ."

" 'Mr.', darling?" Amelia raised her head until her strong chin seemed aimed at her daughter's face, restraining anger only with great effort. "Really, June, you still talk as if you were a child, a silly mincing child! *You are an adult*. Address adults by their first name. After all . . ."

"Yes, Amelia, you're right, I suppose. But I am very grateful to . . . Herm for hiring me. There're a million rock acts out there and if he . . ."

"June?"

"Yes?"

Amelia smiled sweetly. "*Don't* be grateful. No one *gives* you anything in this world. Remember that. This Herm person should be grateful to *you*."

June resisted pointing out the obvious contradiction. What would be accomplished? Undoubtedly, Amelia did her best—so wasn't it best for June to put aside her pride, her sense of her own womanhood, and calmly absorb the hurts that each of these visits brought upon her?

"Yes, I suppose you're right . . . Amelia."

For a moment June could do nothing but stare and admire this habitually elegant woman who happened to be her mother. She wore a burgundy pants suit her daughter had never seen before, bright and almost melodramatic; but June could not take her eyes off the brocade evening cape draped with apparent unconcern about Amelia's shoulders. Not the material, not the imagined price tag, not the radical declaration it made of its wearer's superb good taste—no, nothing more than its placement on her mother's shoulders confounded June. Had Amelia looked into the mirror for an hour making subtle adjustments? Or, if one were Amelia Lockwood, did this sort of natural perfection occur without premeditation?

Now she formed her tapered fingers into a flesh cathedral over which she peered at her daughter. Clearly, she had readied herself to make an important proclamation or frame a crucial question. "June, tell me something, please. From what you've said I gather that you are still performing. But is it true that you are still playing that rock and roll music?"

Why was this so abundantly ludicrous and cosmically absurd? Amelia prided herself on being *current*, yet her careful enunciation of the name of this musical genre was . . . quaint, old-fashioned! June did everything she could to keep from bursting out in a big guffaw of mirth that surely would have meant her permanent banishment from her mother's house. It involved a strenuous act of will on June's part to resist countering with a cliché to match her mother's question.

"Yes, I will play . . . in that style. However, if you consider everything from Pink Floyd to John Cougar as rock, then it's a rather all-conclusive . . ."

"June, are you . . . *on* something? Some kind of drugs? You seem distant and disassociated and out-of-touch. This isn't like you. The only *possible* explanation I can imagine is that . . ."

"As a matter of act, Mother, no!" June's giddy urge to laugh outloud wrestled with her growing anger for control of her voice. "I'm slow enough as it is without burning out any of the few remaining brain cells. I don't drink any longer, either."

"Well, darling, we shouldn't become fanatics, you

know. A little alcohol now and then, in moderation you understand, is really quite beneficial. I've always been a firm believer in the efficacy of the nightcap as a natural sedative, producing the deepest and fullest sort of sleep. Don't you agree?''

Sure, Mom. If you say so, Mom. June held a hand to her mouth. She wanted to touch it again. The bloodrock.

"June, are you sure you're not having some sort of . . . flashback?"

June composed herself by taking a deep breath and exhaling completely. Normally, she had no trouble dealing with Amelia's urge to be master of all she discussed. But tonight. . . . Was some of Larry's rebelliousness rubbing of on her? She'd have to watch it.

"I'm fine. Really I am."

Amelia straightened in her chair like a director who has just been told that everything is ready, that all she has to do is say the word.

"Wonderful, darling. Are you prepared for a little diversion, an entertainment for the evening?"

"Sounds good to me." What could she say? The movie would be screened no matter how she reacted.

"Excellent. Excellent. Alice," Amelia called into the adjoining hallway. "Alice, brandy, two glasses, the screen, please—*Four Women West*, the third reel—and, oh, darling, no calls tonight, all right?"

June squirmed erect in the antique chair. She did not want to be rude, but. . . . "Amelia, remember . . . I'm not drinking these days?"

"Of course, dear." Amelia absent-mindedly stroked her throat, then did a rather dignified double take. "What the devil is that ugly thing around your neck? It looks familiar."

"This?" June pulled the pendant away from her throat to examine it herself. "Just something a friend gave me—a kind of memento, you might say."

"An erotic interlude?"

"Mother!"

Amelia laughed, pleased at the result of her offhand remark. "Oh, aren't I the venomous one? And you thought Mother had been defanged, didn't you, darling? Well, there's no adder like an old adder, as they say." Amelia stared intently at her daughter. "Darling, it's your line. You're supposed to reply instantaneously: 'Why, Amelia, how could anyone possibly think of you as old?' "

Amelia permitted herself a soft but fully-relished giggle at June's expense. "Ah, my darling daughter," Amelia sighed. "You have no idea . . ." Uncharacteristically, she let her voice trail off. She seemed to consider some proposal. "Ah!" she said, reaching an apparent decision. "You know, June darling, how involved I am with Senator Gould's re-election campaign. His positions on law and order, alien emigration, and penalties for drug traffic match my own precisely. Precisely! And then, of course, there's his courgeous stand on standards of public decency in the performing arts. Well, he has a benefit coming up and I'd like and your group to consider . . . Ah, Alice! Darling, our little proposition can wait until later."

Amelia took the brandy decanter and glasses from Alice and signaled the girl to start the film. In moments, the screen descended from the ceiling with a mechanical whir, the lights clicked off, and a clear new print of the film materialized on the silver granules of the screen. June wondered about her mother's proposal but assumed she'd find out soon enough.

"And Hollywood said 'let there be light'," Amelia

intoned in the darkness of the drawing room. "And there was chiaroscuro. And the black and the white were the first day."

Fingering the stone pendant Bosley had given her, June hoped that Amelia's narration would be relatively self-contained tonight and that no reply would be expected. She wanted to relax a little, subside into her own thoughts. It shouldn't be hard. After all, hadn't she seen each of her mother's films twenty times at least?

"Will that be all, Mrs. Lockwood?" came the voice from the darkness, the perfect stewardess voice. "I know you'd like to be alone with your daughter."

"Yes, of couse, Alice; fine, very good. Now I want you to notice, June darling, how evident it is how Charles Ennistone felt about me. There's a certain pervading dullness in his performance in all the scenes with *her*—ironic when you consider that they gave *her* the romantic lead. But just watch his eyes when I come into the scene behind him, dusting, arranging figurines; note the supreme effort he makes to keep his eyes off me. But notice, also, the increased intensity, the life, the marvelous way he . . ."

June had no way of evaluating the accuracy of her mother's version of the celluloid past. Tonight, however, she found herself drifting into it. The credits ended. Figures moved around the screen. Shadowy and vague at first, they soon became clear, specific, as if illuminated from within—props managers, sound people, costumers, make-up technicians, spare actors and actresses, cameramen walking away from their rigs to scrutinize the shot from a different angle. Amelia seemed no longer to be in the room, although her voice remained. No, there she was. Behind the screen. "Mother, why . . .?" But Amelia did not hear.

Removing the maid's costume she had worn in the now-concluded scene of the film still unfolding on the screen, she appeared to be ready to dress for an evening's engagement, a more personal kind of diversion or entertainment.

The bloodrock glowed hot in June's taut hand.

"Mother?"

The man slipping the cloak so gallantly over Amelia's sensuous shoulders was garbed entirely in red, two pock marks blistering his otherwise smooth forehead.

Chapter Six:

When Our Costumes Consume Us

How could this be? Her mother, young, vital, almost frighteningly sexual, driving crosstown (what town? Hollywood?) with her queerly costumed leading man?

June increased her hold on the pendant as if her contact with it powered this compelling vision. But why did it seem a matter of life or death that she see it through to completion?

Erotic foreplay under the lurid streetlamp glow and submarine wash of display light from passing shops. Whispered words twining together like copulating plants. An animated burst of sinuous motion, tendrils spindling together with impossibly delicate yet inevitable combinations. Life, triumphant, obscene, delirious life—Amelia, her mother. "Move your hand down and hold it there and . . . yes, yes!" He has liquor on his breath, so much the easier for oneself to become submerged in the onslaught of his blood energy. Because that is the Secret, the Emersion, the total engulfment one seeks, the less of oneself in all the pleasures that skin and tongue and ears and . . . "We're here, darling. Come quickly now; the others are waiting."

And he dazzles you on his arm up brocade steps into crystaline light brighter than the sun, each radiant center a person, a star! We are all dazzle ships, all stars, you realize, all glowing, all beautiful, all magnificent! How fine and truly wonderful to be with beautiful people who know what they are—and what you are!

"Quickly now. Someone's been dying to meet you. I think you know who he is . . ."

Squeeze the rock. Rock 'n' roll lives.

Beautiful presence, extended hand, a body imposing and open, an odor of compost, dead pines, the wide stretch of landless sea and nothing but nature, not the slightest whiff of anything dirty and small, anything vaguely human.

"Don't we have marvelous Halloween overtures here?" he askes you. "We've missed you. But, ah, now you are alive with one inside you." He touches you with beautifully knotted hands, touches your abdomen where the selfish little thing has already started to make its hideous demands. "Yes?"

"Yes," you say.

"Good. Tonight. But first you will have the night of your life. All paradise, all love, all . . ." He smirks magnificently. ". . . all pleasure." He nods his huge shaggy head for you to agree, to see that all must be in agreement with him. "And then we will end your misery and bring you back to yourself again, so that we may enjoy you and you may enjoy . . ."

Costumes. Joviality. Liquor. Love. Touching. And more touching. And the flow of everything beautiful. Oh, so right. Doesn't it have to be right if it feels so very, very good?

And that other foreign presence, lingering somewhere in the meagerest moment of dust at the height of the central chandaliers. Like a spirit from the past gathering strength from this party—resolution, determination, a plot. But why can you, only you, feel it fixing on the task, cogitating, working out the details of interference, working out the precise energy needed to . . ?

Squeeze the rock. Rock. Rock.

"Oh, aren't you beautiful when you are intoxicated with this joy!" he tells you. "Dizzy? Yes, of course. Let me help you sit. It's time, you know. If you'll rest a moment, we'll take you into the master bedroom. The instruments are sterilized and ready. There is nothing to fear. He's done it a million times. Feeling better? Perfect. Perfect! Now, if you will . . ."

Squeeze. Blood. Rock lives.

Are you the only one to see the tiny flame materialize from nothing, like a cartoon fairy? You know, therefore you see. You have been told that this is the fundamental secret, that the knowledge yields the seeing; the knowing, the possession, and the pain that must be born over and over and . . .

C'EST VRAI. IT IS TRUE THAT THIS IS HOW I DEAL WITH THOSE WHO BETRAY ME.

Flames feast on the elegant draperies, dance with gay abandon on banisters and skip the light fantastic up and down fancy gowns; and digging deep into pockets, flames spout up as gardens where tuxedos had been before, the whole palace a sudden bouquet of clean burning light. Flames cleanse through to the secret corruptions that the surface of glittering civility had seemed so well to cover. Flames crisp all in seconds, the veneer burned away like the thinnest gauze, and all beneath the skin and wood and plush carpet and hardwood and plants and food and make-up and jewelry and bone and. . . .

VRAIMENT. THIS IS HOW I DEAL WITH FAMILY PROBLEMS, THE FAMILY WAY.

Squeeze. Squeeze.

Flames swallowed the motion picture screen. The projector exploded, showering the drawing room with fragments of burning metal and plastic. The flames climbed voraciously into June's clothing, her lap, her. . . .

"June, darling," Amelia exclaimed. "I must protest. If you're going to sleep through my films, at least pay me the compliment of having pleasant dreams."

When our costumes consume us, the fire of ourselves. . . .

With the greatest effort of will, June halted her frantically flailing arms, made them stop pawing the air, pressed them down to her sides.

"You were pregnant with me. You didn't want me. You . . ."

"Darling, are you sure you haven't been taking drugs? Perhaps someone has slipped an hallucinogenic into your coffee or orange juice? You look terrible."

So, was it to be now—the confrontation with her mother that June had avoided for years?

Amelia leaned forward to cup the bloodrock in her palm, holding it out from her daughter's neck. Gradually the look on her face altered as if she might be listening to a distant but clearly audible voice. With exquisite gentleness she said, "You were gripping this so tightly and fighting so hard that I thought if I divested you of it, you might find relief from the strain you seemed to be feeling. But I feared to awaken you. Shall I now . . ."

"No!"

Amelia shrugged, mild amusement showing on her lips, and let the medallion fall from her hand back onto June's chest. "Oh dear," she said, as if to herself. "It's so ugly . . . and I'd already found such an admirable replacement, far superior in all aspects. Look here, June."

Amelia held out a diamond pendant, a piece she had shown each of her daughters countless times, a cherished memento of the very actor with whom she'd starred in the film still flapping against the take-up reel on the cooling projector.

Amelia placed the pendant in June's hand, closing her daughter's fingers on it like the petals of a flower.

So, was this the final assault? Or was June being paranoid, blind to her mother's affectionate motive? "But mother, you never even let me or Betty touch this, let alone . . . You always said it was priceless."

"I suppose that until tonight I never realized what was really priceless, darling. However, if you don't want it and prefer instead to keep this hideous . . . thing, well, that's your prerogative."

June watched Alice return to attend to the drink tray and remove the projector on her way out. Ah, Mother, Mother. It was easy to be critical, June knew, but what kind of mother would she be herself if she had a daughter? Was there any aphorism ready to assert that rock musicians made better mothers than movie stars?

"Why are you so generous tonight, Mom?" June said softly.

Amelia smiled with a serenity that seemed made up of a million tiny particles of tension, like a fine link gold chain held together by frightening, precise artistry. "I think you're under a terrible strain, darling," she said. "Life in the fast lane—isn't that what they call it?"

As an answer, June opened her hand to show the naked frigidly perfect diamond pendant. She did not want it and would not take it. Did she have to force Amelia to reclaim it? "Amelia, here, please, I can't . . ."

Her mother's shoulders stiffened restrictively.

"I know what your problem is, dear. I know what you young singers do to get ready for a show . . . and then what you do afterwards. I know what's expected of you, darling. Terrible. I know what you must have gone through to get that poor ugly thing you cherish so. A really terrible sort of pressure, isn't it?"

"Mother, what really happened between you and Charles Lombard? You went to a party where there was a doctor who . . ."

A frown wrinkled spontaneously across Amelia's face as if in that moment the tissues had been entirely drained of fluid. Then very slowly, yet not slowly enough to keep the change from appearing grotesquely abrupt, she smiled. "Darling, I want you to do that benefit for Senator Gould! Yes, it's true that he's helping me in my campaign to expunge so-called occult references from the media that our young people are exposed to. But you'd never become involved in anything so foolish and decadent and immature, would you, darling? No, I think your nice little rock group would be perfect for the rally, just perfect."

June could not feel her hand. She sensed the diamond in her palm as a negative presence, cold, lifeless, base. It would do to her whole body what it had done to her hand if she did not quickly give it away.

"No, Mother, I don't perform for people like that. Rock 'n' roll and fascism just don't mix." She placed the diamond pendant back into her mother's hand. She felt an almost uncontrollable urge now to take the bloodrock in her hand, to warm her hand, heal it, win it back to. . . .

WAIT. WAIT UNTIL YOU MUST.

Amelia whipped her head around as if she'd heard a gunshot somewhere in the immediate darkness of her estate. She jumped to her feet, clutching the pendant like trash she could not wait to dispose of, and pirouetted with the exhilaration of surprised anger.

"Alice? Alice, my daughter just remembered that she has a date for this evening. Please get her things."

Alice appeared almost instantly, only to execute a femininely efficient about-face to do as she'd been instructed.

June stared at Amelia who remained facing away at a forty-five degree angle, staring into the middle distance of her enormous house.

"Mother, if you don't want to discuss . . ."

"Someone's been telling you lies, that's all," she pronounced into the darkness. "Hideous, hideous lies. I don't want you ever to come into this house again talking such obscene rubbish. Why, it would have killed your father if . . . Yes, Alice, very good!"

Alice handed June her sweater and purse.

"Thank you, Mrs. Lockwood. Will that be all?"

Amelia gestured magnanimously toward the front entrance. "Shall the three of us stroll outside?"

June told herself not to walk with her head down. To do so while accompanying her tall very erect mother would be to assume the posture of one about to be executed.

Letting Alice move slightly ahead, June whispered, "I'm thinking of going to see Grandma Edna maybe later this week or possibly next week."

Amelia stopped and put her hand on the polished mahogany newel cap at the foot of her spiral staircase. "Oh?" A magnificent pause. "Why would you want to do *that*, dear?"

June let her head bow unintentionally, then forced it back up. She had to learn to hold her ground with her mother. Amelia didn't mean to be imperious or overbearing; simply, she'd got used to being pampered during her film career. Yet how had that pampering affected her while she witnessed the leading ladies receiving even more attention?

June tried to touch her mother's hand, but Amelia moved it away. "Well, I haven't seen Grandma in over six months and . . ."

"Do you suppose, darling, that something has changed in six months? That she is less senile? That she's become somehow responsive, decided to speak? That she's cast aside her morbid senility and found a house to live in that isn't something out of a shabby amusement park?"

June could not reply. All these rhetorical questions built up a tacit yet conclusive "no" in her mind. Yet the real answer was simple.

"But she's my grandmother," June said, her voice revealing how vulnerable she felt her words to be. "I should go to see her. I mean I *want* to go . . ."

Amelia's laugh had little joy in it. Rather, she laughed as a warrior might when, after the battle, he sees how pitiful his defeated enemy looks in death. June knew that the passion of the laugh meant that she was spared a lecture on sentimentality.

Shaking her head decisively, Amelia pushed her daughter toward the massive door that Alice held open.

"Goodnight, Amelia; goodnight, Alice."

"Goodnight, Miss Lockwood."

June started down the broad stone steps toward the van, a toy in the grand driveway. After their earlier encounter, she hadn't really expected Larry to return in two hours as they'd agreed.

"Have a nice opening night, dear," Amelia called down.

June turned to salute the thoughtfulness. But how had mother known that tomorrow night was . . .?

"I hope you're feeling less disoriented by the time you must perform tomorrow," Amelia trumpeted down to her daughter. "Oh, a little advice, dear—start looking for some field of employment more suited to your personality than performing. It's not for the weak, you know. Goodnight!"

Larry revved the engine ferociously as June risked the last few steps to touch the open door of the van.

Chapter Seven:

Hell on Earth

Infernal. Hellish. Horrible.

Blank faces. The desultory drifting strands of conversation. (Sometimes she even caught herself trying to snatch at a word or phrase—what interested them so? Romance, gossip, money?) The clinking of drinks, intentional, sometimes accidental. The ringing phone behind the bar and the increasingly casual way the bartender answered it. (No harm done; it's just the girl singer up there.) It felt like a dream, a bad dream, a nightmare. Too bad she couldn't wake up.

June had wanted to make tonight different. Oh, everything had seemed to sail right along through rehearsals into opening night. God, they'd worked hard to get ready! They'd worked on new songs, new harmonies, new combinations of instruments (trying a new blend of synthesizer, bass and guitar); perfected the vocals, worked hard on their solos, even created a killer new name for the band—Fever Blister (Herm D'Angello pronounced, "It's gross but dramatic—okay!"); and, throughout, they'd talked about showmanship.

Collectively, they were sick and tired of being dismissed as *art rock*, because what they wanted now was to reach their audience.

Danny Driscoll, June's drummer, always chiding the others on being too reserved, was the embodiment of rock showmanship. His habitual dress consisted of white lace with wild seaweed strands of tassels going up his spine and riveting right through the center of all four appendages so that he looked like some impossibly elegant albino lizard. "Give 'em sights!" Danny screamed at the other members of the band. "We're dazzling their ears but leaving them blind. Sights! Treats for the eyes! Dazzle that motherin' audience!"

So Fever Blister worked on the visual aspect of its performance. Bruce Marley, the bass player, returned instrumentally to his first love, the stand-up acoustic bass he'd played in his high school jazz group. Electrifying it with micophone and wah-wah pedal, he threw the five foot tall instrument around the stage like a dance partner, "a member of the fairer sex" as he put it—sometimes gentle, sometimes rough, always amorous. And Larry and June caught the showmanship fever, too, infecting each other to dramatize their vocal and lead guitar playing. It all fit and worked.

June loved the way that Larry, always the rock purist, worked on testing out his hips to see if they would actually swivel and his shoulders to make them shake.

But she knew who held the key, of course. The center of the audience's attention was the lead singer, and if Fever Blister was desinted to ever heat it up, so the primary source of power had to be her. Studying clips of her favorite groups on Duane's home VCR, June worked to incorporate some of their showmanship while coming up with something entirely her own, heatedly sexual yet ladylike, raucous and low-down but always with an edge of enticing refinement. She worked to appear abandoned, furious; but the real excitement, she knew, came from the calm and control she could restore at will. June thought she had it all together—her band and herself.

Then came opening night. Fever Blister knew itself to be a band with real talent, vision, a unique sound—and Herm D'Angello's Club Crater provided the perfect forum for a two week take-off! What happened that first night, however, could hardly be described as a take-off. Oh, the audience seemed eager and ready, everyone agreed later, and the band itself could scarcely be held back from going onstage before showtime. Then what happened?

June blamed herself from the start. Something didn't work, didn't gel. Something had not quite fallen into place for them as a band. Oh, ingredients were there—the high energy, the lyrics, the musical technology, the showmanship—but they lacked a core, a central focus, *something*.

Sure, they called themselves Fever Blister, but no one image as hot and as easily accessible as their name arose from the music. That first night, June had felt an indescribable wrenching in her gut as she put everything into a song and yet saw heads turn away in the middle. If the guy in the third row couldn't keep his eyes off his girl friend's cleavage and the elaborately coiffed blonde in the back had to keep staring at her strawberry dakari, the band had failed rather obviously to catch and hold their attention.

No, June would blame neither the band nor the audience; she knew very well whom to blame. Would her mother be proud of her for taking all the responsibility for the band's failure on herself? Hadn't Amelia drummed this into her over the years?

And so June had gone back to work with her music. She rethought her whole approach to the music and the audience, trying all the while to pick out that intangible quality that some performers seemed to have of reaching out and giving themselves, selling the audience on the notion that they wanted nothing else. Would she ever achieve that? Would she ever find the X-factor that seemed to come naturally to the great performers—as well as to a considerable number of lesser lights who hadn't tried half as hard yet had achieved far more success?

Yes, the engagement had gone on for a week. June had been sure that tonight she had it down. She had come out from the start this evening intent on forgetting everything but the business of giving herself to the audience. Hell, she'd *throw* herself at them if necessary, physically, emotionally, spiritually—and so she did. Eyes closed, fist balled around the mike, June thrust her body and soul at the audience. She abandoned the entirety of herself to them.

And then June scanned their faces in the midst of her performing frenzy. Nothing happened, nothing at all; as far as they were concerned, nothing had happened. They did not react to her. It didn't matter to them. Just another neurotic performer getting turned on by being onstage, she thought—that's how they see me. And so she'd come to this? Caught in this posture in the middle of the first set, June had no choice but to continue gesticulating, thrusting, over-dramatizing her lyrics—a surfeit of performance the audience did not want, and she did not want to give.

Yet there could be no turning back. At least no one had laughed yet! If she changed gears radically now, they would find a way to laugh, yes, they would. And, oh, then, how they would enjoy themselves at her expense! They would enjoy themselves on their own terms, not hers . . . and so on it went, the show, the infernal, hellish, horrible show, the closest thing June had ever known to hell on earth.

Afterward, the club closed, her agony seemingly over, June wanted only to slink off to her apartment and be alone with her growing self-doubt. Spotting Bosley during the last set made it all worse, much worse. She had been so busy giving herself to the audience that she didn't spot him until the show was almost over. Would he visit her backstage? He had looked haggard, defeated, profoundly disappointed—or was she only projecting her own fear of failure, her guilt at having been caught on the worst night of her career by the performer she most admired?

But Bosley was not backstage. So, he'd been so embarrassed that he could not face her. Who could blame him? Then she saw it, tucked into the corner of her make-up mirror. Dead white and foreboding as a curse, the envelope seemed to defy her to touch it. She leaned forward to scrutinize the scrawled words and immediately recognized the handwriting. So he had been backstage to see her.

June thrust the envelope into her purse while Duane's attention was diverted by chasing off a persistent fan. Why didn't she want him to see the letter? Perhaps later she'd share it with him, after she'd first read it.

"June, if you've just got to mope, go ahead." Duane pushed away from the door he'd struggled to close and steadied the lopsided mirror to let her brush out her hair. "Me, I'm going to Faust's Choice to toast the most courageous young woman I've ever known—because that had to be the hostile audience to top all hostile audiences!"

June drew long strokes through her auburn gold hair and watched him in the mirror with despondent admiration. Duane was always supportive, always the gentleman, always there. How could a girl ask for more in a manager? And yet, somehow, that made it worse. Especially tonight. June pulled angrily at a snag at the top of her head. "I don't think I want to go . . ."

He tickled her underarm. "Come on, kid. If you're going to commit hari-kari, at least do it with me in public. That way, I can pass the hat and make a buck or two off the show."

Shaking her head, June tried to make a face but could not keep from smiling. "That's about the only way anybody's going to make money off my performing."

"That's the spirit!" Duane kidded. "What a trouper! Here, let me finish that." He took a few final swipes at her hair before they hurried out toward the front entrance of the club.

In the front lobby near the coat check booth, Larry and Herm were locked in an energetic tête-á-tête complete with finger pointing and shouts. Larry stopped yelling long enough to do a double take as June and Duane strolled past arm in arm. "Ah, just a second, Herm; we'll pick up around two tomorrow, huh? Hey, you two!"

Duane was too much the gentleman to drag June out the door, but he had obviously kept walking for a good two steps after she'd stopped. Had Larry noticed this conspicious rudeness? Wasn't he used to seeing her with Duane by now?

The speed with which Larry approached them made him seem dangerous, a threat. "So where you headin'?" He stopped and stared, waiting for an answer.

June shrugged—not too negatively, she hoped; it was up to Duane to make the invitation. But the glum look that crossed his face showed how hard this would be for him. She hoped that both men would realize how uncomfortable this contesting made her. She did not like being regarded as the prize for the male victor.

Duane was the first to shuffle his feet and look down. "We're just heading over to Faust's for coffee. Want to come along?"

Larry winked at June, then stared Duane straight in the eye. "Well, it'll break the heart of half a dozen groupies but . . . you twisted my arm!"

They agreed upon Larry's van rather than caravaning with three vehicles. The trip to the Peachyard Shopping Plaza passed in relative silence. June found herself unconsciously holding onto the pendant. Was it just her imagination, or was she in fact becoming increasingly nervous and obsessive?

"Are you two forming a new society of the mute?" Larry said as they marched toward the bookstore cafe. "Aren't you curious about why Herm was pulling my coat?"

"Figured it was none of my business," Duane said without looking at Larry. "I figured it was something personal between you and D'Angello."

June felt relieved when they entered the bookstore, each dispersing to a different shelf. Maybe their animosities would smooth over and she could find out what . . .

"Guess again, Duane the Greek," Larry called from over the top of *Biography/Autobiography*, not missing a beat from the rhythm of their dispute. "Because what Herm told me keys into June and Blister and all of us—even you."

Duane wheeled around *Gothic Fiction* to snuggle up to June in *Literature*. "Shall I get you some coffee while you're browsing?"

June shook off his arm. "I'd like to know what the hell Herm was telling Larry!" she whispered angrily. "Why can't you two act like grown men? I'm getting tired of . . ."

"Oh, I'm acting like a 'grown man'," Duane said.

"You're talking to the wrong person." He stopped smirking when he saw the look on her face. "Okay, June, okay, I'll . . . ah, where the hell is he?"

"Right here, sweet stuff," Larry said from behind Duane. Legs crossed, he leaned against the *Science Fiction/Fantasy* shelf, an oversized paperback pulled up near his chest. "Did I hear somebody seeking some information?"

Pretending not to take notice, Duane examined the biography of FDR he'd been holding.

Larry raised his eyebrows to June, who shrugged. "Well," he said, "one in the audience is better than none. Oh, Herm just started out by noting that every night our crowd's been getting smaller and smaller, and he went on to admit that he was probably losing money on us . . ."

"And?"

"But, he has no intention of 'terminating our contract before the expiration date'—I think that's how he put it. You *know* things are bad when you drive a down-to-earth guy like Herm D'Angello to screaming his head off and talking in early American Bureaucrat . . . oh, don't look like that, June, I only meant . . ."

Uncrossing his legs and tossing the book on a display table, Larry hurried to put his hands on her slumped shoulders.

Duane kept staring at the FDR book. "Sure, sure," he said. "I think you've said enough, buddy."

"Oh!" Larry brightened as if he hadn't heard Duane. "He did mention that the good news his accountant told him was that he made more money off the Bosley Broderick engagement than he had on any other act, and that his finances are in the black, at least for now."

June fiddled with the letter from Bosley in her purse. Maybe it was advice on how to turn Fever Blister into a moneymaking act. Oh, sure it was . . . Well, then, maybe Bosley had advice on what to do with two contentious men, neither of whom she really . . .

"Shall we sit down so we can order some coffee—and try to be a little more civil to each other?"

"Take a look at this first," Larry said, retrieving the large paperback and slapping it into her hands.

June examined the scrolled cover. " 'A facsimile edition of the original ancient French manuscript discovered in a monastery in Coulommiers, circa 1237.' What is this, Larry?"

He grunted. "Look at it. Look at the title."

" *'Formulas and Incantations of the Major European Necromancer'* ? You've got to be kidding, Larry."

"Look, June . . ." He came up out of his usual slouch to loom above her at full height. "Bosley got started through Aleister Crowley and other prominent occult authorities when he was down and out over in Europe. Everybody knows that. But what they don't know is that *all* Crowley did was give him a book, a little book on the Tarot, which he'd supervised back in the '40's. Now, I'm giving you this and . . . look, June, don't scoff! Does lightning have to fork through this roof or something? That's not how it happens. *This* is how it happens, a gift to a friend in a coffee shop. Real creative people get their ideas out of little things!"

"What's going on here?" Duane elbowed his way between them as if to protect June from a physical attack.

"Oh, nothing," June kidded, "just that Larry wants us to go satanic and start singing songs backwards so we can get a few people in the audience."

Duane moved his hand over on her shoulder so that Larry was forced to remove his from the spot. "You've got to be kidding. Honey, a sophisticated, visionary adult performer like you can't afford to compromise her image by . . ."

"Duane! We're just *kidding*," she said, casually examining the illustrations in the occult classic. "I agree. It's adolescent, it's silly. Worse, it's selling out. I guess I'd rather go back to peddling shoes or teaching music if the only way I could go on as an entertainer was to put on vampire teeth and sing about selling my soul to the devil."

Duane grinned triumphantly at Larry, who missed it because he had all his attention fixed on June, who continued turning pages. "It's just a gimmick, for Christ's sake!" he said. "We want to have an audience, don't we? Or are we just playing to hear ourselves play? I thought I was the one the rest of you were always accusing of being too . . ."

"Shall we go back to your van so you can drive us home?" Duane said. "People are beginning to stare."

And indeed they were. And June couldn't help feeling that it was her fault. All because she was such a dreadful failure as a rock 'n' roll musician. Casually, she set the book aside.

Reluctantly, Larry drove them back to their respective cars and bade June a rather wistful goodnight. Did he think she was going home with Duane? When it soon became apparent that Duane had precisely that in mind, June had to wonder what he thought when she declined the invitation. Were each of the two men fantasizing about her being in the arms of the other, each certain that she'd tricked or double-crossed him?

Alone at last in her own car, she closed her eyes and tried to relax for a moment before driving home. But all she could see was Bosley Broderick, the raised axe, then everything gilded, everything . . .

She reached into her purse and shredded the unread

letter into bite-sized pieces. She let it scatter in the rising crosswind. She would never associate with that man again. Her life had been far too painful and difficult since she met him and began to wear his manacle on her throat. Look what had happened tonight!

The club parking lot was deserted. Where had all the cars gone? Certainly Herm had to still be around totaling up the receipts. A ground fog curled up around June's car, a fog that she could have sworn was tinted green. She had to get out of there, get home. She turned the ignition to try to start the car. She wished she'd taken Duane up on his offer.

Chapter Eight:

Un Petit Boudeaux

June drove slowly down the broad suburban lane, almost afraid to pull into the dark driveway of her condominium, identical to dozens of others lining both sides of the street. Was she afraid of her own home?

At last, braking, June settled the Volvo over the speed bumps and into the carport stall number 312. She climbed out and locked up, glancing nervously over her back at the massive green dumpster that loomed beside the stucco building. Shrubbery seemed capable of independent movement; she saw several odd shadows she'd never noticed before. Great! Carrying on like the heroine in a grade-B horror flick; terrific, Lockwood! Maybe you can scare yourself to death before the world catches up to seeing what a failure you really are.

June looked around uncertainly. Nothing, really. Someone must have a television set on, an old movie maybe.

She walked briskly up the well-manicured path to her rear door. When the key fit easily into the lock, the sense of being trapped in a grade-B film dissolved. She actually sighed with relief. Inside and safe.

She reached around the corner for the light switch.

Her front door struck something thick and hard and stout that bounced away with the impact. June kept herself from falling by clinging to the doorjamb. Flicking on the light, she saw what had made her stumble. Brightly ribboned, it sat up against the sofa as if placed there—a gift, and a rather expensive antique one from the look of the dog-eared label. But who would give her a bottle of wine?

June bent to examine the bottle. She could make out no more from the almost indecipherable label than the word *Bordeaux*. Well! Quite impressive. If her former roommate Karen Gustaffsen had sent this, her taste and financial condition had certainly improved recently!

The year of bottling had been raked by something—fingernails?—but June smoothed the wrinkled, almost disintegrating paper back into place. It looked like *1928*. Could it really be that old?

It was when she began to slip out of her suede coat that June began to feel something trickling down between her breasts. But the phone rang before she could begin an examination. Tossing her coat onto a straight-backed chair, she skipped into the kitchen to catch the call.

"Hi, sis! It's me!"

"Betty! I haven't heard from you since . . . that double date we had with those two creeps who took us hiking and marrooned us in Alum Rock Park. Have you forgiven me?"

In the brief silence she detected a muffled sniff. "Hey, kid, it wasn't *that* bad. I thought we did a pretty good job of salvaging the evening, driving that poor bus boy crazy and all . . ."

June's eyes trailed casually down as she talked. She

wanted to discover what trickled, what felt wet and itchy.

An opulent little red river threaded between her breasts. She put a finger to the thin rope of fluid. Blood, it looked like. She put the finger to her lips. Blood for sure. Now how the hell had she done that to herself? "What did you say again, sis?"

"It's not the double date I'm upset about, June. It's just that . . . I'm really, really embarrassed to call you about this and . . ."

June tasted the mysterious little red trickle again. Blood, yes; no mistaking it. She began to examine herself.

" . . . well, you know how Philip is about making the monthly child support pavements . . . and even though he's only ten, Ivan's dentist says that if we don't start the corrective work soon he's going to lose . . ."

No. It was all wrong, all wrong . . . "Duane?"

"What, June?"

She stared at her finger, which now appeared rusty, corroded with dried blood.

"June, you said 'Duane.' What's wrong? Is Duane is some sort of trouble?"

She pressed the finger into the path of the trickle, trying to dam it off. It would be depressing and tedious to remove bloodstains from her blouse and bra. "Did I say his name? No, there's nothing wrong with him, except he keeps propositioning me all the time."

"Oh, June!"

"Yeah, that; but he's also asked me to marry him. But that's not . . ."

"But, June, that's great! I'm so happy for you!"

"Don't be too happy for me, Betty. I'm a confirmed old maid, you know that. Now what's this serious thing you're afraid to ask?"

A reluctant pause. June reached for the napkin she'd

left from breakfast to help absorb the flow of blood.

Betty spoke haltingly. "Well, you know how hard it is to call or talk to mother, especially about something like this, so . . . I hate to ask this—especially since I don't even call and congratulate you on playing at the Club Crater and we haven't even seen each . . ."

"Betty."

"Oh, I'm sorry, June. I know I'm always getting off the subject. But it's just hard for me to . . . Oh, what the heck—June, I need to borrow some money."

Somehow she had not expected this. What then? That Betty was pregnant again or in some sort of romantic imbroglio? Hardly. Her sister was irremediably flighty, yet peculiarly responsible. "Ivan's teeth? Is that it, Betty? You may not believe this, but I don't have any money myself right now. Although maybe Duane . . ."

"Oh, June, that's okay! I understand. Really. I'm sorry that . . ."

A ploy? A ruse to break down the miser's defenses? June might have suspected as much of almost anyone but Betty. Because her younger sister, an unemployed person in an affluent society, had remained disconcertingly naive, despite being a very able and determined mother.

For the moment, June had dismissed her bleeding.

"I want to explain," she said. "Because if I were you, Betty, I wouldn't believe that someone who'd just got a great nightclub contract could be entirely broke.

"See, after my roommate Karen moved out, my drummer wanted a raise so I had to raise everybody's salary; and then we decided to buy new instruments, a synthesizer and . . ."

"I feel terrible, terrible, terrible making you apologize when I'm the one doing the begging! I should be the one doing the . . ."

"Shut up, you little twirp! I'm standing here bleeding

to death and you're starting to make me cry on top of it. Listen, I promise that I'll talk to Duane and see if I can get him to float us a loan."

"Bleeding? June, are you injured? What happened?"

Exasperated, June raised her voice, "Did you hear me, Betty? I'll get the money. Am I all right? I have no idea who decided to divert my bloodstream to the outside of my body—other than that, I'm fine."

"Blood?"

Through the reserve, June could hear the incipient hysteria. "Betty, really now; it's . . ."

"Blood? Oh, June! Oh, God! I'll drive you right over to emergency!"

"Come on, kid. That's hardly . . ." Click.

Incredulous, June stared at the dead receiver. Had Betty hung up or . . .? One never knew with her. Giddy as she was goodhearted, Betty could be counted on for precious little, her crimes always those of omission. The line thrummed with static. She could be on her way here—or responding to Ivan's latest emergency, answering the doorbell, remembering at last to attend to the morning's laundry.

Sighing, June set out to examine herself. She could not see the area from which the blood was coming. Compressing her neck and pursing her lips, she tried to see the skin high up under the chin. No—no source. She marched over to the mirror in the record storage shelf built in her stereo for a better view. No, no cuts on her throat.

June lifted the pendant to check just in case she might have . . . Blood bloomed on the back of her hand.

Did the apparently smooth rock have a sharp edge somewhere? She turned the little dark stone over in her hands and found her fingers gilded red from the caress. The stone bled. The bloodrock gave itself away, a mineral eucharist, a geological. . . .

Weird, she thought. Weird. See June Lockwood, standing in the living room of her middle-class condo, holding a piece of bleeding jewelry? Weird? No—ludicrous, silly.

If only she could get the damned thing off!

Well, if Betty did show up, maybe she could free the stupid clasp. What a relief that would be! "Get the bloody thing off me," June imagined herself saying and gave a little laugh out into the cool silence.

Tearing paper towels from the wrought iron dispenser, she blotted the blood on her neck. Then she knotted several thicknesses of paper around the seeping rock.

Silence.

Spooky.

Move. Do something.

She needed some music. Sure, everything'd be find if she just had some music.

June fished a Grateful Dead album out of the wire record rack and slipped the disc out of its sleeve and onto the turntable. She tripped the automatic start tab and watched the clockwork process until she felt satisfied that the album was launched.

Then she remembered the wine. Ordinarily she didn't drink alone; and, truth to tell, she didn't particularly care for wine except as an occasional accent to a good meal. Also, she had no idea where the wine had come from.

"Just like the blood."

Had she said that? She had experienced no sensation of speaking, but the voice had surely been her own. Maybe she'd better have a drink, a glass or two of wine. She had to do something about these nerves.

Taking the bottle to the sink, she carefully inserted a stainless steel tire-bouchon (a souvenir of grandmother's travels, practically an heirloom) into the skin of the ancient discolored cork. The screw slid down in with an almost disagreeable ease.

Slowly, carefully, June pried the ancient cork from the ribbon-bound bottle. She didn't want to have to strain decaying nuggets of rancid cork from this vintage wine that had such promising color.

"Whoa! That smell!"

June made a face and held the bottle out at arm's length. Well, if it were imported cheese, the odor might be promising, but. . . . Hey, kid, where's your adventurous spirit, huh? Loosen up! Hear the Dead—they're loose. Think they'd hesitate to drink that stuff?

Sloshing a little into a long-stemmed crystal goblet, June slouched down into her favorite recliner chair in the corner where her stereo vied for space with the two looming bookcases. The wine rocking gently in the glass left a residue that showed each high-water mark as well as every lesser tidal movement. Could it possibly be drinkable? She wondered if Karen hadn't bought some very expensive vinegar; or was it just a gag all along? The label certainly looked authentic enough and the sludge smelled as though perhaps, once upon a time, it had been something approximating wine. What it was now remained to be seen.

June touched the glass to her lips, tipped it, and rolled out the red carpet of her tongue to taste.

"Wow . . ." She hadn't realized how very, very tired she felt—yet tense, profoundly tense, as if her bones themselves had become charged with some excessive calcium-inflaming energy. Oh, but she'd be okay. A little music and a little meditation should do the trick.

Donning her headphones, June closed her eyes, fingertips together, and pushed her breathing down into her solar plexus.

"Roll away the dew; roll away the . . ."

Yes, fine. But how did it taste?

For a moment she felt like ripping off the headphones to escape the rushing sense of clautrophobia, betrayal from within. She could not remember how the wine had tasted. Had she in fact put it in her mouth? It frightened her that she did not know. Testing her tongue for a residue, certainly some lingering telltale taste, she found that within her mouth she had no sensation but that of a vast and totally unfamiliar emptiness. Nothing else. Nothing but open . . . open . . .

"Roll away the dew; roll . . ."

Her mantra allowed other honest thoughts to filter through. Like the fact that she hated having turned Betty down at first; that she secretly wondered, however, where the hell the money she'd promised would come from; that when her mother bought her movie naked fire . . . what? What the hell the money the where the hell money the hell where money mommy the. . . .

"Roll away the . . ."

body on the road so skinny so small so bloated in the belly so pregnant so dead

"*Roll her off the road!*"

"*No! Throw her in the taxi! We'll never get . . .*"

Zappa, Rundgren . . . oh, the Beatles, Morrison, they all did voice over-dubs through music. But she didn't remember the Dead doing it, not on that album.

June stiffly sat upright as if someone had slapped her.

Because something had touched. . . .

The voices had come clearly through the headphones—but from what source? Some crazy radio drama leaking through the frequencies? Some ham operator?

June had the headset halfway off.

"*Oh, shit*! Here comes that old hag out of the house!

If she sees . . . God, what's . . . what's that behind her? SCCCRREEEE!!!"

Static fierce as a torture scream screeched straight into the headset, pierced right through into June's skull itself. Reflexively, she covered her ears, already covered by the leatherette speakers. After long moments, she groped to adjust the volume down, feeling with her twitching fingers where she couldn't bear to look.

But by the time her fingers found the proper knob inside the stereo beside her chair, the static scream had stopped.

"Whew!"

The headset muffled her voice.

"I think somebody around here needs a good long rest!" And she laughed aloud because what she really wanted and needed was more work. And she knew it.

"Roll away the dew, roll away the . . ."

Clever, the way the record came back on with the stereo off. Such good sound, good separation. Good wine. Good, good wine. Take another sip.

TAKE ANOTHER SIP!

"No, thank you. I don't think I . . ."

ANOTHER SIP! MAINTENANT!

"Roll away . . ."

Something moved on her throat. The condominium lights dimmed, once, twice, three times. The flickering strobe recreated the interior of her home, making it over into another scene entirely where figures and music and the blood of the grape mingled in a fearful warmth, obscenely intimate, a warm darkness filled with the sounds of. . . .

"God, what's happening to me?"

Silence.

Pressure on the throat.

Pressure on the eyes to close. Pressure everywhere.

Stomach, chest, throat. Choking! Pressure!

June did not know how to make it stop happening. She knew now that she should have begun trying a long time ago—back when she was still, before her home had changed.

The small neat stack of laundry that June had placed on the sideboard of the breakfast nook only that morning became. . . . She stared hard, hard. . . . Perhaps if she looked hard enough, close enough, what she was seeing happen would stop and not happen and not. . . . The small neat stack of laundry on the sideboard in the breakfast nook became. . . .

Since she knew it had to be illusion, the first moment was not horror. The first moment was thought. She was in her home. She was sane. Her throat was not bleeding.

Her small neat stack of laundry had not become a thing that moved, green mist curling disgustingly in its wake like a tide of putrified decay. Except that, as it moved, it became clearer, each detail etching into place. Proximity was reality. If the thing had been illusion five seconds before, it had indeed become real as it had crossed halfway to June.

She could not scream. (Not in my own home!)

"No! Please, don't . . . I'm not . . ."

"Roll away the dew. Roll away the . . ."

VOUS EST UNE JOLIE JEUNE FILS. YOU ARE SUCH A PRETTY YOUNG GIRL. DO YOU REMIND ME OF HER? OH, DO YOU . . !

June clawed to get the headphones off but could not. Distance between herself and it. Distance, inexorably bridged, real as two fleshless fingers touching. The distance was no distance. It wanted only to touch her, only to reach out and make itself as real to her flesh as it had become now to her eyes, as real to her touch as. . . .

"No, please! Just don't touch me! I'll do anything if . . ."

The flickering light etched the face in brilliant shadow. Not a skeleton—no, not quite. Flesh so thin that paper might have more width, stretched so tight that when it touched you. . . .

"Please, don't . . ." June could not remember how to beg in such a way that it changed the ongoing bath of reality. Oh, if in your mind, you pledged the deepest most meaningful part of your soul and just gave it right out into the night sky like that—whee!—then it worked. It worked just like that. "Please, don't touch . . ." June's hand wandered up toward her throat. Something was there, moving, nudging, insinuating itself.

The touch on her flesh was real as her own breath. Green fog moistened her skin, her clothing, her loosened hair. June's feet and legs twined uselessly under her as if to lace themselves around the chair she would never leave. The bloodrock had found the center of her hand. Something closed on something not quite dead.

YOU WILL GIVE ME ALL THAT? AND YOURSELF IN THE BARGAIN? IN THE END? ET BON. I FIND THIS MORE THAN SATISFACTORY.

A life-sized slide of her comfortably decorated condominum slipped instantly and brilliantly back into place. "What? What the hell?"

Someone was playing tricks on her. Simple as that. June would accept or consider no other explanation. But what an incredible, incredible job of special effects and illusions! "Ridiculous," she whispered angrily. Her hand hurt from gripping the bloodrock so hard. That damned thing had started all the trouble in the first place. When she got rid of it—then what? June yanked off the headphones and tossed them so that the pleated cord stretched like jangled nerves. She wanted to cry but wouldn't let herself. Not now. Not if whoever played the stupid trick might still be watching.

SZZZRRRIING. SZZZRRRIING. The strident insistent sudden ringing of the telephone made June shiver. The last thing she wanted to do was answer it. But the idea of the phone blaring on unanswered, the image of herself frozen and staring at it in abysmal fear, the disquieting unnaturalness of acting this way in her own home, these were the very factors that would trigger the return of the green mist and the figure.

Stabbing a look at the neat pile of ironed blouses and pants, June got to her feet to answer the phone.

Except the phone was not ringing. Had not rung. Yet she was too frightened not to follow through.

"Hello?"

Dead silence.

"Okay, that's it!" The anger felt awfully good. "I've had enough. I'm hanging . . ."

THAT WOULD BE VERY DIFFICULT, JUNE. THE LINES ARE ALWAYS OPEN FROM NOW ON.

She had not taken French since high school. Then how did her mind manage to translate the words instantaneously into an idiomatic language that seemed to come from inside her own skull? Clearly, she heard the voice in French, yet superimposed over it, like television captions over a newscast, was her own hideously efficient English version.

June faltered, wanting to slam the phone back into the cold plastic cradle. Would that make any difference?

"Listen to me, little sister of blood."

"Bosley?"

"Now you know, little one. Now you know. There is no turning back. There is no darkness. Remember, you are safe in blood. Go in blood."

"Wait!"

(So it *had* been real—a prank played by Bosley all along! But why?)

"No waiting, June. Suffer it now as the others would not. You can't run from the blood."

"But . . .?"

Again June found herself staring at a plastic handle that made no sound other than a buzzing whine.

Replacing the phone, she felt a feather tickle her throat and looked awkardly down at her breast; as if to bisect her body, as if to cut her in half, a thin red river charted its course straight down toward its certain destination.

Chapter Nine:

All Bets Are Off

"It's all Larry's fault—him and that book he made you read in the bookstore. I think we should get rid of him. I never realized before how impressionable you were!"

"Get rid of him? You mean kill him?"

"I'm serious. I think you've put off firing him for way too long. He's disruptive, doesn't cooperate, misses rehearsals . . ."

"Ridiculous," June said. "He's irreplaceable." Her head still hurt from the wine she'd drunk the previous night. Never before had she experienced so much pain from so slight an indulgence.

"Hmmm!" Duane's chin shot up in indignation. "We'll see if he's so irreplaceable after Herm gets through with us. What do you think he wants, anyway?"

"You're the manager," June said, trying hard by her tone to convey her displeasure. "You're supposed to know these things."

Yet she guessed that Duane hated waiting outside D'Angello's office just as much as she did, if not more.

Nightclubs fabricated glamour with the aid of night, but afternoons revealed them as desolate and unromantic, furnished with the bare essentials necessary to scrounge bucks from the customers. Light streamed pitilessly through a dying palm tree beside the two bar stools they'd pull together to wait. June found herself repeatedly studying the red and black carpet, passable after dark, which daylight showed to be a landscape of spots and stains and smudge marks, some gummy to the touch. She kept thinking that she had spotted a larger pattern of malignancy, some hideous grand design fleshed out by the dirt, a design that she could not hold together quite long enough to identify.

"Well, if it isn't Larry that got you into that dangerous state of mind last night, then what did? Huh? Look, June, no more shrouded figures and blinking lights, okay?" He sounded exasperated. "Herm'll think you've been taking LSD or something."

LSD? Could it be? She knew a psychiatrist at the state university who'd be willing to give her some straight information about how her experience connected with acid visions.

"Cheer up, kid." Duane threw an arm around her. "Hey, you haven't been fooling with that stuff, have you?"

Shaking her head, she couldn't keep from responding to his pleading eyes. "It just bothers me the way you reacted, Duane—that's all. You know that I'm a skeptic, a practical down-to-earth person who . . ."

"Yeah, that was before you told me about French ghosts haunting your condo."

June dropped her head again—and there was that vastly stained carpet. "That's what I mean," she said. "*I'm* the skeptic—at least, that's how I see myself. But I try to describe to you a strange phenomenon that I'm trying to understand, and instantly you treat me like I'm a lifelong spiritualist or something. I'm just looking for an explanation, Duane; that's all."

He snapped his fingers for the afternoon cocktail waitress who wore a T-shirt several sizes too small. As she stopped to take his order, June read the words that marched in black block print across her bust line: "Pretty to look at. So nice to touch. But if you break me, consider me yours."

June watched the voluptuous waitress angle herself with sensual ease through the scattered tables back to the untended bar. Maybe if she was built like that her music might get popular. Oh, well, there's always silicon injections.

"A penny for your thoughts, you one-woman rock 'n' roll show, you!"

"What?" She snorted at the idea that she was something special. "Duane, there's something you can do for me."

"Name it, kid."

June hesitated. She had very specific ideas concerning the kinds of exchanges that should take place in a manager-client relationship. Perhaps romance might be allowed if one stretched the rules a bit—but borrowing money? "Forget it, Duane. It was nothing."

But he looked serious now, almost hungry for her words, as if he yearned for her to want something from him, anything. "Go ahead, June."

It sounded like a command.

"You're the last person I'd want to bother in this way, but . . . I need some money."

His hungry look did not change. "How much money?"

"I think about a thousand dollars to start. But . . ."

Duane laughed in a dry empty way that went right into June's heart.

"June. You *do* know that you're my biggest draw?

Now think about that. Think about it, June. How well have we done lately?"

June studied the fibers of the filthy carpet. "Duane, I wouldn't ask except . . ."

"I could loan you maybe half that—unless you can wait a week or two?"

She smiled broadly but tried to stay reserved. "Could you really?"

"Sure. As long as it isn't for something stupid and crazy—like a loan to a relative." Duane laughed at the absurdity of such an idea. It was his stamp of approval on the deal.

Unable to share his laughter, she caught him noticing her seriousness. Oh well, she'd find the money somewhere. If Ivan needed his teeth fixed that badly, well, the money would turn up.

"God, you two characters look forlorn sitting there with your heads down staring into the rotten drinks we put out here in the afternoon," Herm said, only his head out the door. "Come on into the Blue Grotto, kids. Clare, more drinks, huh?"

And so Herm pushed and prompted them into the lush clutter of his office, bright with fluorscent light. On the walls Neapolitan murals fought it out with a variety of old and new Italian memorabilia, two mortuary calendars, a wooden wall hanging with the "Italian Ten Commandments," a faded family portrait taken in the old country with three amazingly distinct thumb prints smeared in its center. On his desk June spotted a youth with his pants down, a figure fashioned from the finest plastic, preparing to urinate in a miniature wine bottle with "100 proof" on it.

"You like that June? Here, I'll show you how . . ." Herm jammed a heavily stained coffee mug under the naked boy, displacing the wine bottle. A little pressure on his tawny head yielded an arching stream of red liquid from the boy's short but wide-open plastic penis.

"Prostate problems!" Herm laughed. "Now . . . will you two sit the hell down!"

June and Duane cleared ship models, magazines and half-eaten loaves of bread off a pair of chairs adjoining the heaped desk. They sat like children waiting to be punished.

Herm laughed at their discomfort and came around to clear a spot atop his desk and sit near them. "Okay, kids, I've got some good news and some bad news. Which do you want first?"

Duane and June looked at each other.

What could they say? Control of this little tête-à-tête was clearly in the hands of the club owner.

"The bad?" Duane shrugged. "I think it's probably best to save whatever's positive for the end."

Smiling—playfully, perhaps?—Herm looked like a sad magician determined to give it his best shot. "Bad it is," he said. "What with the country's economy the way it is and all . . . No, no, no! Don't look like that. I'm not firing you, June . . . not exactly. Look, to be real honest with you two nice people, I've been losing money since Fever Blister started its current engagement at the Crater. Do you have any ideas . . . ?"

Duane almost came up out of his seat, hands shoving hard at the desk top. "Losing? That's not possible, Herm! I've counted the house every night . . ."

"There's more to it than that, Duane." Herm seemed sobered by the younger man's outburst. "The folks June brings in just aren't big drinkers. No, wait a minute, I'm not feeding you a line, just spelling out the truth as best I can. Okay?"

Sneaking an angry look at June, Duane began to examine the hair on his knuckles up close. "I'm listening," he said.

But Herm swiveled on his rump to look straight at

June. "What you have to understand, Miss Lockwood, is that I love your work. I'll bet you didn't know that I was an English major at SFSU, and, well, like all English majors I guess I pay as much attention to the words of songs as I do to the music. We're word people, right? So I love your lyrics, love *you* if it comes down to it! And, well . . . my entertainment manager, Tony C., says to find a way to break the contract, lose you any way I . . ."

"Why that sniveling, Mai-tai swilling son of a bitch!" Duane said.

"Now, now . . ." Herm pretended to caution. "We're all in this thing together. Right? Okay, so I have a proposal. I won't take Tony up on his suggestion about a loophole in your contract. Hell, June, I don't want you out. But I will ask you to go in with me on the risk fifty-fifty."

Cocking his head, Duane squinted unbelievingly at Herm. "Risk? How's that?"

Herm did not hesitate. "We write up a new contract giving Fever Blister a designated share of the nightly gross. That way, if . . ."

"That way if you don't cover your damned overhead, we're left out, financially speaking."

"You don't seem to have much faith in the drawing power of the band, Duane."

"Well, neither do you," he calmly retorted, "or you'd keep the contract like it is."

Standing, June stepped close enough to Duane to silence him by lightly touching his shoulder.

"We'll take the offer, Herm," she said. "And we'll take up the challenge that I think your offer implies. We'll start filling the Crater up with customers—drinking ones, preferably. Maybe this is the incentive that Fever Blister needs to start tearing it up."

"Figuratively, of course," Herm mused, smiling.

"We can't afford any repairs now, you know."

Clearly, his reference was to the band he'd booked no more than a year before that had made local headlines by setting fire to the stage to dramatize their final number.

"Oh, definitely metaphorical, Herm," she said. "I was only an English minor, but I think we understand each other perfectly."

"Perfectly!" Herm relaxed to let a big pleased grin spread freely across his boyish face. "Have some wine?" He tapped the top of the plastic youth's head.

"No . . ."

"No, thanks," Duane said. "My client and I have . . . things to discuss. Excuse us?"

Herm looked puzzled at first, then put his palms down on the desk top to thrust himself to his feet. "Sure. Sure! See you tonight, June. Don't worry. Word'll get around pretty soon that we've got the hottest and most intelligent rock 'n' roll in town right here at the Crater. Again!"

Heading out the door at Duane's signal, June returned Herm's high sign. "Right!"

The time having passed for them to leave for the Club, June and Duane continued to cuddle in the middle of her plaid sofa.

"You're going to be perfect, honey."

She shook her head sulkily. She hated herself when she acted this way, but she just couldn't pull out of it. She thought about the loan Duane had generously given her (to give to Betty for Ivan, but he didn't have to know that) after they'd finished their tête-à-tête with Herm. Would she ever pay it back? And what negative effect might it have on her relationship with Duane?

"I don't know," she said. "Sometimes I just wonder if I shouldn't just give it up, Duane. Maybe it takes a special kind of person to be a rock performer, the kind of . . ."

"You are special, June."

"Yeah, thanks. You've been nice enough to tell me that quite often before. But what I mean is that it takes a unique blend of energy and instinct and . . . oh, God, I don't know! I guess if I knew I'd be doing it. I just don't know anymore."

Duane pulled her to him gently. "Don't worry about anything, little June bug. It's going to be a great night, you hear me? A great, great night for you and the band. Right?"

"If you say so."

"Here, have some more of this antique wine. What's it called . . . Merchant?"

"Duane, I got a terrible headache last night as I told you, and I really do think that . . ."

"No way. Take it from your Friendly Wine Connoisseur Duane Lombard, this brew is too expensive to give you a headache. I mean . . . here, just let me coat your glass."

"No, Duane, I . . . Well . . ."

"That's better," he said, putting the long-stemmed glass in front of her on the coffee table and beginning to pour. "Much, much better. Enough of this stuff and maybe you'll finally let me ask that question from bended knee."

"If that's anything like Wounded Knee, I'd rather put it off until . . ."

But June sensed heat coming from the rock around her neck. She felt inspired. She did! Tonight a great night? Why not? Why the hell not?

Chapter Ten:

A Visit from the Master

Talk about glamour! Shimmering auburn hair cascaded down either side of her severely beautiful, intelligently sensual face; high energy sounds from every side charged the air with a lifetime of brilliant electric connections; the swirling movement of the male bodies, her three musical drones absolutely in thrall to her irresistible leadership, wound and twined about her like the serpentine tendrils of some plant that chose her radiance over that of the sun. Energy, energy—pulsating out of every pore. Ah, she gave and gave, and the giving reflected back a hundred fold so that she knew she could reach a musical climax that would transport the entire room—herself, the band, the audience. The spotlight licked lovingly at her spontaneously contorting body.

Glamour! Glamour!

But why pretend? Right in the middle of "Love on the Outskirts of the Century," she felt like stopping. Why keep her eyes closed? Open them. She knew quite well it was all true—all except the part about the people and their reactions. Duane sat out there somewhere, but she couldn't see him, only the seemingly anaesthetized audience.

I feel the heat, I feel the reality, I feel the absolute down deep inner charge of my goddamn rock 'n' roll soul—so why the hell don't they?

Opening her exquisitely made-up eyes, June scanned the large, lethargic crowd. As Herm had said, few seemed to be drinking. Few seemed to be doing anything, really. Desultory chatter, discreet touches under the table—these were the exceptions. By and large the crowd appeared to be caught in some hypnotic trance that left them marooned somewhere between attention and distraction, involvement and rejection. June saw the effect her music had on men and women; it left them empty, turned them into automatons, robbed them of their essential vitality. But why?

She had no answer, no answer at all.

Should she stop altogether? One song came to an end. She looked at the audience.

With a few classic power chords, Larry blasted them into "No Deposit Universe," the one song that had always found a favorable audience response with an occasional standing ovation. They called it their "flag waver." Okay, Larry—good! Why not shoot the works right now?

She watched the roomful of faces as Fever Blister's unique blend of acoustic and heavy metal rock washed over them like an auditory wave, barely rippling the lackadaisical curtain of their seaweed minds. What did it take to reach them? What the hell did it take? She refused to blame them.

What was that? Someone . . . someone was pulling, plucking at her sequined blouse.

"June!" Larry, frowning, looked to her like a priest frustrated in his efforts to coax the marriage vows from a bride before a very large wedding congregation. "Come on. The set's over. Time to rest up. Come *on*, June!"

She looked out at them, sipping a little, talking a little, staring. Lost, all lost. Everything lost.

"June . . ." Giving up on her, Larry snatched the mike out of the stainless steel stand. "Okay, folks, take a break. We'll be back in ten—stick with us; that is, if you're not afraid to get Fever Blistered! All riiiiiight!"

She saw the tears in his eyes as he helped her off stage. How hurt for her he must have been to do that hokey exit bit. She liked the feel of his strong arm encircling her waist as he gracefully powered her back into the green room where he sat her down on a well-worn sofa. She saw that he was careful to help her settle onto a solid spot, an island of intact material between one section of springs protruding through bare threads and another glazed shiny from use. How nice. What a perfect performance.

June began, very very slowly, to applaud.

"June, snap out of it, huh? Did you know your sister was out there? And that guy Pete Robinson who . . ."

"I know who Pete Robinson is, Larry. Please don't treat me like some sort of festival drug casualty you're tending to in the first aid tent."

"Sorry, I . . ."

"I think it's time we disbanded," she said emotionlessly. "This is getting us nowhere. It's nowhere, Larry. Nowhere at all."

Recoiling from his lead singer, Larry squinted as if to penetrate a disguise; then, at last, he seemed to spy her real identity. "Bosley Broderick's out there tonight. Did I tell you that?"

The cold facade remained in place for a few moments, like an abandoned building detonated from within that briefly appears untouched; then color returned to June's face and her eyes, suddenly bright, opened wide.

"Bosley?"

And then she came fully back into herself. Felt the pain. Remembered, really remembered, where she was right now—the place she'd always dreamt of finding herself, the backstage of her fantasies. The rock star, the vocalist, the center of attention, the woman around whom the world revolved—how could she have forgotten? And Bosley Broderick sat in the audience tonight. He had come to see her again. Again. His presence here certified . . . something, sealed some special secret. Had he seen something in her previous performance that had brought him back? Of all the men she had ever met, he alone saw her as. . . .

"Hello, sister of the blood."

Larry having discreetly vacated the ugly green room, June found herself alone with the man of her dreams. Again.

"Hello, Bosley, sit down. It's even less attractive and more humble than when you played here, isn't it?"

Garbed in a blue velveteen pants suit that looked at first like denim, Bosley gave a grizzled grin and thrust wide his arms. He caught June up in a big bear hug that felt quintessentially parental, only vaguely erotic. She did not want to be let go and pushed him away before he could release her.

"Won't you, ah . . .?" She gestured again to the threadbare sofa, but Bosley instead made for the straight-backed metal folding chair. He sat decorously, grandly crossing his legs and offering a generously expansive smile, obviously a prelude to a speech.

"As my friend Gordon Sumner says, quoting his dear friend the late Arthur Koestler, we are all ghosts in the machine, spirits in this fitfully material world. Yes? As long as our souls are beautiful, June, as long as we are beautiful all the way inside, our surroundings cannot conceivably be ugly. They may only bask in the light from inside us, endure the energy we exude—and wait. Our brilliance glorifies the physical world, does it not, until our Translator changes the language in which we are presented, until our transition into . . . Well, how the hell are you?"

"Oh, just fine." June nodded at him with desperate reluctance. How very badly she needed to see this man whom she had thought to reject a few weeks before! To be in his presence, to hear his voice! To be held again!

She said, "What did you think of the show?"

"Hmmm." Bosley, folding his stubby but powerful arms across his chest, nodded as if agreeing with the pronouncements of a voice only he could hear. "Yes. Quite a show. Yes indeed, June, quite a show."

She sat up very straight, then closed her eyes. What did he really mean? No matter how much it hurt, she had to find out. She drew out of herself in a way she had not dared to do for weeks.

"Tell me," she said.

"Well . . ." Bosley unfolded his arms and spread them as if illustrating the expanding universe. "See? Marvelous, bountiful, ineffable—this I see in you. But this is what I hear in your music . . ." He drew in his arms, fisted his hands, imploded his whole body seemingly.

June saw the man compress into nothing, into a nugget, a kernel of existence, a bare seed of life chastised by the surrounding cold—nothingness.

"Dormant," he said. "I hear an absolute zero of natural emotion flowering from you." He looked over his shoulder at the folding chair as if he meant to sit.

"What's wrong?" June almost screamed. "I can't do any better! What's wrong with me?"

Bosley smiled impishly, the worldly entertainer, and

held up a single finger for her to see. "You don't need me to tell you, dearest love flower, child of deepest blood. You don't need me."

Blinking, June couldn't take her eyes away from him as she half-consciously drew a paper cup of water from the dusty cooler beside the sofa. "I don't understand. If I don't need you, what *do* I need?"

Bosley, nodding to himself, looked away as if everything had been taken care of. He seemed to have phased her out of existence.

"Bosley, please don't . . ."

His body jerked and snapped to a kind of loose-limbed, otherworldly version of military attention. His jaw quivered, shoulders undulating, Bosley threw his head sharply back, mouth open wide. His lips remained unmoving, but words flew out of his mouth as if unbidden, as if he were merely the conduit to an impossibly distant source of communication.

"Look inside yourself, June Lockwood. You know the way to everything you need."

June gawked at the twitching overweight body, small shudders passing up and down his frame as if testing out each set of muscles for any possible weakness or vulnerability before moving on. Finally, however, it was his mouth she could not take her eyes off, certain that at any moment its corners must tear and begin to bleed from being forcibly hinged so very wide. And then, then what would pour out of him?

"Constraints surround you. Ancient words. A presence. A woman. A child. A road. A car. A bottle of wine. Many years and many words. Selfish beings, a failure to resign to Nature. A resistance, a hideousness of surface pretense. Life. Life. You have been blessed with the gift of blood. To suffer the blood that flows through your own body is to know the truth. The deepest push . . ."

A high shrill ringing began to sound in June's ears, the tone of fever in one's head tuned up far too high to be bearable. She clapped hands to ears, remembering wine, remembering stone, remembering images behind the screen.

"Go in blood. Feel the flow of your own blood and the constraints cannot touch you. Yield to the dynamic nature of your blood pulse. Feel it. Free it. Give your blood freely to the world. Go in blood, June Lockwood. Go in . . . Ahhhh!"

June ran to Bosley whose mouth twitched in an effort to close and open simultaneously, a tiny trickle of red creeping down at the corner. "Bosley, oh God! Bosley, don't . . ."

"Die?" The mouth relaxed into normal life. Bosley blinked, smiled at her with mature relaxed good humor. "Me? No way, child. No way. These little vacations from life are what keep me looking young, you know?" And he laughed like someone throwing away a professional secret just for fun.

June touched his face as if perceiving its rough texture as a treasured prize. "Oh, Bosley."

He snapped his teeth at her hand like a movie shark, and she pulled it back in real fear. He caught her eye and both laughed outrageously at her startled retreat. "Silly little sister of truth!"

Trying to compose herself, June bunched handfuls of her costume in her fists. "So what does it mean, Bosley? Do I have to sign some sort of contract with the devil, sell my soul to succeed in rock 'n' roll?"

He brought up both sleeves, angling his wrist to dab with each at the bloody smudges on the corners of his mouth, both hands freezing there a moment as if he were a praying mantis. And then he laughed, bringing his hands down, a big healthy gas engine coughing out the carbon that keeps it from roaring with mechanically perfect life.

"Superstitious child! There is no devil. Only the forces of nature. Weren't you listening? Only what's natural, and what is given to help you get there. Don't tire me, June. Go out as a sister of the blood. All women are most intimately of the blood, but precious few can acknowledge their indebtedness. I did not pass the rock on to you for nothing."

June closed her eyes for a moment as that deadening, all-numbing headache began to return in her skull. She had to shake it. Goodbye, she thought she heard. Goodbye. HAD to shake it.

A sudden commotion at the door made her glance up against her will.

"June, you'd better get back out here; we're starting to lose some of this crowd . . . oh, are you okay?" Larry hung halfway in the doorway, his heel held off the ground waiting for her to respond, his long black hair hanging down like the strands of a mop propped askew in a corner.

"Where's Bosley?" she wanted to know.

Larry, puzzled at getting a question back, let the heel drop. "Bosley? I don't see anyone, June. But then, I've been . . . indisposed." Larry giggled, then clapped his hand over his mouth. "Sorry!"

"Sure you are."

Suddenly casual, Larry confidently sauntered to her side. "Hey, let's get out there before they all leave us, okay? But first, I got this treeee-mendous idea to improve our second set!"

"What's that?"

Flourishing his sleeves like a magician, Larry produced a tightly rolled joint which he held up triumphantly for her to examine, a tiny trophy. "Voila!

Instant showmanship! My buddy Bob's best, straight from the Santa Cruz mountains to your dressing room, my dear!"

"Thanks, Larry, but no thanks. I let Duane talk me into some wine—and the way my stomach feels I'm regretting it. Now let's . . ."

Larry jumped like a cheerleader, thrashing his arms angrily as if he were fighting the very air. "Let's go tear their heads off!" He made a grandiose cavalry charge gesture as he sprinted for the doorway.

"Right!" June said. "Let's!"

Chapter Eleven:

Bloodrock

"Time, June. Let's go!"
Feel it. Do you?

Again and again, night after night, not even her strangle grip on the vocalist's microphone could prevent the nightmare.

She stood alone and lonesome in a deserted windswept schoolyard. Somewhere inside the massive grey building her mother conducted business with the administration. Hours before, it seemed, she had been told to wait, wait and play. But all the children had left before she had arrived. Had they moved here only recently? No children knew her. California winter, bleak and dirty, and the child, alone, tries not to think, tries not to participate in the slowing of the Time that is already so painfully and brutally slow. And the child thinks: The Time for my mother must be faster than this; otherwise she would have hurried out to have me hold her and protect her against It. Only my child's Time is this slow. It isn't real. My Time isn't real. I am not real. I wait. Mother doesn't come. I will never be real. I wait. Time does not pass. Mother does not come. I wait.

Night after night they played "Night After Night," a medley of tunes created by the defunct progressive rock group UK. She felt it always. But the audience seemed to feel nothing. Some started to leave.

"Don't go!" she wanted to yell. I know my Time up here is not the same as yours down there, out there, separated from me by this Wall.

LISTEN TO THE BLOOD.

June looked to her left where Larry almost seemed to be nodding over the fretboard of his guitar, almost asleep.

"The braille of your face I study," June sang, "for a whisper from within . . ."

LISTEN TO THE BREATH OF YOUR DARK BLOOD.

As if a spotlight had flashed on in the sombre light of the club, illuminating the audience, June caught sight of Duane's eager face, sheathed in a pleasant resilient smile. He was determined to like every second of the show if it killed him—and never think a thing of it.

BLOOD. LISTEN. LISTEN!

"Tongue my eyes with salt and sugar," she sang, her voice on automatic, climbing for the high-C on the first syllable of the last word. Then: "Baste them with the lilac singing/Of your veined and pulsing sea . . ."

The spotlight—Betty sitting expectantly in the third row, her face as radiant as that of a child being told her favorite story. What story? Certainly not this one. Then? That Time in the schoolyard when mother never came and the little girl ceased to exist—and knew it? The child with no Time.

No teeth. No audience. No money. No hope.

THE BLOOD. ONLY. ONLY THE BLOOD. LISTEN. LISTEN FIRST. LISTEN FIRST.

But Betty needed the money. Ivan needs teeth. And I need . . .

June had no idea when the automatic pilot began to falter. She heard her voice quaver but thought no one would notice, heard the drums die down but thought nothing of it, heard the bass stop and the rhythm guitar and the lead guitar in Larry's strong hands degenerate into abstract chords that bore no resemblance to anything. But she did not think at all. June heard the music stop and told herself: *the music's over.* Some peculiar auditory hallucination? Hysterical deafness, temporary and curable?

June saw Larry slumped against the drum kit, his guitar lolling on his thigh like the weapon of a defeated warrior, his long black hair snaking down the front of his body like ribbons of surrender.

But the inner music continued on.

YES. BLOOD. YES. ONLY THE BLOOD. YES AND YES AND YES AND BREATH. ONLY THE BLOOD.

Did someone yell? For the briefest moment June got a glimpse of the collective face of the audience—stunned, tense, expectant, embarrassed. In the silence, they would wait for a total collapse or a moment of true genius. Anything in between and . . . well, they'd work that out later, wouldn't they?

The itch. The itch on her throat like the suggestion of a feather's touch there. June had long since learned to live with the maddeningly vague itch that had decided to make itself at home along her throat. She had willed the itch into the back of her mind—far, far back. After all, she could not always be holding the stone out away from her neck. Now she listened.

FEEL IT, JUNE? WHAT DOES IT SAY?

June, eyes closed, gripped the microphone. She wasn't sure. She thought it said. . . .

WHAT?

I want out?

TRY IT, JUNE. THAT'S THE ONLY WAY TO FIND OUT.

But how? How do you lose this fear? How?

TRY IT.

Well, why not? What did she have to lose?

She went down to live with the vitality of the itch that had now become the history of her throat, her pulse, her arterial system, her whole body. Then she knew she had come this far by being so quiet. And so she kept quiet—and listened. Clearly, very very clearly she could hear the music playing, the music she had always heard but never acknowledged.

And if she gripped the bloodrock with both hands the music articulated itself as clearly as own breath.

How perfect! Listen! Just listen!

Did she hear the young man in the front row gasp when the blood blossomed out in a bright bouquet on her white throat? Did she hear the suppressed groans, gasps as she cupped her hands to the tiny fountain that had opened between her breasts?

June felt as alive as a child. Why had she ever resisted? Why had she thought there would not be enough for everyone? Bosley was right—the blood was inexhaustible. Time, money, love, beauty, all there, all flowering, all bountiful and eternal and pure. All answers, all perfection, all knowledge of energy, strength, courage.

She did not hear the hiss of disbelief as her hands instinctively moved to her forehead to paint a triangle and an eye interwoven into a design she had always unconsciously adored. How had she absorbed so much from a book she had only browsed through?

More cheers, crazy sounds. Dangerous persons, wild and ready to do anything, had somehow replaced the sane and bored and complacent group that had sat there all evening taking up space.

June did not know that she had begun to sing a blues, a basic primitive rock 'n' roll blues, a slow blues that increased in speed like a train gathering momentum down an eternal track to crash into the great solid rock face of the final mountain. Because Time had changed. With dexterous ease, June had turned the glove of Time neatly and completely inside out. Now each moment glowed for her. The rest of the world could wait in the playground now, alone with the wind, with the children who would never show, never ever ever if they waited all night and day.

"The deepest push, the deepest push, the deepest push of love . . ."

"OH! YEAH!"

". . . is Blood!" she sang out, voice soaring.

Somehow her whole band had learned to sing with the vocalist she'd never heard before, the strange woman standing with June on the stage. And what an extraordinary performer! Such an ability to . . . to unequivocally release without straining all the energy that flowed! And to think that this woman could perform so well while, simultaneously and intuitively, teaching each band member to play a new tune. And that timing, those colors, that sense of cohesion that you just could not fake! Marvelous!

"Yes!" screamed Danny Driscoll, her shaman drummer, never before ecstatic over a single beat he'd played with her. "Yes!"

"Oh, shit, yes!" some animal screamed from the audience.

Then something went wrong, horribly wrong. A roar, a rumble, that distant monolithic landmass protest of fault wave tension moving inexorably closer and closer. Earthquake!

And only when she opened her eyes at last did she see that they were all on their feet—every man, every woman, Duane, her sister, yes, even Pete Robinson, and Herm D'Angello dancing madly up and down with a cocktail waitress on either side of him and the bartender Sam throwing the phone receiver into the air trailing its severed cord like a torn umbilical. They loved the music, they loved the band, they loved her.

At last June thought her tears were more blood, more blood. But then the salt taste, thinner, yet sweeter, more resinous, reached her lips; and she licked and smacked and began to cry for real.

She looked to her left at the man who played lead guitar for her. "Larry! Oh, Larry!"

They embraced so quickly it could have been an illusion—or pure threatre, rehearsed a thousand times, a perfectly choreographed bit of fluff, just the right touch to send that crazy roomful of lunatics one step beyond into the frenzy they loved losing themselves in. And, Lord, how good it felt to her! And she looked out and caught a quick glimpse of Duane who . . . Oh, never mind, she told herself. Never mind.

"More! More! More! More!"

Sliding easily out of Larry's sinewy grip, June skipped across stage to the bass drum which she freed from its floor brace so that she could face its round skin full toward the audience as she used her nails to expunge the words FEVER BLISTER from its surface. The band, gladly backing her up, buying her time, filled in—not mere noodling but a lovely stream of lyrically improvised rock.

Danny Driscoll discovered the percussive possibilities of the floor of the stage, that it was hollow, that it resounded when struck. And so he struck it—with his foot, then only the heel, then the heel of his hand—again and again.

June scraped. The dangerous audience roared.

"Yes!" someone shouted. "Do it! Change it!"

"A-po-ca-lyp-tic!" shouted another male voice.

A series of innocently obscene catcalls showered the stage with what June knew to be true, true love. Time did not exist as she expunged the false words from the drum. Still kneeling, she began to write, showing her continually glistening, eternally replenished fingers between each stroke.

Everything is music now. Every gesture is music I play in the atmosphere of my life. Listen to me script what's real!

Then she turned the drum back to the audience and showed them what she had painted with her fingers. Whispers at first then an incipient shadow of a chant.

And then the word, bold, vocalized as black lettering, billboards, ball liner screams.

"BLOODROCK! BLOODROCK! BLOODROCK!"

Not holding back an inch of her loving radiant face, June turned completely to Larry who had been calling out her name over and over. He held thumbs up: Yes!

"Yes, June, I think we've finally got a name for our band!" And his understatement and subsequent laughter were drowned out in the cheers.

"MORE BLOODROCK! MORE BLOODROCK! MORE BLOODROCK!"

Somewhere in the tumultuous crowd Herm waved his hands, signaling the staff together. "Wine!" he instructed. "Red wine on the house! For everybody! Call every bar in town if you've got to; tonight we're celebrating!"

June spotted Pete Robinson joining the ranks of fans rushing the stage, but the detail did not register.

All she knew how to do was play music now.

"Okay, everybody," she yelled to the ecstatic crowd, which had begun to swell in numbers as word of what was happening here spread up and down the strip. "Are you ready to hear some rock 'n' roll?"

She had never felt so triumphant, so decidedly on top of the world. What could be better—marriage, motherhood, a mansion, having it all? For now, for this moment, she needed nothing else.

BOOK II
SUCCESS—THE DEEPEST PUSH OF LOVE

Chapter Twelve:

And The Moon Turned to Blood

"Now, are you watching closely? Betty? June? Ivan? It's any moment now."

The soldier retraced his steps along the snowy bank, looking for the girl he had lost and found so many times before.

June concentrated on keeping her hands folded in her lap. She would not let herself become so distracted by the story that she toyed unconsciously with the rock around her throat. She wanted no repeat performance of the doctor, the mansion, and the flames. And, after all, it was not her night to be on stage.

Spotting the rude animal skin coat of a marauding Cossack, the girl could think only to run through the banks of snow fouled by the ridges formed around the roots of dead trees. She fell, panting. Her face, up close, showed terror—and a fierce expectancy. When the male figure surged through the snowy landscape with violent urgency, closer, closer, and then fell on all fours over her, not touching her frozen skin, she knew that she was as good as dead.

"Mommy, why doesn't the movie talk?"

"Ssssh!" Betty whispered in the flickering darkness. "The movies hadn't learned to talk yet, honey."

Fingers snapped as sharply as a stick cracking. The lights came up, the film choking to a stop. "Don't be a fool," Amelia told her younger daughter. "How old do you think I am? I realize you're not quite capable of keeping track of such things. If you had had the sense to ask me, I would have told you about the difference between optical and magnetic sound and the conflicts between our director and recording technician which necessitated . . . oh, never mind. Just watch for *it*." Again, she snapped her fingers, reversing the process, the film churning back into continuous life, the lights going down.

When her eyes flashed open, the girl saw who the figure disguised as a Cossack was. They embraced, snow and tears and skin crushed warmly together. "Who taught the movies to talk, Momma?"

"There, you see?" Amelia called out. She stood and, pointing, went to the light-imprinted screen. "There in the far upper left hand corner—see it swing, out of control, just the bottom of its arc? Now . . . see! There! It drops! See there, once it strikes her, she becomes inert, simply slumps? She never moved. Hans confided to me when he had finished directing the film that the stage hand never did have a proper grip in the first place."

June discovered her hand inching up on the stone and lightly slapped it with the other; perhaps, in some unguarded future moment, a shadow memory of the blow would help her regain her senses. "Tragic," she said. "It's just so . . ."

"Carelessness! Carelessness and stupidity! Like far too many people, she lived carelessly and foolishly, thinking nothing could ever happen to her. After all, didn't the men all tell her that she was the most exquisite, perfect, divine little piece?''

Now the real Cossacks had caught up with the lovers. A piece of lint jumped like a stricken insect across the center of the screen. Her soldier lover looking on in horror, the Cossacks tied the dead actress to the husky high-spirited horses. Proceeding so vigorously through their paces, the myriad extras seemed unaware of the filmed tragedy that had taken place right in front of them.

"Grandmother, did that pretty lady get hurt?"

The tail end of the film snaked through the projector to lash violently against the rear housing. All the customary lights came on in the postcard perfect drawing room. Ivan ran to Amelia to get his answer. "Grandma! Did the pretty . . ."

"The pretty," Amelia mused. "The pretty, pretty lady? You like her, do you? Do you know what your grandmother Amelia thought of that woman, Ivan?" The parquet floor glistening beneath his scuffed shoes, Ivan gave an uncertain nod. "Well, little boy, let me tell you that the pretty woman in question, the *late* pretty woman, was one of the most . . ."

"Mother!" June countered. "I don't know that Ivan is quite old enough to appreciate your candor, which Betty and I realize you intend to be refreshingly . . ."

"Oh, I'm old enough!" Ivan pointed out.

June eyed her visibly cringing sister. Poor Betty! Now it would be impossible to ever get her back here again.

Amelia straightened her spine, her chin held wonderfully high. "Good for you, child," she told Ivan. "I'm sure that if you knew the torment your grandmother had suffered at that woman's hands, well . . . suffice it to say that few mourned her passing. And I'm certainly glad that none of you are like her. If one of my daughters allowed herself to be so willing a victim to each of life's more obvious traps, I would disown and disinherit her. Drugs, alcohol, debauched health—what did she not bring upon herself? And money! Thank God neither of you has let herself get caught in a financial bind in these times of ours when so many women are absolute fools for money!"

Ivan somersaulted on the cushion of the overstuffed chair he'd squirmed in while she spoke. "You gave me $15 for Christmas, Grandma! That was great!"

Betty tried to catch her son's attention, but his eyes were riveted to Amelia, who easily ignored the rambunctious boy.

"Oh, I know people who enjoy being asked for a loan by their friends, even by their children. It gives them a sense of importance, I suppose; it makes them feel powerful to dole out bits and pieces of their wealth to those who are so very desperate for it. Strange, how those who are most foolish and profilgate where money is concerned are the first to grovel and abase themselves so abjectly when the right moment comes. Don't you agree, darling?"

Betty, nodding reluctantly, seemed to sink deeper into the cushions of the plush mauve sofa. Once, June remembered, she had almost resented the attention Amelia habitually paid to the younger of her two daughters. But no longer—no way! That attention, June had seen, became a possessively cruel scrutiny, something like being the subject on a microscope slide, not only under observation but also pinned down by the weight of science.

Amelia placed a cigarette in a long ivory filter and flourished it with gracious ease. "So, I suppose I should ask at this point the purpose of this grave honor, of seeing my daughters and only grandson together in my house for the first time in . . . two, no make that three years."

June knew when to intercept one of her mother's patented ambushes. "Just a social call, Amelia," she said. "As you say, it's just been far too long since we all got together. After all, we're such a small family." Should she risk it now? Her news? "There is one thing . . ."

"Yes! There is this matter of you being in the news, so to speak. I believe I read that our aging hippie Herman D'Angello—'character-about-town' indeed! more like lunatic-about-town—that this colorful Mediterranean type has given you some sort of special contract? What's all that about, June? I shudder to imagine the affiliations with organized crime you've undoubtedly been forced to establish."

June found it not difficult to toss off a polite laugh. "No, Mother! You've got the wrong idea entirely. Herm gave me an open-ended contract making the Crater our home club—that's all; whenever the band's in town, we're guaranteed a place to work."

Amelia nodded with a dramatically ponderous up-and-down movement of her perfectly coiffed head. "I see. Well. And then there's this blood business. According to the media, you . . ."

"It's nothing, Mother—really." At least Amelia wasn't a religious fanatic. All sorts of wild distortions had come from that sector already. June tried to martial inner strength to make her little announcement. "Mother . . . Amelia, I've been meaning to tell you about a man I know. His name is Duane. He started as a computer programmer who somehow got into record promotion and then management and for the last six months we've . . ."

Licking her lips, Amelia leaned forward to scrutinize June and say, "Oh, so the boys smell the money already, do they? Beginning to flock around you like flies, are they? Well, I can't help you at all there."

"Mother, Duane is *not* after money. I don't have any as yet. He's a wonderful man, warm and loving and he really . . . really appreciates me. I thought that I should tell you about him before anything definite is decided."

Ivan, tiring of adult chatter, jumped down from the big overstuffed chair and found his way under an eighteenth century Florentine lamp where he discreetly zoomed his hands through the air to simulate a star ship battle in the far reaches of space.

Amelia looked from June down to the self-absorbed child, then abruptly to his mother. "Betty? Betty, are you awake? Your son—attend!"

Startled, Betty looked frantically around for Ivan and, locating him at last, scrambled down to her hands and knees, a position—it hurt June to acknowledge—that seemed unfortunately natural for her. Without delay, Betty scooted directly over to her son to explain in an urgent whisper some of the intricacies of protocol in grandma's grand house.

"Warm?" Amelia said. "Loving? How long has this tender . . . relationship gone on? Days? Minutes? Hours?"

June stifled the urge to tell her that it was none of her damned business. But why defeat the whole purpose of the visit? She and Betty knew what Amelia was like yet had decided to take the risk of coming here to pay their respects like any normal family. "We've been dating for four months now," June said.

"Four months—ah, an eternity! Such fidelity! But tell me, June, do you really think it's becoming for an adult—after all, you're hardly what they call a 'teeny-bopper'—to use words like 'dating'?"

June could do no better than a shrug that showed no overt hostility.

Amelia gave a little chuckle. "You never change, do

you, darling? You hate me, but you just cannot quite bring yourself to say it."

Stricken with a horrible sadness, June shook her head and tried to meet her mother's steady gaze. "Not at all, mother. I don't hate you. I . . ."

Amelia glared triumphantly. "I challenge you to say that you love me! Now! This second!"

June resisted covering her face with her hands but discovered almost too late that her fingers were compensating by wandering up between her breasts to the pendant. "I'm sorry," she said, looking at her helpless hands. "It's just that . . ."

Amelia rose grandly to her full length. "I think you had better go." She stabbed a look at Betty and Ivan contending on the hardwood floor. "All of you!"

Watching her sister and nephew scramble madly to assemble themselves to the tune of Amelia's commanding tone, June congratulated herself on being ready to go; but then, wasn't she always ready to go whenever she visited this mausoleum? Perhaps it was easier this way, Amelia ordering them out. It certainly simplified the leave-taking amenities.

Still, this was her mother.

"Mother, I really do . . ."

"So, it's definite, June. You are marrying this money man?"

"No. No, he hasn't even asked me yet! But . . ."

"Oh, how very awkward. I never before realized how very presumptuous you are, June. And, while we are on this topic, let me issue a little warning that goes along with your incipient success in this adolescent profession. Many modern musicians have resorted to courting the supernatural to achieve financial returns on the investment of little talent. If you ever embarrass me by getting involved in any of this occult crap, forget that we are related. You will have been automatically disowned. Now what do you have to say to me?"

"I do love you, Mom," June said.

Amelia pantomimed a few polite claps. "Bravo, darling. It took every ounce of will power and determination to get it out, did it not? I commend you. Betty, you're so infernally slow. Aren't you ready to leave yet?"

"Yes, Mother!" Betty said as she bundled Ivan into his coat and crowded him out into the long hallway. "Thank you for the tea and the movies. Ivan, tell your grandmother . . ."

" 'Amelia,' " she corrected. "And do try to stop thanking me. I think it's quite degrading the way you insist on thanking others for every imaginable thing."

Comic strip characters, cute but forlorn, Betty and Ivan trudged down the steep stone steps. Kissing her mother goodbye, June resisted the urge to jump or dance or skip her way down.

Once June had the small car launched out of the mammoth driveway, Ivan began to do chin-ups on the front seat, interposing his head between the two sisters. "Did that moon thing fall down on that lady?"

Betty, delaying, fumbled for a response. "Honey, that was a long, long time ago."

"She was really pretty, Mommy—just like you."

"That's nice, honey; now go to sleep, okay?"

Both women listened until his tired grumbling gave way to contented groans, the sighs of a little boy giving up to the enormity of his fatigue.

"Was it really horrible?" June said at last.

"No!" Betty said. "Of course not, June! It's just that . . . I have a child now and she treats me like . . ."

"Sorry about that. I know exactly what you mean."

"Oh, June, you don't have to apologize—and I'm so grateful to you for all you went through arranging for the loan from Duane. Can you imagine how it would have been if I'd asked our mother tonight, after what she said?"

"Whoosh!" June, appreciating the sentiment. "Can you imagine what mother would say if she knew that next week we're taking this three-ring circus to visit Grandma Edna?"

Relishing the release of tension in their escalating laughter, neither woman noticed the hint of greenish fog that had insinuated itself into the backseat. Stretched out full length, Ivan moaned in his sleep; he struck out fitfully into the empty air with his small hands and curled himself into a tight ball. His continuous self-contained little shudders almost matched the subtle vibration of the engine.

Chapter Thirteen:

Just a Little Mist

It happened the next night after closing time.

June could not have been more pleased with the way things progressed and came together at the club. While the wild man Danny Driscoll enjoyed the "showmanship" of the new act, the artist Larry Ludwig had to admit that the quality of the music had also improved. ("Funny how the intensity makes it seem more . . . real.") And Bruce Marley? Well, he kept on thumping his bass and listening to his Charlie Parker and John Coltrane records between sets, but most of the time he smiled while performing with Bloodrock.

Of course, it made June happy that her band was happy. Of course, it would have been nice to know why. Of course, exactly what had happened, what continued to happen each time they performed—the blood, simply that, the apparently inexhaustible blood—remained a mystery. Perhaps later, when things slowed down a little, she'd find the time to think about it. For now, well, too much scrutiny spoiled a lot of things.

"Oh, June, you just take off like a NASA spaceship

jettisoning the old rockets and just—WHOOOSH!" Herm told her. "What a band!" He scheduled a series of special promotional nights, each of which centered around what he termed "this great little gimmick of yours." One night he had the waitresses pass out small plastic containers of artificial blood he'd purchased at a theatrical supply outlet. Again, Herm had a series of decals made up depicting some of the tranditional occult designs June painted on herself and elsewhere, and any customer ordering a double shot received a complimentary glass with the exotic decal affixed.

"Collect them all," one wit quipped. "Be the first in your bar to have the whole set!"

Yes, the club had come alive. The mood was festive, Dionysian, crazy—yet not really rowdy, not at all. What more could a club manager want from a band? Herm let June know how much he appreciated her; she, in turn, praised the faith he'd demonstrated in the band by keeping it on.

But sometimes it took more than faith to withstand the increasing number of media attacks on Bloodrock. "Lockwood's Luster Dimmed by Bloodbath," trumpeted an early review in the San Jose Herold. Channel Six jammed three cameras and hundreds of feet of cable into the club. Filming for over three hours, they aired less than ten seconds of video tape—June, her face fully gilded in the final moments of the set, sticking her tongue out comically at a heckler who had thrown a Cabbage Patch Doll onstage while screaming out that she should bite its head off. "State of the art rock and roll . . ." the anchorperson had proclaimed over the snippet of film, ". . . irresponsible, disgusting: a true dead end." Yet some of the coverage, Duane assured her, amounted to good publicity, especially the occasional suggestion that the band had stumbled onto something that seemed sportingly sinister yet was, at heart, good clean fun.

Phone calls from two women who were her former high school friends convinced June that the media had succeeded in painting a predominantly negative picture of Bloodrock. Remarkably similar, their diatribes ignored the facts of June's wholesome and productive adolescence—varsity basketball, volunteer work with handicapped kids during the summer, Pep Band. She was an evil woman, they said—a bad influence on their young children, a disgrace to the community. It all sounded frighteningly familiar, like echoes from another life. Finally, the demands: that she abandon her sinful and degrading act which constituted a spiritual and moral hazard to the community, and if not, an organized boycott of the Club Crater or any other establishment foolish enough to hire her.

Tonight, remembering the phone calls, the criticisms, the attacks from out there, June encouraged herself to be philosophical. After all, these people did not really know her.

("Aren't you June Lockwood?" a fastidiously attired woman had asked while they stood in line at the grocery store. For a moment June thought of denying it, but the woman, whose beautiful eyes sparkled with a keen amused intelligence, was exactly the kind of person she would have been delighted to number among her fans. "Well . . . yes," she admitted. "You should be ashamed of yourself," the other told her. "Have you seen the show?" "No, and I haven't the slightest intention of doing so! I know what you are!")

Such encounters were like mini-assassinations in the dead center of the day. Leaning against the bar sipping seltzer water, June shook her head and decided she'd better get herself moving to start the next set.

A dapper tall blond executive-type stopped her with

his arm as she pushed away from the bar. "You're incredible."

"Why, thanks . . ."

"I'm a rock 'n' roll connoisseur. I've heard them all—Zeppelin, Leppard, Y & T, Sabbath, Maiden—and I'm telling you that you're a stronger lyricist than any of them and a better vocalist! And talk about heavy metal! *Adult* heavy metal!" He kissed his fingers and threw them into the air.

"Goodness," she said, feeling like laughing at his extravagant praise. "I don't . . ."

"Take it from me, you're incredible. By the way, what're you doing after the show tonight? I've got my Mercedes parked right out front and the two of us can . . ."

Somehow, she excused herself and threaded her way backstage. Did the whole world have a fever? Sometimes she felt like a nurse with a thermometer which she was perpetually slipping out from under her patient's tongue. Except that the image was wrong; she was the cause of the fever, not the nurse in attendance. Disease? Was her art an illness that her audience contracted each night?

June slid out of her sweater and began to fasten the snaps of her cape. Each night she learned something new from her audience about what they needed from her. Did she learn about herself in the process? It all fell into place—recklessly, dangerously sometimes, but it fell properly and correctly and inevitably—each night, each performance, precisely into place. And just like that, that easy, she was back out onstage and into the last set.

"You've got it now, girl," Larry called over to her.

"Yeah!" she called back, as if a canyon separated them.

"Hang on!" he yelled. "Don't let go! Remember, we're all hooked together by safety lines, and you're the lead climber!"

Each night she felt a certain eager fearful anticipation of the climax, but tonight the slight undertone of dread seemed more acute.

She held the rock with both hands. And the rock bled. The audience lost touch with reality and went blithely insane.

Backstage, Herm watched and listened and clapped like crazy. Not a greedy man, he only wanted to own and operate a club that was "a going thing." Primarily, he loved good loud music and loved musicians and took real pride in telling everyone that his club was the last bastion of quality rock 'n' roll, the real thing.

He hadn't meant anything sinister in wedging the club's backdoor open with that particular book. He hadn't really been thinking, only responding to his sense that the club was more stuffy than usual tonight.

FREE RED WINE—UN PETIT BORDEAUX boasted the red and blue banner strung boldly across the front of the Club Crater tonight. Inside, the wine flowed, as they say, like water; but wine was not water tonight. When this band played, that was *not* the prevalent metaphor.

"Bloodrock! Bloodrock!" the audience chanted, toasting the group's ongoing whirlpool performance, swilling the dark red liquid, and hardly minding at all if some of it sloshed out of the glass and onto their clothing. After all, didn't June do that every night? Didn't a dark red stain appear as she painted her musical hysteria across the face of each night's performance?

Duane himself spilled a little on his shoe as he smacked Herm's broad back. "Remember Gaylord Perry, Herm? They say he was the greatest spitballer of all-time and that he kept the stuff hidden in his glove. With that costume June wears, where the hell do you suppose she hides it?"

Turning his head, Herm looked blankly into Duane's oversized grin. "You should know these things. You're her manager."

Yes, the wine flowed freely. The carpet sopped up what the customers did not.

"Bloodrock! Bloodrock!"

No different from any other performer, no different from anyone band, June and the boys found it easier and easier to yield themselves up to an audience that could not get enough of them—like a patient gasping for breath, like a starving man ready to fight over a crumb of food. What the band chose to give, the audience found to be perfect; and Bloodrock knew it, they felt it, they played it, just like that. All night long. And night after night after night.

But what seemed different, what felt just slightly different tonight? (In the alley. In the darkness. Real. Waiting.)

"More wine over here, huh, Herb?" called a regular seated near the front.

Moving through the medley that would end this last set, June decided that she should try not to mind the drinking. Sure, the audience tended to get sloppy and inattentive when they'd drunk too much; sometimes she worried when she spotted a really tipsy one that there might be an auto accident when the customer tried to drive home. But wasn't all this beyond her sphere of responsibility and control? She did a damn good job of being responsible and taking charge of the music. So what more should she expect from herself?

The final ovation, which used to be a suspended moment, time standing blessedly still, was over increasingly quickly it seemed, no matter how long it went on. Tonight, when she reached her dressing room, June did not remember anything about the sounds the audience had made as she left the stage.

"How about an early breakfast?" Duane suggested. He patted his mouth politely to stifle a yawn, making June wonder if he'd had too much to drink.

She settled in beside him on the worn floral print sofa. They let their torsos sag together, holding each other up. They held hands. Neither spoke. June thought that they both must have drifted off for a moment or longer. She remembered how he used to be squeamish about the dried blood. Now he seemed not even to notice it. How lucky she was to have this relationship with an intelligent, strong, understanding man. And lucky, too, for all the rest the music had brought to her. Lucky, yet tonight. . . .

"Not tonight, Duane. I'll take a rain check. okay?"

"Hmmm, what?" So, he *had* been sleeping. "Oh, breakfast? Yeah, well, I guess you're right. It's pretty late, isn't it?" He watched her go to the make-up table to begin cleaning her face and chest and arms. "Sure now, June? You're not hungry? Well, at least let me escort you out to the parking lot when you finish dressing. This isn't exactly San Jose's best neighborhood."

Squinting, June could not help but fix his mirror image with a look. Was the remark unconsciously racist? If not, then just what did he mean, exactly?

(Out in the alley. In the parking lot. Nothing to fear. In the night. Looming. Waiting.)

"What?"

"Hmmm? Oh, I said this isn't the best . . ."

Lately, increasingly, June now realized, she had felt the need to be alone after the show. Maybe it had to do with being unaccustomed to all the attention, the pressure. So, if not this, then what had she been seeking all these years? But that was just it. Years ago, months even, she would have cherished a few crumbs of praise. Now, public performance was a warm bath of love that left her feeling almost. . . .

(Alive. Real. Breathing. Thinking. Waiting. Salivating for blood, for just a little blood.)

"June, are you okay? You keep looking around the room like you hear something."

Well, she knew the traps of egotism. She'd seen plenty of musician comrades get blinded by the light. And she knew that she had it in her to duplicate their feat, to let her self-image get so inflated that she floated away from Planet Reality into the fine void of madness. And, worse, she knew that when she landed again her little bit of talent would have remained out there in space. No, what she needed now, simply, was a little time to herself, a little time to bring herself down, deflate the old show biz basketball, let the air out of the tires of Ego Auto. A little time to relax herself back down to size.

"No, Duane, really, I'm okay. I'm just winding down tonight and it may take me, oh, another forty-five minutes or so to . . ."

(In the alley. Breathing. Real. Just a little blood. Just a little taste.)

"June? Look, I can wait. If I get sleepy, I'll just doze off on the sofa here. I'd feel better if you'd let me . . ."

"It's okay, honey. Really. I'll see you tomorrow for dinner at Guidon's like we talked about, right?"

"Right! And remember—Pete Robinson afterwards, kid! We're goin' places now and . . ." Stretching his arms mightily, pleasurably, Duane yawned again. "You're sure that . . . Yeah, you're a big girl; you'll be okay.

"So, well, anyway . . ." Yawning once more, he played the fool by throwing both arms across his face.

"Anyway, goodnight and . . ."

They snagged each other for a gently fervent kiss.

"I really love you," he said. "And I wanted tonight to be . . .well, there's always tomorrow, isn't there? So, I guess I'll see you then."

"Right!" June said, trying to act really up so that he'd feel free to go. "See you tomorrow."

His hand slipped out of hers; the door opened and shut. Gone. Just like that. June stood stock still in the silence and listened for the squeak of the service entrance door but somehow missed it. Just like that.

(Real. In the alley. In the darkness. Just a little. Hurry.)

"I've really got to try to get control of my . . ."

With Duane gone, it seemed even harder to relax. She wanted to unwind and forget the positive furor of the evening's performance. But how? For a moment, she wished him back, even thought of trying to will him to return. But she did not believe in that ESP stuff, not at all. She had faith that one could find a cause, an observable logic, behind all events if one had the patience to discover it.

(Waiting!)

June, sighing nervously, dropped back onto the sofa and tried to relax, but when she stretched out with her feet up she felt vulnerable, almost indecent, as if someone were watching her. She sat back up and rubbed her forehead.

Headache. Great, just great. This wouldn't do at all. She'd sent Duane away so she could relax and now she was falling apart. Perfect. See what success does to you?

CHHEEEEKEET!

Sudden sound made June jump to her feet, hands fisted together. Had it come from outside the green room—or from inside it?

"Get a hold of yourself, Queen of the Occult," she

mocked. "Pretty soon you're going to start believing your own publicity. Then off the deep end with the greatest of ease . . . Fssssrrrr. . . ." Gesturing with her hand, she whistled the cartoon sound of some benighted creature falling from an impossible height down until nothing could be heard at all.

Imagining how she must look in this posture, foolish, off-guard, feckless, June shivered.

I'm frightened, she thought. I've talked myself into being really, really. . . .

(Vulnerable. Ready. Just a little bit. Real. In the alley. In the darkness.)

No wine here to change, June. No bottles to trip over. No piles of laundry to move and loom and reach.

She shook her head hard as if to clear away morning cobwebs. But she had never been more alert; in fact, that was what she wanted to shake loose. She thought to rid herself of the sensation of utter comprehension by shaking her head, her whole body—but before she could, she *saw* herself doing it. And words superimposed themselves over the image, words that frightened her. Words and images for which no exact translation existed. Words like. . . .

(Waiting, Waiting in the alley. In the darkness. Real. Just a little.)

"This is stupid," June said. "I'm going to finish getting dressed and I'm getting out of here right now."

Fine. Then do it.

She tried to goad herself into moving through the necessary gestures, but it did not happen; until at last her immobility came to frighten her more than the image of herself preparing to go out into the night. Into the alley. Through the darkness to the deserted lot where she had parked her car.

With reluctant haste June pulled on her casual clothes and shoes and coat, caught up her purse, and shook her shoulders to settle down what she wore as well as herself. Then she faced the green door, unpainted for years. Countless light patches revealed where posters and photos had been taped, then ripped down, leeching the essence of the paint in inchwide tongue marks of contact. Had she locked it? That she could not remember frightened her terrifically. How could she touch the damn thing if she didn't know?

"Now!"

No? Did she want to stay here staring at the door all night? If you can't be anything else, be brave.

The unlocked doorknob turned freely in June's hand. She stepped quickly into the opening, then reached back to flick off the light. ("We've all got to try to conserve electricity around here," Herb had said at the staff meeting. "Why, my PG & E bill last month was larger than my wine requisition!")

June strode down the narrow corridor to the rear service entrance, fishing in her purse for her car keys. Why hadn't she done this in the illuminated safety of the Green Room?

The service door slanted open into absolute darkness.

"How . . .?" But she hardly let the word whisper out, afraid of making a sound, afraid to make the slightest noise as she edged now toward the open door and the short alley beyond.

(Yes. Here. In the alley. In the darkness. Just. Just a little. Just a little closer.)

When did the security force patrol the lot? June stabbed a quick look at her watch. She was afraid to stop walking, but should she wait, crouching in the darkness until she saw a cop car? Or anyone? Anyone at all? Too humiliating.

"Oh, come on!"

June stepped quickly out into the night, into the alley. She held her purse slightly ahead of her waist as if to protect herself. She saw the garbage cans lined up in careless rows and peeked up through the narrow slant of converging buildings to the thin band of stars that seemed to point her way into the open, out into safety.

She did not sigh as she emerged into the open but swiveled her head to scan the elevated terrain of stars sprinkled like dust against the night sky. Deeply she breathed in the night, the beautiful living night. Inadvertantly, her hand strayed to the bloodrock hanging around her throat. To think that moments before she had been crouching fearfully inside that stuffy night club! Now, here she was, truly alive, truly herself.

A little fit of mist came quickly up around her ankles, sudden as a rainshower; it swirled and twisted—and yet she felt no wind, only the clammy, uncanny sensation of being wrapped, enveloped.

She looked up into the trees. No movement. No, the little disturbance had somehow managed to localize itself only around her.

NIGHT AFTER NIGHT I HAVE HEARD YOU CALLING ME. I HAVE COME. TRÉS GALLANT?

It reached greedily up her legs. She felt a tugging sensation at her breasts, tender yet persuasive, compelling, claustrophobic. A sexual assault? Where was her assailant? Some kind of a trick then, a game? But who was playing it?

(HERE IN THE DARKNESS! JUST A LITTLE!)

Putting a hand to her mouth, June turned her head. Her legs felt numb, paralyzed, as if they had become frozen from standing too long in a pure mountain stream.

NIGHT AFTER NIGHT I HAVE HEARD YOU CALLING. YOU OFFER IT, YOU OFFER IT TO ME FROM YOUR CHEST, FROM YOUR BEAUTIFUL . . .

Now the mist had body, substance, texture, hardness.

A firm pressure at her abdomen. She struggled with cloth, skin, smell.

June screamed. As if in echo, some small distant clangor seemed to answer back.

I JUST WANT A LITTLE. UN PEU. NOT ALL, MA BELLE. JUST A LITTLE.

The rotting face, mist and flesh, crooned charmingly into the center of her own face. The smell of wine and rot overwhelmed her. She felt the blood oozing, coming though unbidden, like an unexpected orgasm. Did the blood come from inside her or where?

June screamed again as she felt the constriction, the tightening. As the blood began to flow, the presence that held her had lurched violently down to draw near it. She thought of a beautiful fish discovering the sharp evil in its mouth and the spasm of reaction. But she knew this was opposite, the hideous voracious hunger for life of something already dead.

Being squeezed to death, squeezed! Mist, blood, squeezing her life. Bloody mist, the texture of something once skin; but how comfortable to be enveloped. To be taken inside. To be rescued like this from life. To be taken back into the blood.

NO. FIGHT IT, JUNE. FIGHT! I HAVE NOT GIVEN YOU THE GIFT FOR THIS.

This intervening inner sound shot terror through the center of the beautiful orgiastic numbness. Was it not right to be taken away, to be enveloped, squeezed, crushed?

"June? June, what's wrong?"

That voice came from impossibly far away, another country, another kind of life. It was the voice of ignorance, really. The voice of a two-dimensional creature that crawls forever along the surface of the lined paper and never suspects there is another world.

"June! Hold on!"

It was okay to ignore it. Another moment of pressure and she would hear the exquisite little *pop,* the tiny blood explosion of what had previously been her life. But then it felt like surgical bandages being whipped away by a hypertense doctor; she felt like a newly-bound mummy, just now acclimated to the long long wait, unwound in a fierce bright moment of pain. And her terror returned to full heat as she struggled to free her arms.

"June, stop! No, it's me . . ."

Her arms flailed wildly at the mist flesh that had disolved to nothing but this embracing warm flesh, other arms, palpable, living, dry cloth, solid texture—but she must fight the illusion! She must!

"June! June!"

Shaken and shaken again, not squeezed at all.

Who? This face? This familiar face? But when would the solid impression part, like water, like fog, to show the skull beneath the skin?

"Duane? Oh, I . . ."

"It's okay, kid. It's okay. What happened anyway? From over there under the streetlight it looked like you were a one-woman fog bank. For a second I thought you'd actually disappeared."

June tried to lose herself in his all-too-handsome, all-too-square features. "Perfect," she whispered. "You're always . . ."

"Huh?" He seemed not to hear her. "Hey, listen, since I'm here and you're here and we're both here together, how about that early breakfast I mentioned before? Come on. There's some things we should get straight."

Chapter Fourteen:

No Way in Hell

Sipping tepid coffee, June began to come out of it at last.

Breakfast, lunch, dinner—only once before in her life had June spent a day of meals with a man she was dating. (That day in Golden Gate Park with David Greenleaf when she was eighteen, sticky hand-holding and Ezra Pound poetry—what a joke!) Yet something special seemed to happen when romance and routine came together, a whole day of contact as opposed to the highlighted intensity of a few hours. (Perhaps that was why so many men and women believed in living together these days.)

June looked out the window past Duane's meticulously styled hair to the fog thickening around the little boats floating on dark water. (Hard not to look for mist, green mist.) She doubted that she'd been very good company today—too much staring into space, too much silence. It had taken June long hours to even begin to attempt to outline for Duane the horror she'd felt in that dreadful constriction, that near-engulfment in the mist. Thinking about it now, June shivered. In those hours of coffee and window gazing, she'd known that some of her silence must have seemed almost monumental. Amazing how he'd put up with her! Every other man she'd known would have prodded her continuously with, "What's wrong? Are you depressed? Is it something *I* did? Don't you feel well?" She felt grateful that Duane had enough confidence in himself to let her keep to herself when she needed to.

She looked up at him to express something of this but found that he too was gazing contemplatively at the ocean view. Had she finally strained his considerable patience? Or had it been the story she'd forced herself to reveal, bit by bit, embarrassing as it was, mad as it seemed, the whole frightening improbable encounter? Yet, at last, after hours of give-and-take, June couldn't believe that he'd had her laughing about it. For the last hour or so, however, over a seafood dinner on the wharf at Monterey, he'd allowed her to slip back into . . . whatever.

"Duane, I want to thank . . ."

Duane, meeting her gaze, winked mischievously. "Hmmm? I'm just trying to come up with a rhyme for mist," he said. "Must be lots of good rhymes, hundreds in fact. Let's see—mist? Ah, well, hissed, list, ah . . ."

The tuxedoed waiter made another wraithlike appearance at their table.

"Pissed?" June suggested quite audibly.

"Ma'am?" he queried, so seriously that June and Duane had to turn their heads to stifle laughter.

When the waiter left to fetch a mud pie and a cheesecake, Duane tried to cover her hand with his own. But she just could not tolerate any more reassurance at the moment. She raised her hand and held it out for him to see, fingers wide and extended. "See?" she said, proud as a child with good grades. "I'm not shaking any more!"

Duane ignored the gesture; instead, he studied her eyes like a jeweler searching out the happy secrets of a diamond. "June, darling, I want to tell you how I feel . . ."

Smiling thinly, June ducked, shook her head. She knew what he meant to say. No, the moment wasn't right, not now, not yet. But she didn't want to hurt him by mocking, by being sarcastic, taking his words lightly. No, he had to understand that the other thing, the horrible thing from last night, loomed much much too large in her mind for her to throw open the door to let in the words he wanted to say. Now he squeezed her hand hard, his intensity constricting. "June, darling, I think it's time that we . . ."

"Duane, please. I'm sorry, but . . . I've got so much on my mind. We've got to hurry through dinner to see Pete Robinson, though I'd prefer to put it off. And I promised Betty and Ivan that we'd visit grandmother tomorrow—brrr! And that business last night . . . Well, I . . . Duane, if it's something serious, could we wait until later?"

The pressure on her hand faltered, decreased, then wavered like a pulsebeat. Duane frowned, frustrated and annoyed. "Oh, I'd say it's something serious. But . . . how much later? Later tonight?"

"Well . . ." (What could she say—how about a week from tonight? see my secretary for an appointment? please take a number?) "Well, Duane . . ." (And if you're going to say *yes*, for god's sake don't make it sound like some kind of ordeal!) "Well, I'd say it sounds like the best possible way to end an incredible day."

The pressure increased alarmingly. "Great! Great! Oh, I knew you'd come through for me, kid. What a great, great little gal you are!"

Affectionately tolerant, June tried not to grimace at the pain in her hand. And, sure enough, the pressure subsided in time for dessert. The exquisitely frozen mud pie demanded use of the chilled fork as a pickaxe to chip away at its impenetrable facade. Or she could wait forever for it to thaw. Everything was wrong. Nothing was right. Because, she knew, she made it that way. With her mind—her poor, distracted, overwrought mind.

"I think Robinson's really ripe for the taking," Duane explained while digging into his cheesecake on a diagonal line. "I know you think he's small potatoes—and you're right. But look at the psychology of it. He's really impressed by you, June, so he's out to impress you. Got me? In other words, he's going to offer you a better contract than you'd get from Warner, Columbia, or A & M. Believe me, these small-time guys shoot off some pretty hefty fireworks when they're trying to land an artist they're convinced is going to be major."

Giving up on the frozen mud pie, June considered Duane's insight. "Fireworks?"

"Oh, no gimmicks! Nothing short-term—real substantial ongoing stuff, you know? Hell, we're almost late already. Waiter—check please!"

While Duane was engrossed in digging for his wallet, Larry Ludwig pushed in through the front lobby, a heavily mascaraed blonde hanging langorously on his arm. June doubted her eyes for a moment. This wasn't the kind of restaurant where her guitarist brought his women, as a rule. She gave an uncertain wave to signal Larry but only managed to attract the attention of two men who took the opportunity to jump toward her table for autographs.

Duane, apparently oblivious to June's diverted attention, fended off the middle-aged fans while paying the check. June watched Larry and his lanky companion cross the elegant room. How could he have failed to notice her with all the commotion? Somehow, it seemed to June that it mattered very much that she and Larry not cross paths without contacting each other. It seemed essential. "Larry!"

Duane looked up at her, openly questioning.

"Larry just walked through there into the back dining room," she explained.

"That's nice, June, but we've got to get going—now!"

The fans, a dark-haired man with an umbrella and a bearded giant in impenetrable sunglasses who could have been a hit-man or a scholar, remained within easy pouncing distance; any sign of an opening and they would move in to tear loose a piece of her life, her consciousness.

"Come on, June."

Duane pulled her arm until she began to walk. She fell in beside him, matching his brisk marching step out into the night and the darkness of the wharf. June glanced from side to side. But it was safe. The fog was thick but grey and moist and comfortably insubstantial.

"So you understand this 'non-mortification' clause?"

Wedged securely behind his enormous naked blonde desk, Pete Robinson kept his hand tightly pressed to the contract he'd pushed halfway across to June. Plumes of smoke from the stogy he chewed with narrow jaws filled the fluorescent office with an unevenly ribbed haze.

"Tell us again," Duane requested. "June and I'd like to make certain we're not missing something in the legal jargon."

Pete yanked the cigar out of his mouth and waved both arms like a man flagging down a train. "I'll paraphrase, okay? That way, everybody understands. Okay, so it says that in light of certain occurrences throughout the history of rock and roll music, my co . . ."

"*Occurrences*—such as?"

Pete, rubbing his jaw, almost burned himself with the cigar. "Oh, you know, that thing with the Rolling Stones and Hell's Angels where that guy got murdered; the kids getting trampled at the Denver Who concert; all those nasty little satanic coincidences whenever Led Zeppelin and Black Sabbath perform outdoors; the bat that . . ."

"Okay," Duane conceded. "So you think my client's some sort of heavy metal madonna who's going to incite rape and riot wherever she plays?"

Pete manufactured a steady stream of smoke like a dragon gone mad. "No, no! That's just it. We see Miss Lockwood as the perfect blend for the 80's rock audience—a little MOR, a little sugar-coated occult. Just the right formula to catch both the . . ."

"Sugar-coated occult?" June cried out.

She wanted to get up and leave but fought the urge. She had to act mature; these money men took too much pleasure in seeing a rock artist reduced to the adolescent stereotype that presumably fit them all.

"Miss Lockwood, June, I'm simply saying that you are *not* like those other performers, that you are neither satanic nor irresponsible. In fact, that's why we're interested in you, why we consider you just exactly right. And it's also precisely why we *don't* want you to change, don't want you to feel the pressure to go (shall we say?) in the established direction.

"The 'non-mortification' clause simply asks you to maintain the integrity of your act, not to damage or besmirch it by overbalancing the presentation in the direction of tastelessness or . . ."

June wadded up the paper cup from which she'd been sipping tepid water and hurled it angrily at Pete's Executive Basketball net mounted on a pea green wastebasket. "Isn't *integrity* a strange word to use when you're talking about what you consider an act, an act you won't even allow me to change? Integrity means growth to me, Mr. Robinson; and growth demands . . ."

"Miss Lockwood, we're *not* disagreeing! We're saying the same thing, only from different directions. I agree that as an artist you need to grow. Why, if there's anything I've encouraged in artists over the years, it's growth. And we at RMA want you to grow along the positive lines you've been inclined to choose. We want to guarantee that you won't confuse a step backward with some kind of . . ."

"Sometimes it takes a step backward to get back on the path, Pete."

"Miss Lockwood, I really wish that . . ."

Duane jumped to his feet, waving aside clouds of cigar smoke to gesture for June. "Excuse me, Pete?"

But once he had her outside in the hall his narrow argumentative tone opened up into confidence and amusement. "June, he's a fool. The clause is ridiculous. RMA played God to pluck it whole from chaos. No, but let me tell you, the percentages he's talking about are incredibly good! Maybe he knows something we don't; maybe RMA Is going backrupt and sees Bloodrock as a write-off. We've got to grab this, jump on it, mortification clause or no mortification clause. It's dynamite, June! Two albums and we can retire."

June shrugged, then smiled and pressed the flat of her hand against Duane's expansive chest. "Hey, why not?" she said.

Back inside, the act of signing seemed simple enough, yet Pete's reaction puzzled June. Duane had long since briefed her on Pete's life as a blustering party-giving widower—the portrait of a heel or of a desperately lonely man? Pete's smiling mouth drooped open as Duane put pen to triple-carbon paper. His eyes brimmed with glistening moisture.

"Hey, kids, did I tell you I'd lined up a tidy little gang for tonight's occasion? Just some friends, local DJ's, a couple of other guys from RMA and their wives and girl friends . . ."

From his first words on Duane shook his head with convincing vigor. "Sorry. It's her night off so we've made other plans."

"Just for a little while?" Pete suggested.

Duane eyed the windy seascape in a dusty frame hanging over the desk, his eyes full of distance, goals, resolution. "No, I think June and I would prefer to be alone tonight."

Pete stared down at the cigar he held on his chest. "I just thought . . . since this is a special occasion, a sort of . . ." He sounded ready to beg.

"Sorry," Duane said. "Maybe some other time."

He reminded June tonight of a conquering warrior, self-righteous from his victory. "I don't see why we couldn't stop in for a little while," she said. "We haven't made any definite plans."

Duane kept his gaze moving briskly between June and Pete. "I guess I have to come right out and say I've got a surprise planned."

"Well, I don't want to horn in on anything special," Pete said. "But I just kind of wanted to show that there's no hard feelings and that I really do appreciate you two nice folks coming to me when . . ."

"Sure." Duane extended his hand, the evening's consolation prize. "Some other time, okay?"

"That's okay! That's okay!" Pete enthused as they shook. "Some other time'll be just great, just great! You two kids go and have a nice time, a nice quiet evening together."

Duane nodded to this and put his hand in the small of June's back to get her moving. Head down, she stalked angrily across the characterless newly-carpeted lobby and elbowed her way through the glass door out into the parking lot. She hated rudeness, selfishness, intentional cruelty; brought up in a home void of warmth, she'd waged a lifelong battle to keep some sort of spark alive in herself. And now, just when she found herself really caring for Duane, he showed this ugly streak, this heartlessness. Still, who else could have tolerated her all day, survived her violent mood swings and fits of silence? Who else could have helped her put so much distance in so short a time between her sanity and that incredible attack on her body and soul less than twenty-four hours ago?

"June, look at me." Stopping her, Duane lifted her chin in his hand. "You're mad about something. I can tell. What is it?"

June, twisting her head and shaking out of his grasp, could not answer him. For once, her emotions seemed beyond translation.

"Well, if you won't tell me, I'm just going to assume that everything's okay."

June sneaked a quick grateful glance his way as he unlocked the car to let her in. She felt fortunate to have been allowed the refuge of silence. Her fingers yearned to close on the broach, but she locked the seatbelt and squeezed her hands around the buckle, reading the ornamental front like braille. Two or three times on the long drive back to her condo June felt compelled to speak but did not. Duane appeared resolved and complete, neither in need of nor receptive to any words from her. Soon his compact Cadillac bounced on the radical slope of her driveway, the headlamps crazily raking across the two-story complex like unmanned searchlights. He pulled the car smoothly into the stall and turned off the engine. In that moment she realized they had not even turned on the radio. Her nervous eyes searched the darkness.

"Duane . . .?"

He nodded as if she'd given a command, popping up out of the Eldorado. He whistled softly, tunefully, but seemingly to himself as they walked up the curving concrete path to unlock her front door. "Hey, look at this," he said, bending to pluck the object off her carpet. "Another bottle of that vintage vinegar you like. Guess you've got a secret admirer with his own private—and very old—vineyard."

June hung her coat in the front closet, trying to keep her eyes off the age-yellowed bottle Duane stored away in the lower kitchen cabinet where other liquor gifts had gone unopened for years. She did not want to remember what happened before, did not want to think about it.

Duane plunked down with familiar ease on her resilient sofa. He seemed masterful tonight, undaunted by her discomfort. He had the look of a man who knows he has absolute control.

She watched him watching her.

"Come over here beside me," Duane said, patting the sofa. Why did this bother her? Was he acting too proprietary for her taste?

June stood her ground in the center of her living room as if she were the visitor here; she did not feel like going to him, submitting to his comfortably dictatorial male will tonight. Still . . . he had saved her sanity today—hadn't he?—wining and dining her through both a major depression and a major studio contract. "Duane, I'm grateful, I really am, for the wonderful day and for all your patience and . . ."

"The hell with that stuff!" he said. "None of that means anything to me if you don't come over here right now!"

June faltered, folded her arms, looked away. Hadn't she a will of her own? Or was that the very problem—was she so narrowly willful that she resisted the simple direct impulses that would finally bring happiness?

"June, please. Don't make me beg you. I know you've got a lot of pressure on you now that you're a big star."

She covered her face with her hands. She felt herself swaying and wondered if she might fall. And wouldn't that solve everything? She felt the moisture on her face and the heat from the thing around her neck.

"But remember," he said, "I've been here all along. From the beginning, really. I've been your number one booster and fan and . . ."

True. Yes, true. She took her hands from her wet face to look at him in this new light.

"Right! It's me—Duane! I'm not your enemy. I'm the guy who's been right here all the time."

Yes, he'd always been there, loving her whatever her mood, always positive and asking so little for himself.

So what was the barrier? What?

"June?"

"Duane, I'm sorry. I . . ."

She had not been conscious of having moved, of dropping down beside him on the sturdy sofa, of thrusting her face onto his comfortable chest. But now, comforted, enveloped, loved, she knew only that she had moved more freely than ever before.

BLOODROCK

Then this was it? "Oh, Duane . . ."

They caught each other up desperately, hungrily, each seemingly in need of more than flesh could give. Finally, reluctantly unclenching like wounded prizefighters, they pulled apart. "Is this a good time . . . to ask?" Duane said. His breath resounded in her ear with tender urgency.

Ask? Ask? Oh, *that*.

"Yes," June said, eyes closed. Yes? "Yes!"

Duane pulled his head back a little as if to get a perspective on her face. "Will you think about . . . will you think about another kind of contract . . . with me?"

He sounded so serious, so desperately serious!

"I love you, June," he said. "Marry me."

He squeezed her and for a moment she could not breath. He didn't know his own strength. But, oh . . . he did make her feel good, made her feel like . . . herself. Yes, he made her feel like she'd always wanted to.

"Yes, darling," she said. "Yes."

"June, I'm the proudest man in the world! Now, let's get this ugly thing off from around your neck, okay?"

Could she start their engagement off with a lie? He'd think she was crazy if she confessed that she'd tried to remove the bloodrock and found it impossible. "Duane, the . . . the clasp's broken and . . ."

"Okay, honey. That's all right. Don't worry. I love you and . . ."

Clothing came away like discarded skin. They kneaded each other with fingers, knees, elbows, a choreography of hunger, of the need to be engulfed, taken in, merged with.

June's long fingernails sank into his biceps, as she clung and twisted.

Duane's hand scouted deftly down the ridge of her

long thigh. "Oh, lord!" he said. "O, God, June, you're perfect! Just perfect the way you . . ."

And that was when the pattern of blood sprouted out to make its widening mark on her white breasts.

Chapter Fifteen:

To Grandma's House We Go?

"Duane, I'm okay. Look, I have to get ready now."

One of her best towels firmly clutched in both his hands, Duane moved solemnly toward June like a supplicant come to offer penance.

"Has it . . . has it stopped yet? No! There's a trickle! Let me . . ."

"Duane, I'm sorry but that's a perfectly good towel and I don't want to get blood all over it. Now would you mind?"

Duane made a lunge at her throat with the beige and blue towel. "June, be reasonable! We have to get you to the hospital!"

But he suddenly stopped. Why? Was it something about her posture, perhaps the way she cocked her head to the side as if hearing a distant voice? Oh, she was aware that he was there, painfully concerned. She found his solicitude touching—yet bothersome. Should she tell him?

"June, you're not having some sort of . . .?"

"Breakdown?" June supplied. "Why not? I feel like

I deserve it. But honestly, Duane—no. No, I'm not having a nervous breakdown, although a little rest sounds awfully good right now."

He raised his eyebrows, dumbfounded, as if somebody had undermined his sense of masculinity. "Well, then?"

"I suppose you thought, along with practically everybody else, that the blood that appears on my chest on stage, all those illimitable quantities of blood . . ."

"A trick, of course." He eyed her closely as if to ward off something she might say that would be dangerous, shocking, ruinous.

"No, Duane." Slowly, metronomically, June shook her head. "No, that blood comes from . . . somewhere. From this ugly thing around my neck maybe. I don't know."

"June, this isn't like you to be . . ."

Behind the solicitude she could hear fearful misgivings. She'd made him afraid—but *for* her, *of* her? She could not tell.

"Tell me, June. Please. Please explain it to me. I don't understand what you're saying."

As if relieving a child of a dangerous object, June reached out slowly and took the towel from Duane's hands. She tried her best to smile. "I can't explain what I don't understand," she said.

Eyes furtive, almost desperate, Duane kept pinching a corner of the towel between two fingers. (How innocent he was! He feigned professional shrewdness but couldn't begin to understand Bosley Broderick's bloody theatrical mysticism; and, therefore, he would never understand the gift. If she confided that the pendant could not be removed, he would be persistently logical in arguing that it could. Results? Hours of physical and emotional exhaustion—a horrible and impossibly frustrating prospect.) June touched his sweaty face with the towel he could not relinquish. "So, in light of this . . . problem, do you still want to marry me?"

It had come out more aggressively than she'd intended. But there it was.

Duane's face twitched, an involuntary theatre of emotion. She thought of the time-lapse photography and make-up changes used in films to depict the werewolf's transformation from human to wolf and back. And she was powerless to help him; she had no silver bullet.

"I . . ." He seemed to be choking.

"Yes, Duane?" (Did she sound absurdly eager?)

"June, I love you. I want to marry you. We'll fight this thing together. We . . ."

Had he run out of clichés? June felt cold and distant not to be sharing his generously flowing tears. Oh, if necessary, she could start her own salty flowing—but not from her face.

"You've really made me a happy man," he said.

Embracing, they rested their arms and heads forlornly together, two people who have no choice but to cling to each other for support. Love? Security? Comfort? June wanted to hold him and be held, to let her mind relax into oblivion, but already it had revved up imagining the afternoon's long-delayed visit to the undistinguished house.

Was she engaged? June supposed that she was. Perhaps the bleeding that occurred at the crucial moment was both certification and surrogate ring. Since the media had first pounded her shortly after the birth of Bloodrock, she tended to see the events of her life in headline form: Blood Queen Announces Betrothal to Manager; or He Passed Her 'Blood Test'—But Is He Really Her 'Type'? It was all a simpering grade-B horror film that no producer would be silly enough to tackle.

June watched Ivan scramble up one side and down the other of the sofa. "Bang!" he cried from hiding. "Bang! Bang!" Since she and Duane had embraced on Ivan's furniture playground only hours before, June considered the possibility that she should feel guilty but dismissed it. She had also decided to wait a while before revealing their engagement.

"Laser blast!" Betty cried, clutching her wounded heart. She fell across her sister's lap, whispering, "Should I have left him at the baby-sitter's?"

"No!" June patted Betty reassuringly on her skinny shoulder. "He's a great little kid; besides, we may need the fire power today."

"After all you've been through lately, June, are you sure you're up to seeing Grandmother now?"

"Mom, you're supposed to be dead!"

June shrugged. "If anyone can tell us what's wrong with this crazy family of ours, it's her. Right? And what's a better time than now?"

(Oh, almost anytime. And shouldn't she be killing two birds with one stone by announcing her engagement? Wasn't it customary to pass such information on to one's grandmother?)

"Remember when we were kids, the days we had to go to grandma's house? They were . . ." Fending off a laser blast, Betty searched unsuccessfully for the right word. "I don't know, just . . . a necessary suffering kind of thing. Kind of . . . I don't know!"

"It was like some sort of family ritual," June said. "A dark pageant we had to perform over and over, as if we'd committed a crime we couldn't even remember."

Betty, considering for a second, snapped her fingers. "Yeah—exactly! Gosh, you're terrific, June! You've got such a way with words and . . ."

"Just a reflex," she said, shaking her head. She

closed her eyes. "In five minutes I couldn't tell you what I'd said. Shall we get started?"

Betty pulled her son from the sofa where he'd gotten one arm and a leg wedged between rough-textured cushions. June put her cassette tape recorder and the second bottle of wine into an Alpha Beta grocery bag and rolled the top down tight. They were headed out the door when the phone rang. While Betty and Ivan headed out to the car, June took the call. Less than five minutes later, bag in hand, she joined them.

"June, why are you frowning like that?"

"Nothing, really." Without thinking, she started the Volvo and pulled away from the curb. "It was just Duane. Bosley Broderick's agent called to say he couldn't make it to our first recording session tomorrow. He's sick, supposedly. At least that's the excuse."

"Oh, that's too bad! You really wanted him there, didn't you, June?"

June shrugged as she pulled onto the expressway. Betty sounded so sure of her disappointment. June felt less certain. Was she disappointed that Bosley couldn't be there at her first professional recording—or relieved?

Betty and Ivan wrestled on the seat beside her, more like two kids than mother and son. Betty scored on a side hold and Ivan retaliated by tickling her, his hands burrowing deep into the folds of her blouse. The sublimated eroticism bothered June, and she reflected as she pulled off the expressway onto the residential drive bordered by a city park and lake that next time Ivan would be less likely to feel carefree and playful. Perhaps, as a little girl, she had been similarly lively, animated, on her first visit here. Could she remember back that far? A little girl in a green Sunday dress, smiling, gliding up those old wooden steps, into that dark house, into that dark world. Of course she remembered. Of course she knew that Ivan would never willingly visit Grandma Edna again after today.

"Here we are," June said, deftly steering the Volvo down the long flower-lined driveway. No one had entered through the front since the death of Edna's husband in '47.

They got out of the car; that was easy. But when they turned, collectively, to take a step toward the little house, they stopped.

The sunlight seemed to sink into the peeled paint and old wood beneath—dull, reflectionless, indifferent alike to heat and light and energy. June sighed; no mist, at least. Shadows always appeared around the yard in places they did not belong. Shuttered windows on the sides, drapes drawn shut in back, the house seemed to have taken an oath of silence. Betty touched her sister's arm.

"June, I have to admit I'm scared."

But something up on the rear porch near the door had caught Ivan's attention and the heavy wooden gate creaked angrily as he pushed against it with his small shoulder. "Who lives here, Mommy?" he called back, almost tripping on the little brick steps.

Betty reached out for her son as if she could touch him and began to walk toward the house. Falling in beside her, June answered for her sister, "It's your great-grandmother's house, Ivan. You're going to get to meet her today."

"What makes her so great?" he said, hanging onto the porch rail to swing out and greet them. "Is that why I've never seen her?"

June took Betty's elbow and nudged her forward up the steps to the door. "Turn on the tape recorder," she whispered.

"June, it's useless. You know Grandma doesn't . . ."

"Just do it, please."

For a moment they stared at the door. Then June pulled back her fist to knock and it swung propitiously open. It always did. No one had been invited in, as far as June knew, for close to forty years. The door opened itself. It had to. No one else would open it.

Glancing searchingly at each other, they shuffled into the musty darkness. June took little comfort from the physical pressure of Ivan and Betty at her back as she advanced into the gloom. Objects, odors, a childhood reverie she could not fight back, the smell of old linoleum still curling and crackling underfoot after all these years, the old double-bar clothes wringer, grey and yellow with indeterminate stains. As a little girl she had tiptoed past it, knowing that if she brushed against it the stain would be on her and never come off. Ever. Like a hideously patient lover, the stand-up lamp remained jammed into a corner of the back room, its shade cocked sideways and down, a slumberous head on a slouched body ready to come to life just for her.

June waved a hand for her sister and nephew to follow, then glanced over her shoulder to see them crouching down like disembarking helicopter passengers who imagine they must duck to avoid the swinging blade. The gloom, the musty odor, the absolute and unforgiving stillness of the house made movement seem like an intrusion into nightmare. Shared fear, a comfort? Nothing was now or ever had been shared in this house.

The feeling? As though the trek through the house to find Grandmother must involve an enormous risk that no child can afford.

She had only to follow in the wake of the adults. Mommy moved in front of her, grand and slow as a stately ship, her back filling her field of vision. Mommy's back, her uncaring back, was her only protection. Up ahead was her step-father, quick and energetic until the year of his death, advancing into the domestic gloom with the stealth of an alert native guide using only the terrific sensitivity of the surface of his skin to detect any possible danger. Why were step-fathers always braver than real ones?

Oh, but when you go back as an adult how small it all is, how short that distance you had thought as a child to be a maze of killing length. Yes—and no. After Betty was born, Amelia carried her in her arms through Edna's house on each of these dark familial safaris. June had never had the protection of a body behind her, but her mother and father had run interference before her. And why, after he died, did they never come here? Was it because Amelia would not dare to do what June did now, lead a brave little expedition through this small house?

Yes, as a child it had been hard enough for June to follow her parents, trying not to recognize the objects that clicked into place to taunt her, trick her into really seeing them. She had no words or specific mental image for her fear. But there it was, in her face, as she led a small family of sorts through this little darkness as her Dad had done until his death.

"June, why did you stop?"

June, shaking her head, forced herself to go on. She could see that the house was not a vast labyrinth; she was an adult, and old fears could not reach her. Except that, somewhere in the center of this junkyard of discarded yet obscenely personal objects, somewhere in the center of this maze of self-imposed gloom, was the black hole, the sitting room, the spot Edna chose never to leave. How, as a child, had she felt in the presence of her grandmother? Unable to remember, June shocked herself by turning up the face card of a more distinct recollection: *I've always known she's dead in there. I've always been sure of it on each visit. There, in the dark center of this house, I find my grandmother dead in that absorbed sunlight that gives back nothing. What if this time it's true?*

So, at last she'd caught hold of it. All these years of visiting, creeping through these dark rooms, touching nothing, trying to see nothing, she had been terrified of not finding a living relative at the end of the puzzle, at the center of the maze.

Grandmother, be alive. Don't be dead; please don't be dead! Please, don't hurt me. June remembered her little prayer, her child's self-created incantation. *Grandmother, don't be dead. Don't hurt me.* Over and over. But why? Why had she been so certain that her grandmother intended to die just to hurt her, that grandmother's death was an evil secret sewn into the lining of her own hidden inner life? Had June actually believed that someday she would find herself there at the center of this maze of objective gloom? Herself, alone, in an old woman's shawl, dead?

Light angled through a crack in a filthy yellow shade and slurred through the splotched fly-specked window glass into June's eyes; blinded, she stopped dead, and Betty and Ivan shoved into her back. "June, what's . . . ?"

"Ssssh." She had to gather herself, prepare herself, steel herself to be truly ready for anything, anything that might be there to be seen when she turned the last corner her fingertips now reluctantly tested. The sitting room. Grandmother. Edna. Not a sound.

June stepped forward, closing her eyes as she had as a little girl, feeling her way around the corner with her shoulder against the filthy wallpaper to slide into the high-ceilinged room (As if only by dimming her senses could she tolerate the transition from the world on this side to the one her grandmother pulled blackly in upon herself—and all that entered there.)

"Hello, Grandmother."

Chapter Sixteen:

In the Line of Duty

Finally, it had happened. The arms of her wooden chair were scraped light in deep long gouges as if she had raked her fingernails along them through years of unrelenting anguish. She still wore the faded housecoat that covered her from neck to ankles, colorless, shapeless, a garment as ghostly as a shape with no substance, a life-sized formation of ash that crumbles to the touch.

The room seemed not to have changed—the sewing baskets; the two mismatched love seats tilted oddly together; the ancient Singer sewing machine poised on the sideboard like some black icon of the industrial age; the two thoroughly bleached out oval rugs; the ceiling light and floorlamp, the pallor of their identical yellow bulbs suggesting that bright light might somehow destroy something here not quite alive; and the latest in an endless series of brand-new television sets, the only thing new that ever entered here, still humming, the sound turned down low, its multicolored light washing over the unmoving figure whose closed eyelids seemed as fixed and changeless as every other thing in this room touched by the softly flickering glow.

Yes, it had finally happened—the nightmare realized.

"Grandmother?"

The ancient frame gave not the least suggestion of movement or response. June did not think she could bring herself to touch her. Frightened, she couldn't keep her eyes from darting to the walls, every inch claustrophobic with pictures. Photographs of Edna from infancy to age thirty-nine pushed and leaned and crosscrossed against and into and over each other, a black-and-white congestion of images of a sexually exquisite youth. The house had not one mirror, but over the years the photos had kept appearing, one by one, as if Edna's past took it upon itself to stay alive in a tug of war with fading memory. Perhaps forty or fifty additional photos had crowded onto the walls since June's last brief visit the week after she'd graduated from college. This increase appeared to be the only change in the room (aside from the TV set, which gave the impression of being self-replenishing, updating itself as its owner aged), perhaps the only change in the entire house.

And then June remembered. It had been her Dad's duty. The words had to be right. And she had not as yet spoken the one word that would let the process start.

"Grandmother? You'll only answer to Edna, isn't that right? Edna? Edna, are you . . .?"

The eyes, glowing angrily like the buried embers of an extinguished fire brought back to life by someone's breath, flicked open.

Now what?

"Hello, grand . . . Edna," June tried. "Edna, I'd like you to . . ." (Meet? Watch it, June.) ". . to see Betty, remember? And this handsome young man here, whom you've never met before," she settled her hands on his shoulders to move him forward into the meager light, "is Ivan. Say hello to your great-grandmother, Ivan."

Fidgeting in June's grasp, Ivan looked back at his mother, who nodded for him to go ahead. "Hello, great-grandmother."

The gray eyelids closed again over the ashy embers that were her eyes, remaining so still that for a moment it seemed as though they had never opened. June opportunistically eyed the old face and saw that Betty and Ivan, also fortified by the knowledge that life did move inside the envelope of skin, focused there as well. Each wrinkle on the face seemed an independent frown directed pointedly at each of them. Her skin had the texture of a fine desert sandhill windblown into perfect furrows, serenly inanimate. Now she would never move again because she had no need to move.

"Momma, why doesn't she talk?"

In her purse June's tape recorder hummed on, recording nothing.

"Ssssh! Momma would tell you if she knew," Betty whispered. "For some reason Grandmother hasn't spoken for many years." She shot a glance at June, probably a request for approval.

But June could not begin to respond. Here in the darkness, here in the dead center of her grandmother's lifeless house, why should she feel so utterly at peace? She knew that somehow she belonged here. Would she occupy that chair one day herself, its arms scratched light out of human age and anguish? Something of her destiny lived in this room.

June placed the bottle of wine on the television set. She could not remember if Edna still drank, yet somehow she felt that the bottle belonged here.

"Sit down, folks. Ivan, you and your mom scoot in here." June indicated one of the odd love seats. "And

I'll just . . ." She perched tentatively on the other, trying to make the sound of someone settling in with a sigh. Then she motioned for Betty to begin talking, now, before Edna opened her eyes again. Betty flashed back a shrug of dismay, but June waved her hand to encourage her.

"Well . . . ah, Edna, I hope you like the letter I write to you every Christmas. Did you remember that Ivan's in the fourth grade? And that because his work has been so good they made him yard duty assistant? He has his own little . . ."

Perfect, exactly perfect, June thought, but hoped that Betty could keep it up to allow enough time to carry out her plan, her intended exploration. She wanted to check out a few things in the ninety-year-old basement—the labels on the bottles of wine stored there, for one thing. June stood.

The old woman wheezed horribly, her eyes flickering open and shut and open again like some short-circuiting detection device. Sitting, then subsiding deeper into the love seat, June listened inattentively to Betty's pleasant drone, all the words positive, all about Ivan and his achievements. June's focus narrowed to the crevices and folds of that perfectly aged face no more than seven or eight feet away. She wanted to keep her eyes fixed there as she attempted again to rise silently, tiptoe to the television set to take the wine again, and ease her way out of the sitting room door, a finger to her lips to keep the question in Ivan's eyes from forming itself into speech. Once out in the darkness again, June clutched the bottle to her breast for security and remembered the stone around her throat. Yes, she had to find the stairs to the basement.

YES. IN THE DARKNESS. IN THE BASEMENT. WAITING.

Feeling with her toe, she located the closet stuffed

BLOODROCK

with Edna's gorgeous clothing from thirty and forty years ago. The door creaked open to let out a fragrance of moth balls and dust, the mild rich scent of decay, and the ghost of almost forgotten perfume. June crouched through the folds of cloth antiquity to test the floor but found it solid. Before straightening back up she had the hair-raising premonition that someone would come up behind her in the darkness.

Her feet and legs pressed together, June leaned into the wall and eyed the sliver of light from which her sister's voice droned on incessantly. June had promised herself not to touch the bloodrock, but she knew that she would freeze to this spot if she did not let her hand travel between her breasts to find the familiar warmth, the source of her power.

In a moment she found the right closet, removed the false floor, and reversed herself to angle feet first down into the darkness. Down far enough to clear her head, she caught the wine bottle under her arm and struck a match. A kerosene lantern on a cement ledge indicated that she had not been the first to explore here. Father? Grandfather? All she knew of the cellar came from a few casual words in her childhood about the wine having been brought up. "I brung us up a good one tonight," the paternal voice had slurred, and the adults had laughed politely.

June, watching with pleasure as the kerosene wick caught and held the flame, wondered if she would find what she feared down here. The steps appeared endless; it frightened her not to be able to see the bottom. It was probably not far at all. Who would be no insane as to undermine the foundation of a suburban house by gouging out so much of the earth beneath it? Her grandfather? The previous owner—whoever that had been?

Ah!

Her foot, accustomed so soon to the round solidity of

each subsequent rung, pushed through into nothing but darkness. Startled, she dropped the lantern, the bottle, herself. Dropping no more than a foot or two, for a second June had actually believed she was falling to her death. Miraculously, the lantern had fallen upright, as in some animated cartoon where everything must remain intact in order to go on delighting the children, its flame still brightly alive; the bottle had failed to break open on the hard dirt floor of the basement.

Now June beheld a Lewis Carroll cavern of stairs and wooden shelves crafted into earth; soil, wood and age somehow uniting the manufactured and the natural. She could not tell where the wine rack ended, the earthen boundaries began. Would there still be wine? Oh, but the real question was: Had any bottle been recently removed from this vast repository of spirits? Thick with dust, the myriad bottles winked almost imperceptibly in the flickering kerosene light like trolls hiding in the shadows of the bridge one is crossing.

June leaned into the protective railing to get a closer look. She cocked her head sideways and began to read labels. Story books, picture books, fairy tales swirled alive under her gaze, the dust-muted colors incredibly romantic in their depiction of scantily-clad women and gallant men, buccaneers, vintners, farmers and poets. And the good story moved from one bottle to another so that June hardly noticed the names on the respective labels, hardly allowed herself to be aware of her movements deeper into the cellar as she became increasingly captivated by the enchanting narrative, the story captured in the bottles.

The names, the vintners' names, the labels, the romance of the sound of money poured deep into the rich French soil, the provinces, the land, the love of life, the reverence for the dead: Les Freres Mouches, La Pere Mort, L'Apprenti Imprimeur, Monsieur Méchant. . . .

June might have held her bottle up in the darkness then, the kerosene lantern lifted higher in the other hand, ready to match the label she'd studied long and hard with the one her peripheral vision might have caught. But something happened. The bottle slipped from her hand as if struck away. And when it hit the cellar floor it neither shattered nor rolled but stuck, half buried. And when she bent to test the floor, it was neither solid nor a floor, but somehow rich and pungent and ripe, dark red in color, a palpable stain, a mist with darkened substance.

Then June saw the graves sprouting up around her, the battalions of slanted stones, the haphazard lonely weather-beaten calling cards of the dead. Then the bottle disappeared into the ground. When she turned to catch hold of the huge wine rack, it too was gone.

Then the arms began to come up out of the insubstantial soil, the earth that no longer kept the dead in place; the arms came out, fingers writhing, grasping. And when she turned to run, her grandmother caught her around the throat with the bony fingers of her putrescent hands.

"No! I won't . . . !"

The weight of her chest and lap had to be thrown off, the tombstone of her grandmother that kept her from running. She had to push.

"SSSH! Aunt June, keep quiet! You'll wake momma and great-grandmother."

"Thank you, Ivan. You can get off me now."

"Sure thing!"

He scampered back into the corner behind the love seats to huddle over a hectic pile of mismatched toys. She remembered losing hour after hour among such toys in her own childhood. Of course, they were the same toys.

June massaged her face. Ivan plays while the adults

sleep. Pretty funny. But what about Betty—had she hypnotized herself with her own nasal drone?

Waking her sister, June encouraged Ivan to leave the toys as he'd found them, then set an example by kissing the sleeping octogenarian on her cheek. One eye winked dangerously open as Betty pressed her lips to the ancient skin, but it clicked back shut when Ivan followed suit. "Have we got everything?" Betty asked as they filed out. "Are you leaving your wine here?"

"I thought I left it on the television set," June said. she eyed Ivan. Who else could have taken it? "Oh well, it doesn't matter."

A light breeze with a scent of early winter freshened the late afternoon as they emerged, blinking, from the old house.

"She's not well enough to live by herself," Betty said as they headed for the car. "Don't you think she should stay with one of us? And, June, why in the world did you waste all that tape on me putting us to sleep? What did you expect to record?"

With Ivan bouncing into the back seat, the two sisters settled into the front and June started the engine. "Just a hunch," she said. She eased the car down the narrow driveway, unable to resist taking a last glance at the house. "For a long time now I've had this weird feeling that Bosley Broderick knows something about our family that I'm supposed to know. Something not too pleasant, Betty. There's a . . . a voice I heard in that house as a child that I think I heard again two nights ago behind Herm's club. It sounds crazy but I thought . . ."

"You thought maybe the voice would come through on the tape even though we didn't hear anything?"

June tilted her head in a self-mocking grimace. "Something like that."

"Do you think Bosley Broderick's faking being sick? Do you think he wants to hurt you?"

Without another word, June dropped the mother and son off back at their small duplex. She hadn't meant to be impolite; the fact that she had no answer for Betty made it very difficult to find anything to say.

Chapter Seventeen:

All The Channels Open

Larry casually wrapped his arm around her as if not quite aware of what he was doing. (Should she make a big deal out of it?)

"Pretty goddamned weird, I'd say. Play that last part back again." He pointed his finger at the tape recorder as if expecting it to function on its own.

June looked away to gaze through the soundproof glass. Three orangutans cavorted around the studio's sound equipment, identical crowns of thorns affixed to their golden pates. She stabbed the orange START button.

"*Je vous recevral dans mes bras. Vous etes belle, tres belle, trop belle! Trop, trop belle. Je desire votre sang.*"

"That's it! Larry, that's it!"

She pecked the yellow STOP button.

Larry squeezed her shoulder. "Hey, that's French, huh?"

Outside the booth, the orangutans clowned themselves into a frenzy of fur biting and tail grabbing. Shoving through them, heedless of the collective raspberry they administered as he passed, the session supervisor pressed his hairless face against the glass to see what was happening to his equipment.

Larry pulled June down out of sight behind the room-length console. "God," she said, "it's incredibly clear."

He gave her shoulder an affirmative squeeze. "Yeah!"

"Betty and I couldn't get the right combination to get the words to come. How did you do that?"

Pulling her closer, Larry shook his head to dismiss the idea that he'd done anything special. "I just played it backwards with the treble dialed all the way up and . . . hell, it doesn't matter. Hey, what is it, June? Where did you get this tape? What does it mean?"

"I wish I could tell you." Easy; be clear; be logical. Okay . . . but how? "Hell, I've got to tell somebody. It might as well be you."

Larry pulled away to dramatize hurt feelings, his fingers lingering on her neck. "Gee, thanks, June. Might as well tell old Larry; after all, he's nobody but a mindless burnout who couldn't repeat his own name if he didn't read it off his union card."

She snared his wrist to pull him back; she had no time for games. "Larry, you know that's not what I meant. Listen, I don't speak French, but I'm pretty sure this is part of some sort of family curse, fanciful as that sounds. All the time I was at Grandma's house, I heard this thick humming—like static—and I remember it long ago, when I was a kid and we visited her. And that's the spot on the tape—right there where you . . ."

"And we're the only two people in the world who know!" He scooted closer, working his sinewy arm back around her shoulders.

"That's what bothers me!" June said. "I think Bosley knows about it somehow—don't ask me how—and he's trying to use it against us, against *me*. Maybe he wants me to sell my soul . . ."

"To the devil?" Larry supplied as a joke when it was obvious she didn't mean to go on.

June, aware that he thought she was being defensive, shrugged. "I don't believe in any of that stuff. To me, what makes the mysteries of the universe beautiful is the fact that they are subject to rational explanation. Maybe we're not ready to know yet, but someday we will be. This occult stuff's a cover-up for ignorance."

"Whew!" Larry whipped off an imaginary hat to fan them both. "The Queen blasphemes! Wash your mouth out with brimstone, June Lockwood!" He jumped up to his haunches to better chastise her. "What would the demonic faithful say if they . . .?"

The control booth door swung open. Pete Robinson, bursting in, almost tripped over the two prone musicians.

"Oh, well, don't let me interrupt—but your warm-up session is starting in five minutes. I'd think, young lady, that you'd want to get yourself ready for your first professional recording!" Shaking his head, Pete turned away muttering, "They're all alike," and left.

"That guy's scum!" Larry said as he helped her up.

Still staring in, the hairless session supervisor apparently had not moved from the spot since they'd ducked out of sight.

"They're all weird!" he whispered. "Too bad Duane says you gotta go with the top dollar. Hey, speak of the devil, how come you called me to decipher this thing for you instead of him?"

June followed the final antics of the costumed adolescents; two of them had removed their orangutan heads and were using them like stuffed pillows to slug each other. Larry deserved to know why she needed his help, yet anything she'd say would be a betrayal of

Duane. "He thinks . . ." She massaged the bridge of her nose. "He thinks I'm having a nervous breakdown or something, that all these terrible things that have been happening to me are just my imagination, that I'm some sort of neurotic." Now that she had it out, she searched Larry's face for a reaction. "Well? What do *you* think?"

He looked up from shaping some shredded substance with his fingers. "About what?"

"About me making all this up, having . . . mental problems."

Larry, shrugging, took care to keep the edge of the paper straight as he rolled. "I haven't met a lead singer yet who wasn't a little crazy. But I'd say, on the basis of this weird French shit on the tape, that you're not goin' over the edge without some help." He brought the twisted papers up to his lips and struck a match. "Share a joint?" he asked out of the corner of his mouth.

"Larry! We're scheduled to start recording in just . . ."

"There's my little girl!" Duane announced as he strode into the soundproof booth. Apparently failing to notice Larry cupping the joint, he rushed to June for a quick kiss. "Are you really excited?" He turned his head to include Larry in the question, too.

"Definitely," June said. "Definitely. Are the orangutans through yet or . . .?"

"Naked Ape they're called," he said. Brown tweed sport coat, charcoal slacks, blond hair tailored into place, Duane looked positively professional today, June thought. "Clever, huh?"

She nodded. "Cute kids."

Duane cuddled her close. "Have you told Larry about . . .?" His voice trailed off suggestively.

June picked an imaginary piece of lint off the shoulder of his coat. About being engaged to be married? Catching the two musicians in a tête à tête, how clever Duane had been to hint that she had secrets with all the boys. "Well, I . . ."

". . . . guess I'll get my act unpacked," Larry muttered. He shrugged violently as if hit by an uncontrollable shiver, then lurched for the door.

"It's going to be a great day for you, June!" Duane announced, pulling her closer. "A great day for both of us!"

Over Duane's square shoulder June watched Larry amble off toward the men's room where, she suspected, he'd *inhale m' spinach*, as he colorfully dubbed his pre-performance toke. The downturned line of his skinny shoulders suggested depression, but why should she feel so bad about an unfortunate situation? What was he but a burnt-out guitar player? Sure, he was a good listener—but all he ever thought about was drugs and easy women.

Duane gave her one last decisive squeeze, a quick constriction around the shoulders, then released her as far as arm's length. "There! That's enough to hold you until after the session!" he kidded. "Let's go knock 'em dead!"

June couldn't help but notice that Naked Ape had enjoyed the hour of free recording time they'd won from the local FM rock station. Despite their clumsiness, they'd shown amazing familiarity with the equipment and procedures of the studio. June, admittedly an innocent when it came to recording technology, found that once outside the protective booth she could no longer hide her enthusiasm for the wondrous toys in this auditory playground, this pleasure palace of sound. She had to touch and fool with everything.

For years, while many less committed musicians she'd known had bought thousands of dollars worth of studio time to impress their friends (and themselves), June had avoided delving into even the relatively ordinary recording techniques. The hell with state of the art sound—she'd worked on making good music; of course, no one else had thought it was so good until now.

Only months before she'd caught herself thinking that she'd never legitimately find her way into the studio to record for real. And now, here she was. And—oh, God!—she was determined to make the most of it. June pantomimed what she wanted to Duane who now sat beside one of the two RMA engineers in the booth. She tried on each headset. She picked up the bass and played it, then drums, lead guitar, keyboards. She played and tracked and played herself back. Then she put it together, a girl with multiple personalities gathering them all for a conference, a chorus, a song. She directed Duane to bring up the bass, now the drums, then sang right over the top of it, all the while visualizing herself flying like a bird over deliciously familiar terrain.

"Hey, the female Todd Rundgren!" she yelled when she heard the surprisingly good collaboration with herself played back. By the time the half-hour equipment check concluded and the recording session was due to start, the rest of Bloodrock had arrived, each in his own good time. Drummer Danny Driscoll danced frantically through the studio, striking everything in sight with his open hands to produce various percussive sounds, the acoustic tile walls, music stands, his own bare chest. Danny, clearly pleased with the direction the band had recently taken, seemed to be riding the crest of some immense emotional wave. Did he ever stop moving, June wondered, or did he twitch and dance and lunge even in his sleep? Remarkable, how much of what he invented they used in their music.

"Everybody ready?" Duane's voice piped over the

booth microphone. "Okay, June. We're set up here. Whenever you give the sign."

June nodded indeterminately. Ok, immortality, here I come. Buddy, Jim, Jimi, Elvis, Janis, move over, gang, 'cause June's on the way. And the only thing after cutting a rock record is to cut *out*.

June, smiling at the satire of her little revery, nodded more decisively now over at Larry. But her lead guitarist kept on studying the complexion of his blond guitar as if deciphering hieroglyphics coded into its lustrous finish. How strange to see him with a headset clamped down on his cascading hair, wires running into the guitar and out to the rest of the band like tentacles of some performing octopus. Of course, June realized, she looked like that too.

"Okay," she said. "One and . . ."

Bloodrock played its basic repertoire, concentrating on the sound that RMA had deemed worthy to be preserved on vinyl, their own juxtaposition of intelligence and heavy metal mayhem. "Blood Dance" required three takes, but "Consanguinity" and "New Veinous Surge" came together the first time through. June thought that now she knew how a blacksmith felt—controlled, cool, methodical, forging practical necessities out of fire and molten materials others found too dangerous to handle.

Somewhere in the middle of "Turkish Fizz," June spotted him seated in the sectioned-off gallery among a handful of her friends and well-wishers of the band. Utterly bald, of an indeterminate age (late fifties?), annoyingly familiar, he wore a jet black suit and vest and held a black cane with some sort of face carved into the handle. Enormous, he overflowed the studio chair. And he nodded, not really to the music, but as if in agreement with it, as if Bloodrock had a thesis and he loved the way the band expounded it. June could not keep her eyes off this nodding man. Where *had* she seen him?

Today Larry played with his inimitably controlled passion, his fingers running all over the instrument like frantic mice, but his countenance remained impassive; he might as well have been a corpse reposing in a morgue refrigerator for all the emotion he displayed. Once, however, toward the end of the session, June caught him looking over at her with the timid hopefulness of a little boy frightened to ask an adult for the thing he wants most in the world. What, Larry?

"Okay, you beautiful Bloodrock!" Duane announced over the booth loudspeaker, "Great session! Great session! Let's knock off for today—back tomorrow at the same time. This gentleman here, our senior engineer, says you conducted yourselves like a band that's been living in a studio for twenty years! Great going, group."

Slaps, kicks, happy punches, Bloodrock congratulated itself. June checked her own chest. No blood. Had it been an hysterical reaction all along? Had she outgrown it? She was, in fact, absolutely dry—no sweat, not a drop. A troubling fact, considering that she'd always been a good sweater. But the studio differed from a club, so maybe. . . .

"Oh, by the way," Duane broadcast from the booth, "June and I have a little announcement . . . I think!" Throwing the acoustic door open, he sprinted over to help her off with the headset. Then he whispered the question she'd been dreading all day—he wanted to make it public, official.

Despicable timing, but how could she justify going against it?

"Everybody?" Duane yelled, his voice taking on a more direct kind of authority without the microphone. Head tilted grandly back, he wrapped his arm protectively around June. "Miss Lockwood and I have decided . . . Well, everybody knows I'm a golddigger, so this's a perfect time to tell you that this brilliant vocalist—who as you can hear is about to make a million bucks with what we've done today. This wonderful young lady and I are getting married. And real soon."

Amidst the chorus of questions and congratulations, June blacked out everything but Larry's reaction, or his lack of one. Removing his headset, Larry proceeded to unplug and encase his blond guitar as as if he had heard nothing. The methodical dreariness of impending suicide? Ridiculous, of course. But what must he be thinking? (That June Lockwood woman, she's got secrets from everybody!)

"Miss Lockwood, a word with you?"

The black glove threatened her face; June flinched before identifying the gesture as old-fashioned gallantry.

"Reformer," he said, actually clicking his heels. "At your service, Miss Lockwood. You may remember that I once had the pleasure of permitting you to go backstage to see Mr. Broderick."

"Excuse me a second, Duane," she said.

Reformer bowed to Duane as he and June withdrew to a quiet corner of the studio where someone had left a pile of crushed paper cups.

"Miss Lockwood, I'm afraid that I . . ."

"No, *you* look. You can tell Mr. Broderick that I know what he's up to. And it won't work with me. He can have this damn rock back and he can take his curse! I don't need success that badly. Understand?"

Reformer smiled with disconcerting composure, his bald pate glistening under the fluorescent lights. "Through, Miss Lockwood? Good. I hope that you will do a little better job of controlling yourself when I tell you my news. Bosley Broderick, my employer and beloved friend, is dying. He will die tonight if you do not go to him. Now!"

June, backing away from Reformer's quiet ferocity, almost tripped on a music stand before steadying herself. "Ridiculous!" she said, trying to sound angry.

Again he thrust the cane at her chest. "Not ridiculous. True. Mr. Bosley Broderick has done much for you. Do not fail him in his transition. It is a little thing for you. Surely you are not so selfish as to disappoint this great man by denying his last request?"

"Oh—a last request?—like lending him my soul to use as a surfboard to sail through eternity?"

"Now it is you who are being ridiculous." He extended his huge arm. "Come."

June looked back at the diminishing commotion of the celebrants withdrawing from the studio. Was it all a theatrical gimmick, a grand illusion that would vanish if Bosley Broderick snapped his fingers? She turned away and, without saying goodbye or signaling a single soul, followed the bald figure out the studio door.

Chapter Eighteen:

The Caves of Ice

No one seemed to notice their trek across the parking lot to Reformer's compact car. Was it such a common sight—a young woman in a burgundy pants suit trailing a balding man dressed entirely in black and brandishing a magician's cane?

Reformer drove with such care and control that June caught herself being almost hypnotized by the ride. Had he picked up a few of the master's tricks?

Undergoing reconstruction, St. Dorothy's Hospital had the appearance of a facility abandoned in a war zone. A surprise rain shower that morning had filled the newly-dug foundation with over an inch of standing water. Now June shivered at the sight of the ugly colorless complex as if its forlorn appearance made some final statement about her own future.

"Come."

Trying to disguise her reluctance, June followed Reformer through the open glass doors and down the dimly lit corridors to an elevator that took them up to the sixth floor. She could not escape the sense of unreality, of being part of a movie or a book, living some life other than her own. Shivering again, June crossed her arms on her chest to rub a little warmth back into her shoulders. Spooky, how in a few minutes you can be taken completely out of the normal course of your life.

"Right down this hallway, Miss Lockwood. That's right—in here."

Afraid of being tricked, yet unwilling to look like a timid child, June tilted her head forward to try to see into the room as she forced herself to take one step after another until she was inside. A sterile white curtain surrounded the bed.

"Here."

Assisting her forward with pressure on her arm, the bald man brought them both up to the bed and drew aside the curtain with a chilling whisper of cold steel rings across the stationary curve of the overhead bar.

Bosley Broderick's head scarcely seemed to dent the soft frame of the pillow where it was centered. Eyes closed, mouth open, his hair splayed out like escaping energy, Bosley did not breathe.

"Oh!" June caught her wrist between her teeth. She thought of Grandma Edna.

Nodding meaningfully to her, Reformer, without looking down, reached out to take the dead white hand of his friend. One piece of the puzzle fell into place. June remembered him now. No wonder that car ride through the San Jose she'd known all her life had felt so otherworldly! Reformer, part of the BB retinue from the musician's first excursions into the occult, had posed on close to a dozen album covers, the central image Bosley had chosen to represent himself and his music. But June had not recognized the chosen image until she'd seen him looming over his dying mentor! On "Beneath Oceanic Grounds," Reformer had been photographed buried to the neck, desert sand spilling from his open mouth, his eyes brimming with a joyous insanity. "Hula Kaleidoscope" boasted a leisure suited Reformer leading a flock of geese in perfect V-formation through a luminous winter day.

Reformer was Bosley's alter ego, a shadow about to outlive its source.

"Hello, little sister of the blood."

How long had these steel blue eyes been on her, compassionate yet seemingly backlit by some indecipherable preoccupation? June blinked, but the illusion that Bosley Broderick smiled, staring at her, did not diminish. "I said 'hello,' sister June. How's the music business?"

So his "death" had been illusory—staged, phony—like everything else in his life and career. Never again would she let herself be duped by this pathetically dishonest old charlatan! Relief flooded through June like a drug.

"Sit down, little sister." Bosley lifted a pale, heavily freckled hand out of the covers to pat the bed. "Here. Beside me."

"I'm sorry, Mr. Broderick," she said. "But I'm wanted back at the studio. I just wanted to drop by for a . . ."

"So, Mr. Magic, how are . . .? Oh, excuse me, Miss!"

A dark handsome short young man in a tailored herring bone suit moved in familiarly beside June, but started after a glimpse of her face. "Don't tell me—you're June Lockwood, aren't you? I'm Dr. Sutton. You know, I've met more celebrities since Mr. Broderick's been with us! Doctors aren't supposed to like rock, so I keep a low profile. Would you excuse us a moment?"

Giving her a perfunctory grin, Sutton turned and threw the curtain up around the bed like an illusionist preparing to make a volunteer vanish. Reformer remained inside with the murmuring voices. She paced the remaining space in the room but felt too much like a spy so moved out into the desolate hall.

Dismissed, was she free to leave? It seemed criminal to do so now. Perhaps she'd been wrong about his faking this close approach to mortality.

Turning back toward the room, June caught sight of the dapper young man retreating rapidly down the hall in the opposite direction. "Oh, doctor!" And because she didn't feel right about making him wait, she skipped to close the distance between them. His tolerant smile seemed a trifle forced.

"Yes, Miss Lockwood?"

"Is Mr. Broderick . . .?"

"Yes," Sutton interrupted, nodding as if in agreement with a question he had not heard. "I've taken him out of intensive care because I thought he'd be more comfortable here where he can have friends come and go. He has many friends. Anything is good that will take his mind off his condition. He's quite alert, Miss Lockwood."

An icy steel net seemed to have settled over June's body; invisible hands worked to cinch it tight to her torso. "I see," she said.

"Please feel free to visit as often as you like. We would be very fortunate indeed to have Mr. Broderick for as long as another week."

"Well, I . . . Yes. I understand."

When she shuffled back into the room, June found that the white curtain around Bosley's bed had been drawn aside. His sheet covered him only from the knees down. Had the doctor recommended such radical ventilation? June realized that she had not yet found out what was wrong with him.

"Come close now, little June," Bosley requested.

"Beside me, please."

Without ever having consciously decided to approach him, June found herself stooping a little to touch his white arm. Yes, he had an incredible will. Was he willing himself to die?

The creases in his face revealed the pain of the effort to smile.

"Reformer, you may leave us for a few minutes, if you will. Yes, just for a little while. Now, June." He beamed with the defenseless delight of a child.

"Yes, Bosley?"

For more than a moment the expansive grin that possessed his face seemed hideous to her, premeditated, a mask concealing a terrifically vital evil.

"Would you like me to die a happy man? Would you, little sister of the blood?"

June could not answer. She groped for something to hold onto at the foot of the bed.

"You do not trust me. I must tell you about my last will and testament. And then you must do as I say."

June brushed distractedly at her brow. "Bosley . . ."

He shook his massive head, his hair dancing listlessly on the pillow. "In my will you are the first named. You are the only artist included. I have given you the secret of the blood and you have used it bravely. I have given you the rock and you have born it with the pride of true suffering. Now I must give you the remainder of everything of real importance to me."

Could it possibly be true—a greater burden of gifts? "Bosley! I can't . . ."

"Silence, little sister June bug. You must not waste time, neither mine nor yours, please. I leave you no money. It is unimportant. I leave you no possessions. The only important object you already possess. (Let the leeches slobber over my guitar and copyrights, my stocks and bonds—they are nothing.) I can leave you only my life, the inside of my life. Do you know my life—my security, my strength, my knowledge, my sense of place? When one lives in a house that permits one to move about mentally and physically without barriers, a house whose byways lead always deeper into oneself, then one's domestic environment flowing outside one's skin is as vital as the blood flowing inside. Where is blood without skin, little June bug? Where is the contained without a container? I leave you my house. May the blood of the stone find true peace there at last."

Instantly, the balloon of a headache inflated itself between June's eyes. "No, Bosley, no. I just can't . . ."

The childishly enormous delight remained on Bosley's face, but superimposed over it now was an absolute determination that threatened to turn vicious at the least opposition. "You must, sister June. You must. And you must marry, this very weekend you must be wed so that I may live to perform at your wedding. This you must do. But I have sad news. One of your band must die. I will replace him and perform for the first and last time as a member of Bloodrock for your wedding reception. Don't resist me, suffer the blood. You must know to suffer . . ."

June threw fists out from her throbbing forehead. "You've cursed me, you and this ridiculous rock of yours that I can't get off! You've cursed me and my family! I hate you! Yes, you've made me a success, I admit it. But I refuse to follow . . ."

She blinked. Like a lamp turned down to the brink of extinction, Bosley's face and eyes lost all delight, all determination, and nothing seemed to remain but a steady dim glow that drew her closer like an indistinct whisper. "I did not make you a success. Nor did the stone. The blood, the suffering, the knowing of yourself succeeded for you. All these things will happen, little sister. You must suffer through them near to willingness or all will be lost. You must marry. You must have me perform. You must take my house, ensconce your family, have your child, your beautiful girl child. You must continue to suffer. You must continue to know. The blood must be obeyed. The blood . . ."

"You're crazy," June muttered, but a huskiness, a catch in her voice, made it come out loud, too loud, an announcement, an insult. June knew she would be contradicted now, denounced, Bosley's weak voice growing suddenly strong and thunderous. But when she opened her eyes again, his were closed. He did not breathe. For the first time she knew with absolute and irrevocable certainty how incredibly gentle, how incredibly fragile the poor strange man's life had been. Oh, she had always known, since she was a little girl and first heard the voice and read his lyrics and felt what he was feeling. But then she had pretended not to know. And now that he was gone, now that she had killed him with words, she had no choice but to admit the truth of that knowledge. "Bosley?" She touched his cold shoulder. "Bosley! Oh, Reformer . . ."

The bald man appeared at bedside between her and Bosley. Tranquil, unhurried, he took the bloodrock in the palm of his hand and slowly and wordlessly tugged as if nothing animate were attached. June felt no urge to do anything other than obey the pressure and follow the direction of being pulled.

Reformer pulled the bloodrock toward the bed and down by Bosley's head. His face loomed huge, a pale alien landscape, the planet on which one was destined to land. June saw that she was part of an inevitable pageant, neither good nor evil but somehow forming a central pattern in the fabric of the life force. I must, she thought, I must. When the bloodrock descended to touch Bosley's motionless adam's apple, his body seemed to recoil, contract, resist. June bent to kiss his cold lips and felt the pressure on her throat subside.

Cleansed, baptized, she slowly raised her head back up.

"Bosley, I'm so sorry," she said. "So very, very . . ."

His eyes opened.

He smiled as if he had just told a joke. But weakness ruled his old voice. "Don't be sorry, June. Do what you must. Trust me. I am very tired now. Even the knowledge of the blood cannot keep me alive for more than a few more days. When will you be married? Today? Tomorrow? I must perform for you. I must . . ." His eyes closed.

She bent close. Sleep? Something like that. But it seemed best to answer. "Oh, Bosley, I can't say for sure. I have to talk to Duane first."

Reformer firmly grasped her shoulder. "Do what you must." He nodded her dismissal. Clearly, he did not intend to leave his friend alone.

Feeling like a lost child, June wandered the corridors of the hospital in search of an exit. She'd have to call a taxi. And then what?

Her hands held each other at the wrist like handcuffs. At first she pretended to indulge in doubt. Then, for whatever reason, she knew with absolute certainty that she could only do what she must.

Chapter Nineteen:

The Touch That Kills

Duane called twice in the early evening but June, unprepared for the conversation, said first that she was sick, the second time that she was thinking of skipping her club appearance that night. He wanted to know if she'd feel well enough for the next recording session tomorrow.

After hanging up, she considered Bloodrock as an instrumental group. On the phone Duane had said how disappointed he'd been that she had mysteriously disappeared before the planned post-recording celebration. Where had she gone, anyway? Well, she wasn't quite sure why, but she felt deeply pleased to have avoided Duane's little party. It had been important for her to pay her respects to a dying friend. And who could blame her, after the day she'd had, if she did not show up at the club tonight? Still, what point was there in avoiding the things that kept one going? YOU MUST. YOU MUST.

In plenty of time for the opening set June drove herself to the Club Crater where she found Larry in the green room, excited as a madman.

"Have I got some awesome weird shit to play for you!"

That was all she needed to hear. But she said, "What is it, Larry?"

"Did a little taping of my own this afternoon. Hope you don't mind my borrowing your little machine. Right! The whole session! Right here! Listen!" He pushed START, then, almost instantaneously, STOP. "Oh, I borrowed the studio to do a little remastering; you know, half-speed, backwards and . . ." He stabbed the orange START button once more.

It was not rock 'n' roll that growled with tinny resonance from the cassette recorder. Yet June recognized it, recognized herself. Oh, the Beatles had done it first, on "Tomorrow Never Knows," and then on the White Album on "Number Nine." And others, many others. And no wonder! Listen to that insinuating electric crackle of splayed sound! Like lying on your back to see the ceiling as a whole new world to walk and . . .

". . . recevral dans mes bras." The voice wove through the thicket of backwards slow sound like a needle intentionally left in the fabric of a completed garment. It was there, cold and unmistakable and real. "Vous etes belle, trés belle, trop belle! Trop . . ." Off.

June gripped her chin as if to stop it from quivering. "Is that voice or guitar or . . ."

Larry shook his head. "I've played that patch forward five or six times, June. It's not you. It's no one specific instrument or sound. It's the music, the whole unit, the band. Something, huh?"

June looked at the unwashed window, its grime glaring against the background of night. "It has to be

Reformer. He had to put those sounds on the tape. He and Bosley are trying to drive me crazy, I know it. I just know it."

"Know what, honey?" said Duane, who'd come in through the green door wearing an eager grin. "So you decided to show up after all, huh?"

June put a fist between her breasts. Duane's interruptions came like clockwork. Whenever she felt on the verge of discovering . . .

"I've been listening to what we did today!" Duane breathed with crazy pleasure straight into her face. "The new album—'Bloodburst'! How's that for a title? I knew you'd like it—thought of it myself!"

June watched Larry withdraw to the farthest corner where he sank into the easy chair and propped his feet disgustedly on a tattered ottoman, his head twisted to the side to rest on a supporting fist. Did he feel defeated—or betrayed?

"It's going to be the biggest thing since Sergeant Pepper, June! I'm telling you, you don't know what an amazing thing you've done—and you, too, Larry."

June pushed his chest to move him out into the corridor. If she didn't tell him now, she might never manage it. "Duane . . ."

"No, June, let me tell you the rest! I can't believe the response already—musicians, producers, technicians, everybody's talking whether they were there or not! I've got film directors begging for a chance to do a video! What's-his-name from Oakland left a message that he wants you to headline the first Hour-in-the-Sun concert this summer! Incredible! But, first, we've got to get you out of this dive. People're going to figure that if you're willing to perform here for peanuts, they can get you cheap too. I'll find a way to break D'Angello's contract and then will start . . ."

"Duane?" June caught her lower lip between her teeth, made a face. "Do we still have time to get married?"

Duane reacted as if slapped. He pushed back from the wall where his hands, still pressed on either side of her shoulders, kept her from moving. "Gosh, honey! I didn't mean to make you think that . . . Hell, yes! There's always going to be time for us to get married. Hell, *yes*! I just got all caught up thinking about your career—how great things are going, how perfect they're turning out for us. I guess I got carried away. But sure, honey, in a couple of months, when things start to settle down and we've fulfilled the majority of these offers, we'll talk about it, maybe even set a definite date!"

"Duane?"

"What, honey?"

"Now. In the next two days."

"What's that? What have I forgot? What's in the next two days?"

"For us to get married."

"Honey . . . you're kidding, right?"

She shook her head with a solemnity that seemed close to tears. Duane's jaw dropped as if the bottom had fallen right out of reality. "Honey, you can't be . . . oh, baby!"

He caught her up desperately, hugely, hugging her as if she were in imminent danger of hurting herself or coming apart, as if the strength he put into this hug was the only power on earth that might hold her together. "Baby, whatever it is, whatever it is that's wrong, I promise I'll make it right! We'll talk about it and work it out and make it right, I promise! Okay?"

Should she tell him that Bosley was dying? Should she say the words *I must*? As he relaxed his hold, she shrugged away to straighten herself but kept moving from foot to foot, an illusive target.

"I'll start the planning tomorrow. I'll set everything up. Then I'll let you know."

As if she were a climber slipping away from him inch by palpable inch, Duane reached out with little apparent hope of touching her. "June?"

"I must get ready to perform now."

She turned on her heels and strode back into the green room, closing the door behind her. She selected and donned her costume with an almost angry efficiency. She knew what she must do. It took its toll, knowing, planning, working, never deviating. But she could not betray the most powerful creative urge she had ever felt in her life.

With a nod of her head June launched the band into its first set.

By now Bloodrock had a following that regarded each performance as an event, a happening, an excuse to gather together and celebrate life. Every night they greeted the appearances of each band member with the most wholeheartedly open and loving response they could muster. An evening at the Club Crater was a frolic, a picnic, a church celebration where delight and amusement were ends in themselves. Bloodrock transported its audience to exactly those psychic vacation spots it dared to imagine in its most secret dreams; and the audience, in turn, goaded the band on to new heights by a sheer unprotected vigor of appreciation.

June determined that tonight she would coast. She would put energy and technique on automatic pilot and just cruise along with the show. The audience loved her, loved the band so much that a mediocre night became a welcome opportunity to contribute, shout, offer encouragement, scream, applaud. June knew she could cruise without worry, do what she must.

(In the fingers. In the touch. In the blood. The stroke. Waiting.)

What?

"That's it, June! Do it now! Don't wait!"

What? She saw the bald young regular in the first row, heard him yell (Illness? Radiation treatments? How had such a young man become so obtusely bald?) But it did not register. Did not register until she realized what a vicious tight grip she had on the infamous pendant, those few ounces of rock that had become the focal point of each audience's concentration. She made herself release it.

"Oh, June!" the bald kid groaned. (He looked so healthy!)

Automatic pilot? Taking it easy? See what happens when you pretend to try to coast?

No. She had to be onstage and in her body for herself and her crowd. She had to deliver herself in each note she sang.

June glanced over at Danny and saw at once what had attracted her attention. Head and shoulders back, eyes glazed, he'd taken a little leave of absence, left the stage, left the state, left the planet. His hands worked the drumsticks over the arrangements of skins as if transmitting code, each stroke raising a welt, the story of his life pounded out in braille.

June turned to sing toward him. She bent at the waist, her free hand trailing like a rudder in the air, and ranted and raved in his direction. But he had taken himself too far out on the high narrow trail of frenzy to hear her. And what if every instinct leads you to the solstice of expression and nothing happens—no climax, no flourish, no final plunge—and you're left there at the top, alone and naked? June knew she couldn't do that to Danny. If she had helped him get there, she'd help him get back as well.

But Danny didn't come back. Arms and legs churning with the furious precision of a mechanical toy, Danny smiled beatifically at the club's low ceiling. The sound bounced and jumped and twitched and for a moment June saw Danny as a little boy climbing a massive tree which was the music made by her band. She saw the high crevice he straddled, heard the river singing far below. She saw a skinny acrobat held aloft by the sheer force of his percussive strength. And she saw that if she missed a note, skipped a vocal beat, dropped a single syllable, Danny, a trusting climber who's forgotten his reliance on a shared lifeline, would fall, tumble, plummet. She could kill him by stopping. If she stopped singing . . .

You must. Do what you must. Do . . .

But that was foolish thinking, primitive logic! Would she let herself be ruled by the magical fallacy? The thought irritated, a mosquito alighting on bare flesh. She slapped it down by stopping. She stopped singing.

Danny's drumming thundered on by, oblivious to any other sound on stage—a herd of cartoon buffalo never noticing the feckless character they crush underfoot. And June gave out a raucous snort of laughter as she reclaimed the microphone from the stand once again. Dead? Fallen? Lifeline withdrawn—hanging defenseless on the sheer face of the cliff of his own empty sound? She loved it—loved being absolutely and irrevocably wrong!

Yes, you must!

Yes, the cessation of her singing, the silence from her sector of the stage, had been exactly the stimulus Danny needed to shinny on all the way up to where his drums could do the singing on their own. The drums did sing, they crooned. They yodeled out a vision of a place where frenetic rhythm joins frenetic melody, drugs and innocence cavorting in the blood of the life force, the blood finding new directions to flow and the skin discovering the path to follow, stretching, covering, tattoo taut, the tom-tom rhythm right in the center of his life.

"Do it, drummer! Do it!"

Even the most fanatically devoted were unsure of his name! Yet how they loved him now!

Laughing, June moved sensuously across the stage to her crazed drummer, her celebrity-in-the-making. She had to find a way to congratulate him. True, he had to be *on* something, but somehow her customary disapproval of substance abuse didn't surface and June found herself enjoying Danny's ride on the drug trolley. She laughed again, moved closer to the gyrating drummer.

She saw Larry shoot a wayward glance her way. Was he wondering what had happened to his band's vocalist? It did not matter. She knew that she must move closer to Danny.

And she did move closer. (How could she have been so wrong? Trying to cruise, to put it on automatic pilot? Was that the way to obey the blood, to move directly into the remorseless hot center of one's life? Did it take a drug-crazed drummer to show her that creativity never stops, that each moment opens up to possibilities and choices and directions that could never have been foreseen before now?) She knew what she must do.

June stared at Danny Driscoll. Here was the heart of Bloodrock beating itself insane on this stage. Who would have thought the heart could pound and pulse and beat on by itself without June-The-Mind-Lockwood to direct it? Here, pounding, beating, living, was the automatic nervous system of the band in action.

"Go, you crazy burnout!" someone yelled from near the bar. "Go for it!"

June turned to the audience as if she'd forgot that they were there. She tried to see individual faces through the smoke and glare. She tried to listen to their buzzing attentiveness, their long loud silence. Oh, yes. Oh yes indeed, they were with him. They knew, too. And some laughed out for all the right reasons. And June looked from Danny to the audience and back and then laughed again.

You must.

And she took another step to him. And she could hear him now. Because he sang as he played. And what he sang . . . if she bent close enough, she could hear.

". . . great stuff," Danny said, his eyes shut. His lips moved like tumblers in the lock of a damaged safe. "Great . . ."

Rape? Drape? "Danny, what are you saying?"

"Oh, I drank it down, June. I swirled it round." Sweat poured freely from his ecstatic face. "I found it in your dressing room in your French gown."

June clapped, the pleasure of comprehension. "The wine?" She wanted to sing out a high joyous whinny of laughter. "That moldy old bottle?"

Danny nodded without missing a beat and June laughed. The Guru of Tympanic Tension, she inscribed in her mental marquee. Danny Driscoll, the Demigod of Drummers!

(Here. In the fingers. In the rock. On the stage. Touch.)

Oh, she just had to laugh! Drugs, she'd been thinking! And here it turned out to be nothing but that rotten old wine that was probably rotgut even back in the twenties—or whenever it had been bottled! Probably the most dangerous thing Danny'd ever consumed!

June just had to laugh.

And as she laughed, she found herself moving with the luminous uninhibited yet controlled sensuality that had previously been denied to her on stage—which she unconsciously had denied to herself. Her body broke free now, free to be perfect, perfectly attuned to the undulating patterns of music, the cornucopian resonance that had no cause to ever stop, the sound that welled up from the skins of Danny's drums. The deep blood rhythm.

"Do it! Do it!"

Do what? Who were they yelling at?

You must.

June, laughing still, threw her hands up over her head to clap. And as if the fact that she'd kept them waiting just so long was excruciatingly right, a shriek of pleasure went up from the audience and it all began. All the hands. All the hands pounding together. All the hands slapping out a beat that fell straight down the middle of Danny's impossibly divergent drum solo the way a heartbeat, in the act of love, louder, louder, faster, goes right down the center as the rhythm of one's body branches off to explore every outer avenue of blood.

"Do it! Do IT!"

June laughed and clapped. The audience clapped.

Laughter.

". . . just an old spilled grape," Danny Driscoll said—or sang—in a whisper. "Just red and wet and stale and . . ."

(In the wine. In the darkness. Touch him.)

You must.

June's hands came together explosively over her head, over her swaying body. She studied Danny with fierce concentration. How beautiful. How beautiful he was. How furiously the blood moved through his nervous veins. How bravely he kept his arms and legs and body moving and pivoting in every direction, so careless of the precarious possibilities of blood. And she could see it. She could see the blood. Moving. Waiting. On stage. Alive. Ready to be touched.

June dropped one hand, but the crowd kept their little rhythmic avalanche alive. One hand to her side, June patted the air in time with the other. She heard the sound of it. It was the sound of blood, the sound one hears when one's eyes x-ray the creativity of others. Living everywhere one can see. On the stage. The blood. Ready to touch.

"Do it! Do it!"

With her free hand June took the bloodrock, nestled it in her palm. She stepped closer still to the frantically sweating young drummer.

On the stage. Just the touch. Here.

You must.

The hand she held aloft, still clapping against the air, still making the air applaud, felt warm now, hot, and she brought it down, not from discomfort, but because she wanted to feel her hand become cool. Where it had to be. Where it must be.

"Just some old lonesome grape—just some old lonesome bummed out puking grape juice I made the mistake of slurping one night!"

"Do it!"

And now June saw exactly where Danny needed to be touched, his straining body depicting perfectly through the sweat, the red haze that surrounded them both, the precise outline.

Why, she had only to touch him in all the exposed and prominent places, the places where the tension was unbearable, where the strain, the emotion, the heat of the blood as he pushed himself up so unbearably hard.

The Club Crater's crowd screamed out with crazy joy when June's brilliant wet red finger touched Danny's bulging forehead, touched the protruding veins, tracing the lines of tension, tracing all the places where he was ready to burst open with the exertion of creative effort pushed much, much too far.

"BLOODROCK! BLOODROCK! BLOODROCK!"

The audience writhed at the flood of sound from the stage like a tidepool of sightless life sensing the return of the sea.

". . . I only meant to get a little drunk. Just a little old red puke I lapped out of that bottle."

"Do it!" June etched every prominent straining point of tension, a dressmaker following the pattern. And Danny held himself up high for her to touch, to be gilded, to be anointed. Oh, how desperately he wanted the release of blood!

(The touch. Here. Now. On the stage. Open.)

And June felt herself and Danny transported somewhere inside a bloodred mist that promised them all the sweet eternal secrets of childhood, now and forever, the self-renewing energy of life, somewhere where the blood flows like sweet, sweet. . . .

Danny had stopped drumming.

That was good, June knew. How horrible the tension had been for him, how deep the need for release. And how joyous she felt to have been the vehicle to relax him, to set him free from the compulsion to play a drum solo that went on forever.

Then June dropped her gaze down at the sound of Larry Ludwig's gasp. The stage was hushed, the audience silent. She saw Larry's hand go to his mouth. He dropped his guitar with a horrible resounding empty thunk, a beautiful instrument unconsciously broken. Then she realized that for long seconds she had been feeling the strangest sensation of standing in a puddle, almost as if. . . .

And then she looked down at Danny Driscoll, open wherever she had touched him, as if someone had run a scissors down a dotted line. His mouth and eyes were open, too, and he had sprawled full length on his drum kit.

It was enough. June did not need to see any more.

Chapter Twenty:

Disbanded

Bosley Broderick had been wrong about one thing. Nobody had died. Not quite. Not quite. What a wonderful consolation.

"June, don't make me send Duane away again. Please? Pretty please with sugar on it?"

Somehow, she managed to shake her head. Marriage? Did someone suggest that marriage and attempted homicide could be compatible? Perhaps the same person who thought you could go through with a scheduled recording session the next day after discovering you were a pair of human scissors? And they wondered why she could not look at this person!

"No, Betty, really . . . I'm afraid I'm not particularly good company right now. Okay?"

"Well, you're the boss, but I still think you're being awfully mean."

Bosley Broderick had been wrong about a lot of things. His own death for one. A call to his hospital had confirmed his miraculous recovery and release.

Wouldn't it be an intriguing coincidence if Danny had taken over the old master's bed? She could not be sure, because although she'd traced him as far as St. Dorothy's critical care unit, she hadn't discovered the courage to visit him and doubted that she ever would. Doubted she ever could.

"Aunty, June, mail call! Clang! Clang! Mail call!"

Ivan dumped the cheerful heap of envelopes from the little red fire truck with bell that he had physically outgrown several years before. Down they tumbled into her lap, like manna from nowhere she cared to imagine. And why did Ivan have to play this game each day when the mail diverted from the club and RMA and Duane's office arrived at June's little condo? Was regression as contagious as this?

"Thank you, Ivan. You do a beautiful job of delivering mail in your fire truck."

"Be back in a minute with more!" Clang, clang, and he was gone.

June scooted her hands through the heap of hungry white rectangles. If you opened one, the opening became a mouth that wanted to eat you. It was that simple. One wanted your soul. One wanted your skin. One wanted a piece of hair or the shape your pencil made when you put it to paper and tried to remember whom you were supposed to be. Whenever she tried to stack them up high, they crumbled down in her hands.

Betty came in to stand over her sister. "So many people love you, June. It must be wonderful! Oh, sometimes I wish that so many people care about Ivan and me—or even knew we existed. Is it almost like feeling that you're going to live forever, having so many people always thinking about you, people all over the place? It must be nice. Would you like your lunch now?"

June shook her head politely. "No thank you."

"Have it your way, big sister. But you've got to eat sometime."

Hadn't it been nice of Betty to come and stay here with Ivan at Duane's request? It certainly must be an inconvenience for her, although she had not complained. Then, too, weren't all the others attendants and nursemaids of a sort, too? The letters, the phone calls, the persistent ones who found the front door—weren't these all efforts from the healthy helpers of the world to assist her back to . . . what? Back to what, June?

Shooing the remainder of the letters off her lap, June pulled the fuzzy coverlet up around her neck and watched the patch of late morning sun move inexorably toward her midriff. Sometimes, like yesterday, she let the TV set drone all afternoon so that she couldn't hear anything. Television was the answer, but for how long—weeks, months, years? And what would she do after television no longer worked for her? The phone rang.

Betty yelled from the kitchen. "A Herm D'Angello wants to talk to you. From the Club Crater. He wants to thank you for all the business you're bringing in even though you can't be there . . . June, please! I really think it would be good for you to take some of these really positive calls. This man wants to thank you for . . ."

"Please say that I'll call him back. Thank you, Betty."

They all meant well. They hadn't meant to be part of the rock that she had pulled down on herself when she pulled the bloodrock on her neck. Just like calling the butler, just like ringing the bell, just like releasing the payload poised above one's head. And so here she was buried in the ground with tons and tons of debris piled on top of her. It made it worse that some of it was alive.

"Aunty June! Aunty . . ." The Fire Chief Supreme pulled up beside her day bed for another delivery. Sunlight played like innocence on its shiny surface.

Jeux sans frontiers, said the little voice, the only thing trapped inside with her. *Aren't we happy now, June, my darling, that we know that all the boundaries are down and we can play in any way we want?*

Her only intimate . . . call it *pet*? Call it *love*?

Yes. Probably yes. Because outside were all the pushers and shovers and all those tons of depressing concern. They all wanted to get in to wish her well, take her picture, write the story, seek the real thrill, snag the autograph, pay endless dividends of prefabricated condolence, bask in the midnight sun of her underworld publicity and maybe even—if luck held out and everything went just right—get a chance to touch the rock around her throat. Rock around the throat tonight, B.H. And don't forget to take those comets with you when you fall out of orbit and crash into the sun.

"Aunty June, will you play Old Maid with me now? I'm tired of watching television."

"Wouldn't you rather play the Smurf board game? Why don't you go get it and we'll play."

She had to remember that life went on outside herself even if it didn't inside. It was undoubtedly better that way.

"June, Mr. D'Angello says he's booking a new band that wants to call itself Bloodpearl and wonders if it's okay with you?"

June called back to Betty that it didn't matter to her. No, it really didn't matter to her. Except everyone seemed to assume that it mattered very very much to her. In those first few hours after Danny had fallen when she'd given a handful of interviews, the reporters had all been so solicitous and polite. Oh . . . aggressive, pushy even, but really careful not to say the wrong thing, careful not to imply that in some way she was responsible.

Then she'd sent Betty out for the papers. It hadn't been necessary; unbidden, friends and acquaintances kept track of every scrap of news concerning the Bloodrock incident at the Club Crater on the night of November 23rd. BLOODROCK DRUMMER IN BIZARRE ACCIDENT. LOCAL BAND MEMBER'S SEIZURE BAFFLES DOCTORS. POLICE UNDECIDED IN OCCULT BLOOD INJURY OF AREA ROCK STAR. BLOODROCK SINGER IN SECLUSION AFTER ONSTAGE INCIDENT. CORONARY COMPLICATIONS RULED OUT IN ROCK DRUMMER'S COLLAPSE. SINGER LOCKWOOD ANNOUNCES DEMISE OF REDHOT ROCK BAND. Commentary: WAS LOCAL DRUMMER'S TRAGIC ACCIDENT NECESSARY? Editorial: MORRISON, MOON, JOPLIN—DOES THE NAME DRISCOLL HAVE TO BE ADDED TO THIS TERRIBLE LIST BEFORE THE PROPER COURSE OF ACTION IS TAKEN?

"Here are the dice, Aunty June. Do you want to shake first or do you want me to?"

"Oh . . . go ahead, Ivan. You start."

"Thanks! It was your turn this time, but you're nice!"

June could still see the newsprint of the editorial in the San Jose Gazette—"a generation of musical lemmings heading over the cliff of drug oblivion" and "human time bombs strapping themselves to the nitroglycerin of loud music and too much attention." Wouldn't it have been nice if she could have laughed at this bombast?

"Your turn, Aunty June? Do you want me to roll for you? Which piece do you want?"

June looked at the pretty blue and purple board game. Did they have a homicidal smurf? She could identify with all of them. "That one," she said.

She thought of something that made her bite her tongue. The magic finger. The one that unzipped skin. The one that politely escorted the life right out of your body—unless rude doctors interfered to sew you more or less back together. June took the bloodrock in her hand for perhaps the hundredth time since the accident. She drew a line down her middle from her neck through her navel and down between her legs. Oh, it was all right. Ivan wouldn't see anything, only the fact that she slumped over the board. Then they could go and get the authorities and lay it all to rest.

But she had no luck. It just did not work that way. She felt a mild little tingling itch. And then nothing. Oh, a little residual heat that quickly faded. But that was it. She was zipless, unzippable. And so she kept pretending to be alive.

"Look, Aunty June, you got the blackberries! You've almost won!"

Sure. Wouldn't it be nice to think, since the trick didn't work on her, that she had in fact done nothing to Danny Driscoll? Oh, she'd worked on that one for hours and hours.

No, the only consolation she had was her little French friend, who was no more than a voice. But oh, the games they played, the fun they had trampling over the fence that separated sanity from that infinite schoolyard beyond!

Maybe she shouldn't hate Bosley for giving her the bloodrock after all.

"June, he's really insisting this time and . . ."

"Hello, I'm back. It looks like I'm interrupting

something important. Am I?"

Ivan yelled "no," while June whispered "yes."

"Should I go way and come back later?"

Ivan saw June's head drop under Duane's direct gaze. Even questions defeated her.

"Are you okay, Aunty?"

Now June knew how the scene would go. A moment before it had seemed impossible. Now she knew that Ivan, caught up in his little boy's obsession with gallantry and heroism, would save her. Slowly shaking her head, June demonstrated her agony.

"My Aunty June does not wish that you stay," Ivan told Duane, not quite able to look directly at him. "You must leave!"

"Well . . . of course."

Nodding uncertainly, Duane withdrew.

Why did being saved feel so disgustingly empty? Suddenly, June felt that if she remained here another moment playing cards and board games and watching television that she would burst wide open. Worse, she would not. The emptiness would continue to bulge—like bloat—a static pressure, her only way of denoting that life went on.

"Your move, Aunty June. I wish you would start playing the game right."

True. All too true. She was good only to injure, to rip open, to spill out vitality. Hell, in the old days when leeches were the essence of medicine, she would have been tolerably useful, made damn fine money as well.

Betty backed into June's daytime bedroom, her hands raised in hopeless surrender like a character in a B-movie giving ground to the monster.

Then Duane strode sheepishly in after her, flourishing a handful of dripping flowers. "Here, June. These are for . . ."

"No. I can't take them."

"Because you think they're from me? Come on, June! I was on my way out to the car and your neighbor in the next unit stopped me and asked me to give you these. Fred, I think he said. It seemed very important to him. Here."

She made the fatal mistake of touching this dripping life. Sunlight yellow. A twining curve of shapes. An assault of cut fragrance. Where had he found roses and daisies this time of year? And why did she think now of the huge house, the estate that Bosley claimed he would leave to her in his will? Thirty-two rooms, servants quarters, an olympic-sized pool. Was it because she felt as certainly unsuited to that gift as to this she held in her hands now? And yet, it felt good to take the rude bouquet and smell and crush it gently, petals and moisture and all, to her throat.

"Duane, please take them back. Give them back to the man. They're too . . ."

"No," he said softly. "You're the one that's too much, too far gone." He looked at June's sister and nephew with quiet regard. "Betty, would you and your son mind excusing us for a moment?"

Their nods and shrugs and shuffled steps reminded June of the manner of visitors to a terminally ill hospital patient who are told "it's best that you leave now." And she had to think again of Bosley Broderick.

"Well, June . . ."

She shook her head forlornly. She felt like a mountain that refuses to allow the least suggestion of a fingerhold to an impassioned climber.

"Shall I put these in water?" he said. "No? You can't stay? Won't say? Flowers are too dangerous to talk about, June? Look at me! Putting flowers in water is too dangerous a topic for you to discuss, for you to allow yourself even to look at me?

"Okay, that's my answer. June, you're too good a person to do this to yourself. Everybody knows that you feel terrible about what happened to Danny and that . . ."

"Do they?"

"Yes, they do. Everybody that matters, everybody who knows you. The rest are going to think what they want to think anyway."

"What about Danny? He knows me, he matters. What does he think?"

"Well . . ."

"There! You see!"

"No, June, you've got the wrong idea. Danny is as confused and disoriented by this as you are. Whatever kind of experience he had that night playing that amazing solo, whatever happened, whatever he took, whatever possessed him, he loves what he did but hates what happened to him. He's afraid that if he ever tries to really cut loose and play like that again the same thing will happen. He still loves you and admires your music and knows that you didn't intentionally do anything to hurt him. Yet he's a little frightened of you because he's not sure exactly how much your touching him contributed to the bleeding. Can you understand that, June?"

"You . . . you heard this from Danny? He actually told you this?"

Duane gave the nod of a man who knows he has made his point, punctuating it with the physical gesture only to be polite. "It's time for you to come out of it, June. You've punished yourself long enough. You've excluded yourself from the world long enough. It's beginning to be a sickness, June, an illness. If I didn't know you better, I'd say that you were enjoying cutting yourself off from everybody and everything. Do you think you can languish away here forever, watching television and pretending to play games with your sister and nephew? Do you think a creative person like yourself can turn her back on creating for the rest of her life without paying an enormous emotional penalty? It's time to think about showing a little strength and a little courage, June. I've always thought those virtues were part of you. I love you, I want you to marry me. I want you to go back to performing, to honor your contracts, to keep your commitments—not because of the money that it could make us (though, god knows, that's nothing to sneeze at) but because it's *you* to be doing things, creating, meeting people and responsibilities. The woman throwing herself down in this dismal room at the shrine of the TV is not the woman I love. There. How's that?"

He stood back from the crystal vase bristling with the red and yellow and pink blooms of the home-cut bouquet. Life—he forced her to see it.

"You're right," June said. "I love you. I will marry you. Thank you, Duane."

He scrambled over to kneel beside her. He took her face out of her hands into his own like a man opening the petals of the lotus to find the jewel inside. Mutual consolation turned into a crazily clutching embrace. Hugging harder, harder, each snarled happily at this escape from the long deprivation they'd imposed upon themselves.

"Listen, listen, listen!" Duane said breathlessly. "We'll go out! It's cool—but sunny. We'll go to the zoo or the wharf at Santa Cruz or . . ."

"No," she said. "We'll go get ready." And when he appeared puzzled she added, "To get married, stupid! I've got this notion all of a sudden that life's too short to fool around. So I've got to find a guy who's desperate enough to want to just jump into it without a thought in his head."

"Yeah," Duane said. "I think I just might have the guy you're looking for."

June could not help herself. Holding her blouse away from her white skin, she checked her chest for moisture, color. A nervous habit, necessary ritual? She realized now that it was there she looked to discover emotion.

Chapter Twenty-one:

A Warning, A Celebration, A Fever in the Blood

It was all ponderously informal—the date, the time of day, the location of reception and wedding, the guest list, the catering and entertainment.

Although she did not tell Duane, June decided that she must accomplish one specific thing before the eight days prior to her wedding elapsed. She must return a gift, the gift from Bosley Broderick to be exact. She did not wish to be married wearing the bloodrock. She did not want ever again to do anything of consequence with the bloodrock suspended from her throat. And, since neither she nor anyone she knew could remove it, her only recourse was to find Bosley and demand that he take the bloodrock back.

She smiled each time she let herself imagine the rock coming free of her throat. She felt, she thought, the way ancient mariners had felt when the putrid white bird was lifted at last from around their dreaming heads.

The first day she phoned the hospital once again, only to be told by the nurse at the desk in the intensive care ward that without a doctor's permission no personal information pertaining to former patients could be given out. Great, just great.

The next morning June persuaded Duane to contact Bosley's agent who only could report that he hadn't seen his client in weeks. As far as he was concerned, the flamboyant entertainer was no longer his client. For all he knew, he said, Bosley could well be dead.

Reformer had dropped out of sight as well, June discovered on the third day of her search.

On the fourth day she used her influence with Herm D'Angello to come up with the names of three musicians who had served as sidemen with Bosley during the last year. And the next day she tracked down two of them, finding one in a county-run alcohol detox center, the other in a Campbell pizza parlor where he performed as half of a banjo duo. Neither knew a thing. The third was rumored to have withdrawn from the ranks of the living.

On the morning of the sixth day June called the DMV and state police; she gave up her search for Bosley that same afternoon.

Slamming down the phone receiver on the final frustrating call, June took a hammer from her father's old tool box and attacked the rock that hung from her throat. She had to lean forward so that it rested on the wooden shelf and tilt her head and swing the hammer sideways and in. At last, her wrist aching, she stopped after twice smashing the thumb she'd used to steady the rock, which had not perceptibly changed. The pounding had not even managed to make it warm.

Normally, although she knew that she felt better when she conceived of some force in the universe larger than herself, June did not pray. Amelia had steered her clear in her childhood of any and all religious instruction, which she regarded as dangerous. Later, after leaving home, June had learned to cherish various spiritual philosophies, but prayer never became a part of her beliefs. Perhaps, as her mother had tried to teach her, she still conceived of it as primarily a form of weakness.

But the bloodrock would not come off. And in two days she would be married. What else could she do?

"Aunty June, aren't you through in the bathroom?"

"No, Ivan, not yet. I'll be out in just a minute."

Or just in time to get married? So much left to do!

Poised on the edge of the white porcelain tub, June slapped the wet towel down across her naked legs.

"Please don't let me bleed when I walk up the aisle or kiss Duane after he gives me the ring; please don't make anyone bleed when I touch them in the reception line or greet them casually later; please don't make me bleed when the best man toasts us or we're cutting the cake or the photographer has us posed for everyone to see or when I'm passing out the favors in a little basket; please don't let a lot of news people find out so that I get nervous and start touching the rock without knowing that I touch it; please, though I'm glad Amelia is renting a wheelchair to bring Grandma Edna, please don't let them start in on me again; please don't let people get too out of hand with booze and drugs because they think that since I'm a singer it's okay and even necessary to do that to show how important they think the occasion is; please don't let me have too much time to myself so that I get scared and don't know what I'm doing and can't go on with what I'm supposed to do; please don't let Duane know how horrible I feel sometimes because he wants and needs me to feel happy because I'm marrying him and wants that to be enough to solve all my problems, including this one; please let him be happy and me a good wife to him despite all this; and please don't surprise me with Bosley Broderick and please don't let me ever bleed for no good reason at all ever again; and please, no French voices in my head. Please, please, just let me be ordinary for this little while, with no blood or pain or fear. And please let me be an ordinary mother with an ordinary child, a little girl, and in a nice house that does not have to be a mansion. And please, at the very least until the wedding's over, stop all the strangeness. Thank you."

Okay, do you feel better?

Yes. Yes, I do.

"Aunty June!"

"Okay, Ivan. You can come on in. It's all yours now."

Duane and June agreed to split the wedding preparations between them. They were too old, too independent and self-reliant, they figured, to inflict such chores on others—even if to do so was eminently traditional. Still, friends and acquaintances and well-wishers stepped in to take charge of a surprising number of plans.

Out of necessity, June first told Betty about the rescheduled wedding. And Betty, of course, told Ivan. And together they took over the guest list and decorating duties, which involved daily visits to and from the home of Duane's friend John Fabray, the site of both wedding and reception. "Are you sure you don't want me to get Mom and Grandma Edna involved in this, June? I'm sure they'd both enjoy it, and after all the mother of the bride . . ."

"For God's sake—no, Betty!"

But the first person June had really wanted to tell about her radical decision was her friend and band co-founder Larry Ludwig. She smiled whenever she thought of him. How foolishly sentimental—because he was too unstable and irresponsible to stay with a woman more than one night, let alone a lifetime. Still . . . does the cliché *soft spot* seem to apply, June? Good, good, she could chide herself mildly now, without using the poison-tipped harpoons which had been her self-doubts and accusations during the prolonged depression.

When Larry tried to congratulate her but could not, June understood, even felt flattered. So he really did like her in that way.

"You're sure it's on?" he said. "Sure you're not going to rape somebody or something? Speaking of which, don't bother to invite Danny. He's doing fine but there's some controversy over whether he'll regain sufficient motor control to ever walk again."

That hurt, as Larry certainly must have intended it to. But the fact that he did maintain daily contact with Danny really helped June because she did not yet feel ready to see him. Actually, she hoped, if all went well, that the hospital would be their first stop before leaving for a short casual honeymoon.

"You wouldn't believe the gifts he gets," Larry informed her. "We're talking gifts galore here—five different Grateful Dead T-shirts, a dozen red American Beauty roses in the coziest plastic skull vase you ever did see, an autographezed copy of Kate Bush's new album since he's secretly in love with her. Recreational drugs? You name it, he's got it. Some crazy even brought him a box of candy!"

Later, she remembered to add a prayer for Danny Driscoll to recover fully and find it in his heart to forgive her, somehow.

In those eight days June did not perform at the club but did call the band together for two unrecorded practice sessions. Bass player Bruce Marley brought along his friend from school, Paul Travers, to fill in on drums. He sounded good, June thought. Larry, his thumb up ten minutes into the first session, affirmed her judgement and made Bruce feel proud about his recommendation. Paul—wearing corduroy pants, a button-down shirt, glasses and a fixed expression of nervous discomfort—seemed to notice neither their appreciation nor their acceptance of him.

June, who did not shake his hand when they met, was careful not to go near him during the practices.

"What a war machine!" Bruce enthused. "When are we taking this musical Juggernaut out on tour?"

"Oh, soon," June said.

"Sure, I understand," Bruce told her. "You've got more important things to think about right now. But after a few weeks of marriage, you'll get the itch again. No offense intended!"

Duane continued to claim that they had enough material from the single recording session to release an EP consisting of five or possibly six tunes. Then later, when public demand increased for a full album, they'd take the plunge back into the studio. They had all the time in the world for that. Right now, he had his hands full juggling previous commitments and preparing for their wedding. Right? Right.

Right. They both kept very busy. The eight days went by like nothing.

A variety of cars already clotted the curving tree-lined street when Betty located a space two lots down from John Fabray's house. So the time had come at last. It did not seen so very different from any other moment in her life, and perhaps it was realizing this that frightened June most.

"Betty, would you and Ivan like to go ahead? I'm going to . . . a little last-minute fussing, you know?"

"Are you sure you're all right? Okay, then—come on, my little knight in shining armour! Maybe you and I will get married if Aunty June gets cold feet!" And so they skipped down the street and up the walk to the ranch style suburban home that sprawled easily across an area of two normal lots. Both mother and son were dressed in white and tricked up with every item of jewelry they owned. Married and divorced, how did Betty manage to see each new event in life as a first time experience? Was it simple ignorance, stupidity? Or some blessed talent known only to the pure in heart? June doubted that she believed in such absolute purity. But by such doubt did she automatically sentence herself, slam the door of innocence in her own face?

June locked the car and stooped in the driveway to adjust the hem of her pants. June Lockwood, bride-to-be, why don't you just stroll inside and get married? It seemed too unreal, too casual, too everyday—yet somehow charged, emptily charged, with a meaning that had nothing to do with her. Cold feet? No wonder parents and other relatives had tranditionally shepherded the bride and groom through this penultimate day. Oh, the ocean isn't *that* cold; just one more step, now another, and—yes, jump! You may even survive! Left alone, untended, who would not chose to run? Who was she to marry today? Perhaps if a picture of Duane had flashed across his friend's house, she would have discovered a cause for entering. But these trimmed hedges, manicured lawn and shrubs presented the stolid front of a calendar photo calculated to be admired—but never entered. The murmur of voices seeped through the walls like undiscoverable secrets.

Foliage thrashing, something thrown violently down in the decorative gravel around the front hedge, stomping, grinding, a boot obliterating a living spark in yards of grey rock—that was all she heard, all she saw out of the corner of her eye.

"June, what the hell are you doing out here? I know it wasn't the same thing I was doing!" Larry heaved an enormous Paul Bunyan breath of satisfaction and grabbed her arm to hurry her into the house before she could speak or offer the least resistance.

"June! Hey! Hey! Hey! Everybody, it's the bride herself!"

Larry's hand slipped away from the small of her back as a crush of people separated them just past the threshold. A little boy in a bellhop uniform shoved a tray of high-stemmed champagne glasses at her midriff. Linda Lombard, Duane's youngest sister, fell on all fours and lifted June's left leg to slip a garter under her pants. A bald man dressed as an English butler thrust a bouquet into her hands, a single thorn lightly scratching one of her fingers. A tall teenager told her to hold still for a picture. Click, flash, click. More unreality, life frozen. Yet this flesh on flesh on flesh, hands in her hands and on her arms and shoulders, everywhere, slaps, touches, shoves, pushes, hugs restored June to her body.

I'm back, she thought. Congratulations.

Somewhere out of sight in another room the last cut of side one of "Mendelssohn's Greatest Hits" began to play on a stereo, a light scratch punctuating over and again the triumphant march through musical midsummer. Someone shoved a rough-textured black book into June's hands already occupied with the bouquet. Laughter, shouts, applause, like a single sweet happy sound.

"Come on, June!" said a familiar voice. "It's time."

A piano in an adjoining room sounded thoughtful and contemplative against the brittle thicket of sound made by these many glad voices. Suddenly the piano broke into a grand parphrase of the Mendelssohn march, jazz tinted yet stately. Instead of rushing through this unreal moment, how wonderful and simple it would be to find the piano, find the master musician whose knowing hands made these sounds, and quietly sit and listen perhaps for hours. Let the whole procession hurry by without her, unaware that one of its key performers was AWOL. But to whom could these hands belong? No matter. A sidetrip into the room from which the music came, a room as vast and comfortable and familiar as childhood, would turn into a rosy eternal round of days and years, a lifetime of playful artistry and artistic play. June pictured herself on a throw rug with her legs curled up and her head propped in her hands, listening to music made only for her.

"June? You sure are balky today. Well, you know what they say about the bride who hesitates when the wedding march starts. Come on."

Whose arm did she clutch for the ride outside? See how anonymous it is, being spirited away from the presence of the master pianist? The loud announcement of afternoon sun caught June full in the face. Several girls in pastel formals laughed when she jerked her head aside to protect her eyes, blinded by the light.

Wedding? Her wedding day.

Wrong? The idea made a noisy little commotion in her head. What was wrong? June turned to her escort to ask what was missing.

"June," Amelia whispered in her ear. "Duane's waiting. See him? He's been waiting for a long time and I think you'd better . . ." Her words trailed off, slippered feet descending steep stairs. The stereo blared out the insistently triumphant march, but June could still detect the deft solitary sound of piano improvisation underneath, like sunlight flickering along the bottom of a shady ravine where a creek runs, steady and clear.

She saw Duane standing in the center of the yard, handsome in a very pale pink shirt with a broad wide-open collar. The tufts of his chest hair curled lazily out as if to articulate how easy it was to be casual on every occasion.

Volume raised again, Mendelssohn marched despotically over the delicate muscularity of the live piano. The sunlight cursed her for remaining still. And then. . . .

It was too late now. She had to do it. She had to pretend that nothing essential was missing today. After all, she had only to open her eyes in the bright winter sunlight to see everything and everybody. The rose trellis beside the dried-up masonary fountain. Pete Robinson. A flock of TV antennas stretching away down the suburban block like an exercise in elementary perspective. Larry. Ivan. Betty. Benches. Chairs. Bowls of punch. Rows of friends. Piles of presents. Musicians she knew from other bands. Amelia with her hands on Edna who'd ventured out into the open air in her wheelchair for the first time in many years. Cake. Champagne. An impromptu music pavillion fashioned from an inverted plastic pool and folding chairs, each chair occupied except. . . .

Despite the volume of the Mendelssohn, June heard the piano stop and knew the pianist had left his instrument to move to her side.

Duane extended his hand to her and she took it. He whispered something she did not need to understand. She moved her head and lips in simulated reply. They had begun.

John Fabray directed each of them to read a favorite poem. He handed over a large brown book to Duane, who read from it. Now June recognized the book she held and when it was her turn to read the selected passage aloud she did so. Appreciative silence. Sportive gusts of afternoon wind flapped the ladies' dresses, tablecloths, crepe streamers. Fabray suggested vows, loyalty, trust, compassion, creativity.

"I do," he said.

June's hand fluttered up to the pendant stone.

"June?"

"I do," she said.

They exchanged the rings. They kissed each other. They squeezed and hugged and embraced much much much too hard. Her breath cut short, June imagined that she saw a mist forming along the base of the fence behind Duane's back, a red mist, no . . . green, a mist in which. . . .

"June, congratulations!" "You're so lovely. Too beautiful. Too very beautiful to be real. But isn't that exactly what we've always hoped for?"

The mist shifted, seemingly indecisive. Now June knew what had been missing, who had been missing. He was missing no longer.

"I hope you don't mind our inviting your friend," Larry blurted out. "Hey, I mean, the band needed a fill-in with Paul out of town for the weekend and Danny still . . . Just don't be mad at me, June, not today, okay?"

The serenity of her smile could have fooled anybody—and she knew it. "I'm not mad," June said. "How could my wedding have been complete without him? Thank you—and thank you for coming, Bosley."

Chapter Twenty-two:

His Will Be Done

June cupped the bloodrock in her hand. What had she meant to ask Bosley?

"There's magic in a winter's day such as this—so warm, so sunny, so compassionate," Bosley told her. "Do you believe in magic, June?"

Happy faces eddied around them, water flowing past a pair of stationary rocks. June eyed Bosley's loose white tunic and deck slacks, a surprisingly conservative outfit for "the master of the outrageous."

She realized that she felt glad that he was here. Now, somehow, it seemed that the ceremony was complete. How good to be happy! Yet he looked so fragile.

"Can't you answer, June? Words are magic, little sister. June bride, look at the day. It *is* June. It is *you*. The day has become you. And you, you have become . . ." His arms fanned out in a gorgeous expansive gesture, pure theatre. ". . . radiant!"

How could she have ever imagined that this warm, earthy, loving man meant her any harm? June let herself go, relax, give in. Her sigh became a lilting laugh.

"You know," she said, "a week ago I would never have believed that I'd laugh again. And now here I am—and you've even got me blushing!"

Bosley shook his large blue-veined head. "Beautiful day, beautiful bride, beautiful wedding. Blushing is natural. Blushing means you still believe in innocence. That is my legacy to you, June, to know, to perceive, to act, to be in the vanguard of human experience and artistic expression but still retain radical innocence. Oh, you must get angry, really angry, if anyone tries to take . . ."

"Excuse me!" Duane pushed roughly between them with great good-naturedness. "This is *my* bride. If anyone is going to monopolize her, it's me." Beaming, supremely confident, Duane loomed above them with friendly menace.

June saw that though Duane had tried to make it sound like a joke, he meant what he'd told the sick musician. Of course, she understood. She understood fully. "Duane, remember Bosley Broderick?"

The two men shook hands like friends. Bosley bowed. What courtly tension! Her gaze wandered up to the music stand where Larry paced aimlessly, touching the case that housed his current guitar, then peering out at the happy throng with a lost look in his eyes. He looked as lonely as she felt in this moment of Duane's intervention.

"Listen, honey." Duane's hand squeezed, then lingered on her waist. "I'm going to prove that I'm not a possessive chauvinistic so-and-so by leaving you alone here with this . . . great musician. I'm going to circulate. See? We trust each other already!"

"Wait, young groom." With the air of a parade's grand marshal, Bosley stopped Duane by using his arm as the gentlest suggestion of a blockade. "I want to propose a toast"—and his voice rose to announcement volume, cutting through the quiet winter wind—"to you, Duane, and to your bride and I want . . ." Bosley shouted out now into the open brilliant sunshine above the heads of the chattering strangers. ". . . all of you, everybody, to join me in this joyous and solemn and spiritual moment."

June twisted her sweaty hand in Bosley's soft warm grip. Frightened at the exaggeration, she saw him in his hospital bed, head wreathed by floating hair. Joyous? Spiritual? Solemn?

"Bosley?" she whispered as the dying man lifted what appeared to be an empty glass. "Bosley . . ." (*how's your health*?—ridiculous! But she had to know, had to find out whether or not today, on the very afternoon of her wedding, Bosley might be intending to die.)

"I'm fine," he said sotto voce, then shivering so that his smile constricted into a comic sneer. He tugged at the brim of her floppy hat to bring her close. "No, I can't read your mind. You're a good woman, June. You live by your heart. What else would you want to know? Why else would you interrupt me, a fellow performer, as I'm gathering an audience for our first and only show together? No, I'm fine. I'll last through the day!" he joked.

Now Duane reached across Bosley's broad torso to grip the bicep of the arm that held June. "Mind if I ask what you two are saying?"

"Yes!" Bosley said. Taking each by the hand, he yanked Duane and June up the loose brick steps onto the music platform.

Flushed out of his solitude, Larry made a surly growl and slunk off behind the drums.

Bosley took Duane by the shoulders and squared him up to the audience like a cardboard display figure, then motioned to June to stand to his other side. "Won't you all indulge an aging rock 'n' roller," he called out to the unfocused throng. Men and women paused mid-word, mid-gesture, mid-munch to shift their gaze to this impromptu stage festooned with crepe but still looking like nothing so much as the largest plastic swimming pool around. "Super!" Bosley laughed with a raucous abandon June admired. (Being crazy must be a hell of a lot of fun.)

"Toast!" he said, raising up his water glass. "Alcohol's a poison, ladies and gentlemen, so don't feel that you have to indulge in it to join us. Water's better for toasting. Clean fresh water, pure water, clear cool water! Which sometimes turns to wine, which sometimes . . . But why am I blathering on about water? Absolutely mad, you think? Well, my dear dear friends, I'm here to offer a toast to a magnificent . . . drink of water, June Lockwood . . . what's you name again, sir?"

Duane played it for a laugh, doing a double take off each shoulder, one for Bosley, one for June. "Lombard," he said at last.

"June Lockwood Lombard—it does have a ring of sorts. Water. Clear water. The creative artist. What else are we, the artists of the world, if not a glass inviting the thirsty to drink? We offer . . . well, let me tell you a little of what this one particularly lovely creative young stream has to offer us all . . ."

Swaying, Bosley dropped their hands to gesture. In that second June sensed it, a profound systemic weakness, the feeble little flame inside his impassioned words.

"When an artist marries on a winter's summer day, something magic is in the air. New possibilities are flying just over our heads like invisible birds. See them? Feel them? Reach out and catch a hold of one of them if you dare! June has done this for us all today . . . and Duane.

"I've known her since her girlhood." (Why did he say this lie?) "Beautiful and slender, she lorded it over the other tomboys in this town with her hammer wand of courage. Brave child, brave teenager, but a terrified adult. June's fear should be no secret to anyone who's heard her music. The world terrifies her, and this personal terror may be the most constructive force motivating any artist on the current scene. Drink it down; drink it straight down. And, if you must have a chaser, put on one of my old records—though I don't recommend it because June's *the one*. I've passed the baton—the blood is in her court, the highway opens through her head now. When the snake slithers across the surface of our compass rose, anyone who does not follow is lost. Drink. Drink."

"You've had enough already, I think!" shouted a tall man with a professional beard who wore wide suspenders but no coat.

Bosley staggered against Duane, who steadied him reluctantly, frowning. "No," Bosley said, hanging onto Duane as if such support were a sign of his own strength. "I am not drunk, my friends. I am not ill. I will not die. Nevertheless, everything that I have I leave to June. And you are all my witnesses! My house. My art. She deserves everything I have to give and everything you may offer. She is the artist who dares to think in her art, dares to speak with her heart. I do not know another rock artist who dares to flirt so outrageously with the whole range of human suffering. Sex and drugs and rock 'n' roll? June leaves the adolescent cloud for the heartland of blood beyond age. Listen to the heart, listen to the music. Let June lead you back into your body and teach you again what it means to be alive."

"Why don't you teach yourself how to shut your big fat . . ."

Bosley began to wave his arms wildly as if to gather objects from or gain some handhold on the air. When she saw Duane step aside to give the musician room to play out his fit, June braced her legs and knees and readied herself to catch the precariously erect old man should he go too far.

But Bosley seemed to find his purpose at last. "Don't mistake my foolishness for hers," he said. "She eschews the easy way, the quick love lyric, the simple appeal of cynicism, the ready drama of the fast chic empty life. She offers us a glimpse back into the bloodstream of our humanity at a time when it is profoundly unfashionable to admit to being human. Listen. Drink. She will reward you. She will refresh you. She will show you the way back into yourself. Thank you. *Prosit!*"

Bosley pantomimed for them a prolonged and grateful gulping of the contents of the empty glass, his Adam's apple bobbing with embarrassing realism. At last, he wiped and smacked his lips.

"Wsssh," he said. "Waited too long for that. Been carrying the baton far too long. Now, June, I'm going to play one last tune for you. No, no, don't mind me. Circulate. Greet guests. Listen to me now and then—but just enjoy."

Duane shrugged, stepped down from the impromptu stage and disappeared. How did he do that? June tried it, shrugging, stepping lightly down into the smiling throng of faces, hands, chests, swiveling hips and elbows. But she did not disappear, it all just closed in on her, a seamless garment of friends and well-wishers that fit skintight.

"June, I want to apologize for that drunk old fool. He had no business . . ."

". . . on and on, didn't he? Couldn't really make out what he was saying, though; sounded sort of Marxist or existential or . . ."

"... the poor man, because he used to be quite a musician; and now, obviously, he's just a shell of ..."

"... institutionalized because you never know how much harm someone like that ..."

"... kind of spooky the way he said things that made you shiver and look up into the sky and down at the veins in your hand and think about the fact that one day every one of us is ..."

"June, darling!"

"Miss Lockwood, can I have your auto ..."

"She's Mrs. Lombard now, Dennis!"

Nodding politely, she turned in a semicircle back to face the little stage. Bosley had settled in behind the drums, leaving Paul Travers to slap a tambourine disconsolately against his thigh. Bosley teased the snare with a stick and then began to tap it. Pressing the stick to the cymbal to stop a vibration, he pulled the microphone close, then accelerated the pace of his churning hands.

A woman kissed June on the throat. June touched the rock with the tip of her finger. She saw Larry's hands moving fitfully on the frets of his guitar. She listened to the beat of the drums. She thought she could hear his heart beat in them. She thought that if she kept attentive, concentrated, she could keep the beat steady. Ridiculous, of course. Then why wasn't she breathing?

"Ridiculous,"

"What's that, darling?" Amelia said, suddenly at June's elbow. "The music? Yes, I quite agree."

One tune, Bosley had said. June held her breath again as the song ended. And the next began. June breathed in and held it. Listen to the heart beat. Feel the rock around your throat.

She did not know what she said to the unfamiliar face before her, large and handsome and tanned, eyes squinting into the sun, lips moving with cinematic precision, nostrils flared with just the right hint of civilized passion. Lips moving—but she heard no words. She spoke—something.

June craned her neck to see the impromptu stage. She felt the wind on her face. She waited, listening to the music.

Bosley played a dozen tunes before turning the sticks over to Paul Travers and departing the stage. June did not see the old musician leave and kept searching the throng for him because there were things she wanted to say. Sometime around 6:30 the last stragglers ducked back into their cars and drove away into the suddenly chilly winter night. June and Duane thanked John Fabray before leaving on their weekend honeymoon. Because on Monday, it was back to the recording studio, back to the Club Crater, back to everything that had constituted and continued to constitute their lives. Yes, they had agreed eight days before, laughing, there was life after marriage.

As they drove out to highway 280, "the World's Most Beautiful Freeway," June kept scanning the side of the road, the faces of the few scattered hitchhikers. None of them was Bosley. She caught herself holding her breath on the drive up to San Francisco. She did it again, inadvertantly, as they checked into the Fairmont and had dinner and again as they lounged in the Venetian Room listening to Mel Torme sing "Zaz Turned Blue."

When they were alone in bed in the honeymoon suite, she caught herself again. She had almost broken herself of the habit of touching the bloodrock—but was this breath-holding a byproduct of exercising such will power?

Only when the phone rang at 2:30 a.m. and she discovered Larry at the other end and heard the news about Bosley that she had expected did June begin to breathe correctly. She tried not to think what final statement the artist was making to the world by dying today.

"We're never going to move into that house in Los Angeles," she said. "Can you imagine raising children in a mausoleum like that?"

"Whatever," Duane said. "You're just upset because your friend died. Come on back to bed."

It was not until they had made love for the third time that June was able to cry. She cried all night. She had let Bosley die without telling him that she loved him.

BOOK III:
BLOOD SACRIFICE

Chapter Twenty-three:

House Warming

Nothing had changed. Everything had changed.

"No," June whispered to her husband in the darkness, "nothing'll ever make me retire from music."

Would this be the night she finally found the right moment to tell him her news?

Duane leaned triumphantly over her, hands binding her wrists, his weight all in his strong straight arms. "Great! What a partnership we've got—perfect sex, perfect business!"

And then, hands still imprisoning her wrists, Duane dropped his big torso down onto her slender body. Robbed of breath by the blow, June clamped her teeth on the forced exhaling of air.

"How's that, honey?" Duane asked, moving now.

"Great," June said. "Just great."

Why did she almost invariably think of Larry now, these past three months? Of his thin wiry almost puny body and his frightening, unpredictable, annoying energy? A married woman, she hated the idea of having fallen already into the need for fantasy romance. After all, hadn't she thought of Duane as the perfect man not so very long ago? And wasn't he? Thoughtful, responsible, strong, commanding, he knew what he wanted from both of them—and what wonderful security to be carried along on the coattails of such certainty.

Yet.

"Good, huh, baby? Good?"

"Yes, Duane. Quite good."

Yet. Yet why, if Duane were so wonderful, life with him so very marvelous, why did everything seem so utterly wrong?

Okay, June, answer your own question. Wasn't it the tension, the tension of not telling him?

For a moment she lost her adult perspective on the golden bed, the royal blue bedroom, the cream-colored mansion in which she lived—the past, the present, the future, the landscape and the furnishings of her life. She knew that it was childish to allow oneself to become disassociated in this way, to let the connections go, to cast off, drift free. Childish. Irresponsible. Wrong.

Yet, right now in the middle of making love, the priceless chandelier floating over their massive brass bed was a jellyfish of muted sexual illumination, cut crystal tentacles lifted in the warm green water through which they swam together. And so she sailed her grand brass ship down from the blue ocean sky surface into the dark subterranean grotto where the passengers met great creatures from the nether world who wrestled with them in the madly heated contest of bodies some of them named love.

Yet it was dangerous for the child to stay out long, not even so long as the time spent in the habitual lovemaking that seemed sometimes their sole communication in this inherited house. So sometimes the adult tightened her fist and made the child scamper back inside.

"Honey, what's wrong? You . . . stopped. Did I do something wrong? Don't you feel good?"

Did you *not* do something, Duane? Would you once, just once, *not* do something?

Yet she loved him, loved his almost habitual flexibility, his willingess to find good sane reasons for her maddest intentions—the move to this disastrously impractical Los Angeles monstrosity, this eccentric's notion of a palace. "Definitely centrally located," he had said after the reading of the will. "Hey, we'll be near the recording studios, the really important clubs. And, hey, the place's almost right on the Hollywood Freeway, isn't it?"; and the very successful resumption of her music career despite the media response that portrayed her as a parasite, or, as one Bay Area critic pronounced, "a female vampire who feeds upon the creativity and originality of others," prompting Duane to insist to her that, "It's best you keep busy, honey. If you fold in the face of criticism, you'll never have a good opinion of yourself. And then where'll you be?"; and of her probably ill-advised decision to remove Edna from the shuttered suburban house and install her instead in one of the mansion's myriad guest bedrooms, Duane had offered that, "We won't have far to go to visit now, will we? Really, honey, I'm glad, because as old and sick as she is, you'd just be going back and forth to San Jose to tend to her if we hadn't."

And on and on and on.

Yes, Duane could justify her every whim. In the light of the success, the exposure, the money, shouldn't she regard that as just the most remarkable and wonderful talent ever? Well then, why did Duane's refusal to contradict a single one of her many requests make June feel so powerless, feeble, weak? Why? Want an answer? In giving in to her so completely, he seemed to be saying: I'm the one with the strength; I'm strong enough to go along with anything you want and still be the one on top; aren't I the most subtly commanding man you ever met?

"Well, yes."

"You like that, honey? That good? Oh, you sweet wonderful sexy thing. Are you almost there?"

"Almost."

Where? Which room? The formal dining room? The breakfast nook? One of the thirteen guest rooms? In some rooms sex, in others food. They did not screw on the tables or eat under sheets. Neat and regular and nice. A little husband, even a little wifey for company. See them in their tiny little four-story doll house? What's missing in this picture?

"June, did you make it, honey? What's wrong? You look strange."

I have something to tell you, Duane. Say it!

"Honey, you know, I really liked the way you were moving," he said. "That really helped; that was really good."

Sure it helped. He could be helped so very easily. Jealous, June? Sure. And she knew it, too—jealous of Duane's ability to be distracted into absolute contentment, to be philosophical about every problem known to man and woman and some in between, his ability to float through life like some sort of inflatable pool toy that never took a trip to the bottom of the chlorinated water. How could she not be jealous of someone for whom life was so easy, who succeeded with such facility? Her perfect, perfect husband.

"You're perfect, baby, just perfect."

"No," June softly enunciated. "I have something to tell you, Duane."

Eyes closed, he did not react. Sleeping, unconscious?
"Duane? I have something to tell you."

No reaction, no movement. Perhaps it might be best to broach the subject while he slept.

"Duane, I'm pregnant," June said. "What do you think of that?" So now it was out—her fear of a negative reaction.

Like a whale rising slowly from the ocean floor to feed Duane stirred, stiffened, seemed almost to tremble, and then abruptly sat up to the full height of his strong upper torso. "Pregnant? Pregnant? You're kidding, right?"

So intense, attentive, Duane seemed to have been startled into a hostility of alertness. She'd never seen him this way before.

"June, you *are* kidding?"

Unable to read his mood, she gave a reluctant shake of her head. "No. I'm not kidding."

"Oh!" The way his face contorted made her sure he would take a swing at her and flinched away only to be caught up in the triumphant onslaught of a bear hug embrace. "Oh, you great little woman! You great procreant fertile marvelous creature of a girl! You're going to make me a father? A papa? I'm going to be a daddy by the greatest rock star, greatest woman, greatest sex object of our time?"

June snorted in her effort not to laugh. He was a total madman!

"You're crazy."

"Crazy? Me? You're the cause, then—you sexy little miracle you! I wouldn't talk if I were you. But, hey, how do you feel? Are you okay? Anything you need, honey? How long are you going to keep performing?"

June looked away from him as if a forest vista opened up from the wall of their bedroom, an access to freedom. And perhaps it did. "I don't know," she said. "I really haven't thought about it. I think I'll wait until it's . . ."

Jumping up around her with his elbows, he was the old Duane again, attentive, solicitous, concerned. "Honey, you've got to think about . . . well, I guess it's your decision and all but . . ."

Now she realized why she had waited so long to tell him. She'd guessed at this urge to smother her with care.

"Honey," he said quietly, "I promise not to pressure you, but there's a few things I want you to consider—like trying to get that damned thing off your neck now that you're going to be a mother."

Ting-dong-dong-dong-dong! Ting-zing-dong-dong-dong-dong! It chimed, the Tibetan doorbell Bosley had installed to alert himself to visitors when he traveled to one of the far outposts of his house. "God damn!" Duane said. Not having retained the three attendants, they could choose only to answer or ignore the summons of the peeling bell.

Zing-tzing-dong-dong-dong!

"Shit," Duane said, "just when . . . what terrible timing! What time is it anyway? Well, I'll get it. Just stay here and I'll be back."

He slipped on a terry cloth robe, knotting the belt at the waist, and stomped across the deep shag rug out into the hallway that led to the staircase.

June stared at the smears she'd left on the pillowcase, crimson turning to that ugly rusty brownish-red. Thank god the chandelier was on dim because Duane thought that strange business was over with. She was the Midas of blood; she had the touch.

She slipped into her rainbow kimono and hurried to the linen closet for fresh sheets and pillowcases. It was when she returned to the master bedroom and began to change the sheets that she realized she was not alone.

Chapter Twenty-four:

House Guest

June worked wide-spread fingers into the opening of the silk case to slip it over the plump pillow supported against her thigh. She felt a touch, a tap, a signal.

Someone wanted her.

BONJOURS, JUNE!

"What . . .?" The pillowcase slipped from her fingers. June rubbed at her eyes. She had emerged from the pool, from kissing the pink tile bottom, from keeping her clear brown eyes open far too long. The chlorine afterglow furred everything, fastened a pious gassy halo of green mist to every object in the master bedroom. She rubbed and rubbed. She squinted and blinked. Failing to obliterate the magnetic exactitude of the metal filing mist, June kept her eyes open long enough to see the folds of textured moisture begin to swirl and shape and stand.

JUNE, MON CHERE.

"Yes?"

JUNE, DO YOU KNOW WHAT I LIKE?

"Oh, God!" And she'd been so very, very sure that

she'd licked her little problem, shaken the auditory DT's, hallucinations of the ear—since the success of Bloodrock, since her marriage, since moving into this house.

DO YOU KNOW WHAT I LIKE, JUNE?

Horrible in her head—yet what danger could there be in answering it? In talking back to a voice that wasn't there? (Oh . . . not much . . . just one nifty little snag called madness.)

JUNE?

"What do you want?"

JUST THIS. Something gripped her hands, but she could not look down to see who or what it was. Both palms and the white underside of her fingers felt sticky, as if she'd touched some milky cactus with hair-thin spines. Paralysis pervaded her body. Snap. Now. Lethal plant. Carnivorous vegetable life. Render the victim helpless in the instant before consumption.

Oh, she wanted to struggle. It was her only chance. The lust to struggle was the lust for life. But her body would not work and so all the struggling stayed right here in her mind, a peculiar sense of the world clenching and unclenching like some muscle of perception. Panic became a substitute for motion, confusion for action. Mentally, June thrashed and kicked and fought and resisted what she knew now to to be inevitable.

JUST THIS, JUNE.

I LIKE BABIES.

I LIKE BABIES BETTER THAN ANYTHING.

No!

YES. AND THAT IS WHY . . .

Of course, June started screaming. Her lips rubbery, dead, numb, the scream could only burst out bright and loud in the range war of her brain. Scrreeeam! Scrreeeam! And the room around her went away. The light left, the walls lifted out like myriad pieces of a board game put back in their box and placed on the high shelf in the closet, stored away for the night. Gone, everything that had been here. This is what happens when one sleeps in the room that belonged to someone you loved who died. It is natural. It always happens. Everything is taken away. And you are alone. And there is the attack.

AND THAT IS WHY I CAN WAIT EIGHT MONTHS MORE. IT HAS BEEN A LONG TIME.

(*Screeeam. Screeeam.*)

She heard the voice with which she screamed. She heard it in her body. She heard it in her head. She heard it in the air she breathed. It reverberated through Bosley's invisible mansion, the huge vacuum which had been a house, a massive grey presence, pregnant restless void. Reverberated, strained at doors of perception, to get loose, get beyond, burst on through to the other side. Heard the volume of her own voice, the voice in her mind, the voice of her scream, its strength, its terrified vigor.

For the briefest foolish second she let herself admire her own awesome power. Then she heard the laugh.

In her ear? Over her shoulder? In her lap? Over her head? Modulating like a musical note, the laugh expounded upon her screaming brain, detailing the extent to which it was impressed.

Trapped, imprisoned, rendered helpless by this paralysis, useless, and futile, her screaming, June knew, she had nowhere to go. She could not project it out any longer. But it continued to grow. Size. Volume. Pressure. Heat. Her scream had to burst wide the chamber that confined it, burst open the small rounded bone that packaged it, this little convoluted cavern, this skull jail. Burst, burst!

SCREEAM!

June felt the insidious moisture along her legs.

The hands tightened on her wrists, an irresistible tug and pull, an urge to come on down to where it no longer mattered.

Down. Down.

She had to scream again, and more, and louder, even if her head must open wide, her life split wide apart to accomodate the violence of the scream, volumes of immeasurable emotion, boundless vistas of fear. Go ahead, open. Go ahead, come on out and. . . .

. . . .come on out and play, June!

AND THAT IS WHY, MON CHERE, I WILL TAKE IT FROM YOU, PINK AND SQUIRMING.

Danny Driscoll's bloody grinning ecstatic face filled her field of vision like a giant marine creature rising through ocean darkness to extend beyond the frame of a scuba mask.

"June!"

What a wonderfully deep rich voice that bedroom door possessed, despite its agitation! And how surprising, to find such concern in an off-white mahogany portal. Too bad the woman toward whom such warmth was supposed to be directed no longer had a need for such display. Unhappy woman, unhappy door. Unhappy voice here in this boiler room of bone, in the last possible second before the steam sings its true song and the walls crack, split, and open up all.

"My God, what's she doing down there?"

"June—what the fuck?"

Smash. Steps, thuds.

Heavy hands. Quick hands. Holding. Shaking!

(Too late. Too late.)

"June, June honey, come on! Snap out of it!"

Snap out of it? A Classic phrase on which the needle can ride to put the pressure level . . . just over . . . the top.

"June? It's me, Larry! Hey, what the fuck are you

doing with your eyes glued back in your head, huh? Get 'em back right, damn you! You look spacey like that..."

... just ... over ... the fucking ...

"... and if you don't come out of it, we'll make you go sing with the Starship or something, huh? Lost your way back to earth?"

That hurts.

That switch being thrown like that.

That return to this room hurts.

"Okay. That's better. Those beautiful blue eyes look a hell of a lot more becoming when they line up in front, June, kind of like a row of slot machine cherries or blueberries, I guess. Blackberries?"

Hurts? Laugh?

"Hey, that's better yet!"

June's eyes let light in once again.

"Hi, beautiful," the musician said.

"Hi, Larry."

"What's cooking?" he said. "What's shakin'?"

June laughed, her head thrashing through an involuntary shiver. What was she doing on the floor with her whole body pinned, paralyzed? She tried to struggle up.

Duane, elbowing Larry aside, gave her his arm to help her up and out from under the mattress that wedged her in against the wall. "June," he whispered, his back turned to Larry like an acoustic barrier, "what the hell are you doing down here? Is this some kind of game? Or are you having some sort of ... some kind of fit or something?"

June turned her pert classic profile toward him, since looking away was the only answer she could give to his question.

Duane bent closer and pinched her ear hard between his fingers. "You tell me you're pregnant and then you go and do this! What am I supposed to believe, that you're possessed or something? Come on, June, shape up!" He shot a glance back over his shoulder.

Shuffling nervously, Larry spoke in a mock-cowboy drawl. "I'm butting in on you folks. I'll just let myself out, if I can find the way . . ."

"No, Larry—stay!" June said. "Please." She watched anger spread over Duane's face as he finally realized that she was naked. Rising to one knee, he shielded her body from Larry's line of vision while reaching behind him to fetch the loose heap of folded silk from the rug. "Here," he said. "Put this on. Hurry up." She thought that the quality of his concern was that of a store owner surveying merchandise unsettled by an earthquake. (Nestled in the carpet, she could see it, she imagined—happy, feeding on all this disruptive emotion, growing inevitably stronger, larger.)

YES, JUNE. C'EST VRAI. IT IS ME.

"Well," Duane said, inexplicably sighing as if relieved. "Thank God you're all right." He tugged the mattress back onto the bed with a few quick emphatic maneuvers that seemed to indicate that he wanted no help. "I'm going to straighten this place up." He looked at June as if to say that only a crazy woman could have done such damage to this room. "What did you do in here, June?" he said, trying to smile. "Did you try to stage a one-woman Who finale or something?" He fell to his knees and began sweeping broken shards of crockery with the heel of his hand. Then he stared back at her and Larry over his shoulder. "Why don't you show Larry the rest of our magnificent house. I'm afraid he didn't have a chance to get the class A tour after we heard you screaming."

Larry set his hands on his hips and rolled his eyes in critical praise of the bedroom's decor and dimensions. "Sounds good," he said. "Quite a little bungalow."

"Ummm." Duane busied himself with the patch of rug between his knees.

June tugged the rainbow kimono close around her breasts and watched Larry cock his fingers in the belt loops of his jeans. Scowling, willfully darkening, he seemed to be conjuring all his arrogance to fight the easy grandeur of this house. But why? Resentment? Jealousy?

I'M HERE, JUNE. YOUR HUSBAND IS NOT SO EFFICIENT AS HE THINKS.

She resisted looking back over her shoulder as she pushed Larry out.

"Come on—please?"

Chapter Twenty-five:

Rock 'N' Roll Mausoleum

The moment they were out of her husband's sight Larry yanked her to him into the elegant gloom of an apparently interminable corridor. Somewhere outside, in the night beyond these walls, the western world was pretending that the season was spring.

Squeezing her arm hard and shoving his face to hers, Larry demanded, "Does this shit happen all the time?"

June scanned the hallway. What if Duane were to follow? She looked back into Larry's face, frightened by the ferocity of his apparent concern.

"No," she said at last. "This is . . ."

"The first time? Okay, then it ought to be the last, too. Leave here with me, June. This spook house of a dump's no place for you."

If only you knew, she thought. But instead of saying it she laughed. "Larry, I see you almost every night—I mean, it's hard for me to feel *that* way about you, because . . ."

(did i tell you what i like from them, june, the little ones, the babies?)

Larry relaxed the pressure on her upper arms. "Sure," he said. "I feel the same, so I've . . . got some news for you."

She looked at her feet which were lost in the shadow of her own body on the ugly dark blue and maroon art nouveau carpet. "I have news, too," she said.

Neither spoke. They'd reached an impasse as if her announcement had blocked his in a game that had become much more than casual.

(their little smiles, their little mouths)

Larry looked up at the shadowy vaulted ceiling as if he'd heard something.

"Come on down this way." June's hand pushed air like a swinging door. "I'll show you some of the sights."

"Sure . . . something to tell my grandkids."

"It's not so special," she said. "It's just that you haven't been out before so . . ."

"You don't take me seriously," he said, following with obvious reluctance. "The only men you take seriously are the ones who talk to you about money and mortgages and marriage."

That hurt June. Of course, Larry had meant for it to do so. Still, she had come to depend on him in more ways than she liked to admit.

(stay here, give birth to your child here, june, mon chere)

Larry stopped and cocked his head as if to listen. After months of living with her, Duane had never heard that voice. So how could she hope that Larry would do so? No, it was no more than coincidence.

"See the carvings?" June said quickly, shoving at the door. "All supposedly authentic druidic emblems. And, well, look inside for yourself . . ."

Why was it so hard to be casual about his physical presence, as if some frayed electric connection inside mended when he was near?

Larry stopped just inside the paneled high-ceilinged room. "Dolls? A room full of dolls? Bosley didn't seem like the kind of guy . . ."

"His wife collected them, Larry. Porcelain, paper-mâché, wood, marble, bone, chalk, apple, cloth—she looked for substance first, shape second. After she died, he decided to keep them just as they were. Look at the faces."

Larry nodded, bending to eye the nearest row of dolls, fashioned from foil, aluminum, gift wrap, gold. Each doll had affixed to its face the photograph of a homey middle-aged woman. "His wife? So how does it feel to be the owner of the world's foremost spook house—now that you've replaced *her*, I mean? You realize that you *are* the new mistress here."

She followed him out the narrow doorway, reaching back inside to flick off the light. "Don't mock me, please."

"June, I'm not . . ."

(let me pick, like dolls, like tiny living)

Larry stopped just outside the door, his face showing an abrupt angry uncertainty. "Do you have a radio on around here?"

June shook her head. How good to have him here. If only she could keep him from going!

Larry snapped his fingers. "Hey, didn't the priest throw a doll into the coffin just before they sealed it up? Was it one of hers?"

"It was Elvis. You didn't look under the photo masks, Larry. Each doll's a rock musician; he was her favorite—excluding her husband. Bosley liked to brag that he was the only rocker not represented in her collection, and he said that he and Elvis would be buried together with his wife. Please, I want to show you at least one more room."

Hands in back pockets like oversized wallets, Larry, head bowed, strode down the eerie hallway beside her. "Funny," he said. "Bosley's funeral was really frustrating and almost kind of weird the way it was so normal and humdrum. Just your typical funeral service, as if he were never famous, never into the occult, never . . . owned this place."

"What did you expect, Larry? It was a funeral, not a stage show."

"Yeah, but wasn't his rep always supposed to be that he wasn't putting on an act? That at least some of it was real? I mean, there wasn't even one solitary mourner dressed weird. Now that's really . . . strange.

"Oh, by the way, Danny's doing great and says to say hi. His physical therapist told me he should be walking by summer."

"Good," she said. "Good." All she wanted to do was show the house, this house that spoke more convincingly for Bosley than anything in his life—except his music. "So what's your news?"

"Huh! No way! You first!"

The corridor dead-ended into a massive wooden door bristling with bas-relief figures in a pastoral setting. June pushed; it opened and illuminated itself instantaneously like the interior of a refrigerator. Cold light revealed an artistic arrangement of body-sized boxes made from materials as varied as bronze, maple, copper and pine.

Annoyed, Larry scratched his head. "So this is where you sacrifice your overnight guests? I get it—she collected dolls and he collected . . . these." He reached into the front pocket of his blue jeans and brought out a tiny paper packet, carefully folded and bound tightly with a rubber band that he slipped off immediately. He kept his eyes squarely on her eyes as he undid the thumb-sized packet, as if doing so would prevent her from noticing the business of his fingers. "What do you call a house that displays coffins, June? You're a vivacious, warm, creative person. I can't believe you're living in a fucking mortuary!"

The contents of the packet peeked out now—blue, red, bright green, striped, the pills glittering like serpent's eyes.

"Going up?" he said. "Going down? First floor: vets, v.d., veteran cosmic . . ."

"You're not going to . . .?"

"Of course not," he said, popping a frighteningly abrupt choice of capsules into his mouth. He dry-swallowed and smiled. "Gulp," he said and straddled the handsome mahogany coffin that an inscription identified as a replica of that in which Jimi Hendrix had been interred.

Larry propped a foot up on the ledge of the open casket, hopped up to sit and swung his legs inside. He yawned. He looked longingly down into the satin enclosure. "Kinda sleepy. Mind if I nap in here a minute?"

"Larry, one day you're going to take one too many of those—or the wrong combination—and and it *is* going to be you in there, for good."

"Sounds fine to me," he said, "just fine." He lowered himself into the luxurious box. "Nice. Definitely more comfortable than my last motel room on the road with you. Ah, yes, room service please? Yes, this is Larry Ludwig. I'm a very major, very important rock star and I'd like . . ."

The voice died.

June strode to the coffin and looked down at a stereotypical corpse, eyes closed, hands folded on the chest, a slight smile carefully fixed on the rigid face.

"Hello, hotel maid. It's about time. I'll have a double shot of embalming fluid on the rocks and make it snappy. I haven't got forever."

June felt like stomping her foot but did not want to give him the satisfaction.

"Larry, you said you had some news. What is it?"

The corpse smile came undone. "This weird shit," he said, eyes open now. "I can't take it any more."

What did he mean? This room? The house? The attack on her he'd witnessed?

"The success is nice," Larry said, sitting up in the coffin. "Kind of. But the audiences have been getting weirder—and younger, June; you have to've noticed. And you, well, look at this place. June, this house is a fucking mausoleum, not fit for human habitation. You don't believe me? Call the fucking surgeon general. You've surrounded yourself with money and possessions and plastic people and you're going down, June. I don't like seeing it happen to you. Maybe I can't stop it, but I'm not going to see it through to the bloody end. I'm quitting the band, June. I'm quitting Bloodrock."

"You're kidding."

Larry climbed out of the fancy box, shaking his head. "No way. I don't want to end up as one of your exhibits in here. No way—and you'd say the same thing if you knew what was good for you. Come on, June! Let's get out of here, just like kids again. We can hit the open road in my old van and listen to classic rock tapes all the way down to TJ. Hey, the waves are great this time of year and I know a little bar where . . ."

I'm pregnant, she wanted to say then, to stop him dead. That would be the acid test, to see if he really wanted a pregnant middle-aged woman along to share this adolescent odyssey. I'm pregnant, she would say.

And he would stop and gawk and then he'd say *do you really intend to bring a child up in a haunted house*? And more, much more. But she doubted very much that he would continue to wax romantic about the siren call of the open road. And he would certainly manage to forget to extend again his gallant offer to rescue her from this malevolent abode.

"So what's your news?" he said.

She was almost frightened into telling him. Could he read minds, too?

"Nothing, Larry—just something about the band. Now that you're quitting, it doesn't matter. It doesn't matter at all."

"June, don't be a pretender. Come with me."

"*You* come with *me*," she said, "right down this corridor and . . ." She knew he would follow, not wanting to be left alone in the display room with the lights out. "See that section of ceiling there where the cracks are? Duane's going to put a skylight there for me so that I can have a plant room with a sprinkler system and . . ."

Larry touched her shoulder, just with the tip of one finger. "No matter how many living things you drag in here and sacrifice to this ridiculous pretentious joint, June, it's still going to be a death house. Can't you see that?"

She bowed her head. "I never knew you were so superstitious."

"Yeah?" he said and pinned her against the rough plaster wall, and arm on either side of her shoulders, his head dipped dangerously close to her chest. "Yeah?"

June turned her head to take the warmth and welcome claustrophobia of his breath on her cheek. What did he mean to do? Oh, she knew. Duane would come and find them posed like this and assume—what was the cliché?—the worst. And sometimes in Larry's company she knew she came close to relishing the idea of letting the worst come to pass. Nice fantasy, sure. But the reality was that her husband was back there somewhere in the manageable darkness, crawling around on hands and knees to clean up after her. He was an adult; why could she not be the same?

"Larry, would you please let me . . ."

"Have you looked at yourself in a mirror lately, June? Stage pallor? Fine—we've all got it; look at me. But you haven't got a lick of color in your face anymore. For a while I thought it was part of the ghoul routine for the show, like Ozzy with his vampire teeth and werewolf make-up. But when I saw you and Duane standing next to each other after he pulled you out from under that mattress, you with your ghost face and him with his Tab Hunter tan, I . . . Where the hell's he find that much sun, huh?"

Averting her eyes, June did blush a bit. "Okay, I'll use more rouge—just for you." She bit her lip at the stupid flirtatiousness of this. Inappropriate, June, absolutely unconscionable!

"Don't be ridiculous. You know I'm only saying stuff about your face because it's a picture of what's going on inside you. I'm talking about what you've become, June. You used to be political, concerned about people. You used to be an artist. You used to be a thinker, a person, a mensch. Now look at you! S & M metaphysics instead of ideas; gimmicks over real emotion; glitter over directness and substance. You and Duane don't have a marriage; you coexist in a partnership! Bloodrock has become a corporate asset instead of a performing band. Me, I'm sick of the whole thing."

June risked engaging his eyes, then wished she hadn't. "So you hate us. You're leaving Bloodrock. Great.

Terrific. But just leave me alone, alright?"

"No." With monstrous slowness he shook his shaggy head. "I got selfish reasons to want you alive. I want your body for myself. I want your body to serve my sexual whims whenever. Duane may not know how . . ."

"Oh, Duane does very very well."

"Uh huh. Sure. What's he do? Take a roll of hundred dollar bills and ream you out? Money. Possessions. Status. Security. He's fucking you over with this shit, June. I can't give you any of that crap, haven't got it. Only got this old wasted body of mine and a few half-smoked joints—oh, and a little thing called personal freedom. You know? F-r-e-e-d-o-m? Freedom? Ever heard of it? Seems like something you don't know much about these days."

(in the darkness, around this corner and up the stairway, i am waiting outside the old woman's room, june, i'm waiting)

"You'd better go, Larry. Just go."

June didn't expect these lame words to have the slightest affect on him; in fact, she realized that she probably hoped they wouldn't.

"Yeah," he said, releasing her, spinning on his heels to stride away. "I guess you're right. Damn right!"

He moved away like a machine, not a friend, not a fellow band member, not the warm breath that had been all over her face, so accusing, so painful. No, she'd made a mistake; she had to tell him.

"Larry? Larry?"

But he had already managed to make good his escape.

June is aware in her dream that she thinks she is dreaming. This awareness strikes her as reminiscent of consciousness. It is possible that it is not a dream? She

BLOODROCK

struggles to move as if awake. The universe shivers into bright color. She sees herself onstage performing. Larry is with her—and Bosley, too. How happy, oh, how happy she feels!

She listens closely to the music she is playing. Bloodrock! The sound is unmistakable—rich texture, jazz undertones, sophisticated shifting rhythms. Yet it is quite different. The difference is disturbing. The difference is reminiscent of being confused over whether one's waking moments are a dream or reality or, in fact, a dream of reality.

It feels good to be performing again. She hefts her almost weightless rhythm guitar and guns the group into yet another marathon of unrelenting creativity, improvising, tying together two three four tunes from their songbook into some impossibly lovely musical mutation. Singing feels good. Improvising feels good. It feels good to be surrounded by virile young musicians giving everything they have to this auditory world view.

She looks somewhere. She looks stage center. There is a dais there, a little low table draped in blue, fringed in white. She tries to see the dais as a separate object in all the universe. There is an urgency to do this. It is something important. Something important to her. She focuses her mind to the dais. It deflects momentarily.

She sees Larry smile. It is a signal, prearranged to look spontaneous. She congratulates herself on this sleeper's awareness. They move down-center to the little table. They play music. She sings. The crowd responds. The group triumphs in the air and walls around them. The music comes to a crescendo of lyrical bedlam. She sees they have reached the moment of theatrical climax. She looks down into the crib ensconced on the dais with the blue cover and the white fringe. How beautiful her baby is. She hears the voice.

It is Bosley's voice. Larry smiles. It is time. It is time for the sacrifice. The act must be concluded. All shows have a final act. The final act should be dramatic. He raises his axe. And she raises hers. It is necessary. There is no other way. It is for the blood. We must suffer. For the blood. No other way.

"No!"

Chapter Twenty-six:

More Guests

"Try to get a hold of yourself, June. No more fits, okay? OKAY? We've been married—what?—three, three-and-a-half months now? I was humiliated last night in front of that hobo guitarist of yours, you wallowing on the floor with nothing on like a madwoman! And then going off God-knows-where with him for hours . . ."

"Less than an hour," June said.

She handed Duane his briefcase without looking at him. He'd made it clear that he'd had the engagement for weeks and was not, certainly not leaving because of this little disagreement.

"You're a star, June, a sophisticated star, not one of these self-destructive highway-to-hell types. Right? RIGHT? And now, now you're a mother-to-be, to boot. Please, June! Please promise me that there'll be no more fake fits, no more of this play-acting about psychic attacks and voices and visitations in the night! Please? Please, sweetie pie?"

June straightened the starched lapel of her husband's

peach-colored pin stripe sport coat, the one he always wore when he'd psyched himself up for closing a deal. She felt very lucky not to have revealed her most recent dream. Yet this secrecy made her feel like a . . . like a what? What was she?

"I'll do my best," June said.

"That's the ticket!" Duane seemed genuinely warmed by her tepid words. "Oh, and by the way, I'll call your bass player Bruce and ask him if he knows an up-and-coming young lead guitarist who's hot. Also, I've got an appointment tomorrow to see that fusion drummer from Laguna just in case our dear Mr. Travers continues to miss rehearsals. So everything's proceeding just great and right on schedule. Right?"

"Right," June said. Yes, she had to remember she would be a mother. She had to regulate herself, systematize herself, to wean herself away from the occasionally chaotic life she'd led as a performer. With Larry gone, that part of her life was gone too. She had to start her new life now. "Have a good trip, Duane. Please take good care of yourself; make good deals. Call me?"

"Of course, honey! And hey!—don't worry about Larry. He'll be back. Begging. We'll hire another guy until then and we won't even let him know that we're interested when he comes crawling back. Right? Right. Now listen, you take care and . . ."

And he trailed off as he shut the door behind him.

. . . leaving June with words in her mouth. "Don't bet on it, Duane. Larry isn't like you."

(don't forget your future dreams, so soon, so real, so soon)

Knock. Knock. Knock.

She shook her head, something she'd caught herself doing rather frequently. Questions. Why had she steered Larry away from her grandmother's section of the house?

Knock.

Perhaps Duane wanted back in. Perhaps one of the habitual denizens of the shrubs on the far side of the gate had overcome at last the mental barrier of a fan and dared to apply his actual knuckles to this actual door. Perhaps what knocked out there was no more than the figure behind the voice in her head.

To live like this alone.

To live a day without performing, without writing.

To live a day without friends, without Larry.

To live with the baby in her belly, the voice in her head, the soul gone from her body.

She could not. She could not.

Knock. Knock. Knock.

(petite, june, only me, remember let no one else into this house of ours, you need only me, and the baby, remember our baby)

June Lockwood Lombard stared at her front door. She could not stand being alone in the house for nine months. She taught herself to be frightened of what could be outside. And so she stood and stared at the door. She stared at the door that spoke in sudden spiky percussive coughs of sound.

Was this like her? To let herself get paralyzed out of the normal flow of life? To think her way into a mental corner of passivity? Was this the *real* June Lockwood . . . Lombard?

"Hello? Who's there?"

But she knew the answer before it came—it had to be Duane. No, no, of course not! Betty and Ivan were coming up sometime this week!

"It is me. You remember me. I am a friend of Mr. Broderick."

Remember? A thousand grotesque faces splashed across the empty screen and jammed together, a wad of film spliced too thick to pass through the threader.

"Duane?"

Knock.

"Please. It would be good that you opened. You would feel that the benefit went to you."

June touched the round brass knob. Huge pictorial fingerprints, germs, a pair of eyes and animated tongue.

"You know who I am. Like you, I believe in the eternal spirit that is Bosley Broderick. I want to help you. I cannot help you if you do not . . ."

June twisted the living knob that pushed voraciously into her hand to rush against her abdomen as the door swung fully open.

"Oh."

"Hello, June Lockwood Lombard. I hope you are pleased to see me here. It is the one place in this world where I belong."

"Yes, of course, Mr. . . Reformer."

For a moment she had been sure it was the mist, green and persuasive, subtly putrescent, traveling backward somehow to the bright blooming moment of blood. It was a relief to see Reformer. But much, much too inevitable to be comfortable. It was the relief that comes when the body has taken at last the full weight of the lowered stone.

He resembled nothing quite so much as a civilized caricature of the massive genie newly freed from the lamp. His blue three-piece suit fit over his frame like the blanket from a moving van over a formidable chest of drawers. Staring down at her from a certain height, he seemed easily capable of standing absolutely still for a considerable period of time. June imagined engaging him in a staring contest and began to blink repeatedly, as if she felt her eyes to be drowning.

"It is all right that I am here? I would like to stay here. It is true that I belong here."

June's hand fluttered ineffectually to her throat. She could not feel the bloodrock that had been so conveniently available whenever a bloody act had wanted to occur. Her hand wandered on her chest like a child lost in the dizzy familiarity of its own house. Ah, she had it. And now she could feel it throbbing in her hand. If only she could pull it off and end the horrible visions, the green mist, the voice, the decay within, the blood spattering her legs and feet, spattering the endless grey corridors within.

"No."

The single bulbous hand softly enclosed her hand and squeezed until her nervous twitching stopped entirely.

"Never do that. Never try to take the Bloodrock from your neck. It is all that stands between you and your prescribed death. It is all that intervenes between your unborn child and . . ."

"You can't know that!"

"Yes. I can know that."

"Well . . ." June's eyes strayed, searching for any way out of the focus that burned and hurt and strained them.

"It is Mr. Broderick's wish that I live with you always in this house in which he first made contact with the ancient and eternal truths."

She did not look, did not speak, did not think.

"Your husband will be happy. He will understand. It will be good with me here."

June did not try to think of a way of getting him out of the house. Reformer was here. An image actually flashed into her mind of the mansion being plucked right off the entire extent of its acreage, leaving the bald giant standing there naked and alone like a doll a child tired of sheltering.

"Yes, you will need this. And, of course, you will need also your own courage, your own great courage . . ."

Did Reformer have a terminal grip on the rock? At the bottom of her field of vision June could see his hand shaking with the object in his grip just under her chin. Had the intensity of squeezing melded hand and medallion? Because blood trickled artfully from the open crevices of his hand, running down his wrist and dripping on the imported oval carpet under their feet, eyelets of darkness in the multicolored pattern.

June tried to step back, but the chain around her neck stopped her, digging into the folds of flesh in her freckled neck. She saw how loosely he gripped the rock, how his fingers curled around it like the petals of an unfolding flower.

Then the blood that flowed from his hand seemed to change. No longer oozing or flowing, it bubbled up now like a spring that rises out of itself, only to subside eventually back into the confines of itself, a liquid phoenix whose brief life she alone was being allowed to witness. As images began to appear, June decided that it had to be a trick or illusion perhaps a holographic projection. (Perhaps the rock was—had been—some kind of holograph all along.) Unbelieving, aware of being deceived by her own eyes, June watched shapes, scenes, stories, a narrative of blood. A face, tiny—yet immensely present here in the fluid film—grinned, laughed with crazy passion, gave a zany grimace all the more shocking when one realized what a large effect came from such miniaturization—Bosley Broderick. He raised a dagger, clearly delighting in the ponderous theatricality of drawing out the gesture. Seeming to glint from a nonexistant light source, the blade appeared to be a smaller version of the instrument June had witnessed used on the squalling peacock. Except it was no bird depicted there in the liquid illusion but a dais with a blue coverlet on which a child rested, a baby, perhaps asleep. The very precision of miniature detail drew the viewer into the significance of the sight. Now the huge face changed, the laugh changed, the blade fell.

"Oh, God, no! What are you doing? Why are you in my house?"

As if awakened from a trance, Reformer closed his fingers on the dry medallion, snuffing plumes of flame, staunching a gushing wound, shutting the projector down. He let it slide out between his fingers to slap quietly back into place on June's pale chest. "You saw nothing but what will happen if you leave this house. I must live here. You must live here forever to let your baby live. Here Mr. Broderick protects us."

June pointed down at Reformer's fist. "But it was Bosley that . . ."

"No." He shook his bald head slowly so that the whole upper hemisphere changed in response to the chandelier in the cathedral ceiling high overhead. "No. That is not what you saw. There is no magic. You saw the future that is contained within you. Sometimes this is given to us just as sometimes we dream."

"Then . . .?"

"I am tired. I wish to sleep now."

Reflexively, June gestured toward the stairs rising to the second floor where the closed doors of bedrooms ranged away in both directions.

"Yes," he said, "that is true."

She did not have to show him the way.

Fretful, frustrated, June patted the cushion of the Empire sofa on which she rested and watched the dust gently churn in the plane of sunlight warming her knees. She wished she had watched Reformer choose his room.

At the time she had been so certain that she would be able to tell afterwards, that it was not necessary to watch him, to spy. But now she could not tell. And because she could not tell, it seemed very important to know. She imagined Duane returning home, exclaiming at the news, questioning her as to Reformer's whereabouts. The fact that she could not answer he would take as further evidence of increasing instability, an impending breakdown.

If only she had watched him.

Somewhere in the middle of her self-accusatory reverie, June became aware that the front door was at it again. How strange that she had positioned herself on the one sofa that directly faced it!

knock

"It's Reformer again," she told herself. "I saw a 'Night Gallery' like this one time—a woman meeting herself at her own door over and again—except it'll be Reformer at the door forever. So I've found my purpose here . . ."

knock

She had nervously wandered through the house for most of the late morning and early afternoon. She had touched her knuckles to the door of her grandmother's bedroom twice and once put her ear to the cold white-enameled wood to hear the eerie perpetual drone of soap opera voices, like sounds from another dimension. And she had tested each door on either side of the stairway. She could detect nothing. It was the utter absence of any sense of life behind a single door that had jangled, had disturbed, had shaken her. Had she imagined it all, the knocking, entrance, dialogue, vision?

knock knock

Wasn't it always like this when she wasn't performing, when she wasn't actively engaged in the

Chapter Twenty-Seven:

The Gorgeous Patient

A sunlit green paradise floated all around her. She saw it through the narrow slits.

"June? June? Open your eyes."

No. It was wonderful here. Here she lived each moment of a child's life with the exquisite enjoyment of a grown-up. She would die before relinquishing this sun-flooded green world.

"June, honey?"

Don't answer. Don't dare let loose of the warm bright flowers dying to breathe in your moist little hand. Keep your fist deeply embedded in the lion's hot dry mane, his fur thirsty as harvest wheat. Do not be tempted by the perfect regular dead ticking, the flickering of pretend life on the other side.

"June, you can do it, honey! I know you can do it! Come on and . . ."

Too many years had passed since she had entered this golden forest paradise. How fortunate to be offered this final miraculous chance to live eternally as an adult-child in the kingdom where pleasure and pain compliment each other like lovingly seasoned foods.

"June, the doctor says you can wake up if you want to. Please, try, June. If not for yourself, then think of your . . ."

No, she did not want to be a baby. What she wanted, she had—the body of a youth, the conscious apprehension of maturity, the appetite for unending pleasure and experience of an adolescent blessed with the bounty of eternal life.

Now, for the briefest moment in this twilight kingdom, she glimpsed her own lithe body, turning in the purple gold of the sun's last rays. She spied the meaningfully beautiful round of flesh atop her pelvis, sharply outlined against the electric blue sky. She saw herself reach down to touch her mound of a stomach.

"That a girl, June! It's alright! It's alright. Open . . ."

June risked letting the narrow slits gape wide. But what she squinted into life was not the wrong side of the screen, the world of her mother. The hanging green growth, the man, the lion, it all seemed to have reappeared . . . out there.

"June, this is Dr. Frederick who's been nice enough to remain with us through the, ah, crisis that . . ."

"Think nothing of it," boomed the roguishly mustached doctor, a walrus of a man.

The bloodrock throbbed on June's throat.

Danger near. Danger near.

She squinted again, then ventured to open her eyes by degrees.

Yes, somewhere on the periphery of vision the green mist waited to be ushered in by . . . her mother? Impossible to say. But what a delight to see her sister, her nephew, an enormous bald man, and other recognizable figures here with her in this gorgeous floating place of plants feeding in the yellow diffused glow of sourceless light. To know how a dolphin feels. To arrive at last in shallow warm water to sing forever in the slanting sunlight only feet below the surface.

"Please, June," Duane begged. "The doctor assured me that you could speak if you really tried, if you really cared about me, about our baby, about yourself. See, there are people who love you here and all they want is . . ."

Focus faltered. Husband wavered . . . and green mist took his hand. When he walked away forever into mist this garden would go grey forever with death. No! She had to make them stay. "Please . . ." The attempted voice faltered into silence; she'd pushed too hard. "Please." That felt right, just the right degree of force. "Please don't go away from me now."

Duane took her hand but she did not feel his cool dry skin.

"Stay with me," June said. "We'll all have so much fun here—I promise! When I came here as a little girl, I always thought I'd have to play by myself forever. But now you're here!"

"June? June, honey?"

"Just think," she said, "we always dreamt in our most secret fantasies of a perfect place where there was always pleasure and always anticipation of pleasure—no guilt, no fatigue. And now we're here together."

"Sssssh!" Duane said, his mouth inches from her ear. "June, sssssh."

"And even if they should close the door now, we're all on the right side of it, aren't we?" She seemed to get a signal from their faces. "Aren't we? We are on the inside, aren't we?"

Standing, Duane spread his arms expansively, a host at a failed party.

"Well, that's going to be it for today, everybody," he announced, gesturing to the door. "June's just a little . . . a little disoriented this afternoon. I'm sure you can understand, with everything she's been through . . ."

Betty jumped up excitedly, as if the group had made a triumphant decision, and yanked her son toward the open door. "Congratulations again, Duane!" she called. "Father-to-be—so exciting!"

"Yes! Thanks!" He waved them out. "Be with you in ten minutes," he whispered to Dr. Frederick, who lowered his head to exit, pulling the door quietly shut behind him.

Duane swiveled on his heels, slapping his hands together, a nervous comedian uncertain of the crowd. "Well, June . . ."

"They all went away, didn't they? I'm not really inside, am I?"

No longer constrained to maintain an appearance, Duane moved closer now to take a good long look at what had become of the woman he loved. "June, do you know who I am?"

"Taxman. But I did declare the pennies. You forgot to set up the silver screen."

"Duane. Yes, I'm Duane, your husband. And I love you very much. And no matter how long it takes"—he snatched up both her cool passive hands—"no matter how long we have to work, I promise you, June, we're going to get you better. We're going to get you better than better!"

"Why, Duane? What's wrong?"

"Huh?" Her sudden alertness, made Duane rock back as if a firecracker had exploded in his face. "I . . . June, are you . . . ?"

She scrutinized the details of the absolutely unfamiliar room. She had no answer for her husband.

Duane buzzed around the bed like an insecure tour guide compensating for his inexperience by an interminable flow of solictious energy. "Like the plants? I know we discussed an arboretum under the central skylight, but this room gets beautiful morning sun and all this lovely afternoon light. You don't mind, I hope. Well . . . recognize the hangers? Remember that little white-haired lady at the bank down on Santa Monica who you talked to about Picasso? She did them all specially for you. Just finished yesterday! Think you're going to like the room?"

Had she blacked out? It had felt so good imagining that she was a child—but enough was enough. How much incoherence had they witnessed from her, the gathered well-wishers? What had become of the happy stable well-adjusted June Lockwood once alleged to be too sane and normal, too level-headed to succeed as a rock star?

"Right, honey? A perfect opportunity, huh? No excuses. No hard feelings. We just tell everybody we're not breaking any contracts, we're just taking a hiatus. We won't even say 'maternity leave'; let them come up with that. What could be more sensible. Right, honey, right?"

He did not mean to play the jailer to her inmate. No, one would be deemed mad, quite mad, to hint that the rest cure Duane outlined in any way resembled a prison term. Right, June, right?

"And Reformer showing up—what luck, huh? I mean, just when we need a sort of butler or whatever, not that he'll do much other than look good. And even Betty isn't allergic to a little mopping and dusting; her kid's hyper but he's good at washing dishes. So there you are! We all love you! Everything's great. Everything's taken care of! Your job is to sit back and relax. Sound good?"

Why? June lifted an absurdly pale arm. Hubris? Because she had got carried away with delusions of grandeur concerning her flimsy artistry, the meager life force she transported of this 110 pound frame? Was she a female Faust, faltering, falling? Was that it?

"A great publicity angle once we decide to unretire, huh? Wasn't overexposure our one big fear? So—one, a nice long rest; two, just let Dr. Frederick work through this with you until you feel like yourself again; three, have our beautiful child and rest and take care of both of you and then in a year or two . . . But first, get that 39.5 hemoglobin count up, right honey? Oh, called your mother. She can't make it this weekend because of her volunteer work for the campaign but she promised to see us next week. Great, huh?"

June appreciated his concern. Of course she did. But she had no way to show it without simply lying. She was a little girl making big girl money. She couldn't help it that she had fooled people. If she got real real lucky, maybe someday she too would believe that she was big enough to have a baby.

"Right, honey? June, are you crying?"

Duane seized her with ferocious conviction. "It's okay, little girl. I love you, I love you! It's okay!"

"Please help me, Duane. Help me!"

Duane rocked her back and forth with an almost violent rhythm on the early American bed, chanting reassurances all the while.

Then she felt it, the familiar itch, the warm trickle starting its trek down the delicate contours of her throat. She held his chest off just enough to avoid staining his argyle sweater; he didn't need to know.

Chapter Twenty-eight:

Carry the Blood to Term

June wanted out. Of the bed. Of this room. Of the God damned house. She wanted out.

Now!

Confined, claustrophobic, antsy, ready to do anything for a stroll in the garden, June daydreamed strips of rhetoric to plaster on her husband's restrictions. Look here, darling, if I'm going to deliver the kind of healthy baby we both want, I need more exercise than I can get in here. Duane, honey, my legs are cramping—do you think they could be starting to atrophy? Sweetheart, if part of my problem *is* mental, as you and John Frederick seem to feel, then wouldn't it be a wise move to extend my range of personal contacts?

But Duane had an answer for every rhetorical foray, as if this were a game of psychic baseball and he was stealing signals from her brain. No, the hope hidden in June's rehearsed arguments turned, with each exposure to frustration, then to anger—first at Duane, then at the others in the house, and finally, of course, at herself for being so stupid as to make the attempt to get out. And when this anger turned to resignation and eventually to contemplation, June realized just what a lucky young lady she was to have a husband who loved and cherished her—when he could, in fact, be exploiting her "growth potential," marketing her as a rock 'n' roll commodity, distributing her commercial flesh. Lucky, too, to have a platoon of folks right here in the house to do the things she could not do. And from this gratitude had grown the knowledge that all cricumstance had contrived to make her free. Because her mind, not imprisoned by these physical restrictions, had come untethered from the normal constraints of everyday life, her imagination cut loose, her mind set free to roam at will—wherever, whenever, however. Wasn't this the golden land behind the green door, one's hope for eternity?

Fans and aspirants envied the rock star who cut records, gave interviews, performed concerts, made public appearances, traveled, always meeting the demands of the timetable, sticking to the schedule, pushing, pushing, pushing herself. But June, and only June, knew the secret. When one lost oneself in that welter of quasi-glamorous activity, one lost . . . oneself. But now fate had granted her at last the opportunity to be that long distance voyager of the mind she had always dreamt she might become. How glorious to face a day with no restrictions, no requirements, no commitments! In her delirium she'd imagined herself a child; now she *was* a child. No one to talk to, nothing to do, only the immense and particular and unfenced pathways chosen at random by the sublime flashlight of her mind and imagination.

The wall of hieroglyphic figures, its narrative progression revealed by the directing hand of the archaeologist, her face revealed at last when the camera pans back—the invalid, senile, infantile, one truly free member of society. And wasn't her pleasure enormously enhanced by the fact that she'd been, just three months before, such an unwitting slave of her ability to function effectively in that superficial world? Four months pregnant and totally free.

And June slept. And she dreamt. But she is not dreaming. Not this time. She is onstage, reunited with Bloodrock, reunited with Larry. And they are playing festively around the dainty dais on which her child perches. And the music is good and loud. And the audience ready. And she must do it now. She must do it. And if she does it the voices will stop. And the world will be good again. And she will begin to enjoy her freedom. She will reap the fruit of freedom. And she raises the axe. And she raises it over her child, over the body of her baby. And she yanks it up high to sever the chains and shackles which bind her down, tie her down to this. . . .

"Are you dreaming again, June? You're just like an old . . . never mind. Listen, I just got the call from the airport. Your mother's finally here. I'm going to get her. So I'll . . ."

She said she was going with him.

He said that she needed to stay home and rest. She needed her beauty sleep for both herself and for their unborn child.

Duane beamed as he flew out the door. She imagined him flapping his arms to wing his way over the freeway to the airport. Pulling the sheet up around her face, June smelled her own thick odor of sweat and confinement and inactivity. Freedom? She wanted out. Her mother was coming. Coming here. She was no longer in bed as a patient; no, with Mother on the way, she was a target, a dumping ground, a scarecrow, an arid field with an enormous red X of phosphorous burned into its hide. June flapped her bedclothes and sheets. She felt crazy, crazy and frantic to get out of the room—anywhere, anywhere!—before Duane brought Amelia back to this house.

Did she sleep? Did she dream?

"Hello, darling," her mother told her, pushing aside a hanging plant as if it were a curtain hiding the identity of the patient.

"Hello, Amelia," June remembered to say. She watched the swinging plant, an out-of-control pendulum directly behind her mother's head, dry chunks of soil spilling over the edge of its wicker container. She knew how the plant felt; her childhood had been exactly the same. Wherever she went, into sickrooms, into movies, into lives, Amelia's entrances were casual and disruptive with never a backward glance.

"Well, you don't look terribly glad to see me." Amelia removed hand-dyed calfskin gloves from either hand. "I rather thought . . ."

And in her wake? June had spent a lifetime witnessing and experiencing the irresistible pull of the vacuum produced by her mother's forced departure from any scene in which she had chosen to be involved. No, it would kill her now. That lingering hint of mist, the mind on the outskirts of ether sedation. . . .

"I don't know how to thank you for coming! At times I'm . . . frightened, and I know you'll . . ."

"Of course. Your first. You haven't the slightest idea what it means to be a mother. No, your fortitude has never been impressive, but I will do my best to see it increase."

Nice. June saw the swinging plant slowly subside of its own inertia.

Amelia slapped the calfskin against the stainless steel serving tray parked at the foot of the bed. "And what's this I hear about you bleeding again, June? You know how I feel about people who give into psychosomatic illnesses! Remember that your grandmother was a practicing Christian Scientist until she fell into her present deplorable state—what dramatic irony for you to house her now! Traditionally no member of the Lockwood family has survived who kowtowed to her own weakness, who failed to achieve self-reliance."

Christian Science? Why was this the first June had heard of her grandmother's religious convictions? And why did that innocent white puff of cloud on the horizon of her childhood memories suddenly seem to resemble a blurred glance at a newspaper headline?

"There's been very little bleeding lately. I'm trying hard to control it. I *am* controlling it."

"Good." Amelia thoughtfully stroked the wooden bedstead with her fine gloves. "Hysterical bleeding is not only distasteful but—dare I say it in this age of so-called feminism?—unladylike, decidedly unladylike. Agreed?"

"I thought blood was unisex."

"What's that, June? Speak up when you're talking to me."

"Nothing, Mother."

A high-pitched silence.

"*'Amelia,'* darling. Please don't be tiresome. I've traveled too far to . . ."

"And I'm exceedingly grateful—really! But . . ."

". . . fence with words, to play games. I just won't have it, darling. You know that I am a woman who speaks her mind, and you know how deeply this petty quibbling annoys me. And while we're being forthright, I feel I must inform you that I find this house absurd." Amelia rose momentarily on the toes of her beautifully polished black patent leather shoes. "It's no wonder you make yourself sick and bleed. This place is pestilential, decadent, ugly. Although it does not surprise me in the least that Bosley Broderick would have owned such a house, since he always did have the most abominable taste. I find it more than alarming that a daughter of mine would think of spending a single night here, let alone goading her own grandmother and her sister and her nephew into taking up residence in such a disgusting and pretentious dwelling."

June tried not to gape, not to smile. Although she'd heard her mother speak her mind on countless occasions, today marked the attainment of new heights of candor and directness.

"Don't be so inhibited, mother. In my house, I want you to feel free to let down . . ."

"Has someone been telling you that sarcasm becomes you? It doesn't." Amelia swatted at her mouth as if a fly had tried for entrance. "Especially under the present circumstances—pregnant, in this foul noxious place, victimizing us all with your self-induced instability. Are you so very attached to a piece of real estate inherited from a megalomaniac? Is it not bad enough to have bedraggled our family name with this continuous tawdry media exposure?"

"Mother."

"No, I will be heard. If I'm going to subject myself to the siege of a pregnancy brought to term, I will expect the most scruplulous accountability . . ."

"Afternoon, ladies!" An immaculate silver service platter with carved pentagram handles appeared in the open doorway. "Now, I'll just put this . . ."

Duane moved cheerfully into the sunlit tension.

Amelia gestured for him to unburden himself. "I was outlining for my daughter the proposal I made to you as we returned from the airport, Duane. Perhaps you can do a better job than I of convincing your wife that it would be best if she came to live with me as soon as practicable."

"Voilà!" Duane whipped off the service lid,

unveiling a seafood soufflé still steaming from the oven. "This place?" he said, turning to Amelia as if he had just heard her. "It's not so bad. Here, honey! Have some. It's good!"

"Well!" Amelia cleared her throat angrily, coming dangerously close to an old man's petulant *harumph* which she averted at the last possible moment by coughing. "I'll leave you two to your own devices. I think I shall visit Edna now. Where is she?"

June's arm flew up as she began to explain, but Duane had already jumped to his feet. "I'll show you the way, Amelia," he promised brightly. "It's not far. I'll be right back, honey." He bent to give June a gentle glancing peck on the forehead, staggering slightly as he swung himself erect. "Dizzy, I . . . See you in a second, babe."

Allowing Duane to pilot her, Amelia shot a triumphant glance back at her daughter as she passed through the doorway. Swaying, skipping for balance, they exchanged looks of mutual appreciation. June thought they looked like childhood playmates who did not yet know that they were in love.

Chapter Twenty-nine:

Weapons of the Midwife

June slipped out of the warm bed without turning on her bedside light. It was the first time since being placed in it that she'd been out of the bed unaccompanied. She fitted her hand between the door and jamb and inched out into the unlit upstairs hallway and glided toward the telephone on the stand near the banister.

Leaving the room, leaving the bed was like . . . what? Being expelled from school? Being born? Venturing out to find a job? Yes, others wanted her in a particular place. And what if they found her wandering in the dark? What then? Would they restrain her after returning her to the bed? Or perhaps padlock the door?

Smiling, she touchd the lovely bulge of her stomach. THE PREGNANT WOMAN PROWLS—coming soon to a theatre near you! Keep your door locked! Just when you thought it was safe to go back to the laundromat. . . .

To get caught? (And *then* how do you act dignified?)

Now, dear, wandering in the dark again, are we? Got up to go potty and lost our way?

Oh, I get restless and . . . But what if you begin to bleed, dear? Bleeding in the dark, all alone, no one to tend you? But I'm perfectly fine, these spells . . . Oh, but we're here to care for you. and that's precisely what we are going to do.

And so they did. Such efficiency. Such smothering efficiency. Quite commendable. Except that she could stand it no longer. Not without going crazy. And how to tell them, each of them, all of them, that their loving solicitude was the very thing that eroded the precarious balance they meant to restore? Please stop being so nice. Please stop being so careful. Please stop tiptoeing, kowtowing—and let's ban whispering! Could somebody shout now and then? The patient's a rock 'n' roller, not a librarian!

But she could no more say these words during the daytime than she could jump to her death with her baby nestled in her womb. But the alternative—PREGNANT ROCK STAR DIES MYSTERIOUSLY: MENTAL SMOTHERING INITIAL DIAGNOSIS. She could feel her brain cells dying out like distant stars, expiring with that quiet little pop snapdragons make when one pinches them.

June shivered as she touched the cool smooth handle of the silent phone. She dialed, the clicking rotation seeming to resound enormously in the paneled corridor. At last, she heard inside the receiver the cranky repetitious ringing at the other end.

"Hello?"

"I have to whisper so they won't hear me."

"June?"

"You haven't come to see me."

"That's true. I've been busy."

I need you. No, that wouldn't do. That was premature—like the baby?

"Larry . . . how are you?"

June eyed up and down the dark long hall, sighting along the protective wooden railing that stretched to infinity like a surrealist canvas.

"Well, I've formed a new group—Muscleman. Remember Gary and Joe, the brothers from Australia? And we picked up a topnotch techno-punk drummer that's scared everybody shitless. You're lucky to get me 'cause we just got back from a short tour of the Northwest where . . ."

"That's just wonderful, Larry."

"Why are you whispering?"

"I don't want Duane to know I'm using the phone. I'm supposed to be in bed."

"Because it's late? Oh, because you're that far along with the baby? Yeah, I know. Doesn't everybody? Don't worry. I'm not mad. A little late maybe but. . . . congratulations! Is everything, ah, normal?"

Normal? This phone call was the only normal thing she could remember in the last three months. "Well, more or less. Except . . . I had an accident."

"An accident! Are you okay? Is the baby okay?" Larry's voice was so loud in the receiver that June, holding it away from her ear, feared that his concern would be audible throughout the house.

"I'm feeling okay," she whispered, softer still, hoping he'd follow her example. "I really should be . . ."

"Wait! June, have you been reading the papers? Have you heard about all the shit your mother's been giving different groups—including mine?"

"Part of that Senator Gould's campaign? You know, Amelia's here with us now."

"Living with you? God, June! And so you must

know all about the rumors about me and you . . . that's probably why you called."

A finger touched the base of June's spine so that a sudden electric shiver jangled her whole body. She could feel her jaw moving.

"You hadn't heard? Maybe Duane's keeping that shit away from you because of the baby and all. Well, you got to know, it started in *The Midnight Questioner* and just took off from there. The word's that a panel of swamis or something has agreed that after you have your kid you're going to make a comeback and, well . . ."

June tried not to hold her breath. "Yes—and?"

"And . . . well, you know how the press crucified Ozzy for that bat thing and the way the so-called Moral Majority sabotages Black Sabbath and Iron Maiden concerts and . . ."

"Please get to the point, Larry!"

"Okay. These mediums or swamis or whatever are predicting for these scandal rags that you're going to put your baby in the show and . . ."

She could not bear to hear it said. Far worse was this torture of letting the concept dangle between them without articulation. "Yes?"

"Sacrifice it. June . . . I'm sorry. I shouldn't have . . ."

"I'll sue them. They can't get away with something like this! They can't! Why didn't Duane tell me? Think about it, Larry. We can make more money by suing these idiots than we ever could from the band. Right, Larry? Right?"

"I shouldn't have said anything, June. Sorry."

"Nothing to be sorry about. I guess I'd better . . ."

"The Muscleman tour did okay, but the critics clawed the shit out of us. They said we were Bloodrock without balls. Ironic, huh? They said . . . Ah! June, everybody's saying there's nothing new in rock since you went away. Everybody! I'm sorry I . . ."

"Is the world so boring that a pregnant woman with a psychosomatic illness who never even gets out of bed is the main topic of conversation?"

"What can I say? Have you heard our album? Your mother has—and so has her little organization. She's outgrown her senator, you know. Look, is there anything I can do?"

Good question, Larry. Because this conversation had done little for her that every other conversation she had during this convalescence did not do. It had made her feel like returning to bed, staying in bed. She had risked the call to be uplifted, exalted—or at least to get in a little laugh. Instead . . . "There is one thing. Could you go to the downtown library and do a little research for me—maybe for both of us?"

She explained what she wanted with a vagueness she knew had to be irritating. Yet Larry seemed willing, projecting an enthusiasm that was probably intended to cheer her up.

June heard a sound like slippers near the foot of the stairs. She remembered that her own feet were bare and realized how cold they were on the bottom. "Don't call me," she said. "I'll call you."

"Does that mean I don't get the job? Listen, just for you, I'm cutting back to two joints tonight."

Duane sat at the foot of her bed. He stared out the window past the corner of the right wing of the estate where the sun seemed to be settling into the deep well, once functional, now only decorative. "I've never met anyone so politically knowledgeable. Really!"

Where had this childlike enthusiasm been hiding since their marriage? Why hadn't June been able to bring it out in him? "Politics was a hobby with Mother even before she started acting. She seems to enjoy it."

"Enjoy it!" Duane whipped around to face her. "It's more than that! She sees things so clearly. I mean, the world financial crisis, the need for international law-and-order, communist aggression—she makes it all so clear and simple and important! Gosh, I'm going on as if you'd never met her! I guess you've had some great talks with your mom over the years, huh?"

Unable to look at him, June fussed with a big white button dangling loose on her pink pajamas. "I guess so," she said. "Sure."

"What are you. . .?" Duane began, angry, but instantly calmed himself, a sprinter skidding to a stop. "Well, that's okay, honey." He pushed up to his feet and started for the door. "I know you're tired. Get some sleep. I'll see you a little later."

"No, Duane, please. I don't want . . ."

"That's okay, honey. Have a good rest. I'll check on you later tonight."

Gone again. She never seemed to hold anyone substantially any longer, only glancing pieces of them, only broken shards of their time, crumbs of moments, catching only stray fragments of their attention and their energy. June felt like requesting that cardboard likenesses of friends and acquaintances be set up around the room so she'd have something to talk to. A joke, of course, but, frighteningly, better than what she had now.

Best to subside back into that comfortable playhouse where there were no walls and all the toys were hers. But she seemed unable to shut her eyes these days without remembering her phone call to Larry and the little walk she had taken to make it—that short walk in this vast house during which she had passed the rooms of various sleepers. Behind her husband's bearishly celibate door she sensed a comfortable mass of warm darkness;

behind Betty and Ivan's door a nervous fitful yearning for a vagrant innocence that escaped from their world like compressed air through a hole in a tank. Behind her mother's door an almost imperceptible light stuck a furtive tongue out into the hall. But, of course, all that had been what psychiatrists used to call transference, mistaking her own feelings for those of others.

Yet when she had passed—or tried to pass—her grandmother's room, she had felt something change. She remembered when as a child she had first encountered "magic" or "electric eye" doors leading into grocery or department stores; looking at the little light beam her body was breaking, she had imagined that she could feel its actual touch. She felt the same way outside her grandmother's door that night as she entered a cold spot. June had reached out a hand to touch her knee, her shank, her ankle. They were warm, but they felt cold. She could feel the cold on the back of the testing hand. Then something touched her hideously, obscenely—and she thought she saw the floor and walls steaming as if a temperature change were causing all the moisture to rise and coalesce and move toward her.

Back in her sick bed, hiding under the covers for the first time since she was seven, June thought *my baby, my baby, my baby, my baby, my baby, my baby, my baby*

So, she taunted herself now, go ahead and shut your eyes. Go ahead and get your cheap little thrill. Go ahead and dangle your baby over the abyss and pull it back, dangle and pull. You're addicted to the rush, aren't you?

"Hi, big belly!" Betty cried, skipping in with a vase filled with yellow roses, red-tipped chrysanthemums, and varicolored daisies, artificially tinted.

"Just what I need," June tried to joke. "Flowers!

You seem especially cheerful this afternoon, Betty, what . . .?"

But Betty had frozen at June's first words, the vase held up in both hands, suspended above the nightstand where she meant to place it. "You know, June, I shouldn't say this," she said slowly, as if the words were painful, "but Mother's right. You *should* try to be more positive about things. Maybe if you tried to look on the bright side more, you'd feel better about yourself and about . . ."

"I see."

As if the projectionist had solved his problems with the projector, Betty completed the gesture of setting the vase full of flowers on the crowded nightstand jammed against the bed. "It's been funny staying here," she said thoughtfully. "Funny and . . . and strange! For the first time I've actually had a chance to talk to Mom—I mean Amelia!—to *really* talk to her. And you know what, June?"

June knew. She'd had a lifetime to memorize the plot. Didn't Betty remember her mother's habit of sizing up each segment of life for the upstage area—and then moving to occupy it? "No, what?"

"Oh, I can tell you don't want to hear this, but, well, she's a wonderful person, really a wonderful caring person! I'm so grateful to you, June, for giving me this opportunity to find out! Because as kids we . . . well, you know! Oh, she loves you so much, so very much! For instance, there's a retrospective of her films—just for her, June!—in Montreux, Switzerland scheduled for next month and—just for you, and the baby, of course—she cabled them to postpone it indefinitely! Can you imagine? And she's been offered the lead in three really wonderful movies. She brought them along and let me read one. June, you wouldn't believe how good it is! It's all about this strong-willed woman with two really different . . ."

Giving what felt like a poor facsimile of the Mona Lisa's smile, June closed her eyes on Betty. She had discovered that this was her best technique for sending visitors scurrying off, muttering, as a rule, ". . . just let you rest. You need your . . ."

But Betty persisted. Puffs of air on her face made June open her eyes to see the counterfeit money her sister was gleefully waving. "See! See! I finally got a little ahead of her! For the first time in my life, June, I'm beating Amelia at Monopoly!"

"How nice." The trick was to sound groggy and cheerful simultaneously.

"Oh, we're having some real marathons! I can't believe that Reformer never even heard of the game since it was famous and popular during the Depression and all. But now! He plays like some shrewd old conservative banker or something!"

June nodded.

"Well, I guess I'll get back to the game. You have to get your . . ."

June nodded sleepily.

". . . rest. Bye-bye!"

Rest, yes. June knew the truth of this. Because tonight, tonight. . . .

Chapter Thirty:

Bloodbirth

What if she lost the baby on one of these nocturnal excursions? Oh, then they'd be sure to see her as certifiable—Duane and the rest of them. ROCK STAR LOSES UNBORN BABY IN ACCIDENT. And the kicker floating emphatically above: SHE 'FELT COMPELLED' TO WANDER AT NIGHT IN DEMONIC MANSION!

No. No slip-ups. No accidents. (But accidents will happen.) And certainly no intrusions of imagination—no green fog, no blood, no hoary bottles of wine suspended in air like Macbeth's illusory dagger.

June let both hands roll down over the country hill of her belly, full and comfortable as a Grant Wood landscape. In the distance, a farmer plowed under a cloudless sky. Come on; time to test out that cold spot.

Time to test.

June inched her way out of the room and down the dark hallway, feeling like a fat French detective whose belly is the most formidable of his investigatory attributes. Frightened? Yes, very. If she had to run, could she manage to crawl like a pregnant lizard?

Once more she edged past her husband's bachelor chamber, light flooding out from underneath like love. (Derek and the Dominos powered through the classic "Layla." She could hear Duane singing off-key to the electrified lyricism, a big mumbling voice.) She wanted to push the door open and walk in and hug him and force him sexually to forget she was an invalid. But then he'd know she walked. And walking was her only remaining tool of discovery.

And she walked on down the hall. And she came to the room where her mother was.

Rubbing eyes fiercely, she could not get the colors out of the landscape of darkness. Reds, greens, yellows, everything etched, executed, a delicate patina, a pointilist's inside look at the reality of black. Chill swirled through or around or past June. Where the cold spot? Where the world? She stopped dead in darkness.

A kick inside. Either baby wanted her to lie down, stop agitating around so much; or maybe baby had its first little whiff of mortality, its first little encounter with the void right there in the first darkness, and after birth this bleak meeting would lead to designated oblivion, glue, grass, pills, booze, needles, nostrils, bottles, nipples, only to be turned back into its first and only home. June patted her womb reassuringly. There'll be time enough to sleep.

Frightening how easily distracted she'd become. Running on empty. . . .

HELLO, JUNE. BON SOIR.

. . . leaving herself so vulnerable . . .

I SAID HELLO TO YOU. ANSWER ME.

June clapped hands to shoulder blades—freezing! Freezing!

Control. To try. Line up stairway with last hanging plant over banister. Is. Yes. Somehow stumbled into. It,

cold spot. Unprepared. Vul. Ner. A. "Hello. Who?"
THAT DOES NOT WORK, JUNE. YOU KNOW IT. (TRY THIS.)

June pressed a hand tentatively against the wall to steady herself. The wall stayed. Somehow. But to lean against it, ah, her body making thump to alert house, L.A., the world.

"Like . . .?"
LIKE THIS.
"Like . . ."
LIKE *THIS*.
like this?
BETTER. MUCH BETTER.

Hunching her shoulders, June hugged herself with one arm. She did not know what she was doing. Telepathy, dream talking?

DO NOT DOUBT. DO NOT WONDER. DO. DO AS I SAY. NOW, GO TO THE BANISTER.

June tried to see in the darkness. Not possible. The voice (could one call it a voice?) came from EVERYWHERE, NOWHERE. She had the peculiar sensation that if she stepped TO THE RIGHT or TO THE LEFT she would shake it, lose it, much like discovering one stands on a hot air VENT and then moving aside. DO NOT DELAY IF YOU WISH TO DISCOVER MY MESSAGE. GO TO THE BANISTER. MAINTENANT.

So, should she? June became hideously aware of the living particularity of her body. The slippers felt loose and dangerous on her own feet, her belly sagged insistently. How could she resist the urge to sit, to rest, to let nature take its course? Sweat sneaked up from countless pores like tiny nocturnal animals prepared to frolic. Frolic? Her head pounded with migraine pain. Her heart took on a dangerous life of its own, a drummer ignoring the rest of the band as he takes off on a crazy experimental solo.

JUNE! GO TO THE

Voices in her head preached contradictory advice at the top of their lungs. How with this CONCATENATION of silent noise could she choose correctly?

WE CAN NOT SPEAK IF YOU DO NOT DO AS

She put one foot in front of the other. She reached out, bent-kneed, to try to catch the banister before she bumped into it. And neatly vaulted over and down to her death. And the death of her BABY. And certain headlines. Wonderful headlines. ROCK SINGER PLUMMETS TO HER DEATH IN HELLISH MANSION; BOSLEY ESTATE CLAIMS VICTIM AS VOICES PROMISE REDEMPTION.

STOP THAT. OBEY. DO NOT PROFANE THE SERIOUS GOOD WE HAVE MADE HERE TOGETHER. GO TO THE BANISTER. TAKE IT IN BOTH HANDS.

June felt forward, hands out like twin divining rods, ready to intercept anything steady in the solid darkness. There! Smooth wood. Cool wood. She pulled herself snug to the balustrade, pressing womb secure between conical balusters. LEAN OUT.

Instantly, intimately, below her womb, something touched her. Something . . . as if the air had slipped on a glove of flesh, invisible, cold, palpable as fear. She had no thought to bat the touch away. It would mean taking hands from the life-grip she held for herself and her baby. She knew she could not touch what touched her. That was the terror that reached her heart.

Grip TIGHTENED! June felt her womb might tear. The TOUCH fisted into and around her swollen vagina, kneading, ICELIKE kneading as if it thought to tenderize a piece of meat. LISTEN, JUNE. I WILL NOT HURT. I WANT ONLY YOUR ATTENTION.

BLOODROCK

She struggled to get away from the PAIN, wrestled with panic that ran up and down her arms and legs like quicksilver rodents. STOP STRUGGLING. SUBMIT. Exhausted, June yielded to, gave herself over TO MY DOMINANCE. LEAN OUT OVER THE RAILING. LEAN OUT ON YOUR TIPTOES. LEAN OUT SO THAT YOUR BELLY PROTRUDES OVER THE TOP OF THE BALUSTRADE.

June tried to crouch lower, digging her heels into the plush soft carpet beneath her feet. NO! DO IT! The touch became a PART of her, as if the pain GREW out of her own flesh, a byproduct of her own body, of living, forever and ever.

"Oh, God! No! You're hurrrrrting me! Please!"

NOT THAT WAY. THIS WAY.

"Please, you're . . ." Hurting me. YES. I KNOW. Why? Please. YOU KNOW ME NOW? YOU REMEMBER WHEN I TOUCHED YOU LIKE THIS WHEN WE FIRST MET BACKSTAGE? Yes. THEN YOU KNOW I WILL NOT HURT YOU. YOU KNOW I MEAN YOU NO HARM. YOU KNOW. Yes. THEN DO AS I SAY. A child compelled to do the impossible by an irresistible adult force, June could only straighten herself, stand and. . . .

LEAN OUT. POOCH UP YOUR BELLY, YOUR BABY. LEAN OUT.

June did. And all the pressure CAME OFF her womb in a flood of relief. (Was her baby still there? Was *she*?) She knew what the next COMMAND would be and she felt a thrill of relief that the ordeal would be over. She would no longer have to endure the daily tidal wave of tyranical emotions that her solitary life had become. Because she was not one to survive such a lengthy inner cataclysm. Better this way. Better while she was still herself.

Better to do this while I am still myself. NO, JUNE.

FEEL. JUST FEEL, LITTLE GIRL. NOW, TELL ME . . . *WHAT* DO YOU FEEL? "I feel . . ." NO. "I . . ." Feel . . . free. I Feel . . . GOOD? YOU SEE, JUNE? YOU ARE A CHILD. WHEN THE OTHER COMES FOR YOU AND FOR YOUR BABY, WILL YOU GO AS WILLINGLY AS YOU WOULD FOR ME? JUMP, JUNE!

"I . . .

JUMP! She could not help but love the grand authority of the command. Of course, she would jump; she would jump so far and high and so gracefully that when he parabola of descent began it would be so LOVELY . . . so LOVELY . . .

NO.

Like a sudden stabbing sickness the flesh-air-touch knifed back into the heart of her vagina with clinical decisiveness. June groaned as the touch brought her back, pushed her back. Forced her down to her knees. In the dark. In her house. Alone. Ashamed. Ridiculous. June did not know she was sobbing until she tried to identify the pathetic sounds she heard. When she recognized them as her own, she forced herself to HUSH, HUSH!

WHEN HE COMES, IS THIS WHAT YOU WILL DO? IS THIS HOW YOU WILL ACT? June stared out into the darkness. She felt as spent as if she had spent an entire night making love. Both questions and answers seemed superfluous, impossible. I THOUGHT YOU WERE STRONGER THAN THIS.

"What are you telling me, Bosley? It is you, isn't it?"

YOU ARE NOT STRONG ENOUGH. YOU WILL KILL YOUR OWN BABY. WON'T YOU, JUNE?

"No! That's ridiculous . . . I'd never willingly kill my baby. I'd never . . ."

The cold subsided. Light seemed to lift from the walls, the floors, as if the natural process of the rotation of the earth had been allowed to continue, to catch back up. "Bosley? Bosley? I want you to tell me what the hell you're talking about? And where did you learn French?"

No answer. Not outside. Not inside. When her mood turned to one of frustration, then to one of anger, June stalked back to her room and slammed the door. She did not care who heard tonight.

The next night June found bitter dregs left in the bottom of the green bottle that had arrived with Amelia. She drank. Mists began to appear. And then she vomited on the flower patterned linoleum into a bright spot of sunlight. But Bosley was not there. Nothing felt cold. The mist left with the vomit. But June knew that she was alone now.

"Feeling stronger today, June?" Amelia asked repeatedly. "Feeling stronger? Feel perhaps like going for a little walk—as far as your grandmother's room, say?"

And what did it mean, that smile with which she punctuated the question?

Loneliness haunted June during the latter months of her pregnancy. She felt that people in general—and old friends in particular—were avoiding her. Duane confessed at last that he had read about the rumors. And, yes, everyone in the house probably had heard them, too. But how had she found out? June began to form an image of this web of lies, this ring of rumors, creating a force field or some sort of spectral moat around the estate. No one could get through to her. Larry had been the last. And then it had grown too strong.

In these moments, in these long afternoon hours when the sun tilted endlessly through the drowsy warmth of her bedroom forest, June grew closer to the life evolving inside her stomach. My baby, she thought, my friend. They frolicked together in Edenic glades, vistas of a mauve and purple Maxfield Parish landscape, asexual, poignant, painless. She would take up painting after her baby arrived; rock 'n' roll could do without her.

"Talk?" Reformer asked, his huge bald pate glistening in the afternoon light, formidable, charming. "You have seen him. You have seen the Master."

A question? No, she'd heard in the inflection nothing but certainty. "Why, I . . ."

"Do not lie. You sought him out. You almost died. He warned you at a cost to Himself that a spoiled child such as yourself cannot conceive. You have seen him escort your mother on his arm; now you've seen him on the balustrade of the house that once was his. Do not test him again."

June propped herself up awkwardly on her elbows to get a more direct look at Reformer. "I don't understand . . . are you saying that Bosley—or whatever it was that I ran into that night—is evil?"

"You always underestimated his strength, his integrity, his endurance. You never understood the beautiful destructiveness of his creativity. You inherited his house, yet you dishonor his death by failing to take seriously the profound and terrible gift of the audiences he permitted you."

Such passionate intensity! June could only nod to signal compliance. She began to see that Reformer might well be jealous of what had not been left to him.

"Auntie June?" Ivan pestered. "Please, please please please sing the song about the Chinese cheese candy! Please? Please?" He jumped up and down on the foot of her bed, flexing his knees and springing mightily up into the air, striving for a trampoline effect, extra altitude, extra hang-time. "Cheese, please! Cheese, please!"

How many times had she told him she could not sing? How many times had they told her not to sing, not to risk the strain?

"Cheese please! Cheese please!"

Hyper, impatient, stubborn, willful, unmannerly—but what terrific company! She had no words for the way he included her in his secret community of play to share the real goods, the sweets, the achingly beautiful sweets of discovery in his little boy life.

"Auntie June, you're crazy! You're crazy, Auntie June! You're crazy! You're crazy!, Auntie June! You're crazy; you're crazy! You're out in space! You're on the moon! You're flying away with the big stars!" He bounced to the bop rhythms, bounced to accentuate his anger at her failure to respond, to come across, to sing for him. Then suddenly Ivan dropped to his rump and bounced to a stop. "You know what I think, Auntie June? I think that you can't sing any more. I think that you've gone *horse*!" He pounded his sides to gallop.

Hoarse? Her voice gone? June tried not to smile at this marvelous ploy. Certainly a Machiavelli of Ivan's stature would be offended by a smile.

"You think so, huh?" she taunted and began to sing, a lovely vibrating note that soared into joyous glissando, then sank down to slink into a low and diryt rock 'n' roll blues.

"Auntie June! Auntie June!" Clapping his hands, Ivan jumped with glee. "Auntie June is singing! Auntie June is singing!"

A dream? A reverie? She thought she was a child again, sick, feverish and . . . her mother's hand, cool and gentle, on her forehead. She could feel warm morning sun on her closed eyelids; inside a celebrational red shot through with gay balloons of black, living membrane watering sunlight down to the cozy rose hue of a bedside lamp. But if she opened up, it would all be gone, the hand, the warm inner light, the sensation of. . . .

"You're warm, dear. You have a slight temperature. How are you feeling this morning, otherwise?" Amelia lifted her cool dry hand from June's brow.

June felt too good to answer. She felt luxurious, expansive and secure; she felt like an overjoyed child in the body of a reserved adult. She remembered reading that a mother-to-be welcomes being mothered more than she has at any time since being a child herself. June smiled at Amelia.

"Well, that's pretty enough, I suppose, but the fact is that you are flushed, feverish. Still, I see no reason that we shouldn't begin to take Dr. Frederick up on his advice to start you on an exercise program." Amelia dropped onto June's chest a sheet of paper showing an annotated chart with gridlines running its entire length. "Darling, read that closely. Follow the directions. Obey it explicitly. It's time we whipped you into shape for a safe delivery. I *am* looking forward to enjoying a little granddaughter."

Why now? Why so late? *Your bleeding* would be the inevitable reply. They had used the bleeding to justify the invalid treatment and to sanction their cruel indifference to her emotional needs; why then, now, did they want her to exercise?

"Will you do that for me, June?"

"Yes, later this afternoon, I'll try to . . ."

"Good. Good. Oh, by the way, remember that guitar player who used to be with your group? Larry something? He had a bit of an accident, I'm afraid."

"Oh God, no! No!"

"Oh, I'm afraid I can't tell you anything at all about his condition. Try to rest now, dear. And promise me you'll start exercising as soon as you feel up to it."

"No Chinese cheese please? No Chinese . . .?" Finally, she'd had to ask Ivan to leave because she felt very, very tired. This time she was telling the truth. The doctor had examined June the previous day and proclaimed her overdue. Talk of induced labor, possibly a Caesarean delivery, danced glibly from various mouths. Those who came in and went out forgot to say goodbye. She had become no more than a situation they were dealing with.

She felt horrible. She doubted she would ever sing again.

Late that night, after Duane had checked in and read to her for a few minutes, the pains grew unbearable. Yet somehow she could not force herself to press the button on the device Reformer had installed to summon help—the Pregnancy Hotline, Duane had named it. Why was she still sleeping alone? What had her mother told Duane that had convinced him that she should remain isolated like this?

No, the baby hadn't arrived, just great pain. A great, great pain. She did not know what to do. She tried the breathing method; she tried transcendental meditation, repeating her silly single syllable over and over again, forcing her breathing to center down deep in her abdomen, her eyes pushed up in her skull. This served to triangulate her sense of being, opening it up all the way to the pain. Nothing but the pain.

"Do imaging," Dr. Frederick had told her on one of his weekly visits. But she had dismissed it, secretly offended by the easy presumption that came with the use of jargon. But now she was desperate enough to try anything. She would *do imaging*. Make Pain the Bad Guy. Give him a black hat, black gloves, a big cigar and evil leering eyes. Good. Antagonist fully formed—and, oh, how Big he was! Now what do we have to combat him? Let's see.

Well, nothing in here. Let's look around the house. No, no, wait—how about the scrawny but noble figure of her nephew Ivan? Smile into the teeth of Pain and imagine Ivan brandishing a Star War umbrella to stab the Bad King of Pain in his belly. Jab, Ivan! Jab! Suddenly his face contorts and he turns to glare into June's eyes. Auntie June, he screams, you didn't tell me this was real! And, just like that, he's gone. Listen—a snapping sound that could have been the bones of a neck, a popping that could have been the package of a skull, a grinding that was almost certainly. . . .

So would she similarly sacrifice her image version of each citizen of this house so that she might soon come to hate herself as hugely as she hated the Pain? The Bad Guy—that's a handle, and she refused to let go, release the leash . . . but if it began to run and drag her with it?

Wait! It's him, the aprotagonist, her savior! Surprisingly, he drifts into sight from the far side of the Pain, like a heavenly object approaching from the far side of the sun (a particularly black and malignant sun). But feel the warmth of this object as it draws near! The shape takes definition now, a dark silhouette of a man, recognizably European, garbed in black. A faint green mist licks at his ankles. This is fascinating; don't change a thing—just watch. If we can't defeat the Pain, perhaps we can devise a show of sufficient interest to divert us from feeling It.

For long moments the tall dark man motions to June with his arms, gestures of greeting, welcome, comradeship. As she begins to tire of this lengthy prelude, he turns directly to face the Pain, which is no longer black. The Pain has changed now, changed utterly. Only Its intensity identifies It as what It was. Because It has the color and the vitality now of a raw throbbing heart. Beautifully bright, gorgeously red, It beats with a vicious urgency, a tattoo of soundless vibration that seems destined to send her a message, a visual tom-tom, a choreography of pulsating tissue. She does not think she likes to look at It now. Let the Hero, the dark man mantled so beautifully in a shroud of living green, move up the hill to take the Pain. Kill It, she thinks. Kill It!

But the dark elegant man, her Hero, bowing, gestures with open hands to the Pain as if introducing It to her, as if suggesting thereby that she get to know It better. Familiarity breeds madness, a voice tells her. Suffering willingly is the key. But she can only watch as, ringmaster and performer, slave and master interchangeable, the tall green-shrouded Hero and the great red throbbing Pain dance and cavort and perform in an unending series of theatrical constructs, each concluding with a perfect transition into the next. She understands that the dynamic balance of their relationship has no end. No end.

Then something terrible happens. Without warning, the dark Hero turns to her, winks conspiratorially, reaches around the throbbing Pain mass with both arms and squeezes. The heart of Pain swells, bulges, and bursts in His grasp, a soundless explosion that seems to fill the universe with red and diffused energy. Then the mist-shrouded Hero moves toward her.

Duane was the first to respond to June's screams, but soon the whole house was awake. Hallucinating, June saw Frank Zappa garbed as an obstetrician, his hands groping blindly for her cervix while he watched cartoons on an overhead VCR.

At 3:37 that morning June, assisted by her mother, her sister, Reformer and Duane, gave birth to a seven-pound baby girl.

Chapter Thirty-one:

Bloodbrother

Closing her eyes and turning her head, June batted away the aromatic offering with the back of her hand. "No, Larry!" she cried and covered her face.

"Hey!" Incredulous, he spread his arms in benevolent surrender. "It can't hurt the baby—you're not pregnant anymore, remember? And here's the evidence right here. Little . . . little . . ."

"Dianette—after Duane's grandmother. Who let you in? My mother told me you'd had an accident. I thought that maybe . . ."

Larry let loose of the baby to snap his fingers. "Dianette—sure!" He bounced the little lace-covered ball of pink on his lap and held up the joint for her to see. "Here, try a puff? Let's see if you're braver than your old lady."

"Larry, she's only two months old! That's criminal—even if you are kidding! So, the story about the accident, all that, it's nothing?"

"Don't let me get your goat, June. You know I love kids." Larry dangled his fingers between the baby's crossed eyes. "Hell, I'm a fanatic about innocence; that's why I smoke grass and such—to preserve my own."

"You're incorrigible!"

"Thanks." He nuzzled his new girlfriend whose tiny ferocious hands were embedded in his cascading hair. "God, you're beautiful. You're so damned beautiful I could bite your little face off, you know that?"

June shook her head in mock disapproval. "Look out, Dianette, he just might do it. Larry, why won't you answer my question? What happened? Did you have an accident or not?"

Larry jerked his head around like an eccentric searching the room for insects. "Funny, I felt more comfortable talking to you on the phone. The accident? Yeah, I had an accident, June. No big deal. Maybe I'll tell you about it sometime. Right now, I'm just going to play with this little one for a minute and then hit the road. Got a lot of . . ."

"Please, Larry, no paranoia. No one can hear us. Please tell me what you found out."

"Sure . . ." He bounced Dianette on his knee with the nervous distraction of a man who'd done this for years—of course, he was used to the feel of his sleek blonde guitar! "How much do you know about the thirties and forties in Hollywood when your mom went from kid actor to big star? Not much? Well, I do . . . now. I'll admit that my motive wasn't unselfish; I figured that if I raked up some muck on this bitch—pardon me, I mean your mother—maybe I'd come up with something to get her to unhitch from my ass, you know? So when I got into the files of the L.A. Times, right there in the dead center of the gossip columns—Amelia Lockwood, Amelia Lockwood. And always the same. Look, you don't mind if . . ." He gave June a glance out of the side of his eye before striking a match to light the joint he'd been waving for emphasis. He took one long greedy pull, a moment of pure preoccupation. "There. Yeah—whooooo." He exhaled with profound reluctance, a miser releasing his life savings to a stranger.

"Larry, I really wish you wouldn't do that in here with . . ."

"Here. You take her. Okay, where . . . oh yeah, her name—and always in an occult context. Do you know what I mean? Amelia Lockwood with Madame La Fifi, Seer; Amelia Lockwood with Swami Ridpathpani; Amelia Lockwood attending seances, psychic conventions—you name it! She even knew Bosley when he was starting out and probably even dated him! Supposedly she donated this enormous sum of money to finance a cult dedicated to reviving Egyptian funeral rites. I can still remember this one caption to a picture of her inaugurating a so-called church that used to be a burlesque house in downtown L.A. I've got the notes here somewhere . . . 'Amelia Lockwood,' it said, 'well-known patroness of . . .' "

" 'Amelia Lockwood . . .' it has a certain ring, doesn't it?"

June's mother filled the doorway rather too humanly, rather too particularly; and, as if she could read her daughter's mind, Amelia said, "Isn't it peculiar how, when someone surprises us in the process of gossiping about them, their presence often seems an affront, a slap in the face, a painful reminder that the ogre we have painted is rather larger than the one standing before us."

Larry, averting his eyes, nodded to her words as if he heard in them the music of a song he'd been struggling to compose.

June wanted to find something strong to say, something that would not sound defensive. "Mother, I don't want you to get the impression that . . ."

"Oh, I don't get impressions, dear; I pick out details, deal in facts, dote on the actual. Unlike my children, I have a predilection for reality."

Instead of inhaling, Larry expelled a lungful of pungent smoke into the antiseptic atmosphere of the enclosed room.

Amelia glared, then looked from one to the other. Her eyes settled automatically on her daughter. "Is this behavior wise, do you think, with the baby present?"

Probably not. Certainly not! But June would not betray a friend by saying these words. "Mother, we all know that . . ."

"Sometimes, darling, I really do wonder if you know much of anything at all."

Larry jumped to his feet with an exaggerated hopping stomp. His grotesque grin turned his face into that of a poor circus clown who fails to paint over his emotions. "Well, I won't say it hasn't been nice—'cause it hasn't! See y'all!" He loped out heroically like a little boy whose dignity is in a shambles.

"Your husband was a fool for letting him in," Amelia said. "I'll have to see that he doesn't make the same mistake twice. Have you made the change in the baby's formula that the doctor recommended, dear? And are you remembering to test it on the back of your hand the way I showed you? Really, the bottles you give her are always much much too hot!"

"*The Hollywood Bowl*! Remember those three words!"

"What, Duane?" June had been dozing with Dianette nestled between her right arm and breast. It was a natural way to nap now.

"I haven't got time to explain in detail, but we're shooting for the Bowl for your coming-out or coming-back—your return, that's what I'm trying to say! Sound good, sound great?"

June tried to wake up, to clear her mind. Had she missed something? "You mean you want me to . . .?"

Duane angled his body back out the door. "Oh, I've talked to Larry and everything! Don't worry—it'll be the biggest thing since the Doors made their comeback after Miami!"

And then he was gone, as he always seemed to be.

"That was your daddy, honey," June whispered to her baby in a mock-plaintive voice. "Sometime I'll introduce you to him." Oh, he was always in such a hurry—and always so positive. But why, at this particular time, did that seem so very unsettling?

Amelia returned to San Jose the day after walking in on June and Larry. The next day Dianette turned two months old. Two months—had it been that long? Seven days after assisting in the delivery, Reformer had turned up missing. Gone—just like that—not a word. Ivan and his mother stayed on, with Betty landing a job as a beautician at Hollywood Coiffeurs and becoming quite independent of her sister. Ivan loved being with the baby, but his mother insisted that he finish all his homework first, and then gave him a choice of playing with Dianette or watching television.

It fell to June now to take Edna her meals and attend to her when necessary. From being waited on, June had become the waitress. Amelia, Reformer, Betty—all the assistance she'd had during pregnancy had magically lifted like some fog from another world. And now, June did everything, including household maintenance in all its many forms.

Yes, when Duane rolled through between business trips, he was full of news of negotiations almost consumated, contracts ready for signatures, halls and auditoriums just waiting to be booked, waiting for that final confirmation. June did not want to complain, but the truth was that it would have been much easier for her to have performed while pregnant than to attempt to do so now.

Performing aside, once Amelia was gone, the number one priority in June's mind became the matter of Larry's investigations; yet, every time she called, he was out. At least, no one ever answered the phone. She tried friends, musicians, but she had lost or forgotten many numbers and had no better luck reaching him through others. She searched Duane's personal phone book but found no number for Larry other than the one she already had. Yes, to keep on phoning became an obsession with her. She was afraid for Larry and for herself but could not say why; nor could she say why she never felt any fear for Duane, any sense that his well-being might be endangered.

When Duane was home they slept together, their daughter's frilly pink crib safely ensconced around the corner in the carpeted entry to the master bedroom. But on the more numerous occasions when he was gone, June found herself gravitating back to the hanging plant room of her pregnancy confinement. She felt comfortable there, settled, stable, even permanent. She felt that she and Dianette belonged there. Both seemed to sleep better when they spent the night in the room that had been their prison.

Besides, its proximity to Edna's bed chamber eased the tedium of eternally caring for her. The feeding and clothing of her grandmother and the increasingly minute attendance to her bodily needs—June could tolerate these ageless rituals and took pride in performing them well. The only aspect of the little play that killed her, took something alive and essential from her each time, was the act of adjusting the petulant little color TV set that Edna watched all day and all night. Like a human hypochondriac, the fussy machine, arrogant as a pampered pet with its rabbit ear antennae out proudly, required—no, demanded!—daily adjustment. Her grandmother's unblinking eyes focused on her back throughout the process, June felt absolutely degraded by the simple process of fine tuning the portable set.

"Aren't we lucky that Grandma hasn't rung for us tonight?" With Duane gone and the large house gradually quieting itself down, June had plucked Dianette from her royal crib and tiptoed into their favorite room, their favorite bed to be in together. Yet they were both fitful and restless. Dianette squirmed, arms flailing as if waging an infant's war with the universe.

"What's wrong, little honey? Want to phone Larry again?" The muted little gagging sobs hurt June more than outright howling. Such a good baby, so reserved—as if she'd already learned the necessity for restraint in hiking through the strange terrain called life. The tiny muffled suffering seemed so desperately contained and personal, so quietly intense, that simply to offer a breast seemed to June somehow wrong, somehow insultingly inadequate.

"You're not quite old enough to need a man just yet, so that can't be what's wrong. Still, why else do we girls sing the blues? Philosophical considerations . . . like the fact that Daddy's out of town again? I don't think so. We don't really need him, do we? Lonely? Mamma's right here, you funny! Hungry? Well, like Bessie Smith said, food ain't no cure for the blues, but it sure as hell don't hurt."

Slowly, cunningly—half burlesque, half the love of relishing a habit of usefulness—June slipped off her shoulder strap to gradually unveil her ripe white breasts.

"Supper's ready," she said. "Does madame have a reservation? No? Well, we'll see what . . . Did you prefer a booth or a table? Dining alone tonight, I see. Well, well. Smoking or non- . . ." But Dianette had had enough fooling around and with an impatient little squeal homed in on the chosen breast. "Okay, okay! Oi vay, your manners! I just can't take you anywhere!"

Okay, so you can be cute and clever with an uncomprehending audience, an uncomprehending audience you love. Is this the extent of your ability to communicate? "Bet you wouldn't be such an eager eater if you knew the confection was a hundred percent mean metal rocker who tried to kill her faithful drummer. Bet you'd pull those little gums away if you knew Mommy made people bleed when she touched them. And that funny little rock around her neck that you like to play with . . ." June shrugged her shoulders at the quick twinge of pain in her lower back. Dianette lost her purchase, looked zanily around her and fizzled out a little bubble-mouthed complaint.

June helped her find her way back home and then, cupping the baby's head, leaned back with a sigh into the double-mounted pillows. "You're right, honey. We've got to call Larry. Just got to get in touch with him. It's almost like I'm depending on him to live the life I'm missing.

"Sleepy? Want a little song? Let's see . . .
  Oh, momma rocker had her kid
  And a fair-haired child had she
  She touched its pretty little skin
  Who bled like sap from . . ."

Never before had June abhorred her glib little talent for inventing nonsense ballads on demand. Never before. Abhorrent! Oh, God! Squeezing Dianette with all her pent-up frustration, she finally felt the tiny arms and head trying to root up through her implacable flesh. "Oh God, Dianette! I'm sorry! I'm sorry, sorry, sorry, sorry, sorry . . .!"

But as she heard her voice trail off, June knew that she could not be sorry for her passion here in the privacy of her secret bedroom nursing her own child. No more than she could be sorry for the passion of her creative or performing life. Angry at guilt in an instant, June felt ready to fight, ready to take on anyone who might cross her or her infant girl.

"Honey, Momma doesn't know. She doesn't know if she's a good person or not. She doesn't know if the rock around her throat is divine or diabolical. She does not know if it's good for us to be living in this house that we were given by the same strange man who gave us the bloodrock. Mommy doesn't know why she feels that the only chance for us to survive is to reach out for Larry Ludwig who may not even . . ."

"HELLO! HELLO! HELLO, LITTLE PEOPLE!"

June froze, afraid to look toward the voice. They were supposed to be alone in the house.

"I don't want you to worry about this, honey—because it's in the past, really, even though it just happened day before yesterday—the Bowl's almost certain, and the guy up in Oakland says he's anxious to get you for his first Hour-in-the-Sun this year, and the album just went platinum! Yeah, huh? Yeah?"

Duane rushed the bed and they embraced. "What are you two doing in here, anyway?" He cupped his daughter in his hands and placed his face against her little body, prolonging this makeshift embrace, his eyes closed, his hovering body blocking out the light.

"Is there something wrong, Duane?" She put a hand into his hair and smoothed it down before recognizing a gesture she used repeatedly with Dianette. "Is the

Oakland concert going to be . . .?"

"Danny's dead. He died two days ago. In his sleep, they say. He probably didn't feel any pain at all. I debated with myself whether to tell you or not, but I figured that you would hear sooner or later and I didn't want anything ever to damage all the good momentum we're building up for your comeback." He had not looked at her as he spoke but had played with the baby's hands as June played with his hair. When he finished talking she waited, but still he did not look at her.

"I think I should call Larry," she said at last.

"That's not necessary . . . I just talked to him. Shall we go to bed?"

June toted the diaper bag, while Duane carried Dianette back to the master bedroom. Watching him undress for bed, June kept seeing an actor preparing himself for a performance. And when he dove under the covers with cartoon vitality, she knew what he wanted tonight. She said *cramps, diarrhea, maybe some sort of virus*, and rolled over on her side to wait to hear the deep regular breathing that would tell her he had abdicated to sleep. "Have to check the baby," she said as she eased up from the solid mattress. And then, just in case he might be half-awake, "I think I heard Edna calling."

How foolish could she be, sneaking out of bed to place a call to another man, a man for whom she had feelings she did not care to acknowledge? Tiptoe, June!

She brushed a hand over the baby's blanket as she moved past the bassinet and thought of the wind outside. If Duane caught her . . .what? At Edna's room she tried to ignore the omnipresent cold and shut her ears to the sound of static coming from the out of tune TV set. All she had to do was to go to the telephone and pick it up and dial. That was all. That was all. That was all.

JUNE? JUNE, LISTEN TO ME. ALL I WANT

"No!" She bent to squint closely at the round dial and fit her fingers in the right holes, hurting her back by prolonging this unnatural position. Her finger slipped off on the last number. "Shit!" Had she twisted it around far enough to take? As the ringing began, June nervously eyed the darkness crowding up from both directions in the hallway.

"You're a sickie! Have you ever thought of getting psychiatric help?"

So she had got the wrong number, yet. . . .

"Larry!"

"June? Christ, you've got to pardon me; I've been getting crank calls like every half hour or so and it's drivin' me crazy! How 'bout you?"

"Yeah, I've been crazy too—from not knowing what's going on. Please tell me!"

"You accused me of being paranoid. Okay. You don't have to believe this, but I think I'm being followed. I'm almost sure my phone is being tapped, but I can usually tell and . . . what the hell time of night is it anyway? Jesus Christ, June, what did you do, get out of bed to call? It doesn't sound like they're listening right now so I'm going to make it fast. Okay? I mean, I'm going to have to leave out almost everything that might give this shit some credence but I'm afraid that . . ."

"That's fine." She tried not to let him hear that he had scared her. It had not taken much. "Just tell me."

"Yeah? Okay, you asked for it. First, that accident I didn't . . ."

"Oh, Larry . . . I'm sorry but Duane told me something tonight. He told me that Danny died."

"I told him to keep his mouth shut about that."

"Then it's true?"

"I'm sorry, June. Listen, it isn't . . . Your husband

got some screwball idea about re-forming Bloodrock and selling out the Hollywood Bowl and he talked me into going to visit Danny at his mom's house. Next thing I know I get a call from Danny's sister saying that . . . It had nothing to do with the original accident, June; believe me. Some sort of viral infection with complications."

"Complications," June said.

"Sorry I haven't got time for niceties. I thought I heard something on the line. Danny's funeral's tomorrow afternoon. I'll come by and pick you up about one-thirty. So, you want the report? Okay, I told you how your mother was up to her ass in the L.A. psychic scene in the forties and how . . ."

"Larry, I just can't accept that. My mother's obsession has always been politics and she laughs at anything that resembles ESP, let alone the supernatural!"

"Okay, June. I can't explain what I found, but I worked my ass off. See, at first I just felt so goddamned pleased to have the goods on her. I thought, 'Great, she's a hypocrite! Wait until the media finds out that this ultra-right senorita who crusades against the occult was one of Hollywood's biggest dabblers in demonology.' That was at first, see, but once I got this taste, June, I just couldn't let it go. June, I've been at this like a full-time job, you understand?"

"Go on, Larry."

He sighed; angry at first, loud and high, the sigh dwindled down to a scarcely audible sound of fatigue and resignation. "Okay. Yeah. Well. See, what I found tells me that the bad stuff that's happened, like Danny, hasn't been your fault. Because . . . okay, just let me get through this. Your mom dropped out of the psychic scene for no apparent reason back in '52, but then right after you were born all these rumors started again. Did you know your picture was on the front page of the Police Gazette? I've got it here—'Courageous Actress Refuses to Sacrifice Baby.' It shows Amelia holding you upside down and smiling at the camera. The story says that all these psychics and fortune tellers had gone to her and told her that you were a danger to her, kind of a female Oedipus thing. You never heard that?"

"No," June said more quietly. What was she supposed to believe?

"So look, June. The pattern's there. You're in danger, and your baby . . ."

"Okay, so what else did you find out?"

"Well, that's it, but . . ."

"You worked full-time all these months and unearthed this supernatural conspiracy and all you came up with was a photo in a cheap newspaper of my mother holding me upside down?"

"June, you cut me off when I tried to document all the psychic stuff. It's here. I've got it. It's here! You always told me she treated you weird—now here's the reason. And the deal is that it hasn't stopped yet. Your grandmother's still alive; she's living with you. She's the one to ask. She knows about all of it. All of it! In every story, it's 'Amelia Lockwood and mother,' like she was a saint or something for taking her mother to a frigging seance. Go ask your grandmother. Then *you* can fill *me* in!"

"So . . ." What could she say? He wanted her to converse with a woman who seldom spoke—and when she did, the sole topic was the fine tuning of her portable TV. "So how's your music?"

"My music? My career? Well, we got out an album, self-produced, the Muscleman label; our logo's a dog licking its butt. Sales up to thirty-four-hundred so far. We break even at around twenty thousand, so . . . I mean, who gives a shit if Muscleman gets repressed, if there's a conspiracy to keep them from being heard? The asshole political types look the other way because we're into metaphysics and the apocalypse instead of their brand of revolution. Well, the joke's on them 'cause it's them that gets the John Birch-SPCA treatment next! Wait till you see the morning paper! Just wait, June!"

"Larry, you're ranting, do you know that? I thought your phone was tapped."

"Don't, June. Please. I love you. I want to get you out of this. I want . . . I'm *going* to get you out of this, get you away from all these people. Listen, we're going to form a new group, you and me and whoever we can find; Bloodbrothers we'll call it. Because we are, you and me! We're that close!"

"That's nice, Larry, but . . ."

The connection terminated with a series of loud chortling clicks that made her yank the receiver off her ear as if it had become a hissing snake. An electrical storm. Lightning on the line. Electronic laughter.

And then finally June could identify the sound she'd been standing and listening to in the darkness. Dianette! She ran soundlessly and with no regard at all for her body.

When she reached the silent bassinet, June kept her cold arms locked to her sides. When she saw some movement inside, she would reach out and touch her baby. Because her baby had cried out and then was silent and now. . . . "Dianette!" June plunged her hands down through the coverlet, batting away blankets from her infant's little face. With voracious determination, as if rescuing her from a ring of fire, June yanked Dianette out of the cold bassinet.

"No! No! No! Oh, my little girl . . ." June, checking the tiny throat for obstructions, saw the color slowly seep back into the baby's fat face. And then it came, the cry, the protest, the announcement that the struggle was not yet over.

"Oh, thank you! Thank you for not going away! I promise, oh, I promise that I'll never ever let anything happen to you. Not ever! Not ever! Not ever!"

June did not spot the headline until she set down Edna's breakfast tray. About to test the doorknob to see if this was one of the days her grandmother had not locked herself in, June noticed the words in heavy type on the newspaper she had propped under the side of the plate. "Civic Group Successful in Stopping Rock Performance—Details in Local Section." And quickly delving into the middle of the thick paper she found: "Muscleman Gets Sand Kicked in Its Mascaraed Face." A subhead stood out in the middle of the text: "'Fight?' said Larry Ludwig, guitarist and titular leader. 'How do you fight somebody who claims to represent an entire town, a whole country? We're just a band looking for an audience.'"

June, wedging the newspaper under her arm, tested the knob and found Edna's door locked. Apparently the TV set was working today, because laughter emanated from the dark interior of the old woman's solitary room.

Chapter Thirty-Two:

A History of the Vines

JUNE
 "What?"
 Disoriented, terrified, alone, she awoke in total darkness. Who had screamed? She sat up, pushing the heels of her hands into the mattress, and decided that it was no dream.
 Keeping her head thrust up into the alert horror of the black stillness, June patted the mattress where Duane should have been. Why did it feel so cold?
 And then she remembered. "Dianette, honey?" June yelled out. "Are you okay?" (Foolish woman! Your baby won't be talking for years. Now get a grip.)
 YES, JUNE. GET A GRIP ON YOURSELF.
 (hideous nasal laughter)
 "Bosley? Bosley, is that you?"
 YOU KNOW WHAT TIME IT IS. DO NOT PRETEND.
 She tried to place the sound in the darkness. If she could identify the direction, she would run at the source of the sound, throw her body at it—and hope that her

death saved the child. "Time?" June said, stalling.

TIME. TIME FOR ME TO TAKE THE BABY. LE TEMPS, MON PETIT.

"No!" June screamed. "No!"

THIRTY YEARS AGO I HEARD THAT WORD. NO. I WAS MADE TO PASS YOU AND YOUR GENERATION. I CAN WAIT NO LONGER. YOU MUST GIVE IT NOW.

June bit hard into her lower lip, drawing blood. She licked the salty laceration. Voices, hallucinations, wild imaginings—she had hoped it would never happen again, that the illusion of Bosley's ghost had been the last, that she could concentrate and keep it all from ever recurring. And just when she thought she'd rid herself of all this! Now she pressed thumbs to temple and gritted her teeth.

IF YOU DO NOT CHOOSE NOW, I WILL CHOOSE FOR YOU. THE CHOICE IS SIMPLE, YOUR BABY OR YOUR

"No! I'm hallucinating! No!"

SIMPLE, JUNE. TRES SIMPLEMENT.

The snippets of French, the phony accent—hadn't the illusory Bosley used such a voice in his alleged warning? But when would he make the revelation? He had said the next time would be for . . . Where was her baby? Where *was* Dianette? Afraid to move, June frantically scanned the darkened room. She was a mother now—how could the horror still go on?

OF THE GRANDCHILDREN. HER SON YOU'VE KNOWN TEN YEARS. LONG ENOUGH TO LOVE AS I LOVED MY GRANDDAUGHTER.

June wanted to tear her hair. She wanted to hurl a chair at a wall, to break glass, to damage herself or anything she could lay hands on. The voice was an itch, a swollen cyst on the skin of reality that she had to shred open to keep herself from going crazy.

YOU HAVE KNOWN YOUR BABY FOR SEVENTY-SEVEN DAYS, LONG ENOUGH FOR NATURAL LOVE TO MULTIPLY. PARFAITMENT —CHOOSE.

Shaking her head ceased to be enough. June thrashed about in the tangle of sheets and blankets while the disembodied voice, half-croon, half-croak, droned on. Until a phrase froze her hysterical motion. "What? What?"

IN ENGLISH, AN EYE FOR AN EYE, N'EST-CE PAS? THIS IS YOUR WHAT.

June unconsciously wrapped a section of tangled sheet around one fist and dug it into her mouth. "Please," she said, "I don't understand . . ."

YOUR BABY OR YOUR SISTER'S CHILD. CHOOSE. ONE OF THEM I WILL TAKE.

"Little Ivan? But he's just a . . ."

EXACTEMENT. AS WAS MINE, MON CHERE. I ORDER YOU NOW: WITHIN THE NEXT THIRTY DAYS YOU WILL MAKE YOUR CHOICE. YOU WILL PERFORM ONCE MORE YOUR MUSICAL ACT. YOU WILL TOUCH THE CHILD. YOU WILL TAKE THE LIFE FOR ME SO THAT ALL MAY SEE IT. YOU WILL RETURN TO ME THE LIFE YOUR FAMILY SO WILLFULLY TOOK.

"Who are you?"

IF YOU DO NOT CHOOSE, JUNE LOCKWOOD I WILL TAKE AS MANY OF ALL YOUR GENERATIONS AS MY APPETITE DICTATES ON THAT DAY.

"What did I ever do to you to make you say these things? I'll never do it! Go away—leave me alone! Leave . . ."

OH, MY DEAR! REST ASSURED I WILL NEVER LEAVE YOU ALONE. JAMAIS. JAMAIS. TOUJOURS JAMAIS. BECAUSE I DO NOT HATE

YOUR BABY. I LOVE BABIES. I LOVE ALL BABIES. THAT IS WHY I MUST HAVE ONE WITH ME.

The next morning, shortly before awakening, June dreamt of a cheerful pop rock stage show that featured a giddy demonstrative baby. It was all silly and slapstick, glitter and stupid gags. At the end of the show the baby was gone, the entertainers milling around unconcernedly, looking for a party. Soon a custodian cleaned the area and did not seem surprised to find the bloody remnants of a skinned chicken in a small plastic container colorfully decorating the center of the stage. Removing a big discolored sponge from his back pocket, he sopped up and wiped away all evidence of the bird ever having existed.

Her relief at discovering that this was no more than a dream carried over to the hallucination of the night before. That's all they were—dreams, hallucinations, projections of her own sad fears. And, as long as she remembered that, she would be okay; she and Dianette would be okay.

Already the nightmare had shrunk from the proportions of an overwhelming widescreen down to the manageability of a stereoscopic viewer one holds to the light. One may hold it to one's face and peer in and let the illusion loom larger than life. Or one may hold the little plastic toy safely away from one's vision. June knew now that she had her demon contained.

Liberated by a sense of having overcome so many obstacles, she skipped down the hall to Betty's room.

Didn't everything always turn out for the best? Hadn't Duane returned to bed when her nightmare was over, confessing that he'd fallen asleep downstairs watching a basketball game on television? And wasn't Dianette exactly where she was supposed to be, in the wonderful antique bassinet at the foot of their bed?

So June had placed her hallucination in this common context and emerged victorious. So why not skip down the hallway of her very own exquisite mansion on such a beautiful, beautiful fall day?

"Wake up sleepyheads!" she called as she skipped into Betty and Ivan's bedroom. "Rise and shine! Rise . . ."

The mind knows immediately that it is a scene that cannot be dismissed as long as the brain lives. A cellar door is thrown open to frame a dead child, a little girl, looking up from eating her father. Her eyes are made hideous as they contact yours by the lust to consume the human flesh you wear. Turning from her ministrations to her stricken son, her eyes bejeweled with a mother's tears, Betty's smile was hideous and hateful and . . . hungry.

"You did this," she said. "You're the only one here who causes bleeding, who disfigures, who kills! You're the only one who bleeds! Mother warned me, but I wouldn't listen! I wouldn't listen because you were my sister and I thought you loved us! Why did you touch him? Why did you touch my baby?"

June stepped forward. "Ivan, let Auntie June see what . . . Oh, my God."

"Are you satisfied? You had to come back and get a good look—and now you have—so get out! Get out of our bedroom, monster!"

To speak would be a sin; not to speak would be evil. "I didn't do this, Betty."

"Oh, you!" she growled. "Get out!"

Banished from the immaculate little bedroom, June checked on her own child. Dianette slept with a smile of delight and contentment on her tiny face. June watched her own sleeping baby as long as she could stand to do so with the pattern of blood crisscrossing the face and shoulders of her newphew superimposed across her still form. She had to move, had to walk, get away.

June wandered the vast confines of the house she'd never really wanted, feeling an ache, a tug of emptiness, and absence of life, of anything good; but mixed in was a pinch of claustrophobia, virulent, intense and as immediate as a face fully covered by a hot pillow. Wandering, June saw herself as a zombie, one of the undead. Would it ever stop?

Sunlight slashed her belly and her baby's face. June looked through the dining room sunlight to the impenetrable darkness of the hills beyond the freeway, the crisscrossing traffic in the distance crazily underscoring the sense of blindness.

"Hey, June! Hey, child! Hey, world!"

Duane sprinted in, waving a sheath of wrinkled papers. "I didn't want to bore you with the details what with the excitement of our first baby and all, but we did it! We got it! We got the Bowl!"

"We got the Hollywood Bowl?" Was this nonsense supposed to be a joke? "Do you mean like buying the Brooklyn Bridge?"

"We've booked you—June Lockwood Lombard—into the Hollywood Bowl," he slowly explained. "Don't you see? You're going to be playing your music in the Hollywood Bowl because everybody has seen your video and heard your album and they want to see you. A chance for you to get back with Larry and the boys and . . . No? Well, if you don't like the outdoor setting, we could head the concert back up north to Davies or . . ."

"Just fine," June said, punctuating the two words with her best smile. "It's probably time that I did something constructive again."

"Oh, that's wonderful!" Duane said, jumping up and catching June and Dianette in a stooping embrace.

"Just wonderful, honey! I'll tell the promoters to go ahead with the package. All systems go!"

June watched her ecstatic husband bound down to the sunken living room where he began dialing the phone atop the wet bar. All systems go? Dianette had stopped crying. June, sure her child had fallen asleep, gazed lovingly down only to discover Dianette's eyes open wide and staring.

A fairly continuous bombardment of positive propaganda from Duane and the three skin specialists he'd called out to the house to attend to Ivan finally managed to force Betty to allow herself to be consoled. Now, each day, she eagerly searched her child's face for signs of improvement, healing, a reduction in swelling, a return to his natural color. After three days, when Ivan came out of shock and began speaking, Betty consented to a reconciliation with her older sister.

June felt faintly embarrassed during her brief reunion with Betty. But she had been putting off an even more uncomfortable encounter for almost a week now. Edna never left her room. And June entered only to feed the old woman and adjust her TV. Larry had told her what she must do. But she had not been able to get a hold of him again and he had not called. And so she had tended the baby, changed diapers, smoothed her hair, washed her face again and again, and nursed her and played with her and talked to her and held her and hugged her. Love is a drug? So what's motherhood—heroin?

But she had failed to extricate from her mind the image of Edna's carved mahogany door at the top of the stairs. The harder she willed herself to dismiss the idea that this adventure was *essential, imperative*, the more strongly the notion came crowding back. Dancing. Fires. Fierce quick words of love. Maniacal music. Magnificent men in white furs. Amelia spirited away as if by magic. Grandmother there. Always. A scattered handful of images from her childhood—but what did they mean?

June suddenly became aware of herself with knuckles raised before her grandmother's door. Had she knocked? How long had she been here? Was there still time to run? June saw herself turn to run as Edna inched open the door, catching her in the act. And why should that image frighten her more than the prospect of going inside to have the conversation Larry had suggested? (What conversation? How can you converse with someone who doesn't speak?)

The door eased open like a sigh. And June stepped in as if compelled by the suggestion of a vacuum. Three steps inside altered reality forever. Two steps, bend, and place the tray atop the portable TV, precisely the depth to which June had penetrated for seven months, no more, no less. But today she had taken the third step into the heart of this darkness, one step beyond the set.

"Si . . ."

"Grandma! Are you alright?"

"Siiiiiiiit."

June stabbed looks into corners, into deep piles of darkness, into deeper piles of horribly specific possessions.

An old-fashioned dressing screen rested in the corner parallel to the set. Silk stretched on a light wood frame, the reds and greens of kimono-clad women, the translucence of naked bathers, the cascading blue of a rushing mountain stream and . . . which side of the screen was this scene on? Weren't these the gauzy mutings of reversed color, color viewed through the wrong side of silk? "Sit, child," she said.

Careful of muscle and bone and skin that might very well tear open, she eased herself down on the closeted day bed. Terribly tired, she sighed at the cessation of exertion. Oh, what she would give to never ever have to rise again.

She had almost missed her afternoon repose, her afternoon wine. See, the glass sat where she had placed it that very morning, its base wedged against the bamboo superstructure of the glass inset table. Reaching out carefully with one liver-spotted hand, she took the glass unsteadily and brought it with uncertain ease to her trembling lips. Oh, the exertion, the hideous exertion!

How long had she been gone from her room? She thought that she had taken on some other life, had lived in the forest out there, that house.

But now, thank God, she could rest. Rest . . . forever, if she chose. Forever, never to rise again—what a blessed, blessed thought.

But today she could not struggle free from images of the past. Her free hand grasped a great weight that had appeared on her throat. Intermittently, whenever the energy came, she lifted the object up off her skin and would have removed if altogether if it had not been bound down in some way. And, as always, always, her lips began to move as she confessed to the silence the secret cherished sins at the heart of her life.

"When I was young I was beautiful; men attended me, presented me, lavished me. I was beautiful, I did not know I would grow old, I went to Paris with a man who loved me more than his life, he did everything for me, I did everything, I danced with a naked black woman in a jazz cafe. He liked that, he gave me everything, we found new ways of using our bodies.

"I wanted to go somewhere now. We went to a cemetery where I danced on a grave of a great sorcerer who was dead but lived and still lives; after, we killed his granddaughter by accident. When my daughter was born He came to me and announced Himself as

Méchant, He was charming, He brought a bottle of wine, He made the shape on my belly that the spilt wine had made on his tombstone, that the blood had made on his granddaughter's belly, that would be the mark of the sacrifice I would return, He told me everything about love, He told me everything about myself.

"And then He asked for her, for my daughter Amelia; I was weak; I did not know what to do, Amelia knew, however, she knew, she howled, screamed and blared out her tiny strident animal voice until He left, saying that Amelia was not the gentle sensitive loving creature his granddaughter had been, He said Amelia was a horrible self-centered dark thing like her mother, He meant me, of course, He meant me, and He said He would be back later; and, of course, twenty-seven years later when . . ."

The lips went on moving, but she made the words halt. A bright red burst of good clean claustrophobia struck and she fought to get out, burning out what remained of her diminished energy so that she subsided back willingly onto the cushion.

She sipped her wine from the fine old bottle with the obscene, stained, half-torn label.

". . . where? Ah, Amelia's children, children, my daughter's children, my grandchildren, my first grandchild, heh, heh, heh, still laugh to think of what she did to Him, how she goaded Him into thinking that she would give them up, oh, she led Him on, she called to Him at a thousand seances, hand in hand we attended a thousand parties where a joining of hands was the core moment of the evening, the high point of our delicious entertainment; oh, yes, she would give Him her first baby, and perhaps even her second, oh, He believed, He had to believe, He saw those public displays, He visited a thousand parties, a thousand seances, and people applauded, the right people applauded, how could

Amelia not follow through? how could my daughter not give him what he asked?"

She chuckled aimlessly to herself. They were so beautiful, so beautiful, her hands. She commenced a close examination of her two favorite white objects. She did not use a mirror to see them because Méchant hid in mirrors to tell lies. She knew that her body had not changed since the summer of 1923 when she was the one woman in the world who could get any man to do anything. Anything. But Méchant wanted to hurt her.

For a moment, her thoughts skittered off into the abyss where narrative and chronology fall to their death, where sequence and logic and consequence die of terror long before hitting the bottom. Then she returned to her favorite possession, her body, tool of endless pleasure, her church, her movable feast of herself. And her words, her guilty pleasures in the perfection of debasement—for only she of all the many pretenders, only she had possessed the courage to lead a truly self-loving life. Although her daughter had learned and taken.

"Heh, heh, the Old Fool never has understood us, either of us; my daughter let Him be the entertainment, let Him make His fancy European display and then she cut Him, she denied Him, and all the rumor, lovers knew that she had wrested her baby from the jaws of supernatural death and damnation, and all the gossip and all the talk lived with my daughter, Mother of the Year, Mother of the Decade, Hollywood Mother of This Century, she saved her baby from the Demon that had pursued her for years, bravely, she stood up, heh, heh, heh . . ."

The sound of this dry laugh, autumn leaves trod beneath light leather heels, made her look around the room. As if there might be someone else. As if there might be another on the other side of the screen.

"Stood up to Him? ah, that one thing they did not know, stood up to Him? made a fool out of Him? yes, made him realize He'd been a public display for nothing? yes, infuriated, enraged, revitalized his waning hatred of this family? yes, but stood up to Him? no, no, no, heh, heh, heh, weren't you wonderful, Amelia? weren't you wonderful when you . . ."

The voice box contorted with the strain. Someone wanted words to come out that weren't spoken. Oh, yes, there were a few words that were never spoken even here. But today, today. . . .

And the strain, the terrible tearing at the ancient words that made the sounds, brittle bits of fiber and nerve barely held together by tight dry tendon that almost yielded.

". . . can't get me to say it! won't say it! Amelia, wondrous mother! Amelia, Amelia, couldn't care less for her daughters' lives, but oh and oh and oh to be Mother of the Century, heroine to the secret few initiates, the two or three hundred who knew, lady and queen of women to the public, loving, motherly, protective, goodness personified, ah—the joke, my daughter, my love—the joke is that they loved us so much, we who showed them how to love us by loving ourselves only and more, much much more than they would ever manage with their puny egos, their puny, their tiny . . ."

Wracking cough tore at the disintegrating vocal tissues, but even this could not stop the forbidden words from being dispensed from the ruined mouth. "Yes, cared nothing for your daughters' lives, let their babies die, let little what's-his-name die, why did You say You didn't take him, Méchant? a boy, a boy—and that You would not give up your one chosen moment, ah, You wanted to hurt us, You wanted to wait until the most delicate and sensitive member of our Family grew to the point of maturity where You would give her an impossible . . ."

CHOICE. PACT. IN WRITING. IN BLOOD. THERE IN THE POOL. IN THE BLESSED INDOOR POOL OF HIS HIDEOUS MANSION. THERE IN THE WATER WHERE WE PLACED THE ANIMALS FROM THE PRIVATE GAME PRESERVE.

"I told You never to come into my bedroom when you're like this, never, never, never . . . will you violate the . . . will you forfeit the right to destroy that sensitive little bitch who pretends to love people other than herself? oh, I've seen her, so good and so . . . oh, I held here on my knees, oh, I hated her, oh, I hated sheltering her, but it was all for Amelia, all for my daughter, like me, just like me . . . get out!"

She released her hold on the heavy weight on her wrinkled throat. The back of her hand caught the glass of wine halfway up the stem and overturned it. With great ponderous difficulty she rose through layers of fog and fatigue, something really human like a geological formation yielding to an eruption.

She did not know. She thought she stood.

But on which side of the screen? The green and red kimonos flared with vivid immediacy. They had changed. They had shifted, reversed. Yet she had not moved herself.

"Grandma? Grandma, are you alright?"

At last June found her grandmother behind the dressing screen, unconscious, delirious, her lips moving but emitting no sound. A bright spot of blood shaped like a heart peeked from the center of her throat—glistening, alive.

Night. She knew she had staggered from Edna's room, dazed, nauseated, dizzy. She knew she had fallen somewhere in the darkness. And she knew she had just now awakened hearing this scream. Scream? She knew she had never heard the scream before, but she could instantly identify it.

June had never heard Dianette scream. She had heard her cry but never scream. Babies don't scream. Unless. . . .

And she was running full speed and blind, insane in the pitch black house before her mind could begin to catch up to what her instincts compelled her to do.

YOUR BABY SCREAMS. RUN TO IT. RUN, IF YOU VALUE YOUR . . .

Afterwards, June knew how close she had undoubtedly come to killing herself as she sprinted through the darkened house from one unknown location to another she could identify only by the sound of Dianette's last scream. She jumped down stairs, heedless of the punishment inflicted on hips and feet and knees and thighs, thinking only *how could I have let my baby get so far away*? She vaulted landings, banisters, the hulking obstacles of black antique shapes, bounded, avoided, stumbled over, indifferent to the thrumming of her luridly alive body and brain, thinking only *please let her scream again, please make her scream just once more so that I may know if* . . .

Only one chance. Only one room. And June had gone there, to *their* room, to the plant room, the favorite room, the pregnancy room, the prison room, the cell in which they had grown together. And she had gone to the crib. And June had looked inside.

The crib was occupied. There was a bottle. There was a night-lite. Only one thing was missing. But June was so happy that at first she did not allow it to register.

"Oh, God, honey! don't scream ever, please? Any sound you want to make is okay with me, but please just don't . . ."

Life is made up of details, a voice said. Read them, June. Them? Yes, read the details. Survival is attention to detail. Perhaps her. . . .

"Oh, good baby. Oh, so good! So quiet and . . ."

. . . . life depends on it.

Details? A list appeared. First, June put her ear to the tiny chest. Nothing? Fumbling in the darkness, June tried to finger the bright little hair of a pulse, first in her flesh toy arm, then her neck.

Dianette opened her eyes. Her mouth roared silently open.

June recognized the unequivocal force of infant terror. She saw every sign that her child was screaming, quivering in horror, screaming.

"Oh, my little girl! My little lover, what's wrong?" She fought down hysteria like dark water trying to bubble up over her head. "What's wrong, little baby?" Details. She had to keep checking. Fingers alertly darting into sopping wet diapers for the stray pin, the clip of sharp label or convoluted cloth. But . . . nothing. Palm going flat, feeling down onto feverish moist baby skin slippery as the inside of a rubber mask worn from door to door on Halloween, feeling for something . . . anything.

Nothing. Everything okay. Fine. Something horribly, dreadfully, unbearably wrong. Something. June touched a wayward trembling fingertip to Dianette's small warm throat. Wet—not moist, wet!

June hoisted her child by the armpits to the pine end table with the big brass saucer lamp. She snapped on the lamp and stared at Dianette's tiny pulsing throat. Blood. Clearly blood. A heart-shaped drop of blood nestled there on the baby's perfect neck like a bas-relief tattoo, like a new form of jewelry one grows out of one's own flesh. "Stop it!"

June hugged her little girl, crooned, sang to her,

improvising lullabies that would never again be heard on any world in the universe. Not ever. But no sound came from Dianette's throat that night, no sound at all.

June fell asleep sometime before dawn, Dianette cradled awkwardly in her aching arms, knowing Méchant had been here, had left his calling card, had lead her to the brink of some kind of choice.

Chapter Thirty-three:

Blood Sacrifice

June watched morning traffic move and coagulate on the Hollywood Freeway beyond the green confines of her estate. She felt herself to be at the center of something but could not imagine what it was.

Rocking Dianette absent-mindedly, June stared at the lone sycamore that hung dowdily down over the tiled roof of the front terrace. What *did* she remember of being in her grandmother's room? Had she heard Edna's voice—or had it been herself she heard? She remembered the sensation of being trapped inside the words, the voice, as if she had become locked in the mechanism of an artificial woman. So, had she experienced her grandmother's thoughts, her life, through some sort of mutual ESP? Or had it been no more than just another hallucination? Actually, she remembered only enough of the experience to feel totally frustrated.

Funny, the business of getting used to things. It had been, oh, thirty-two or thirty-three hours now since Dianette had last made a sound with her throat. And the mother had come to accept it; the mother compensated by performing a kind of casual frisk on a regular basis, hands checking for needles, for moisture, for anything. But mother had learned to accept so very much.

ZAP! PABAP! "You're dead, Auntie June! Why don't you die?"

Startled, June leaned away from her little nephew who aimed an electronic weapon. Good question, she thought after regaining her composure. Ivan, his face swathed in bandages like a child mummy, pointed the space pistol at his aunt's head and made one more gallant attempt to disintegrate her. Every time she saw his covered face June remembered the pattern of marks that she had seen beneath, like cracks in the earth of a dried-up river. Would this be the next stage for Dianette—disfigurement? Or did Méchant have a unique series of afflictions in mind for each victim? If, in fact, there *was* a Méchant; if, in fact, Méchant meant something more than the attempt by her mother and grandmother to personify and create a scapegoat for their past sins.

"Die, Auntie June! Die!" Scrambling athletically into her lap, Ivan swung his knees and elbows, kicking her thighs, jabbing her breasts. She had not the energy to repel him. Since the accident and subsequent diagnosis, he was not her nephew but a walking, talking compendium of frailities and symptoms, a persistently mobilized reminder of her culpability. The invisible boy disguise enhanced this illusion. DO NOT TOUCH ME; YOU'VE HURT ME ENOUGH ALREADY. "Auntie, June, it's no fun at all if you don't fight back! Come on; come on. COME ON!"

"Take that!" June yelled, almost frantic. "And that!" She threw fake blows that were pitiful specimens by any child's standards; yet, she knew, Ivan was inclined to delight in what he managed to get from adults, however meager it might seem.

"Oh, you terrible!" he shouted, truly aroused, redoubling the pummeling of his close opponent with elbows and knees. "You *are* a terrible thing!" June smiled at the irony of a right cross that caught her nose flush and quite perfectly; Ivan would never have heard of the punch or have any way of evaluating what a fine thing he had done. And what a fine thing if this onrushing performance date of a reunited Bloodrock coincided with the period of time during which both her eyes would be black. Would the critics have fun with that! Of course, the wonders of modern make-up. . . .

"No!" Ivan shouted, swinging both fists at her face. "Don't stop fighting, you terrible bad monster Auntie! Yes!"

He looked so ludicrous, a blur of white bandages, that she did not have the heart to call a halt to his brutal shenanigans. So, doctor, you say the marks are not physically serious? You say you can demonstrate that stigmata runs in our family? You think that Ivan would thrive and become wholesome and whole again away from this noxious house, away from this kinky crazy rock-and-roll aunt? Well, I got a prescription for you, doc—up your ass with this fucking space pistol!

"I love you, Auntie June!" The assault has ceased, his arms have encircled June's throat. "You play with me so good! I hope Mommy doesn't make us go like she says because I want to always play like this. Always! Always!"

Holstered, the space gun dug fiercely into June's side. She would touch his face, touch the bandages that brushed his face, part them, cure the boy, brush aside all doubt, all care. How could she blame her sister for wanting out?

"Do you love me, Auntie June? When we go to Disneyland like you promised, I'm going to marry

Dianette and then I can kill the Green Blood Monsters whenever they start to attack again! I'll kill them all dead!"

"I believe you," June said. "I'm so happy to know you're going to save us all."

That night, when it started, June put her hands over her ears, bringing the flaps of her arms in to hide her face. Screams! She could not stand it. Over and over and over, her life a nightmare, each separate terror fingered into meaninglessness. She could not stand it. She heard Duane talking but ignored him. She stayed in bed until she could not stand it. It was horrible walking to Betty's room, thinking of her nephew. June carried Dianette, gently jostling her, shaking her, without realizing it, as one shakes a box to hear what is inside. Ivan had a heart-shaped spot of blood in the center of his throat. He had lost the power of speech.

Some of his gesticulations, however, took on an unfortunately intelligible significance. Duane had to restrain Betty from doing things; then he assisted in translating Ivan's frenetic pantomime. A strange man had come to the boy in a dream and told him that he would lose all of his senses one by one if his aunt did not perform music quite soon. Duane joked that the boy would go to any extreme to get June to sing. Betty, grim, apparently provoked, tried to start another fistfight with her sister, but Duane stepped in again.

Ivan pantomimed an association of himself and Dianette as if the stranger had drawn a specific connection between them, as if somehow their fates were linked. Duane could make no sense of it at all and said it was all very sad. Two hours later a taxi rolled through the Spanish arch into the courtyard of the estate and parked near the decorative well that no longer functioned. When the taxi pulled away, two small heads showed as dark nodules on the back seat, Betty and Ivan departing. "What a shame," Duane said. "What a shame. It's all just one big misunderstanding. Ready for bed, honey?"

What a shame? June felt relieved. Having Ivan around had been far too painful, both for his own pains and for those that might be visited in turn upon her daughter. He had become for her a torturous previews-of-coming-attractions. What a shame, but that was what she felt.

In bed, Duane made the fingerman hop up onto Mount June to play. Fingerman was in a fine mood, Duane said. While she felt like screaming at him that she was in no mood for silly little games, June had made a rule in her mind that she would never discourage Duane on those rare and increasingly infrequent moments when he relaxed enough to get playful in bed. (Oh, he had an ulterior motive tonight—he wanted to coax her out of what he probably supposed was a bad mood brought on by Betty's sudden departure. Because he cared, sure, but then, we can't have grumpy performers on stage now, can we?) The fingerman traversed "valleys and beautiful little hillocks!" in Duane's continuous narration, "venturing where no finger has gone before; his seven minute mission, to boldly stimulate . . ." And then, throwing the covers up to dive under, he made movie music, shark music, and began to dorsal fin his way toward his helpless wife. And June did herself the favor of relaxing a little, relinquishing her body over to the prospect of pleasure for a few minutes at least; soon, there would be time enough to return to what was real. And so the shark caught her, and the feeding frenzy began.

But when June felt the different texture of the moisture, less viscous, more friction, more gritty, she knew that this had been just another trap, one more bead on the rosary string Méchant had made of her life. Duane reared to growl menacingly, grizzly now, and the blood on his chin was no more than a quickly penned comment by the teacher near the top of the student paper. There was no flow, no gush. She had it under control. June had control.

But then the grizzly quit its act and said, "I'm really sorry, honey. I hope you're not disappointed. But . . . did you really have your heart set on the Bowl? We had to move the concert back up north. Is the Theater for the Performing Arts okay?"

It was a moment of high humor. In another lifetime she would have roared with laughter until her funny husband joined in, enlarging his limited perspective in the process. "Sure," she said. "That'd be just fine."

Snap.

Details, preparations—little of it fell to her. She made a pleasant litany of the phrase *it's out of my hands*. She could see it all the way Duane pictured it for her. From all over the United States, all over the world, musicians and technicians and artists, each the best in the business, were converging on San Jose, California, to ready the theater and themselves for the reunion. "Just sit back and relax, June. You're the Queen Bee, and we're all the drones, here to serve you!" Why was she afraid to correct him, to remind him that hopefully they were the workers? Did errors, mistakes provide the real foreshadowing of our fate? She'd find out in five days.

And then there was the one about taking them into your own hands—matters, fate. June looked at hers before dialing Larry's number and relating a very tardy summary of what she had discovered in Edna's room and what had happened afterward. She liked his reactions. She liked the way he responded to her meager attempt at a plan of attack. "Fucking aye!" Larry said.

And they both hung up.

Of course, Duane would see that they had no choice but to take Dianette along with them. No newborn should be away from her mother for four days. Besides, all the live-in babysitters had scattered to the winds, first Reformer, then Amelia, then Betty and her son. They must take Edna with them because, as they had agreed, she was simply not able to take care of herself. Imagine leaving Dianette alone with a babysitter, a stranger, in this house! No, as far as Duane was concerned, it was all set; he had made the phone call to make sure that his mother-in-law was available to take care of the baby for as long as they were in San Jose. It would be a reunion all the way around, he said.

And during the last two days he seemed to talk more than ever about how he'd taken care of everything, arranged every detail, made everything perfect. And she had not had to do a thing, had she? Had she? (So shouldn't she be just absolutely berserk with glee?—wasn't that the implication?) June granted that Duane seemed to have an absolute mastery of business, of the superficial, observable world. And for him, of course, that took in everything. Too bad. Too bad. She whipped it up into soap opera: THE SEPARATE DIRECTIONS OF THEIR LIVES DIVORCED JUNE AND DUANE FROM EACH OTHER.

June tried to ignore the ringing of the downstairs phone as Duane loaded the last of their luggage into the back of the station wagon they'd borrowed from another record producer. Whatever it was, whoever wanted to say it, she felt that she could wait until they landed in San Jose to find out all about it. Somehow she felt safe in assuming that everything would, in fact, be waiting for them in San Jose. June took one last look at the house, at Bosley's estate, before Duane pulled out onto the access road that almost immediately had them on Hollywood Freeway North. Move. Coagulate. Flow. They would be at L.A. International in no time.

June had brought a ridiculous pair of matronly sunglasses to hide behind at the airport and during the fifty-minute flight, but not one person spoke to her; and, once on the plane, no one so much as leaned out into the aisle to stare. What were the odds of the Sorceress of Demonic Rock avoiding recognition in the midst of seventy-six TV viewing, magazine thumbing, record borrowing denizens of the modern world? Was she offended? Halfway through the flight, June removed the scallop-shell glasses and suddenly felt that she was back home in Bosley's mansion, safe and flying high. Dianette tried to cry only once, at a sudden rolling heave of turbulence, her tiny mouth opening wide on a single silent scream. Edna gestured that she was thirsty; June noticed that whenever she ministered to her baby in any way her grandmother would request an equal measure of care. And perhaps at this precise moment Méchant was winging his way on trans-supernatural airways, flying high and straight toward his reserved perch. SEE him SET UP his ectoplasmic amplifers, ADJUST his ghoulish maps, TEST occult acoustics, and TUNE his insubstantial harp and horn to the music of the Infernal Spheres. Safe? Of course she felt safe. Duane and Edna played cards.

They circled San Jose once before landing, a long looping pass that seemed to size up the terrain below as if it contained a combat zone. Yet, once down, few of the pyrotechnics June had feared seemed evident. Disembarking, the only obvious disturbance they could spot was a group of women cordoned into a remote section of the airport near an exterior conveyor belt for luggage. Most of the marchers seemed to carry signs, the messages indistinct from the distance; they may have shouted in unison, a muted cough of sound, but the shriek of the jets of an outgoing airliner consumed any other vibration that entered this air. As June emerged into sunshine from the afternoon shadow of the plane, then plunged back into the artificial lighting of the passenger bridge returning to the terminal, a group of fans ranged along the window caught sight of her and gave out a polite roar. June unconsciously adjusted Dianette higher on her chest, above her heart, where her own face and hands could shield the little warm body. Then they came to the end of the ramp and the group congesting the gate converged, and airport dispatch personnel and security guards, obviously forewarned and ready, moved in to shove back the surge of eager fans. "See, honey?" Duane said. "Everybody remembers!" He eased Edna ahead behind the shoulders of a burly guard, her rented wheelchair brushing the legs and shins of the solid wall of bodies.

Winter sunshine, streaming in unobtrusively to bathe them all, so reminiscent of the warmth visited upon her wedding the year before, jarred June's memory so that her reply seemed a non sequitur. "It's hard to believe that in eight days we'll have been . . ."

"That must be Kirsten Peters! I recognize her from the junior chamber brochure the city sent us—she's our official greeter!" Bypassing the security guard, Duane thrust Edna forward like a life-sized calling card.

And the process began. Kirsten Peters introduced herself as Mayor Aspen's representative; she extended official greetings, the city's welcome, and indicated that she was at their disposal as official guide and facilitator. She moved them quickly without rushing them, gesturing at each turn to indicate that the humdrum, the tedious, the routine, the burdensome had been, was being, would be attended to—and never mind! And right this way! And don't worry yourselves! At regular intervals Kirsten touched a finger to Dianette's pale dry cheek, an act of unpremeditated concern, a functionary breaking down the boundaries of official courtesy. And June smiled—San Jose sure knew *how*! And she admired the way Kirsten seemed so pleased to put a hand on Edna's shoulder as Duane rolled her along the designated route, an act she performed apparently without noticing the old woman's pervasive odor or the insistent sucking sounds she made with her mouth.

Kirsten had a nice surprise for June and Duane and family, she said. They would be sharing a floor of the Le Baron Hotel with the rest of the band, the crew and authorized entourage. Wasn't that convenient? (Gesturing them into the limousine waiting at the curb with a smile and a fixed posture that was somehow reminiscent of attendants for certain Disneyland rides.) And the grandmother would have her own room—with a view, of course. Kirsten understood that this was to be a reunion of sorts; therefore, the room separating the two main suites had been reserved to host a small buffet brunch with optional wet bar. Was this satisfactory?

Oh, thank you! Skeletal trees in this merciless winter light, row upon row of them as they drove past the civic center and into the downtown area, dry and glistening and naked. She did not care about the buffet or wet bar or the ease of accomodations but was anxious to see the boys in the band just as soon as possible; she felt shy and embarrassed and wanted to get the difficult things over with, a few words, what to expect, maybe a warning or two. Just certain things. Kirsten assisted them from the limo, showed them through the main entrance to the front desk where they were introduced to the available hotel management. Now they were in good hands, she said; she would in ample time escort them to the theater for the evening's performance. She hoped they enjoyed a pleasant and restful afternoon in San Jose.

Their spacious suite featured a sweep of windows opening to the busy street, the curtains billowing voluptuously in the afternoon breeze like the skirts of festival dancers. June gave Dianette a bottle and fretted a little as a pimply bellhop pushed Edna into her adjoining room. Duane offered to accompany her to the reception for the band; when she declined, he left for the theater to check out the acoustics and see that everything was set up just the way she wanted it.

June could hear the party through the walls, waiting for her in the next room like a hungry animal. A stereo cranked up with too much bass so that the music seemed more felt than heard—Buddy Holly, Sandy Denny, Minnie, Moony, Vicious, Vicious. She touched the wall and felt it throb in the tips of her fingers. Yes, they were in the wall, all those great artists, dead—but alive in this wall. Then what was it waiting for her in the next room? Push the button on the right, Kirsten had said; push the button and the partition will open and you'll be part of the party! She did, and she was.

"Hello, June. How's the little mother? What a beautiful baby—gorgeous as her mom!" (On drums, Paul Travers!)

"Well, as long as this stuff's on the house . . . hey, it is on *them*, isn't it?" (On bass, Bruce Marley!) "Okay, then, let's have at it!"

Muscleman (soon to become the current edition of Bloodrock) descended like locusts on the artistically arranged buffet set up along the stark white wall away from the windows. They fell upon the food with all the nervous preoccupied zeal of men trying to pretend they're at ease in an awkward situation.

He made no move toward the food, did not look her way. Slouching against the wet bar, arms and legs crossed in a classic surly rock 'n' roll pose, he seemed intent on portraying *worst enemy* to anyone who might glance his way. Larry nodded indeterminately. The nod led him to saunter toward her.

"Zee food, she is poisoned, eh?" he whispered into her hair. "That is why we are not eating, no?" He cupped Dianette's symmetrical little face with a nicotine-stained hand. "Beautiful child, June—wild."

"Thank you."

All he did was hold his hand on the baby's cheek, his hair hanging down almost to her face. "I can't believe we're going to do what we're going to do tonight," he said.

"No,"

"You're sure she can't speak? Is this the mark here, this little heart-shaped bruise? She has such a pretty throat . . ."

"Larry, I told you what happened to her . . . to us. I hope that you believe me."

His eyes flicked up to hold her a second then dropped back to rest on Dianette. "Yeah," he said. "But I've been thinking that maybe we should try something a little less . . . extreme first. Something not so . . ."

"Larry!" June pushed into him, traveling through his hair to the clearing behind it, her lips touching the lobe of his ear. "I told you about Ivan! I told you about the stairs! The voices! That thing that put its hand on my . . ."

"So you're going to have him come out dressed like that? And Dianette laid out like a lamb for the slaughter? But what happens then?"

"Larry, I've had nightmares about this for a year. If I knew . . . Look, us progressive musicians are supposed to be able to wing it, right? Right. So, we'll get out there and . . . wing it."

The three young men who comprised Bloodrock's rhythm section had just about completed their all-out assault on the contents of the buffet. Strolling over to the table, Larry took a single celery stalk which he scraped along the side of a crystal bowl that had been filled with some sort of curry dip. His abbreviated open-handed gesture was meant to convey to June that the wasteland repast awaited her indulgence. She laughed to think of trying to find something edible in this culinary rubble. "Good," Larry said. "That's what I wanted to see."

June took a similar stalk of celery and smiled. The very fact that he'd felt the need to make her laugh demonstrated that he was, in fact, convinced. What a struggle! It had all been so long coming. Oh, she felt tired and . . . close to him. The sense of mental and physical intimacy with this sometimes dangerous young man whose wardrobe consisted of varying degrees of faded jeans and workshirts frightened June and made her momentarily dizzy.

Larry reached out to steady her. "Say, you're not . . . pregnant again, are you? I'll escort you back home to rest." And he lead her on his arm back to the other side of the partition to wait until the fall of night for the culmination of their musical reunion.

June never saw her grandmother leave the hotel with her mother. Duane, upset at what he saw as a foul-up, suggested they leave Dianette with the babysitting service provided by the hotel. He said he was angry because he had worked hard all afternoon making sure that everything was ready and set now, when they should be leaving in no more than ten minutes, this important matter had not been attended to.

"She'll be fine," June told him. "She'll be onstage with me."

She remembered the look he gave her now. She remembered how he had looked at her when they'd first made love and the blood from her throat had matted the hairs of his chest. "Onstage?"

"Yes. She'll be with me. She'll be part of the act."

"June . . . I think that after this performance we'd better think about getitng you another series of appointments with Dr. Franklin. The stress and tension really are too much to . . ."

"Shut up," June said, balling her fists and bringing them up. "I'm not crazy. I'm going to be saving my daughter's life."

Duane's head dropped, his hand coming up to cover his face. "Oh, June . . .! June, June!"

He seemed closer to tears than she had ever seen him. Yet the sight of despair on his face while dressed in a carefully tailored three-piece charcoal tweed suit seemed absurd, almost surrealistic. "Everything will be all right, Duane," she promised. "Dianette and I will be perfectly fine—after tonight. Please don't worry." She tried to take his hand from his face.

His eyes came up out of hiding now, dry and frightened but trying to be cunning. "What if . . . what if something happens to her?"

June resolved neither to raise her voice nor to scream. "Nothing is going to happen," she said. "Now, shall we go? The limousine is waiting by now. Duane . . . I am going to take my daughter onstage with me tonight!"

He nodded as if hearing her voice from a great, great distance. "Good. Yes, that's wonderful, honey. And after this we'll go on a long vacation and get a real long rest. And, just as you say, everything will be fine, wonderful!"

June watched him closely all the way to the theater. She would not have put it past him to have some security guard wrestle Dianette away from her at the precise moment she mounted the stage. No, she would watch for whispers, would make such communication as difficult as she could. In the limousine she positioned herself behind the driver, who was decked out in a Greek sailor's cap and drove with one hand as he guided them through the ranks of angry shouting pickets who cricled the theater. Had Amelia arranged their presence here? June wondered if the protest against Bloodrock and herself would affect concert attendance but dismissed the thought as too trivial to be considered.

Surprising midwinter heat yawned hungrily at them and licked its lips as they disembarked from the air-conditioned limo out behind the theater where they were discreetly ushered through a short alley that led into the backstage dressing area. Just inside the huge steel loading gate, June stopped, her eyes scanning the rafters, the ceiling, the backstage superstructure. "What's wrong, honey?" Duane wanted to know.

"I'm listening to the air-conditioner," June said. She lowered her head to give him a mild look and smile.

"You're sure you don't want me to take Dianette? I mean, she'll only hamper you up there since it is your first time in more than . . ."

"No, we'll be fine."

"Well . . . okay then, I'm going to go and check out the . . ."

"Yes." June studied the tiny face of her daughter, sleeping, powerless. She knew that her baby trusted her. "Do what you have to do, Duane."

Duane kissed her, deep frown lines on his forehead, and kissed the baby, the furrows subsiding momentarily before he looked up again to say goodbye. June hitched Dianette a little higher onto her shoulder as she watched her husband go off to find the stage manager. June knew that the gesture had become habitual to her, a nervous tic, hoisting the sleeping infant even when she had not slipped down, even when she was very high up on her shoulder to start with, near the crest in fact. June listened to the hungry purr and knew the theater air-conditioner was in league with the heat, the coming of nighttime. Yes, and one day she'd hitch her daughter up too high and too fast and too far, too far, and Dianette would fly right on over. . . .

"Miss Lockwood, would you care to come with me? I'll show you to your dressing room. I think you'll find it quite satisfactory."

June said hello to Kirsten Peters by name.

"Very good—you remembered! No, I'm not being sarcastic—you've had a busy day and you've got a busy night ahead of you and a beautiful daughter to tend, and remembering my name's the last thing anyone would expect of you. Yes, right in here. Good luck. I'm looking forward to hearing you again."

June thanked Kirsten Peters for everything and settled into a straight-backed chair she'd been told had been used by the symphony conductor and by such luminaries of the music world as Beverly Sills, Count Basie, Ella Fitzgerald and Peter Gabriel. "Just think, kiddo," she told Dianette, "you're going to be up on that stage where the greats have performed. And you only three months old! Top that, Judy Garland, Shirley Temple!"

June nuzzled Dianette's face with her own until the baby, trying vainly to push the huge heavy shape away, began to cry fiercely.

"Oh, so you're resisting being the youngest American performer ever, huh? Me?—the worst show biz mother *ever*? Well!"

The play-acting helped. It helped to push back the encroaching certainty that she would not be the one to finally control the results of tonight's performance. "Don't you want to be a rock 'n' roll star? It's every kid's dream, don't you know? That, or making a million in the computer business. Isn't that what you want? You aren't un-American or something, are you, baby? I'd hate to think that my baby daughter was some kind of . . . communist! Yes, my little subversive, my little anarchist, that's right . . ."

Closing her eyes, Dianette drifted off to sleep to the tune of her mother's nonstop banter.

"Bored, huh? Listen, what do you want, loud music? You want me to play 'Louie, Louie' at a million decibels? Well, it can be arranged . . ."

So innocent, so delicate, the features of Dianette's face seemed forever frozen by the fluorescent lights into a timeless sculpture in which energy and repose had found, for the briefest enduring moment, that perfect balance. She was so beautiful, so good, so wonderful. "Oh, my little girl! My baby!"

June gently crushed Dianette to her, aware of her own immense sophistication in the handling of her child. No one else could squeeze her just this hard, hold her just this near, come quite this close to smothering her without alarming Dianette into the most frantic screams of mortal terror. Only me, only her mother, only me.

Knocking. The dressing room door opened like a hatch in the ceiling in a Greek play. Deus ex machina, intrusion into this world of mortals, this paradise where June and Dianette should have been the only two living beings.

"Miss Lockwood? It's time to . . ."

"Yes."

There had been a time when a folk rock musician named June Lockwood had considered it an affectation to dress differently for a performance than she did on the street; however, June Lockwood, the high priestess of occult rock, had learned that dressing appropriately was part of one's obligation. After all, Ozzy Osbourne did not stroll out onto the stage in one of Don Ho's Hawaiian shirts and sandals, sipping a pina colada.

June did not think of her performance garb as a

costume but rather as equipment, props, part of the created imaginary ambience of her routine. The shaped colored plastic, the lengths of chain and foil, the medieval studded tunic, the severe high heels, the translucent tights, the diabolical cape of many colors she would twirl away from her shoulders like a weapon—these were tools; they helped June assume a certain role, helped her chosen audience find their way into a certain forbidden terrain of their inner lives, guilt-ridden yet greatly cherished.

June's fingers worked with a myriad of satisfyingly fitted snaps, each connection closing down like a little moment of sex. Some mother—all decked out in this science fiction vision of sado-masochism! What would the Daughters of the American Revolution say if they could see what had become of San Jose's Favorite Daughter?

The dressing room door flew open, and June was caught with her shapely breasts out in the air. She turned her back, readying angry words as she hurriedly finished buttoning up.

"Listen, Kirsten, I don't want you to think I don't appreciate . . ."

"Well, aren't you something, darling?" Amelia moved into the center of the room to scrutinize her outfitted daughter; she held one hand to her chin in speculation, a dress designer wondering if she's found the correct model for her new line of fall fashions. "Very interesting. Very . . . interesting. And this is what you wear in your act . . . onstage, June?"

This late in the day, was it possible that her mother could still make her feel guilty? "Yes," June answered reluctantly. "Yes, this is what I wear."

"You know . . ." The very fact that Amelia kept the same speculative pose created a kind of tension. "I wore a costume very, very similar to that in a film about the

French Revolution, a dreadful thing. I'm sure you've never seen the movie, darling; it's too ghastly, really, even for the TV late show. They think these days that they have a corner on soft-core pornography—hah! would you believe I played the Marquis de Sade's favorite whore? He'd make me wear *that* costume. Then he'd do horrible lurid things to me—all suggested, of course, not shown—and then he'd go off and spur the peasants on to cut off more heads or some other atrocity. Not too historically accurate, I'm told. And now you show it all, don't you, darling? Nothing held back?"

June tried to keep her hands from shaking as she fastened her cape to the snaps on her shoulders. "No mother. Nothing."

"Oh, and here's my little granddaughter all sort of crammed into this pile of your discarded civilian clothes! Let's see how much weight she's . . . oh, yes, aren't you a hefty little tyke now? How much—oof!—how much does she weigh, June?"

June resisted the urge to yank her child away from Amelia; she relaced her sequined boots. "Oh, Dianette's up to eleven pounds now, but I'm very careful with her diet even when . . ."

"How nice," Amelia said, tapping the baby under the chin. "You know, June, your grandmother and I are very pleased and happy that you have brought Dianette here tonight to be on stage with you."

June felt like a fish transfixed by a hook that has passed through her esophagus to snag her entire frame. "Oh?"

"Yes." Amelia looked only at the child. "Yes, we've lived with this thing a long, long time and we're very pleased that it will all end tonight. Yes, darling . . ." She looked coolly up at June. "I know that you know; I know *what* you know; in fact, it could be said that I programed—is that the word they're using these days?—yes, that I *programmed* you to find out at just this appropriate time. Doesn't that make you feel useful and needed?''

June's mouth opened helplessly and her hand instinctively fluttered up to the rock that always hung in the center of her throat.

Amelia laughed, pointedly annoyed, disapproving. "Oh, that stupid piece of worthless stone! And this pretense that you can't take it off—this psychosomatic notion of yours that it won't come off your throat!

"I never in my wildest dreams expected you to make such a clear-eyed and practical decision as you have in bringing Dianette here to the theater tonight. Now, you can make everything quite perfect by turning that useless ugly thing over to me before the show. Otherwise . . ."

A good firm strangle hold on the baby, Amelia reached out to pluck the bloodrock as if it were a weed in the crannied wall of June's chest.

June, stepping back, held up a hand. "No, Mother. It's a sort of good luck piece. It was given to me by . . ."

"Good luck? The way you bleed? I know the fool you received it from quite well; he gave a similarly pleasant curse to me. Aren't you tired of suffering? Give it to me."

Amelia held Dianette as if she meaent to relinquish her only at a very high price. June fingered the chain. Impossible . . . but the catch was loose, she felt it. The bloodrock *would* come off her neck. She could remove the burden, regain her child, perhaps resume a normal life and end the suffering and the madness.

"Yes, he tried to give that thing to me, but I knew better than to take it. The blood of sacrificial virgins indeed! That old pervert—he's better off dead."

Amelia's grip on her grandchild looked entirely lethal. "Give it to me, June."

Perhaps, if she took it off now, gave the rock to her mother, perhaps . . . perhaps she could walk out of the theater; she could leave here with her baby and turn her back on the occult and a year and a half of accumulated evil and begin her life again.

"Take it off and hand it to me, June. You and Dianette will find that everything will go smoother and easier tonight during the show if you are relieved of the burden of *that* around your throat. Now . . ."

June took the bloodrock off her neck. She held it in her palm to see how it looked. Then she offered it to her mother.

(june, if you are not sister of the blood and daughter of the blood, then who will be? will you give it over to be destroyed, the stone? will you give away the one path we have to make our pain have value?)

As Amelia reached out to take the stone, June's fingers closed around it reflexively. She brought her tight fist back to strike her own chest with it. "Mother, why haven't we ever loved each other the way a mother and daughter are supposed to? For just once I wish that . . ."

"Here. Take this. I don't want it." Amelia jostled Dianette loose from her shoulder and held her out from her body as if she stood atop some perilous cliff and meant to drop her to test the distance down. And, slipping her hands under the tiny arms, June felt that she had arrested just such a fall, that if she had been a second later Dianette would have been gone.

"I do love you, Mother. I do. Remember that beautiful sunny morning when I was in my eighth month and you sat on my bed and . . ."

"Good. Just keep remembering that, June. I'll be glad to see it over with, but don't look for me after your performance. After all these years, I have a great deal of celebrating to catch up on. Because, if you do love me as you say, you will not let me down. Isn't that right, June?"

"Yes, Amelia," June said. "I'll do my best to put on a good show."

"Splendid," Amelia said.

June, who had propped her baby on the dressing table once again, cinched the broad bright red sash and crossed herself with her laser ammunition belt. These were silly things and she kept her back to her mother to honor their respective dignities. "I dream that one day we will be closer, Mother. I dream that one day we can walk together holding hands and simply spend an hour . . ."

"Knock, knock? Are you in there Miss Lockwood? The warm-up band has finished—Judgement Day, quite good; you might want to catch them some day. Shall I accompany you out to the performance area?"

"No. No . . . that won't be necessary."

June put the finishing touches on the tiny costume she'd purchased for Dianette at a specialty shop on Sepulvada Boulevard. How much of what she'd said had Amelia heard before leaving? Oh, well, maybe one day . . . June supported Dianette on her forearm, giving them both the once-over in the full-length mirror. Nodding, she stepped to the door to flick off the dressing room lights, then stopped. She was on her way out onto a stage where she might be called upon to simulate the sacrifice of her baby daughter. And yet she'd turn off the lights to save electricity? What a dreadful failure of perspective. Feeling pathetic, she snapped the switch off anyway. She could not stand waste. But now, with this good night all around them, it occurred to June that she and Dianette did not have to go out there. They could hide. They could go anywhere and do. . . .

YOU MUST, JUNE.

Oh, God, no! Did this have to start again?

I GAVE YOU THE BLOODROCK. I GAVE YOU THE HOUSE. IF YOU WOULD USE YOUR INTUITION, YOU WOULD KNOW THAT I GAVE YOU LIFE AT THE BEGINNING. NOW I GIVE YOU THIS COMMAND. YOU MUST GO OUT ON THAT STAGE AND PREPARE YOUR BELOVED DAUGHTER. PREPARED HER AS HE WANTS.

June fell to her knees in the dark dressing room. "Please! I can't! I . . ."

YOU MUST. YOU MUST. I CANnot speak a g a i n . . .

June got to her feet. She hitched Dianette higher on the rough shoulder harness and stepped out into the corridor. To her left was the stage. To her right, down a brief corridor of hospital brilliance, was the service entrance, a black rectangle as tempting as the steep view down an empty elevator shaft. June moved decisively, to save her child, to save her soul, to stop the cycle of suffering her family had endured for better than sixty years.

First she saw the lethal arc of glare coming off the rim of the drum kit, then the other instruments rising into view like a forest made of acoustic and electronic components, no soloist's microphone within twenty feet of the next.

"Hi, June," Larry said. "Want a hit?"

He offered the obligatory joint, she made the customary refusal. "Larry?" Tonight he had pushed his experimental aircraft beyond the limits of endurance, had gone too fast and too far and had floundered at the crucial moment when approaching the point of no return. "Larry?" He did not so much sway as waver, his physical presence as reliable as a mirage on the shimmering horizon. Oh, she should have known; she should have figured that he'd turn up stoned at the decisive moment, that when she was finally forced to rely on him he'd prove to be ultimately unreliable. And where did that leave her? The plan? Her baby?

"It's not as bad as it looks, June. I'm here, more or less. Try some?"

If you can't beat 'em, escape with 'em. Was that the way it went? "Well . . ."

"Why not? After all, tonight's a special occasion. You're going to need all the fortification you can get—come on! Breakfast of Champions—here you go."

Holding tight to her baby, June took the tiny twist of smoking paper and put it to her mouth and sucked. The acrid smoke filled her mouth like some teasingly sensual intimation of the pleasures of hell. Puffing out her headfull of smoke, June started to cough with mechanical regularity. Larry pounded her hard on the back until she stopped. "Just like getting burped, huh? I thought I was going to have to catch the kid for a second there. Some people just can't handle their pot."

June's half-hearted laugh became a final cough.

"You sound great," he said. "Think you can still sing?"

She put a hand to her long throat. "Me-me-me-me," she sang with toneless ineptitude.

"Perfect!" Larry kissed his fingers and threw them to the air. "Never heard you sound better! Well, let's do it. What do you say?"

Since there had never been a nationwide Bloodrock tour, there was no massive Bloodrock stage show to prepare. No imaginary wall would be erected to obscure the band, only to be torn down in the finale. No smoke bombs or carefully orchestrated light displays. No guillotine, no snake. No electronic bat hovering against a backdrop of black. Bloodrock featured colorfully dressed musicians and their instruments, their energy, their talent, their ability to project an imagined reality. With the exception of costumes and rudimentary lighting effects, this band presented something like the antithesis of glitter rock, something like no-frills heavy metal; except that Broodrock was a band that easily transcended categories, and if their sound could be heavy and metallic, it could also be light and dry, lyrical and angry, passionate and relentless.

The instruments were set up. A NASA center of recording equipment surmounted the stage, one small red nipple of light pulsing READY. Pete Robinson eyed the stage and did not move. There was nothing left to do. June wandered off to be alone in deep shadow, taking a moment to be with Dianette, to be quiet before the unrelenting clamor of the show. She felt absurd, a mother quietly rocking her very good baby, a mother whose costume would vex many an upstanding citizen. In a few moments June would put Dianette on the little dais the stage manager had assembled upon request, the very focal point of the promiment down center area. How would Dianette feel to be alone under the scrutiny of those thousands of eyes, those baking lights? June hated to let her go, to put her down. Perhaps she wouldn't.

"Do you think we've kept them waiting long enough?" Larry called—and when June nodded *go ahead*, he transferred the message to the technician who passed it on to the stage manager, smoke signals sent great distances between friendly tribes. "Ready, June? Ready, everybody? Let's do it!"

June ran to place Dianette on her blue dais decorated with a white fringe. She kissed her child lovingly, started to run back, then hesitated. "Dianette, I won't let anything happen to you. I promise. I promise. I promise."

As she stood up, June saw Pete Robinson stretching

his torso between the closed curtains, a bottle of wine in his extended hand. "Just a little something to inspire you!" he said.

Chateau Méchant, 1923. Touching the precious antique bottle and faded label, June thought of a classic car whose opened hood reveals a battery flecked with corrosive acidic grey-white foam.

"Remember, we'll issue this as a double live album if it goes right. Give us a good show, June!" Pete passed on the smart little salute of a fellow conspirator.

"Come on!" Larry yelled.

June trotted back to the lead microphone. She closed her eyes, hands on the long smooth stand. She may have nodded.

"All right! Are you ready for a little rock 'n' roll?" asked a disembodied impresario. Behind the curtain, the crowd cheered with mad inarticulate glee. "All-riiiiiight! Then here she is in her first performance in over a year, the high priestess of Apocalyptic rock, June Lockwood and Bloooooooodrock!"

And before the curtain could even shudder prior to drawing open, Bloodrock was playing, at the volume the critics termed mega-decibel, their traditional straight-ahead theme "Blinded by the Blood."

The curtain came open, roaring. Of course, it was really the crowd that roared. But, to June, the impression was that of a mouth opening with long-restrained hunger, hideously ready to devour everything in sight that sounded like rock and roll. Screams of "Bloodrock," and "June," and requests for a score of songs rang out as hands came up over heads to applaud. The cliché *sea of faces* took on a new significance for June as she realized that the overhead hands clapping together resembled nothing quite so much as the tendrils of a tidepool full of sea anemones waving to the delicate currents of the quiet ocean.

Bloodrock played as if their lives depended on it. They played a medley of their more familiar and segued into the songs Larry had been doing with Muscleman.

Several years before, the Theater for the Performing Arts had gained national attention for having an adjustable ceiling that tended to collapse and a suspended balcony that some said might one day demonstrate the same proclivity; and though the structural difficulties had been corrected, June felt frightened by a self-destructive undercurrent she seemed to detect in the frenzy of the audience. Would they welcome a disaster? And how should one judge music that so inspired an audience?

The band blew into "Pumping Iron."

"Flex and muscle," June sang.

"Lift that killing weight."

"Cut that bicep

"And show the strength of hate . . ."

Then she saw them, Amelia and Edna, in the center and three rows back. Amidst the Brownian Movement of young bodies caught in a suspension of auditory perpetual motion, the two mature women stood out for their absolute stasis, untouched, unresponsive, unmoved. They're waiting, June thought. None of this interests them. They're totally indifferent, totally uninvolved. Mother may pretend to hate rock music, but it's only her urge to suppress any passion alien to her own; it's only her obsession with squelching any energy with a coloration and tone that diverges from hers. Grandmother. Mother. Neither approves of what she hears, neither disapproves. She does not hear, she waits. Behind those unresponsive masks there is only patience, the sheen of sun on the wings of the dragonfly, sheer anticipation, and a sense of inexorable joy.

"Cut the muscle down the middle

"Strip the tricep of the brain . . ."

Duane, his face distinguished from the rest of lines of tension that ran up and down, vertical to their horizontal. Horror, said his face. I have horror. His eyes were not on his wife. His eyes were with his baby daughter, his Dianette ensconced on what he must have recognized now as a sacrificial altar. Would he try something? Would he order the curtain closed, the show canceled? Would he rush the stage himself?

Before they had begun to play, June had thought only of the purpose of this evening, the indeterminate climactic moment she hoped to effect. She had virtually forgotten that she had a concert to give. But now, making music, she found that she could pass the time by allowing herself to get caught up in the creative process. She almost forgot about Dianette and the terrible responsibility that had come to be so nicely giftwrapped in her brain. She found herself almost able to forget about everything, everything but the music. The new Bloodrock finished the Muscleman medley to a roar of religious fervor from the animal congregation at their feet.

June strode to the microphone, a smile where her face had been. "And now," she said, "we're gonna play some rock 'n' roll!"

An avalanche of mindless approval cascaded over the stage as she summoned Larry and the band into "A-Positive Iron Capsule Blues," a surrealistic survey of obsessions with personal and political health.

"I was into pills
"And I was into love
"Into countin' those stars above
"Told my Master I wanted some Blues . . ."

For the first time in her life she ceased to be a performer, an entertainer, an artist. She was no more and no less than a woman living out her life in public view. I am the music, she thought. I used to *think* the music, now I *feel* it. And those people out there, that sea of hands and hair, that sea *knows*. They know.

And that felt good to think, that felt very very good.

And then Larry went into the solo that carried her away. She'd always wanted him as her lead guitarist, always loved his playing; and yet, for all his apparent wildness, his willingness to take risks, June had always felt that Larry held something back, something of himself, not just that necessary edge of reserve, something that formed the essential connection between himself and his music.

So as he began to solo now June realized that he had made the decision (consciously or otherwise) to let go, to kick free of the earth, to release that last fingerhold on sanity and order. So he came at her, came prancing at her, mincing, high-stepping, flouncing, jiggling, wiggling, all this indeterminately sexual abandon—so unlike him, Larry Ludwig, who despised the premeditated concert cavorting that he called "show-off-manship." So, guitar held up on hip like some sexual icon, he angled to within inches of June's enticingly garbed thigh. And at point blank range he whirled and wheeled and windmilled his body as he played, miraculously keeping the microphone cord unsnarled. And all of it, the cascade of notes, the whirling dervish torque, turned into a dust devil, a tornado of sound and flesh that would surely be lethal to touch, like a high-powered drill biting through solid steel. Oh, he flew, he jetted, a one-man rock 'n' roll version of the Blue Angels, flying in a formation all his own. One false move and he killed himself and his wing mate, the entire squadron. And the blast and fire and din of their collision would take the audience along for that long strange trip to the killing floor far below.

So June felt frightened to encourage him as much as she wanted him never to stop. What if she moved as he moved? He was blind, oblivious, yet. . . . Snapping her fingers, beginning to make a soft purring coo of appreciation from a space deep in her throat she had never felt before, June fell in with his heavy feedback fling.

Guitar solos are seldom applauded at rock concerts. June did not know if she joined the applause or actually initiated it. She did not even know if she had been immediately aware that the solo had ended. The sound made by this audience, an audience accustomed to applauding by means of certain preconceived patterns that passed for spontaneity, this applause broke down on eardrums with tidal wave abruptness and size. June gritted teeth as she clapped. How did Larry know all that about her? How could anyone know? How could anyone love her after knowing all that?

But Larry kept moving, veering easily away from June toward the center of the stage where the dais holding Dianette floated beneath the baking intensity of spotlights and fresnels. Dianette reached for the tongue of the guitar as Larry glided by, continuing the solo that had begun with her mother.

June could not believe what she heard. She could not believe what Larry played. She knew him to be dangerous, unstable, an irresponsible young man who had somehow managed to harness these flaws into some pretty positive musical expressions. But where did this tenderness come from, this sensitivity to fragile strength of child flesh and blood? Did Dianette see it too, the long trailing strands of crystalline seaweed floating in a sunlit bath of air fresh as infinity, the birds and airborne creatures moving without effort along the roads to freedom?

June began to sing along—not words but sounds, not scat because this was not jazz but something closer to the purest tone a sitar can make when the morning prayer is sounded and children look to the East in the utter joy of innocent devotion. She sang notes that rose and fell around the notes that Larry played, incredibly delicate strokes of equally incredible strength that resonated warmly and fully without touching.

So she had become lost in the creative process, in the audience's ambivalent sensitivity, in the artistry of attempting to concoct a show. So if the showdown were to occur, it was now or never.

"Reformer!" she shouted out to finish off a soaring clarion note. "Reformer! Reformer!"

And the audience picked up the call, uncertainly at first, then with a profound unanimity: "Reformer!" They liked the idea of conjuring up the male muse of Bosley Broderick. They liked the risky urgency they heard from June. They relished this promise of total disruption. (Of course they knew him. Some wore Reformer T-shirts. Some had album covers with his likeness affixed to their walls. Others, both men and women, had his name tattooed on the private areas of their bodies.) And so, when he did appear, June having resumed that ringing note, the audience stomped and shouted and beat on their seats.

The hooded figure, axe in hand, stalked out onto the stage. He stood nearly seven feet tall in the black knee-high boots. The hood was adorned with cartoon splashes of red and green and yellow paint that eddied expressively around his eyes and around the holes for nose and mouth. And although his eyes were invisible in the darkness of the cut-outs, the holes themselves appeared to glare with unadulterated malice. The axe was the two-headed variety favored by barbarian metal groups on their album covers and in their video performances. Hands far apart, Reformer held the axe like a snake trainer displaying one of his lengthier specimens.

Once Reformer emerged from the wings, a trite phrase ganged up on June to block any further rational thought: *no turning back, no turning back*.

"Reformer," June called. "Here." She gestured for him to stand beside the blue dais. Reformer moved with the absolute obedience of a man incapable of hesitation. How many times had he posed this way for Frank Frazetta and Roger Dean?

Now Larry raised the guitar as a weapon that only moments before he had used to achieve eloquent self-expression. He held it out toward Reformer as if to ward him off, drive him away.

"No, Larry!" June called across. "Remember? It's okay. It's okay." It's okay? And who was June to reassure Larry? Since when did a mother strive to convince others that her child's vulnerability was tolerable?

Larry dipped his head down to his guitar. He strummed, came up with chords that said what he felt about having to step aside and leave Dianette unprotected, about having to trust this gargantuan flesh and blood stereotype. His playing fell in perfectly with the Bosley Broderick medley June had initiated to honor Reformer's appearance.

"A tribute to my mentor," June said into the microphone. "The man who put me on the path of blood—Bosley Broderick."

A modest reverential furor of shouts and applause. They seemed almost to remember.

Reformer raised the great two-headed axe and stood near the dais but not quite within striking distance. June eyed him nervously. She waited, waited for some kind of signal as she raced Bloodrock through the master's medley. She felt the sweat begin to bloom all over her body, a renaissance of anxiety. Where was Bosley?

She tried not to see the tension in Reformer's

straining arms, the way the tendons in his forearms tightened and subsided, the quirky little spasms that made his brutal biceps seem ready to fail at any moment. He looked like a man ready to faint. But consciousness did not matter, life did not matter. Dead or alive, his body would perform the task to which it had been called. After all, it was only a matter of relieving tension.

June moved the sweat from the side of her face with a quick sweep of her wrist. Bosley? Are you there? Isn't it time?

No answer. (Seven years? Seven years times three.)

June stepped back from the microphone and let the band surge on by like a runaway freight. "Bosley?" she whispered. "What should I do?"

No answer. (Seven years? No, multiply that by three.)

Now Reformer beckoned to her. Come here, June. And she knew that it was time. And she knew that she did not know what would happen. And June saw the faces of her mother and grandmother and knew that it would finish here tonight, now, somehow, no matter what she did.

"Come here, June," Reformer commanded into Larry's back-up vocal mike. And then more quietly, more gently, but with ferocious vehemence, "He will come only if you call him by the right name."

June put a hand to her forehead to stop the fire of sudden frontal pain. The Devil? Satan? Beelzebub? Did she have to find a copy of Paradise Lost and recite a ridiculous laundry list of diabolical appellations? What else could he mean by *the right name*? Only seven years older?

Reformer shook his head at her with all the condemnation of a petulant professor who believes that the answer to his question should be apparent to the least of his students.

And the gentle beast of an audience roared. What a moment! Bosley Broderick's living emblem, his bodyguard, commands the high priestess of this world to come to the altar, the dais where her own child has been prepared as offering. Who among them, asked to construct a fantasy concert, the perfect dramatization of their perverse needs, would have dared to imagine the moment live before them now?

"Here! June Lockwood, now!"

June moved with uncertain grace toward the center of the stage where Reformer stood near Dianette. He took one hand from the suspended axe to gesture that she was to place her hands on the weapon with his and join him in the terminal act to follow.

"No!" Her cry, narrow and lost at first in the furor of the audience's growling anticipation, turned supple and rose up like a thin reed into the rafters of the theater.

Angry, reinforcing the shuddering axe by slapping his free hand back into place, Reformer jerked his head for her to comply with his order.

A whinny of derision from the audience. Disruptive shouts. Mocking applause. Someone played a cavalry charge on a pocket trumpet, tinny, inept, nihilistic. And then June saw him working his way up the aisle after having fought through the audience. He pushed past those who stood, stepping and crawling, his purpose more than clear. A comic moment? Not quite—his determination was too nervously desperate.

June whirled back to her lead guistarist. "You've got to stop him, Larry."

Larry put a hand to the strap of his guitar at the back of his neck. "I know. But I almost wish . . ."

Duane bounded up onto the stage with a highjumper's grace. He sprinted forward toward his daughter with his head low like a combat veteran.

But Larry was there. "Duane, I'm sorry!" he said, twisting out of the strap like a frantic stripper and bending to put his instrument aside. Duane, shoulder down, rammed Larry as he released his guitar.

The animal audience yelled ambiguously. The band continued to play without any discernible change of sound, yet a low guttural accumulation of crowd complaints puddled up around the music. Some doubted that this intrusion was part of the show. They resented it. They clenched their fists on theater armrests and did not move.

June, frightened they would dump the dais and send Dianette tumbling, moved away from Reformer's side to kneel beside her baby.

Duane and Larry tumbled down center over a snake nest of electric wires and bumped to a stop against one of the six-foot speakers that blared out the riding music of Bloodrock's tribute to Bosley.

Duane came up on top with Larry's throat in his hands. "You're as crazy as my wife! I have to stop you!"

"No, you . . .!" Larry kneed him in the groin, thrust his weight back for leverage and flipped Duane off to free his arms. He rubbed the fire brand of pain in his throat and stood simultaneously with his opponent.

"Take him," Larry rasped as best he could as a security officer sprinted toward them. "This wasn't part of the act, officer. Just . . ." Larry waved vaguely toward June and Reformer the bassinet at center stage.

"Listen, I'm the father! I forbid . . .!" But when Duane felt his arms pinned behind him he went limp like a man admitting total defeat. A second and a third security guard came out to help the first drag Duane backwards off the stage. Duane's eyes closed. He had the appearance of one giving himself over to death.

June watched Larry massage his livid throat and

reharness his guitar with pained reluctance. Who was it who was only seven years old? Some performer, some musician?

"June, how long do you expect that I am able to do this? Put your hands on mine. Call to the master by his rightful name, the name that he deserves to hear from your lips."

June moved to front Reformer and gingerly placed her hands up on the handle of the two-headed axe as if she feared it might fall the moment she made contact. Her back was to the audience. She had violated one of the standard commandments of performing. She had allowed herself to be upstaged by ritual. She tried not to think. If she thought, if she let her mind work, she knew that she would stop this. And then it would all go on and on, the blood, the disfigurement of children. And who would stand up for later generations if she declined now? Too insane to reason out. June clamped her hands harder on the handle, squeezing Reformer's hands as if she wanted the hard wood to splinter in their combined grip.

YES.

PERFECT. AND NOW, MON CHERE, YOU AND YOUR BALD SUPERNUMERARY WILL FINISH, NON?

Reformer, closing his eyes under the hideous mask, nodded to the rhythm of the voice June had heard. "Yes," he said. "That is the last. I have told you what you must do. I have no strength left."

"Reformer?" Hands locked over his, June looked imploringly at the tall hooded man.

Various members of the audience yelled out ideas, decisions, a course of action. It was not necessarily that they were so cynical that they would gladly see a baby killed onstage. They were no worse than those who roared when Ozzy inadvertantly bit the head off a live rabid bat. They were no worse than those who had started the rumors about stomping live baby chickens on stage—nor than those who believed that Bosley had actually decapitated a peacock that night in San Jose. No, they were a menagerie of an audience, but they lived like everyone else with the ongoing tensions and contradictions of the twentieth century. At its religious best, their art would reflect all of that, reflect it in one splendid unified tableau.

And they wanted more—participation, power, the two prime elements they sensed a lack of in their own lives. And so they yelled.

"Do it! Do it! Do it!"

And so they yelled.

"Chop its head! Chop its head!"

And so they yelled.

"Kill the pig! Drink its blood!"

And so they yelled out. And some yelled a feeble "no," reluctantly but with a certain nervous conviction; these were the ones who had begun to realize that what they witnessed was no show. This was real. And yet the feeble objections stayed mainly back in their throats, like the voices of witnesses to a rape or an accident who, half from curiosity, feel unwilling to tamper with an event from which they may learn something precious about the nature of life. And when would the opportunity to see such picturesque horror present itself again? Yet, again by half, they knew the outcome in advance, knew the guilt they would live with, the remorse, the long tedious suffering of sleepless nights. And so they yelled.

VRAIMENT? YOU DEFY ME STILL? THEN WATCH. WATCH YOUR CHILD'S FACE. WATCH THE FLESH PUCKER AND BOIL. WATCH.

Screams rose like steam from the vast zoo of an audience. In that moment, many saw—or thought they saw—something . . . a vast black shadow that engulfed the stage? A green mist seemed to fill the auditorium. Later, many would compare the experience to military gas training or to the irritation that results from the exposure of eyes to chlorinated water. Many felt themselves to be strangling, unable to breath; some pawed the air as if they could not speak, could not call out for help.

June, frozen, felt the sweat trickle down her straining arms. The audience terrified her almost as much as the sudden atmospheric change. The crowd could distinguish theatre from reality—and the dreadful reality that most of them realized they were witnessing began to transform their mood and made them dangerous in the way that any frightened caged animal is dangerous. Some now yelled "Do it! Do it!" with the vicious determination of persons lusting to survive at any cost, at all costs. Yet a louder contingent, a shroud of caring voices, moaned in disapproval, a low growling sound of denial, of humanity with its back against some final wall.

DO IT NOW, MON PETIT. SEE HER SKIN? PRETTY? QUAINT? ANTIQUE? WOULD MADAME CARE TO EXAMINE?

June watched Dianette's face shrink and pucker, shriveling as if undergoing instant mummification down to the proportions and appearance of a tiny defiled head of her great-grandmother Edna. And then the wrinkles began to glow red and swell. An excruciating pain stabbed into June's groin, a pain almost reminiscent of prenatal contractions. But wasn't that the pain she'd felt whenever . . . ?

"No!" June freed one hand from the axe and let it travel in aimless distraction down to the center of her chest. Reformer's lips trembled, tried to move; she tried to read them. His mighty arms trembled terribly. June knew that she had to call Bosley now, call him by his right name. "Oh, Dark One," she whispered, knowing this was wrong even as she spoke. *Seven years*, to whom had she said that, it seemed, so long ago?

DO IT NOW, MADEMOISELLE— OR I WILL CLAIM HER THIS WAY. IT IS YOUR CHOICE.

C'EST VRAI.

YOU HAVE PUT ME IN POWER NOW—AFTER YEARS OF DENIAL AND FRUSTRATION AT THE HANDS OF YOUR FOREBEARS. I THANK YOU. MERCI, MON CHERE. WITNESS YOUR CHILD BECOME IDENTICAL NOW, ATOM FOR ATOM, TO MY GRANDDAUGHTER WHO DIED SIXTY YEARS AGO AND WHOM I LOVED.

"No!" She had to say it. She had to find the one word she needed that would give her strength. Because, she knew, neither she nor Reformer were strong enough to resist the sorcerer's righteous imperative. She had a word. She had a lack in her life, a loss, an empty spot, a hole. She had no. . . .

Seven years older than me, a performer, entertainer, magician; seven years yet ancient, old enough, in fact, old enough to be. . . .

June's fingers closed on the bloodrock. She squeezed until her hand began to bleed. The blood ran down her hand, down her arm, down her throat. The blood ran down between her breasts.

YOU PLAY WITH THIS TOY? IS THIS YOUR ROCKING HORSE?

And the laughter that sprouted out of the voice was physically repugnant, odiferous, noxious, the smell of decay of something too selfish to give itself over to the wholesome process of death, the putrid flesh carried as an infernal souvenir the ego would never relinquish. And now Dianette turned to something . . . something that June would have to bury, something that she would have to. . . .

"No! Oh, Bosley, please! Oh . . ."

(june don't you know who i)

Seven times three, the rocking horse, the lack, the hole, old enough to be

(don't you know don't you know)

shape by my bed good warm comfort beard dark don't go mommy out to doctor fire a barn shun? a barn baby? now for edna? no? now mommy? body in the road seance wine stone japanese screen larynx bloodrock long hair and a full belly in the lovely parisian moonlight, but no man no man ever again but i want (him) i want

(don't you know)

June's fingers bit the rock like fangs. Her blood came hard. All her life long she had wanted. The pain. All her life long the only thing she had ever wanted.

Old enough to be my

"Father? Daddy? Bosley are you my . . .?"

LET GO, JUNE. NO NEED FOR YOU TO SUFFER, TOO. LET GO, YOU FOOL . . .

YES, JUNE. I'M HERE. I'VE ALWAYS BEEN HERE.

The pain in her groin had become enormous, larger than her body. "I can't hold . . ."

NO, JUNE. HANG ON. SQUEEZE. HOLD THE BLOODROCK THAT I GAVE YOU. YOU HAVE SUFFERED THIS MUCH. YOU HAVE SUFFERED THIS FAR. DO NOT LET GO NOW.

The crowd seemed to yell. The band seemed to play. Would her real father ask her to suffer more? Clinging desperately to the rock around her throat, June watched the tip of the axe catch the floodlights beaming down from the control consoles. The lamps swiveled. The tip of the great axe, its massive two-headed top, wavered. It was a lethal ouija board held with an almost pressureless touch by two searchers, trusting that when it moves it will move under the direction of Beings Other than themselves.

Reformer? How firmly was he . . .?

"Oh, God! Reformer? Reformer?"

She could no longer see into the mask. The mask, in fact, seemed vacant. And then June knew that Reformer had lost the battle, given up; his hands, his grip on the axe now at the mercy of. . . .

The rock hurt June's throat. What if she passed out from loss of blood? No, she had to release it, had to put both hands onto the axe in case Reformer. . . .

YES. DROP THE ROCK. PUT YOUR HANDS ON THE SWORD. DADA—DADA! LES BEUX MAINS! MAINTENANT!

Identities scrambled. Whose hands were these? Too many pairs . . . and those funny voices, to whom did they . . .?

NO, JUNE. HOLD THE ROCK. SQUEEZE THE BLOODROCK. ONLY SUFFERING. ONLY SUFFERING TAKES US ON THE TRUE VOYAGE, THE REAL TRIP. IT IS THE WAY WE MOVE AND MOVE BEYOND. SQUEEZE IT, JUNE. SUFFER, MY BELOVED DAUGHTER, MY ONLY LOVE. SUFFER FOR MY GRANDCHILD DIANETTE. SUFFER FOR US ALL.

Closing her eyes, June concentrated on gripping the stone medallion, on going on and going through.

LET IT FALL. MAINTENANT! SEE THE SHRIVELED THING THAT WAS YOUR DAUGHTER? BE MERCIFUL. KILL IT. KILL IT!

The band played brilliantly, perhaps absurdly on, chorus after chorus of high energy blues. Dianette had begun to cry, her shriveled lips parting in pain, the first sound she had uttered in two weeks. Many in the audience began to interpret the near-hysteria they had endured for so long as boredom, a misunderstanding of themselves that they had been over time and again in their lives without dealing with or learning from. They began to call out of their impatience with and ignorance of themselves and this still painful world that they had tried to voyage through for too many years.

"Do it, you bitch! Stop faking, cunt! Do it!" And there, in the front, that one face, that one terminal smile, welling up as if from a deep inner source of satisfaction. Click, snap. The shutter of June's eyes focused and caught the perfect image of her own mother. And, next to her, grandmother.

Blood ran down June's arms, striping them like tapered barber poles, May Day streamers wrapped around the most exquisite pale skin.

LET GO IF YOU VALUE YOUR STUPID PALTRY LIFE! DO AS YOUR MOTHER AND HER MOTHER BEFORE HER! DO! YOU ARE INCAPABLE OF SAVING YOUR LIFE ANY OTHER WAY!

"I . . ."

SQUEEZE, JUNE. AND KEEP YOUR EYES OPEN. SEE YOUR MOTHER. YOU MUST TELL HER NOW. YOU MUST SUFFER THE BECOMING OF YOURSELF.

"Mother, I . . . Mother, you . . ."

June opened her eyes to the change in Dianette's sobbing. The tiny face unwrinkled, blanched, the angry red furrows vanishing like heat dots from a soothed retina, her features swimming innocently back into place once again.

"Mother, you may not have my life. You may not have my daughter's life. You may not . . ."

YOU DID NOT GIVE ME BACK MY BABY! SO! NOW, JUNE LOCKWOOD, DAUGHTER OF THE EVIL, I WILL TAKE *YOU*!

"June?" Larry screamed. "What's happening to you?"

She slumped to her knees, all her energy gone, and gripped the medallion with both bloody hands. In her own way, to her own sense of what it was in the universe that was larger than she, June prayed. She had nothing else left to do. To have retained her one-hand hold on the axe, even with Dianette restored, would have been to risk toppling Reformer with the weight of her own exhaustion.

From where she knelt it seemed to June that Reformer brought the axe up all the way to the floodlamps and fresnels. And then there was an audible grunt as he mustered all his strength to bring the sharpened weapon down on her.

Then it all happened very fast as Larry swung his guitar to deflect the blade away from June. The altered course saw Reformer swinging the deflected axe down on a line to bisect the tiny form that had subsided into the safety of sleep inside her blanket. But the touch of the guitar to the blade he wielded seemed to restore Reformer to himself quicker than any slap. Perhaps an objective observer would have said that he seemed to regain control and to tap into a psychic strength even more formidable than his physical strength—because he did two impossible things simultaneously. He changed the course of the axe. He released the axe. It sailed from his hands with the satisfying sigh of terminated tension one associates with the strongest and most aesthetically disciplined target archers.

The wayward projectile seemed to hang in the air with the relaxed carry of a lazy fly ball as it sailed in the lights of the Theater for the Performing Arts.

YOU HAVE KILLED MY BABY! YOU HAVE KILLED MY BABY!

YES, JUNE! HOLD ON ONE MORE MOMENT! YES, JUNE, IT'S YOU!

The axe still suspended in air, June saw the explosion of light and fire, she saw mother and daughter holding hands—or was it an illusion? If real, which of them had initiated the contact? And the motive? A last plea for love, a last effort to transcend the total self-absorbtion that had been each of their lives? (Or was it the opposite? *This* will save me. If I hold this hand I will not take the long cold trip alone.)

And in her mind June knew that both were dead. She saw them both dead.

Quick as a subliminal image, the wrinkled skin incinerated with a lurid luminescence—then the explosion. Just as the axe hit the back of the empty blue plastic seat, shattering it into fragments from which a score of frightened hands protected their owners' faces and torsos.

And it was over.

The music was over.

It was indeed the end. The blue bus had arrived at its final destination. And all the doors fell open like dominoes in some surrealistic lithograph. Reformer, collapsed on the stage, had ceased to breathe. Larry yelled for oxygen, a stretcher, an ambulance. June slumped beside him, rocking her baby and crying, rocking and crying, all she had ever wanted to do, all she would ever be able to do again.

And June's grandmother who had danced on the grave of a famous sorcerer known as Méchant stirred in her seat as the audience was ushered out by the security guards ringing the aisles and stage. Impervious, unblinking, unknowing—just there, sitting, slouched down, her hand still held in the air where it had gripped that of her vanished daughter.

For the rest of her life June would come awake at odd moments in the middle of the night trying to comprehend why Méchant had chosen to take Amelia with him as he passed out of this existence forever.

Epilogue

They watched the kindergartners and first graders stream out of the old adobe school house to wend their way down the garden path that led to the street with its waiting parents and buses. The children took time to dance and punch each other under the summer noontime sun.

"And how . . .?"

"Oh, that! He's doing much better, much, much better—I'd forgotten you hadn't seen him in a couple of weeks. The doctor says there won't be any scarring. He's sure missed you, Sis!"

"I've missed him," June said. She squinted out into the bright open light for a sign of her nephew. "I'm looking forward to this weekend. You know, I haven't been there in a long time myself. And I guess I'll admit I kind of have to get away from it all . . ."

"Yeah," Betty said, sketching her hair back along her forehead with two fingers. "What they *called* a funeral and . . ."

June hugged Dianette a little tighter. "Funeral in absentia. Not even any ashes to scatter."

"Yeah! Spooky! Two weeks! It still doesn't seem

real—and all those weird Hollywood people and that fan club of hers holding a seance out in that old unused section of the graveyard! Gave me the creeps, even if it was my own mother! But I guess, after everything you've been through, June, it didn't have the slightest affect."

"No way!" June dramatized her reaction by hiking shoulders, raising eyebrows. Then she carefully eased Dianette back into the back seat of her car. "They scared me plenty!"

"Oh, I tell you, June, some of those people really made me wonder if . . . Hey, isn't that Larry across the street in that van with the crazy painting on it?"

"Sure is," June said, but she was already watching her guitarist and friend disembark from his van and come trotting toward them.

"I thought I'd find you here," he said. "Beautiful day, huh? This came in the mail today—I think it's the one we've been looking for. We'll celebrate tonight, huh?"

June tapped the letter comtemplatively. It bore the return address of the firm of lawyers she'd gone to see several weeks before. "Thanks," she said.

Larry shifted boyishly from foot to foot. "I've got to get back to the studio and do some work—unless we want to release this album posthumously. Anybody want to share a joint—no? Well, see you, girls!"

"Bye . . ."

June slipped the letter inside her purse. The day after the concert Duane had instructed her that he had visited Finch, Lyborg and Ross and asked her to do the same. She could see no reason not to do so; they wanted the same thing. Her only worry was that he'd make a last minute grab for custody.

But now Betty was smiling like someone who can't wait to reveal that she'd learned your secret. "June! June, are you and Larry . . .?"

"Bingo," June said. "Since two days after the concert. Do you think I'm loose?"

"I think you're wonderful!" Betty said. "And I think Larry's a pretty wonderful guy . . ." She looked dreamily away. She had meant what she said.

"So my love life's great, but I may be pennyless in no time."

Betty took this seriously. "How's that, June?"

"Didn't you see it in the papers? The theater management was talking about suing Bloodrock for damages? Oh, I think it was just talk but . . ."

"Oh, you poor kid! Is that what the letter was about?"

Whoops. Was it premature to mention the legal proceedings to her sister? Was she, in fact, moving much too fast? Slow down.

More children streamed out of the old well-manicured school. June liked the acres of rolling lawn that fronted the building on both sides. Undoubtedly, the children were told not to play there—no rolling, certainly!—but it was pleasant to imagine them doing so.

"Isn't that Ivan over there walking with that little black girl with the ponytail and glasses?"

"I bet I can guess what the letter is you're hiding from me."

June let her head loll over to the side to eyeball her sister. "I'll bet you can, too."

They both laughed.

"Probably because of the critical reaction to the show," June mused. "I mean, Duane's always been business. Betty, never believe it when they tell you that the rats are the first to leave a sinking ship. No, the money men are the first to go—the financiers, the finaglers, the ones with their long fingers stuck down inside your pants."

"Gosh, sis, you sound . . ."

"Hey, Auntie June! Take that!"

Ivan pointed a new Star Troopers Laser Blaster which fired real space projectiles right at June's chest. She held her hands up in front of her face and flinched away, only half-faking.

Ivan's hysterical appreciation bubbled out in laughter. When he'd calmed himself, he leaned into the passenger side of the car to whisper confidentially that he had a secret, a plan.

"A secret plan? You mean about this weekend?"

"No, but . . . well. . ." He suddenly turned very shy and actually seemed to regret that he'd mentioned this momentous scheme. He'd seemed much more comfortable assassinating his aunt with the blaster.

"What is it, Ivan?"

"Well . . ." He raised his face, brightening at his own burgeoning courage. "Well, I've decided that when Dianette grows up me and her are going to get married!" The words out, he threw hands and blaster alike across his reddening face.

Rolling their heads together, June and Betty exchanged terrific eye shots. Both pantomimed efforts to suppress laughter, both finally failing.

"Just you wait and see!" Ivan spat out, beyond embarrassment, angry now. "I will! I'll show you!"

"Get in, kid," June said casually. "I'm not letting my daughter date for at least another couple months."

"And by then," Betty said, "who knows, you might have a different daddy to ask for her hand."

"No way! One hand? Sheeesh!" He scoffed at this adult stupidity with his superior haughty laughter.

June turned the key and the car purred to mechanical life. She felt very good about picking Ivan up at school, one of those everyday miracles that a few weeks before she thought would be forever denied to all of them. She felt very good about Betty's attitude, about her forgiveness, her understanding, her always being . . . herself.

"I love you, Sis," June said.

"I love *you*, silly big sister!" Betty mocked. They hugged. June steered the car away from the curb. Her hand wandered purposefully to the rock that hung down on her long throat.

THE CURSE

"You must . . ." His voice was that of a dying man. "You must . . ."

June touched cold fingers to her warm lips. He was going to die right there in front of her.

"What, Mr. Broderick? What?"

His eyes—was it a trick of the light, or did they actually roll back in his head? "You must . . . you *will* perform, on stage, a more outrageous act than any I have ever conceived. You will ease my memory from the annals of grotesquery. *You!* You will grow to become one of the greatest artists in the history of this music. You will marry, you will conceive, and then, using your own child alive on stage, you will . . ."